KATHY LYN

LADY APPLETON'S WORLD

THE COMPLETE SHORT STORIES

sixteen stories featuring Susanna, Lady Appleton
Elizabethan gentlewoman, herbalist, and sleuth
and her friends from the
Face Down Mystery Series

Table of Contents

Introduction 1
The Body in the Dovecote 2
A Note from the Author 23
Much Ado About Murder 24
A Note from the Author 50
The Rubaiyat of Nicholas Baldwin 52
A Note from the Author 74
Lady Appleton and the London Man 75
A Note from the Author 92
Lady Appleton and the Cautionary Herbal 94
A Note from the Author 117
The Riddle of the Woolsack 118
A Note from the Author 142
Lady Appleton and the Cripplegate Chrisoms 144
A Note from the Author 167
Lady Appleton and the Bristol Crystals 168
A Note from the Author 197
Encore for a Neck Verse 199
A Note from the Author 223
Confusions Most Monstrous 225
A Note from the Author 251
Death by Devil's Turnips 254
A Note from the Author 283
Any Means Short of Murder 284
A Note from the Author 307
A Wondrous Violent Motion 308
A Note from the Author 327
Lady Appleton and the Creature of the Night 329
A Note from the Author 342
The Curse of the Figure Flinger 344
A Note from the Author 366

Lady Appleton and the Yuletide Hogglers	367
A Note from the Author	384
About the Author	385

Lady Appleton's World: The Complete Short Stories

© 2025 by Kathy Lynn Emerson
All rights reserved. No part of this book may be reproduced or transmitted in any form or by any means, electronic or mechanical, including photocopying, recording, or by any information storage or retrieval system, without permission in writing from the author.

"The Body in the Dovecote" © 2004
"Much Ado about Murder" © 2002
"The Rubaiyat of Nicholas Baldwin" © 2001
"Lady Appleton and the London Man" © 1999
"Lady Appleton and the Cautionary Herbal" © 2001
"The Riddle of the Woolsack" © 2004
"Lady Appleton and the Cripplegate Chrisoms" © 2003
"Lady Appleton and the Bristol Crystals" © 2004
"Encore for a Neck Verse" © 2004
"Confusions Most Monstrous" © 2004
"Death by Devil's Turnips" © 2003
"Any Means Short of Murder: © 2009
"A Wondrous Violent Motion © 2013
"Lady Appleton and the Creature of the Night" © 2015
"The Curse of the Figure Flinger" © 2004
"Lady Appleton and the Yuletide Hogglers" © 2010

illustrations by Linda Weatherly S.

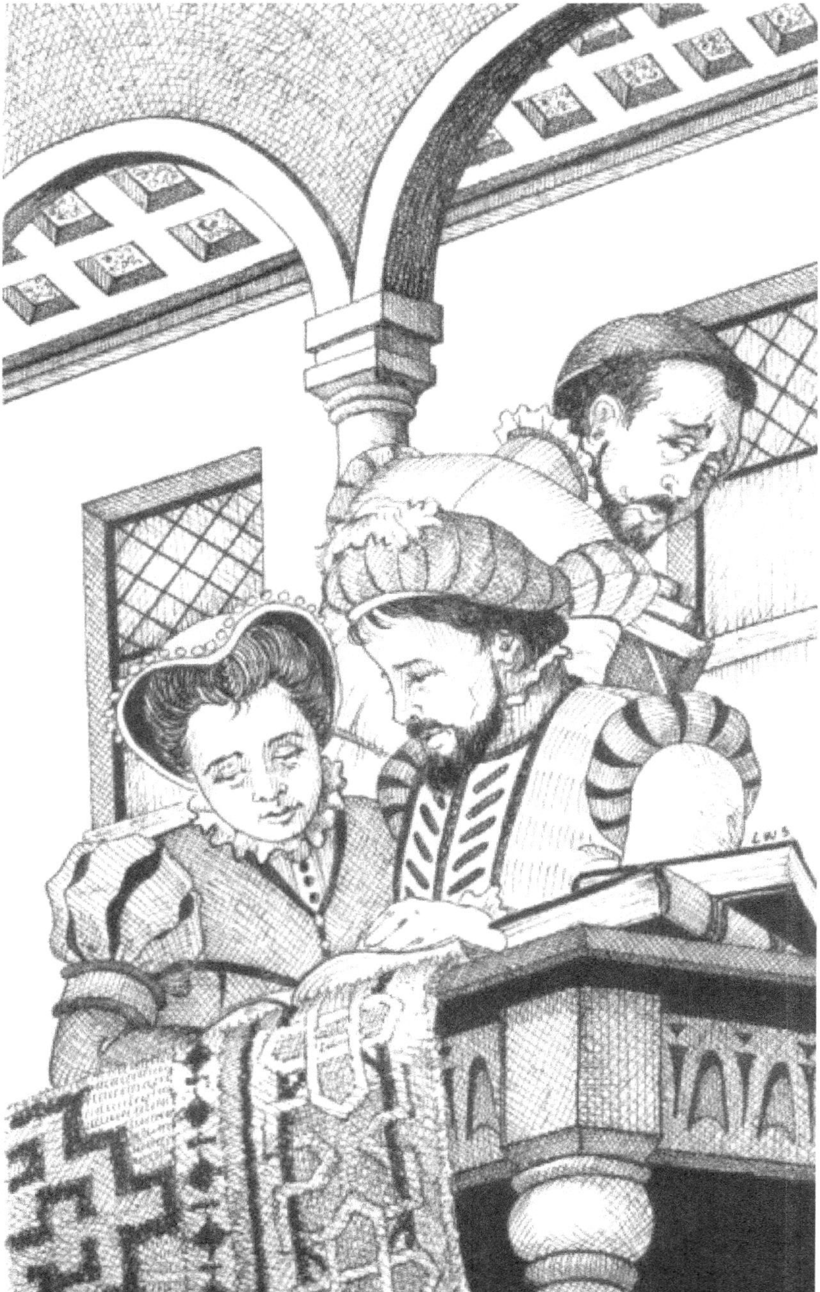

Books in the Face Down Series

Face Down in the Marrow-Bone Pie
Face Down Upon an Herbal
Face Down Among the Winchester Geese
Face Down Beneath the Eleanor Cross
Face Down Under the Wych Elm
Face Down Before Rebel Hooves
Face Down Across the Western Sea
Face Down Below the Banqueting House
Face Down Beside St. Ann's Well
Face Down O'er the Border
Lady Appleton's World: The Complete Short Stories
spin off series (Mistress Jaffrey Mysteries)
Murder in the Queen's Wardrobe
Murder in the Merchant's Hall
Murder in a Cornish Alehouse

Praise for the Face Down Series

"Highly recommended for readers who appreciate suspenseful historical mysteries." *Booklist*

"A nice rural flavor, complete with authentic rustics, living conditions, and social customs, blend with family secrets and a slightly twisted plot to make this an enticing historical." *Library Journal*

"A solid bet for historical mystery fans." *Publishers Weekly*

"A fascinating mixture of fictional and historical characters . . . there are twists, flashes of revelations, and some great titles. It's a fun, easy read." *Historical Novels Review* on *Murders and Other Confusions* (short story collection)

"Emerson takes us on a wonderful jaunt through Elizabethan England." *The Purloined Letter*

Introduction

This collection includes all sixteen short stories featuring characters from the Face Down Mysteries. They are arranged in chronological order rather than order of publication to create a more unified picture of Lady Appleton's world.

Minor corrections and numerous changes in word choices have been made in the course of preparing this collection. This was done to make the text read more smoothly and with less wordiness, and because short stories accepted for publication undergo less editing than book manuscripts. I am grateful to readers who caught mistakes in the earlier versions. Any that remain are entirely my own. There have been no changes to plots or characters.

Please note that the first two stories take place before events in *Face Down in the Marrow-Bone Pie*.

Kathy Lynn Emerson
    Wilton, Maine
    February 2025

The Body in the Dovecote

England 1552

Delighted with herself at having escaped, if only temporarily, from her duties as a waiting gentlewoman to the duchess of Northumberland, Susanna Leigh slipped into the overgrown garden at Otford and set off at a brisk pace along what remained of a wide graveled walk. She craved solitude and an opportunity to indulge in pleasant daydreams about handsome, charming Robert Appleton, to whom she was betrothed, but she had not gone more than a few yards before she realized she was not alone among the tangled flower beds, knots, and works of topiary.

Anne, countess of Warwick, wife to the duke and duchess's eldest son, danced past on an intersecting path bordered by a low hedge of rosemary. Susanna skidded to a halt and would have turned and fled, but it was too late. The countess had seen her. She reappeared at the point where walk and path met, her expression fierce. "How dare you follow me!"

"My lady, I would never intrude upon your privacy," Susanna protested. "I did not know anyone was here."

Lady Warwick considered that for a moment, then nodded. The two young women were of an age and had both been raised in households that supported the New Religion and believed girls should be educated in the same manner as boys, but Susanna was the daughter of a mere knight. Lady Warwick's father, before his execution for treason, had been duke of Somerset and Lord Protector of England.

"It is a large garden," Susanna said. "I will stay well out of your way."

The suggestion seemed to amuse Lady Warwick. "Shall we imagine the Picts' Wall down the middle?"

"If you like. I will take the half that includes the dell and the dovecotes and leave to you all the pleached bowers and arbors."

This time the nod of acknowledgment contained a hint of approval. Without further ado, they set off in opposite directions.

For the space of a quarter of an hour, Susanna enjoyed the peace and quiet of a bright morning at the end of May. The only sound was the gentle stirring of leaves, distant birdsong, and the crunch of her own leather-shod feet on gravel as she strolled beside the dell originally intended to be a trout stream. From the wooden bridge that spanned it, Susanna spent several minutes watching fish flash through the water below. She wondered if the duke meant to restore Otford to its former glory. It seemed a waste to let the manor and its grounds fall to ruin, and yet what need did he have of it when Knole, even more grand, lay less than three miles distant? Both manors had come to him from young King Edward the Sixth when Northumberland replaced Lady Warwick's father at the head of England's government.

Lost in contemplation, Susanna reacted slowly to the sound of running footsteps. By the time she turned, she saw only a blur of brightly colored skirts before the small form wearing them barreled into her. With a sob, Lady Katherine Dudley, aged six and a half, lifted her tear-streaked face to Susanna's and blurted, "There is a body in the dovecote!"

For a moment Susanna wondered if Lady Katherine was playing a trick on her. "Show me," she ordered.

Lady Katherine, youngest child of the duke of Northumberland, blinked rapidly at the command. Then, with a lack of reluctance that both surprised Susanna and heightened her suspicions, she led the way toward the three round brick structures that were home to nearly a thousand pigeons.

The smallest dovecote sat in splendid isolation in a sheltered copse. To lull the doves into taking up residence, their houses were always at some distance from human habitation, but no cooing issued from within this structure and there was no flapping of wings as birds flew in and out.

There should be something, Susanna thought.

There was activity around the larger dovecotes. The inhabitants were foragers, setting off each day to scour the countryside for seeds. She shaded her eyes against the sun, trying to see if the internal shutters were closed, but from the outside she could make out nothing but exterior landing ledges. A protruding stone course around the outside of the building, designed to prevent vermin—weasels, rats, and martens in particular—from climbing up to the entrances and devouring the birds, further obscured her vision.

"In here," Lady Katherine called.

"Wait."

Susanna spoke too late. Lady Katherine had already opened a low, heavy, wooden door and stepped inside the dovecote.

Ducking her head, Susanna went after her. The height of the entry was deliberate, intended to enforce a slow entrance so that a person's sudden appearance in the dovecote would not panic the residents. *No fear of that,* Susanna thought. The inside was eerily quiet and appeared to be empty of feathered inhabitants.

The walls of the dovecote were nearly three feet thick, shutting out both sound and light. The roof, dome shaped and constructed of slates, was topped with a wooden cupola which, when unshuttered, provided air as well as ingress and egress. The shutters, closed as Susanna had guessed they would be, made the interior too dark to see much of anything. As she stood upright, she stepped to one side, allowing in a square of daylight full of dust motes from the earthen floor.

"There," said Lady Katherine. At the far corner of the square, lying atop a thick layer of bird droppings, was a dead dove.

Susanna let out a breath she had not been aware of holding. It was a bird and not a person. Relief surged through her.

"I did not mean for it to die," Lady Katherine said in a choked voice.

Puzzled, Susanna squinted at both bird and girl as she fumbled for the lever that opened the shutters. She found it after a few frustrating moments but admitting additional light illuminated only enough of the interior for her make out the potence, a revolving wooden pole mounted on a plinth at the center of the dovecote. It rose from floor to roof, its two great arms extending outwards. The ladders at the end of each were used to collect eggs and squabs.

It resembled a gallows, Susanna thought, and shivered.

Rows of nest boxes, each about six inches square at the opening, lined the walls in a checkerboard pattern. They appeared to be empty, but Susanna knew that each nest was L-shaped, about eighteen inches deep and twelve across the back, and fronted with a small raised ledge to keep the eggs from rolling out. Were there more dead doves inside, or had they all flown away before the cote was shuttered?

Abandoning that question for the nonce, Susanna returned her attention to the body in the dovecote. She could see that the bird's beak was open. Its dead eyes stared at her, sightless but accusing. She had no difficulty imagining the effect of such a sight on an impressionable child. "Come away, my lady."

Instead, the girl knelt by the body, dragging her jewel-toned skirt in the dirt. "I killed it."

Startled, Susanna stepped close enough to see that Lady Katherine's tears flowed unchecked. Susanna was uncertain what to say. The doves were raised to feed the household, not as pets. Lady Katherine's despair seemed out of all proportion. Had she been a boy, Susanna suspected she'd have learned by this age to hunt birds smaller than this with bow and arrow.

Lady Katherine stroked one hand over the ruffled feathers. "It was here, abandoned," she managed to say between sobs. "It was on the ground, huddled into itself. I collected some seeds to feed it and make it well." She delved into the dirt beside the bird and came up with one.

Susanna accepted the seed from the child's grubby hand and held it in the light. Black and about the size of a wheat seed, its surface was pitted with small warts. She did not know what plant it came from, but she tucked the seed into the little leather pocket suspended from her waist to study at her leisure. She had for some time taken an interest in the identification of herbs.

"It seems most unlikely that you caused the dove to die, Lady Katherine." Susanna helped the little girl to her feet and dusted her off. "If this bird was left behind, it must have been ill." She stooped, examining the small corpse. "See here? This dove could not fly because its wing is broken."

No doubt being seized by small, determined hands had not helped the poor creature's condition, but Susanna did not say so aloud. Lady Katherine had suffered enough guilt on the dove's account.

"I would have cared for it," the child murmured. "I could have kept it in a cage, safe from harm."

"Even beloved pets can die, my lady," Susanna said in her gentlest voice, slinging a comforting arm around the girl's shoulders. "Come away with me now. The dove was already mortally wounded. You could not have saved it."

They had just left the dovecote when a man entered the copse. At the sight of them he started and let the rake he was carrying fall to the ground with a dull thump. "Your pardon, mistress. My lady." He tugged on a greasy, chestnut-colored forelock before he remembered to take off his cap to reveal thick hair full of tangles. "I come to clean out the droppings," he stammered, backing away all the while.

That explained why the shutters had been closed. Bird lime had considerable value as a source of saltpeter for making gunpowder and was collected on a regular basis. Happy to have that minor mystery solved and anxious to escape the pungent smell that clung to his ragged clothes and hobnail boots, Susanna told the fellow to continue about his business.

Forthwith, she escorted Lady Katherine back to her governess, pausing only long enough to suggest that the child might like to have a linnet or a lark in a cage as a pet. That accomplished, Susanna put both the workman and the dead dove out of her mind. She thought of the latter again, but only in passing, when she rose the following morning to news of another death.

"It is Lady Ambrose, mistress," her tiring maid announced. Susanna shared both Ellen and the bedchamber with two other gentlewomen of the household. "They say in the kitchen that she woke in the middle of the night in a terrible sweat, then swooned upon rising and suffered most horrible pangs and fits, worse than anything she endured when she was ill before, and at six of the clock, she died."

"Poor lady," Susanna murmured as she broke her fast with the bread and ale Ellen had brought.

Throughout the simple meal and while Susanna, Margaret, and Penelope dressed, helping each other with their points, they spoke in subdued tones of poor Lady Ambrose's sudden demise. Penelope seemed to think the duke might consider her as a candidate to be Lord Ambrose's next wife. "He is the most pleasing of all the brothers," she declared.

Susanna doubted that Penelope knew Lord Ambrose well enough to judge. Some years older than Lord Henry, Lord Robin, and Lord Guildford, Northumberland's second son spent most of his time at court with the young king. All the brothers did. Susanna smiled to herself. Although she had once been kissed by Lord Robin and found it pleasant, she had never had any matrimonial interest in any of the Dudleys. Besides, Lord Robin already had a wife and it was, or so everyone said, a love match. He'd married a girl named Amye Robsart in a quiet, private ceremony one day after the splendid wedding between the earl of Warwick and the duke of Somerset's eldest daughter.

Inevitably, speculation turned to the cause of Lady Ambrose's death.

"Mayhap her husband tired of her," Margaret suggested with a giggle.

"I am certain it was a relapse," Penelope declared.

A month earlier, Lady Ambrose had broken out in spots. One of the duke's physicians had said it was the measles. The other had diagnosed her condition as smallpox. Whichever had afflicted her, she'd recovered in spite of their care.

Ellen turned a face that had suddenly gone pale toward Susanna. "What if it is some horrible plague visited upon us for the duke's sins?"

"You must not say such a thing," Susanna warned her.

But panic made the maidservant careless. Her voice rose. "Some say the duke deserves to be struck dead for all the evil he's done."

"Silence!" Susanna glared the foolish young woman into obedience. "His grace the duke is a good man."

He'd become Susanna's guardian upon her father's death. To ensure that her interests were protected, he'd quickly arranged her marriage to the dashing and debonair Robert Appleton, a gentleman from distant Lancashire. Although Susanna had only met him a few times since their betrothal, Robert had charmed her with his manners and a pretty attentiveness. He even professed himself pleased that she was well versed in the classics and had studied mathematics and geography.

Annoyed by the chatter and speculation, Susanna left the chamber ahead of the others. She thus chanced upon the duke just as he was leaving the rooms allotted to Lady Ambrose. Attended by his chaplain, his physicians, and his steward, Northumberland seemed uncommon agitated. He was not much given to any show of emotion and further surprised Susanna by hailing her.

"Go and keep Lady Ambrose's maid company," he said. "She is in no fit state to wait alone for the women who will wash the body and wrap it in a winding sheet."

Uncertain how to deal with the sobbing servant she found within, Susanna managed a few disjointed words of comfort. Her effort felt inadequate before such a heart-wrenching display of grief.

Tears streamed down the woman's deeply lined face and dripped off the end of a wattled chin. She was of an age to make Susanna wonder if she had been Lady Ambrose's nurse. The deceased had not been a duke's daughter like Lady Warwick, Susanna reminded herself, but came, as Susanna herself did, from wealthy gentry stock. There were many in the household at Leigh Abbey who had served the Leighs for generations. They'd mourned the death of Susanna's father as deeply as she had.

"Lady Ambrose was surpassing sick," Susanna said. "There is naught anyone could have done to predict a relapse." Her illness, whatever it was, had left her with a lingering cough and a hoarse voice. "Mayhap she'd not fully recovered and fell ill again. You must not blame yourself for that."

"She was well." With an angry gesture, the woman dashed the moisture from her cheeks. Her eyes were red with weeping and her lips quivered. "It was not the same ailment that killed her."

Frustrated by her failure to soothe the old woman's grief, Susanna stopped trying to find the right words and fumbled for a handkerchief instead. Taking it, the maidservant mopped her face. The honk when she blew her nose reverberated in the awkward silence.

"The duke says we're all to be kept here," the servant said after a moment. "No one's to leave, he said, until the moon be at the full. His grace's physicians think it may be the sweat, or worse."

Susanna swallowed back the instinctive fear aroused by any mention of the sweat. That mysterious disease had devastated England the previous year, killing without mercy or discretion. "Death can come with no warning from a hundred causes," Susanna murmured, more to reassure herself than to ease the maidservant's suffering. She had the best of reasons to know that. Her father had been taken from her in a shipwreck. Her only sibling, a younger sister, had met her death through accidental poisoning.

"Lady Ambrose was sick to her stomach and feverish and giddy," the old woman said. "She grew weak from delirium and pain until she slipped at the last into a deep, unnatural sleep."

Susanna frowned. That did not sound like the sweat, or smallpox, or measles.

"She was in such high spirits before she went to bed," the maid lamented. "She said she felt herself again after so many weeks of illness." A brief and poignant smile showed a flash of yellowed teeth. "She filched three cakes from the high table for a midnight treat. She did love sweets, but she gave one to me." She smacked her lips, as if recalling the taste, and with an absent gesture indicated all that remained of Lady Ambrose's portion—a few crumbs scattered across the top of a small table and a single black seed.

With a sick feeling in the pit of her stomach, Susanna rose and went closer. She inspected the seed without touching it, leaning close enough to smell the honey with which it had been coated and to note its deeply pitted surface.

Coincidence, she told herself. Lady Ambrose *must* have suffered a relapse. But she turned again to the maidservant.

"Tell me about your lady's condition when she was ill." During that time, the rest of the household had been kept well away from the sickroom.

Sensible enough to be alarmed by Susanna's abrupt question, the old woman nevertheless complied. "She had a rash and a high fever, mistress. It began on the second day of May, as I remember me, and she was most terrible ill for a week thereafter, but by the twenty-third, she was almost herself again, save for the cough."

"Today is the first of June," Susanna murmured.

Bracing herself, she strode to the bed and threw back the coverlet to inspect the corpse, even turning it over to examine it for spots. It was the duty of every gentlewoman to learn how to lay out the dead. Girls were trained young not to be squeamish.

The only fresh marks were dark bruises between the shoulder blades, an indication that the body had lain on its back for some little time after death. Susanna knew, from her grandmother, who had prepared a good many dead kinfolk for burial in her time, that this often happened.

Although she could see no outward indication that Lady Ambrose had died of eating poisonous seeds, just as she had no proof the dove had, Susanna took the seed from the cake away with her, determined to discover what plant it came from. If she did not, she feared she would forever be tormented by the possibility that telling someone about the dead dove might have saved Lady Ambrose's life.

She sought Lady Katherine first. Susanna did not want to alarm the child and racked her brain to think of some reason to ask where she'd found the seeds to feed the dove. In the end, Susanna's interest in plants—the simple truth, if not all of it—sufficed to broach the subject.

"I hope to make a collection of seeds, roots, and leaves and label them," she explained, "that I may one day identify in an instant, by comparison, any plant that comes into my possession, but I am mystified by that black seed you showed me. Can you describe the plant it came from?"

Lady Katherine, preoccupied with conquering a new embroidery stitch she'd been told to practice, shook her head. If she was disturbed by the death of her brother's wife, she showed no sign of it.

"A pity we are in quarantine," Lady Katherine's governess remarked, overhearing. "There is an old cunning woman at Sevenoaks who is renowned for her knowledge of herbs."

It was an even greater pity, Susanna thought, that no one had yet compiled a complete botanical reference book in English, one with accurate and detailed illustrations. Only the first volume of Master Turner's *A New Herbal* had so far appeared in print and, as he'd been physician and chaplain to the late duke of Somerset and was currently out of favor, no copy of his work graced the duke of Northumberland's collection.

"Did the seeds come from one of the kitchens?" Susanna asked, doggedly pursuing her interrogation of the child. The kitchens were separated from the duke's living quarters as a precaution against fire but they were close to both the gardens and the dovecotes.

Lady Katherine looked up, frowning with impatience. "They were in a box in one of the dressers."

"What kind of box?"

"A box of seeds!"

When the governess seemed about to interject a question of her own, Susanna retreated. She suspected she'd learned as much as she was going to.

She went next to Otford's kitchens. If they'd been in good repair, they'd have rivaled those at Hampton Court, containing a dozen or more separate departments, from a spicery for storing spices to the confectory that turned out sweets and pastries. At present only two small rooms between the great kitchen and the serving place were in use. There special dishes were dressed and garnished before they were carried into the great hall to be consumed.

A quick peek through the hatch into the first dresser showed Susanna the roast carcass of a peacock. It had been reunited with its feathers for presentation above the salt. In the second dresser, one of the undercooks was glazing marzipan. Forcing a smile, she went in.

She received a glare in return. "What do you want, mistress? I have no time to waste today on idle chatter."

"I need but a moment," she assured him, and produced one of the seeds from her pocket. "Can you tell me what this seed is? It was atop a cake."

He spared only a glance before disclaiming all knowledge. "Not a cake I decorated."

"Where else could it have come from? It was on the duke's table." She bit her lip, fearing she'd let too much slip, but the cook was intent upon his work.

Susanna's gaze roved the small chamber, searching for the box Lady Katherine had mentioned. There were several small wooden containers near at hand, each carefully closed to preserve the contents. She opened the first without being noticed and was disappointed to find ginger within. When she reached for the second she was caught.

"I have told you, mistress. That is not a seed I use." So fierce was his glower that eyebrows like two wooly caterpillars nearly met above his bulbous nose. "Do you think I cannot recognize mine own ingredients?"

Lifting the lid of the second box, she saw that this one contained seeds, but they were caraways, translucent and slightly curved with pale ridges, not at all like the one in her hand. "Could a few of these seeds have been mixed in with the caraways or some others?"

"I would have noticed," the cook insisted, but she saw the flicker of doubt in his eyes. In the rush of preparing for a meal for hundreds of people, such a mistake might easily be made.

"There were cakes last night, topped with seeds in honey." Once they were coated, would anyone have noticed the difference? Honey would hide any unusual taste, too.

"*Caraway* seeds," the cook insisted. "Look you, there is naught else in the box."

It was true. If any of the other seeds had ever been there, they were gone now, used up, Susanna was certain, on one or more of the cakes. Mayhap it was fortunate only one person had died!

She had been thinking that Lady Ambrose had been poisoned by accident. It was common enough to mistake one herb for another with fatal consequences. Her own sister had consumed banewort berries thinking they were cherries and died a terrible death. But accident, she realized with a sudden, sickening lurch in her stomach, was not the only possibility. What if the seeds had been put in the box deliberately, by someone who knew what their effect would be? A second frightening conclusion followed hard on the first. Lady Ambrose was unlikely to have been the poisoner's intended victim. She remembered what the old servant had said. Her mistress had filched the cakes because she had a sweet tooth. They had been on the high table, placed there for the duke himself to consume.

Susanna knew then that she must talk to his grace and tell him her suspicions, but she needed a breath of fresh air first. Besides, she had just thought of one other person she might question about the black seeds.

She made her way through the gardens at a brisk pace and in a short time she reached the dovecotes. Somewhere nearby, she assumed, would be a keeper. She found him deep in conversation with the very workman who'd raked out the dovecote. She stopped and studied both men. *No harm in either*, she decided, and neither was likely to have gotten into the kitchens unnoticed to add poison seeds to the cook's supplies. Besides, the workman would have discovered the dead dove in the course of his duties. Susanna saw no point in dissimilating.

"Some of these were given to the dove that died," she told them, once again displaying the black seed. "Can you tell me what this is?"

"Corn cockle," the keeper said at once. "What fool fed those to my flock?"

"A child," Susanna said quickly. "There was no intent to hurt, and only one dove died—the one in the shuttered dovecote."

The keeper's brow arched and the workman's face took on a look of alarm but neither said a word as she described, without naming the girl, what Lady Katherine had done the previous day.

"Corn cockle," the keeper said again. "It is dangerous, but rarely eaten. It grows in wheat and oak fields, chicken yards, and waste places."

"Is it only fatal to birds?" Susanna held her breath.

"It will poison cattle if they graze on it, but an animal would have to eat a good many seeds to take in a fatal dose."

"What if it were already ill?" She did not dare suggest a person had ingested the poison. The workman's panic was already excessive, as if he feared he would be blamed.

The keeper scratched the bald pate beneath his cap. "Might take it off the sooner, same as with the dove."

* * *

An hour later, Susanna was admitted to the duke of Northumberland's private study. The duke had a formidable glower. Between a forked beard and a jutting nose, his full lips thinned. Finely arched brows crept toward a receding hairline as he studied the young woman before him.

"You demanded a private audience?" The sheer audacity of her request seemed to have won it for her.

"Yes, your grace." She fought the urge to break eye contact, determined to convince him that the request had not been a foolish whim on her part. "Someone tried to poison you last night," she blurted. "Lady Ambrose died in your stead."

"Explain," he ordered.

When she had told him what she had guessed, as well as all she knew, he studied her in somber silence for a long, unnerving span.

"Your grace? Do you know who might want to kill you?"

A wry smile twisted his mobile mouth. "A great many people, I should think. Today was the day upon which I'd intended to set out for the north. The reason for my journey is no secret. King Edward means to make a summer progress through Sussex, Hampshire, Wiltshire, and Dorset. Rather than accompany his majesty and risk letting the king observe first hand my great unpopularity with the public, I excused myself to inspect border fortifications. The perpetual threat Scotland poses is at times most convenient."

Susanna frowned. "Would your enemies not see your departure as a good thing, your grace? You'll be away from court for months."

"Which means," he explained, "that someone knew they must act now or lose the opportunity. Someone in this household."

"Surely not a servant. They are loyal to you."

"Some are. You knew William Huggons?"

Susanna nodded, puzzled. Until a few months ago, he'd been a permanent part of Northumberland's household. She'd never heard an explanation for his abrupt departure.

"Huggons's wife was in service to the duchess of Somerset. When the Lord Protector was executed, Mistress Huggons declared I was better worthy to die. That and other remarks, some of them treasonous, resulted in her commitment to the Tower, where her old mistress already resides." His intense gaze focused on her, colder than she'd ever seen it. "Tell me, Susanna, have you heard any one in my household utter similar sentiments?"

She shook her head, but she could not help but think of Ellen. She was grateful when the duke broke eye contact to send one of his men to fetch the keeper of the dovecotes and the workman with the rake.

"We will leave the kitchen staff for the nonce," he mused aloud. "You say the cook denied any knowledge of the corn cockle?"

"He did not recognize the seed. Nor did I. It is a weed." Once the keeper had given it a name, she'd been able to call it to mind. Tall and spindly with pink flowers, it was a common plant. Anyone could get seeds and keep them as long as necessary. That made her wonder if someone had planned the duke's murder for many months or acted on impulse.

It was then that she remembered the exact words the cook had used.

"What do you want, mistress? I have no time to waste *today* on idle chatter," she repeated aloud. "Did he mean he wasted time yesterday, with someone else who did not ordinarily visit the kitchens?"

Approval writ large on his countenance, Northumberland sent another henchman to ask who had been in the kitchens the previous day. The answer was not long in coming. The undercook had been twice interrupted, once by Penelope Stilton, one of the gentlewoman who shared Susanna's bedchamber, accompanied by a maid, and the second time by Lady Warwick, soliciting scraps of gingerbread for her lap dog.

Northumberland's eyes narrowed. When the messenger left, he said, "Lady Warwick has good reason to wish me dead. No doubt she blames me, as others do, for the death of her father."

"But she is married to your son," Susanna objected. "To harm you hurts him as well."

Northumberland's laugh sounded bitter. "If I die, Warwick succeeds to all my titles and estates, scarce a hardship for him or his wife, but I doubt Lady Warwick cares what happens to her husband. Her father and I arranged their marriage without consulting either of them."

"But she agreed. She swore to—"

Northumberland waved aside her sputtered protests. "I have seen no outward sign of hatred toward me, but who can tell what rage, what desire for revenge, seethes inside her?" He sent Susanna a sharp look. "Do you have some reason to think Penelope Stilton a more likely suspect? Or the maid?"

Again, Susanna denied it, but she remembered Penelope's desire to marry the new-made widower, and Ellen's talk of the duke's sins. *There must be some way to find out the truth*, she thought.

"Your grace," the duke's henchman announced, entering with the keeper of the dovecotes in tow, "the workman you sent for has fled."

Susanna felt a surge of hope. Mayhap her suspicions of the women of the household were unfounded.

"Fellow's been stealing bird lime." The keeper sounded indignant. "I knew naught of it, your grace, till the gentlewoman here mentioned that the small dovecote had been shuttered."

Not murder, then, Susanna thought. *Only theft*.

"Send out a search party," Northumberland ordered.

As he gave further commands, Susanna slipped from the room. There might be a way to prove guilt or innocence. If she pretended to know more than she did, she might shock one of the three suspects into revealing herself.

She found Ellen in the bedchamber, mending a smock.

"I know what you did," she said in an accusing voice. "You were seen in the kitchens yesterday."

Bristling, Ellen glared at her. "I only do what I'm told, madam."

"Is that your excuse?"

"I am expected to obey all three of you." Ellen's agitation grew so great that she accidentally stabbed her thumb with her needle. She stuck it in her mouth. After a moment, she blurted, "Mistress Penelope gave me a shilling to do as she asked."

Distraught, Susanna left the maidservant without saying more. She had been wrong. Lady Ambrose had been the intended victim all along. Penelope had been serious about wanting to marry the widower.

Her duty was clear. No one should be allowed to get away with murder. She must return to the duke's study and tell him what she had learned, even though doing so would result in arrest and execution for Penelope and dismissal, at the least, for Ellen.

To reach her goal she had to pass through a gallery that overlooked the gardens. Glancing out, she saw Lady Warwick sitting on a stone bench under an oak tree. She appeared to be weeping. Susanna hesitated, but she knew that a few moment's delay would not matter to Ellen and Penelope. Changing course, she went outside.

"My lady?" she asked in a tentative voice. "Are you unwell?"

"Go away," Lady Warwick said on a gusty sob. "I grieve for my poor sister, cruelly taken from us by the sweat, and for all the others who may yet die of that dread disease."

"Lady Ambrose's death was caused by something she ate," Susanna said, thinking to ease the countess's distress. "The ailment is not contagious."

Lady Warwick stiffened and lifted her bowed head. "What do you mean? What caused her death?" There was such agony in the question that Susanna felt she had to answer.

Moving closer, she retrieved one of the two black, pitted seeds from her pouch. "This is what killed her."

The sudden loss of color from Lady Warwick's face betrayed her.

Susanna swallowed hard. "Do you recognize them, my lady?"

"No. How could I? I know naught of seeds."

Susanna did not believe her. "They come from a plant called corn cockle. They are poisonous. Somehow they were added to a glaze used to ice cakes and those cakes were taken to the high table. Anyone there might have eaten them, but as it happened, only Lady Ambrose did."

"No." As if the idea were too terrible to contemplate, the noblewoman's eyes abruptly lost their focus.

"Where did you get the seeds, Lady Warwick?" She kept her voice level but firm.

"From my father! From my poor, dead father! He gave them to me the last time I was allowed to see him and told me how to use them. But I never meant for anyone else to die. Only the duke."

"Are there more? Do you mean to try again?"

"No! No! They are all gone, and I thought I had failed. I thought I had done all I could, and I was *glad* nothing happened. I did not know she'd eaten the cakes." She'd grasped Susanna's arm with painful force as her voice rose.

"You tried to kill the duke of Northumberland." With an effort, Susanna broke free, rubbing the bruised forearm.

"No. Yes." She was sobbing now. "I had to obey my father."

She broke down completely then, and had to be helped to her bedchamber. Susanna sent for a soothing posset to sedate her and stayed with her to make sure she drank it.

"I swear I will never attempt such a thing again," Lady Warwick vowed. "You must not tell anyone what I did." Her eyes pleaded with Susanna.

"I wish I could promise that," she said with genuine regret, "but the duke already suspects you."

Lady Warwick turned her face to the wall.

Only when she was certain the other woman was deeply asleep, did Susanna leave her. She went first to her own chamber to confront Ellen once more.

"What did you do for Penelope?" she demanded.

Ellen blinked at her in confusion. "I thought you knew."

"Tell me." Her tone left no room for refusal.

"She wanted a potion to bring down her courses," Ellen grudgingly admitted. "My aunt is the old cunning woman of Sevenoaks. I know what ingredients to mix. Mistress Penelope distracted the cook while I searched for wormwood and rue."

Susanna was both relieved and dismayed. An ounce of dried wormwood mixed with a pint of boiling water and drunk three times a day could bring down a woman's courses, but wormwood and rue, especially in combination with myrrh and lupines, were more commonly used only when one wished to expel a fetus. She did not ask Ellen for any further details. She did not wish to know.

Still reeling from all the revelations of the afternoon, Susanna made her way back to the duke's study. Northumberland sat behind a table littered with papers, leaning on his elbows, his fingers steepled under his chin as he listened to her account of Lady Warwick's confession. He was silent for a long time afterward, as late afternoon sun filtered in through the mullioned window behind him, making a hatchwork pattern on the rich red velvet of his doublet.

"Lady Ambrose's death has already been attributed to the sweat," he said at last. "That verdict stands. Once you leave this room, you will never again speak of what you know, not even to me."

"Do you trust Lady Warwick to keep her word?"

"Both reward and punishment must be apportioned." His eyes bored into Susanna, as if he would bend her will to his own. "My son's wife must be watched, lest she lapse again into mental derangement."

Susanna held her breath. Did he mean to imprison the countess? Would he send her to the Tower, where her mother was already housed?

"I am pleased with you, Susanna. You have served my wife well as a waiting gentlewoman. It is time you had more responsibility. From this day forward, you will serve Lady Warwick as her chief lady. You will sleep in her chamber and provide soothing possets as necessary."

"From this day forward?" Numb, she repeated the phrase. She found it difficult to distinguish her reward from Lady Warwick's punishment.

"Your coming marriage need be no impediment," Northumberland continued. "You'd have remained part of this household afterward in any case."

Susanna wanted to object. Her daydreams had included blocks of time spent with her new husband in their own house, but Northumberland's attention had already shifted to his preparations for the journey north. With a sigh, Susanna let herself out of his study.

In the future, she resolved, she would try harder to ignore any mysteries that came her way. She was certain she'd have no difficulty doing so.

A Note from the Author

Susanna, Lady Appleton is a fictional creation, but in order to write *Face Down in the Marrow-Bone Pie*, I had to develop an extensive biography for her. I decided that Susanna would be just a little younger than Elizabeth Tudor, who ruled England from 1558-1603, and that she would be trained as a gentlewoman in the household of a real person, John Dudley, duke of Northumberland. In the story you have just read, Susanna Leigh is seventeen years old and not yet married to Robert Appleton.

Most of my stories and novels use a combination of fictional characters and real people. "The Body in the Dovecote" was inspired by a letter from the duke of Northumberland to Sir William Cecil in which he described the death, on June 1, 1552 at Otford, of his daughter-in-law, Lady Ambrose Dudley. There is no mention, of course, of poison.

After the events in this story, the duke attempted a rebellion that would have placed the Lady Jane Grey on the throne of England. He failed, was tried for treason, and was executed. Northumberland's eldest son, John, earl of Warwick, was released from the Tower of London in 1554 but died soon after. His childless widow, Anne, daughter of the duke of Somerset, remarried and lived until 1588. By 1566, however, rumors of "mental derangement" had already begun to spread. That, too, inspired me.

To find a poison capable of killing a person as well as a dove, I contacted Luci Zahray, "the Poison Lady." She put in a good many hours of research to come up with corn cockle, for which I am immensely grateful.

This story was first published in *Murders and Other Confusions* (2004), my first collection of short stories featuring characters from the Face Down novels.

Much Ado About Murder

"The vii day of March began the blazing [star] at night and it did shoot out fire."
Diary of Henry Machyn (1555/6)

An ominous portent first appeared in the sky over England on the same evening Robert Appleton brought Lord Benedick and his wife to Leigh Abbey. It was a blazing star with a long tail. Half the size of the moon, it much resembled a gigantic torch burning fitfully in the wind.

"A sure sign of disaster," muttered a maidservant, casting her baleful glance at the comet high above. She sent an equally suspicious look toward the new arrivals dismounting by rushlight in the inner courtyard.

Ignoring her tiring maid's comment, Susanna Appleton wrapped a wool cloak more closely around herself and went forward to greet her husband and his guests. Jennet could find evil omens and harbingers of impending doom in the twisted branches of a bush or the discolored grass beneath a mushroom. She relished dire predictions, although she always professed herself well-pleased when they came to naught. No doubt she imagined her warnings had somehow prevented catastrophe.

The visitors were a richly-dressed young couple traveling with two elderly servants. As Susanna watched, the husband lifted his wife out of her saddle and set her gently on her feet on the icy cobbles. He pressed her gloved hand to his lips, then held it tight as he slipped the other arm around her waist to steady her. He was rewarded with a smile of such radiance that Susanna felt a twinge of envy. True devotion between spouses was rare and it was sadly lacking in her own marriage. Robert would always love wealth and position more than he cared for any woman.

"Lord Benedick comes to England from Padua," Robert said after he'd presented Susanna to that nobleman. "Padua is part of the powerful Venetian Republic, where he is held in great regard. And his wife here is niece to the governor of Messina."

Titles impressed Robert more than they did Susanna, but she was as well informed as he on the subject of various political alliances. He did not need to tell her that Messina was part of Sicily, or that Sicily was under Spanish rule. So, some would say, was their own land, ever since Queen Mary's marriage to King Philip.

Robert's reason for inviting Lord Benedick to visit his home was just as clear—he hoped a friendship with this well-connected young sprig of the nobility would ease him back into favor at court. He'd made the mistake of backing the Lady Jane Grey's attempt to take Mary Tudor's throne away from her and had spent several uncomfortable months in prison before being pardoned and released.

Susanna had also supported Queen Jane. Now her loyalty was to the Lady Elizabeth, Queen Mary's half sister, although it was not wise to say so. These visitors, she decided, must be looked upon as the enemy, a danger to certain clandestine activities practiced at Leigh Abbey during Robert's frequent absences.

Forcing a smile, Susanna gestured toward the passage that led to the great hall. "If you will come this way, Lady—"

Impulsively, Lord Benedick's wife took both Susanna's hands in hers. She spoke charmingly accented English. "Let us be comfortable together, Beatrice and Susanna. What need for formality when we are destined to be great friends?"

"Destined?"

Beatrice laughed. "It is written in the sky." She gestured toward the comet. "Under another such dancing star was I born. How can any doubt this new one is a sign of good things to come?"

With great ease, Susanna thought.

As she led the way into the house, she realized that Beatrice's "dancing star" must have been the one that streaked across English skies in 1533. Susanna had not been born until the following year, but she had heard the stories as a child. That particular portent, it was said, foretold the divorce of King Henry from Catherine of Aragon. To those of Susanna's religious upbringing, putting aside both Queen Catherine and the Church of Rome had been cause for rejoicing. Catholics viewed the matter in a different light.

The divorce of her parents had been one of the first things Queen Mary set aside when she came to the throne. Now it was her sister, Elizabeth, daughter of Anne Boleyn, who was accounted a bastard, and those who would not renounce the New Religion and return to the Roman Catholic fold faced arrest, even martyrdom, on charges of heresy. The plight of many of Susanna's late father's friends had driven her to devise a way to help them escape persecution.

When wine and cheese and dried fruit had been served, Robert spoke. "We have been granted permission to hunt in the royal deer park on the morrow," he announced. "We will retire early to be up betimes."

Seated before the fire in the great hall, Susanna shifted to allow the warmth to reach more of her. Because Robert wished to impress their guests, he kept them in the largest and draftiest of the rooms instead of retiring to one of the smaller, warmer chambers. While beads of perspiration formed on her forehead from the heat, her back felt cold as a dead man's hand.

"Do you go with them, Beatrice?" she asked.

"I take no pleasure in killing." Beatrice sipped from a glass goblet containing a Gascon wine.

"She prefers slow torture," Lord Benedick commented, *sotto voce.*

Ignoring him, Beatrice remarked upon the color of the claret. "Bright as a ruby, as it should be."

Susanna could not resist. "I am told that if a claret wine has lost its color, one may take a pennyworth of damsons and stew them with some red wine of the deepest color to make a pound or more or syrup, which when put into a hogshead of claret wine, restores it to its original shade."

One foot resting on the back of a firedog, Robert stirred the fire with a poker. "The study of herbs," he confided to Lord Benedick, his manner implying a shared masculine indulgence of female weakness, "is my wife's little hobby."

"A very proper occupation." Lord Benedick lounged on a bench with a low back, his legs stretched out in front of him with the ankles crossed. He lifted his goblet in a toast to both women. "Mine delights in devising new uses for holy thistle."

"A universal remedy," Beatrice said with a smug smile. The twinkle in her eyes and the quick exchange of glances with her husband alerted Susanna to the play on words.

"*Carduus benedictus,*" she murmured.

Belatedly catching on, Robert laughed.

Jennet hovered close by, ears stretched to catch every word, but she did not understand the pun. Beatrice's companion, an old woman named Ursula, also seemed oblivious, or else she'd heard the joke too many times before to find it amusing. She sat near the hearth, placid as a grazing cow, her gnarled hands busy with a piece of needlework.

"If you have an interest in herbs other than the one that shares its name with Lord Benedick," Robert said to Beatrice, "you must ask my wife to show you her new storeroom."

Concealed by her skirts, Susanna's hands clenched into fists. Trust Robert to focus attention on the one thing she wished to hide.

"I fear it is most noisome," she protested. "I have been conducting experiments to determine which herbs are most effective for killing fleas and other vermin." She'd intended the pungent smell keep Robert at bay. Now she must hope the odor was also strong enough to deter curious visitors.

"Poison would never be my wife's weapon of choice," Benedick remarked. "No more than the bow. She prefers a blade."

"He means I speak poniards and every word stabs." Beatrice gave her husband a playful swat on the shoulder.

This couple bandied words like tennis balls, Susanna thought, and yet each one was served with affection. She glanced at Robert, then away.

Benedick grinned at his wife before returning his attention to his host. "I cherish the hope that this visit will allow me to gain some small understanding of English women, for I find my wife to be a most puzzling creature."

"*Your* wife, sir?"

"Did you not know? Beatrice was born in England."

"My mother," she explained, "was Spanish. She came to these shores in the entourage of Queen Catherine of Aragon and married an Englishman."

"Have you family here, then?" Susanna asked.

"Alas, no. When both my parents died, Ursula was obliged to take me back to Spain to be raised by my mother's sister."

Hearing her name, the old woman glanced their way. She sent a fond smile winging toward her former charge before once more taking up her embroidery.

The conversation turned to the delights of travel in Spain and Italy. To Susanna's relief, there was no further mention of the new storeroom she'd caused to be built in an isolated spot beyond her stillroom and herb garden.

***

Before dawn the next day, Susanna rose to watch the hunting party depart, then made her way to what she privately called "the mint room." It was well, she thought, that the three "heretics" she'd had hidden at Leigh Abbey a few days earlier had left before Robert and his guests arrived, but a great pity that another had turned up right on their heels.

She glanced over her shoulder as she turned the key in the lock. No one was in sight and the sun had yet to burn off a concealing early morning mist. With luck, she could spirit the fellow away before Beatrice or her servant rose from their beds.

About the members of her own household she had no concerns. None would betray her. They had been loyal to her father in his time and they were loyal now to her. Further, they regarded Robert as an interloper and doubtless always would. He'd gained legal control of Leigh Abbey only because he'd married her.

The near overwhelming scent of mint rolled out of the storehouse the moment Susanna opened the door. Inside the small, brick-lined, stone building were great bales of garden mint, watermint, and pennyroyal. Taking a deep breath of fresh air first, Susanna plunged inside, skirting the bales to reach another door, this one concealed by a panel in the back wall.

She did not see the body until she tripped over it.

Susanna knelt beside a man sprawled face up on the floor, an expression of agony on his face. She knew even before she touched him that she was far too late to render aid.

As her fingers found a lump on the back of his skull, her own head began to swim. Startled by her find, she'd forgotten to hold her breath.

Was this how he died? In fear of suffocation, his heart failing under the strain of trying to take in untainted air?

Eyes streaming, coughing fit to choke, she fled the storeroom. In the yard, doubled over, she inhaled in great gulps, all the while fighting for control of a roiling stomach. When someone took her hand to guide her to a nearby bench, she let herself be led. She assumed Jennet had come to her rescue, but it was Beatrice's voice that spoke, in calm, well-modulated tones.

"I have heard the odor of pennyroyal attracts fleas, then smothers them, but I'd not have thought it would work so well on a man. Was he your particular enemy?"

Susanna stared at the other woman in shock and horror. "I did not kill him!"

"He is dead." Beatrice looked distraught, as who would not, having come upon such a scene.

"A tragic accident."

"Yes." Beatrice did not sound convinced.

What else could it have been? Susanna buried her face in her hands, although she had no intention of giving way to tears. For just a moment, she needed to hide from Beatrice's too-perceptive gaze.

The odor in the mint room had been well nigh overpowering. If he'd dropped the key she'd given him, then panicked as he tried to find it and could not, confusion and the struggle to breathe could have caused him to stumble and fall, striking his head. On what, she had no notion, but she'd felt the lump. The blow alone might have killed him. Or, as she'd first thought, he could have had a weak heart and been snuffed out by sheer terror. She was certain of only one thing. The pennyroyal alone was not to blame. As Beatrice had implied, a man was a great deal bigger than a flea.

"Inconvenient, no matter how he died," Beatrice remarked. "If he is found here and can be identified as a heretic, his presence will endanger your efforts on behalf of the Marian exiles."

Startled, Susanna sat bolt upright. She felt a chill that had naught to do with the cold, damp morning. "What do you know of the work we do here?"

The calm, composed countenance above a sable-trimmed cloak of red velvet inspired confidence, as did Beatrice's words. "Benedick and I have many friends in the English community at Padua."

Susanna's head pounded, an after-effect of her coughing fit. She found it difficult to order her thoughts. Did she mean Benedick had befriended men driven into exile by Queen Mary's religious policies, or that he was acquainted with Englishmen already there before Mary took the throne? The University of Padua had long drawn students from England, in particular those with an interest in medicine, but not all of them were followers of the New Religion.

"I see I must be blunt with you." Beatrice glanced around to make sure they were unobserved. "Some of the most recent arrivals reached Padua only because of your efforts on their behalf." She named several men Susanna had hidden at Leigh Abbey on their way out of England. "What you do here is of vital importance, Susanna. Benedick and I may not share your faith, but we approve of saving lives."

"Robert would not, if he knew." The bitter words slipped out before she could censor them.

"I am glad to hear that you have kept your ambitious husband in the dark."

"He is a loyal subject!" She stood up too fast, making her head spin.

"Aye, so loyal and so bent on advancement under your present monarch that he might be tempted to betray his own wife. There would be a risk. He might be blamed for your folly. But if you alone were found guilty, he would benefit from your downfall."

That Beatrice spoke the truth did not make her observations any more palatable, but her words also reminded Susanna that she had a more pressing problem. "I dare not call in the coroner. He would ask too many questions."

"Then we must remove the body from the premises at once," Beatrice said, "before anyone else comes along and sees it. Have you a barrel or a buck tub to hide him in while we transport him?" She glanced toward the dark interior of the storeroom, as if considering the dead man's size. "Or mayhap an empty wine butt?"

Susanna rejected Beatrice's more colorful suggestions. "A plain blanket to wrap him in will do. There is one in the stable." After closing and locking the storeroom door, she led the way there. "He rode in on an old bay mare. We can use her to carry him away again."

"Is there a river or stream nearby?" Beatrice asked. "If we leave him in the water, it will appear that he was thrown when he attempted to ford it and drowned after hitting his head on a rock."

"And the rushing water will wash away the smell of the mint." Susanna had to admire Beatrice's quick thinking. In spite of a tendency toward the over-dramatic, she had a practical bent.

"But what was he doing in your storeroom? Why did he come out of hiding?"

Susanna covered her hesitation by fumbling with the stable door. Beatrice appeared to be an ally. She knew Susanna smuggled heretics out of England and that one of them was dead, but she might not realize that the storeroom had a secret inner chamber concealed behind its back wall.

"You must have told him to remain out of sight," Beatrice said.

"When do men ever do what they are told?" Susanna felt a wry smile twist her lips when she heard the asperity in her voice. "Had it been Robert, he'd have risked venturing out at night to make sure his horse had been cared for." He doted on Vanguard. "That, I think, is the most logical reason for the stranger to have been wandering about in the dark."

"Why go into your storeroom?"

"Curiosity?"

"Do you know his name?" Beatrice fired questions in a barrage and Susanna volleyed answers back.

"I never ask for names."

"Then how—"

"A password."

The system had been devised with the help of Sir Anthony Cooke, a dear friend of her father's. He was himself in exile now, but one of his daughters had remained behind to maintain a station along an escape route for fellow "heretics" similar to the one at Leigh Abbey.

"Saddle the bay and two other horses," Susanna instructed Mark, one of her grooms. When he hurried off to do her bidding, she turned to her companion. "You must not involve yourself in this, Beatrice."

"You cannot manage the body alone."

"Mark will assist me. All else aside, you are scarce dressed for the task, and you can better serve me by staying here. It will help allay suspicion. You can pretend to be closeted with me in my study while I am gone."

Common sense warred with an overabundance of zeal, but in the end Beatrice agreed to Susanna's suggestion.

* * *

"Does he appear to have struck his head on a rock?" Susanna asked. Although the brook flowed fast and deep with spring run-off, a strong man in good condition, such as this one had been, might have been able to pull himself out if he had not been knocked unconscious.

Even with her stalwart young groom's assistance, it had been no simple undertaking to move the body. The deceased had been dead weight.

"He'll do, madam," Mark said, "and we must be well away before anyone comes upon us."

"Free his horse," she ordered. "Set her wandering in the woods." She was tempted to order Mark himself to "find" the bay and instigate a search for its rider, but she was loath to do anything to call attention to Leigh Abbey.

Had she thought of everything? She wondered as they rode home. Belatedly, she remembered that he'd had a pack with him when he arrived. That might contain some clue to his identity. All she knew at present, from his appearance, was that he had seen more than forty winters. The better to go unnoticed on his journey, he'd worn plain clothes that gave no hint of his occupation, but he'd had the speech of a gentleman.

The ride back took less than a quarter hour. She'd not dared transport the body any farther in daylight.

"Go to the kitchen and dry off," she told Mark. His clothing was soaked from positioning the dead man in the water.

Susanna went straight to the mint room, pausing only long enough to collect a lantern. When she'd locked herself in, she hurried to the inner door, her key at the ready. A moment later, she was safely inside the second room and had shut out the overpowering smell.

No one had disturbed the hiding place she'd had purpose-built to conceal refugees from Queen Mary's religious persecution. Long and narrow, it took up one end of the windowless storehouse and contained sleeping pallets, a chair, and a table. Food and drink were stored in a tall, free-standing cupboard.

Suspicions had begun to nag at Susanna as soon as the initial shock of discovering a body had passed. In the aftermath, transporting it and throwing it into the brook, she'd had no time to ask herself questions, but now that she had leisure to consider them, she became aware of a disconcerting dearth of answers.

Susanna contemplated her surroundings. The dead man had arrived with a pack. She remembered seeing it. It was of brown leather and of good quality—the type of bag that hung over a saddle.

It had to be somewhere, along with a key, a duplicate of the one she had just used.

She began a methodical inspection of the chamber, end to end, floor to ceiling, but she reaped no more reward for her pains than a splinter in one thumb and sore knees.

No pack.

No key.

Covering her mouth and nose with a cloth, Susanna conducted a quick but thorough search of the storeroom before she emerged into the crisp afternoon air. There was nothing in the mint room but mint.

The hairs on the back of her neck prickled as she made her way to the stable. She glanced over her shoulder, certain someone was watching her, but there was no one in sight. Had the dead man felt this way? She wondered. For all that Mark and the other grooms slept in the room above, he could have entered the stables unseen and unheard. Then what? She studied the neat rows of stalls. Had he merely checked on his bay? Or had he come to hide something? More to the point, had he feared some enemy, someone who had, indeed, caught up with him?

As long as the duplicate key to the mint room remained missing, Susanna was forced to consider the possibility that the stranger had been murdered—that someone had trapped him in the storeroom, struck him on the head, left him there to die, and locked the door on the way out.

"Oh, there you are, madam!" Jennet exclaimed, rushing into the stable. "Mark said you were back."

Beatrice arrived a moment later, closely followed by Ursula.

"Can she be trusted?" Beatrice demanded, glaring at the tiring maid. "She had the whole story from your groom before I could prevent it."

"I am obliged to trust you both," Susanna told her. "There is no time to waste. It will not do for Robert to return and find me here. I have never shown an interest in the horses before."

"Why *are* you in the stable?" Jennet asked.

"To search for the stranger's missing pack."

When she had described its appearance, they spread out. Beatrice spoke rapidly in another language to give Ursula instructions. The reminder that both women were foreigners, for all that Beatrice had been born in England, gave Susanna pause. It seemed odd to her that Beatrice was so determined to help.

For a short while, no one spoke. Susanna inspected the stall where the old bay mare had been kept, the one in the darkest corner, where its occupant had stood the best chance of escaping notice. Stabling the refugees' horses was the riskiest part of her enterprise. Robert paid little attention to people, but he was devoted to his cattle. There had always been a chance he'd notice unauthorized additions.

Mare's droppings aside, Susanna found nothing in the stall. She moved on to the next one.

Jennet's cry of triumph brought them back to the center aisle of the stable. She had found the missing pack in the tack room. She hurried toward Susanna, carrying it in one hand and waving a paper in the other.

"A letter!" Beatrice cried, intercepting Jennet and plucking it from her fingers. "This must be destroyed before it can be used against you."

"Wait!"

But Susanna was too late. Beatrice had opened the nearest lantern and thrust the paper into the candle flame. By the time Susanna reached her, it had been reduced to ash.

"Now, then," said Beatrice, pulling at the pack, "we must do likewise with this."

Jennet tried to keep hold of her prize, but Beatrice was a strong woman. She tugged it free. Giving Susanna no chance to protest, she swept out of the stable with it. Ursula trailed along in her wake.

"Is she mad?" Jennet asked.

"It is my hope that she is only overzealous. I intended to destroy the pack myself, but I had planned to examine the contents first."

"It is the fault of the star with the long tail," Jennet muttered darkly. "It was an evil omen. Did I not say so? Death and destruction. Terror and—"

"Enough! Nothing supernatural caused that man's death, or Beatrice's actions, either." She fixed Jennet with a commanding stare. "What did the letter say?"

"Oh, madam, how could you think that I—"

"What did it say, Jennet?" Susanna tapped her foot and waited. All Leigh Abbey servants were taught to read, and if Jennet had one besetting sin, it was an overabundance of curiosity. She'd been caught more than once hiding behind an arras to listen to the private conversations of others. Susanna had no doubt that she'd skimmed the letter before announcing her discovery, or that she'd found it in the first place by searching the pack.

"It was a letter of introduction. I did not have time to read the whole of it." Jennet's affronted tone spoke volumes.

"Repeat the words you did see, exactly as you remember them."

"To Sir Anthony Cooke, Strasbourg. I recommend unto you Master William Wroth."

"Go on."

"That is all I saw, madam."

"What of a signature? Who sent it?"

"I could not make out the name, but the letter was written from Staines on the second day of March. Where is Staines, madam?"

Susanna frowned. "It is some fifteen miles west of London, along the way to Salisbury." Of more importance was the identity of the person in that place who'd sent William Wroth to Leigh Abbey.

"Fetch Mark," she instructed. "I've a message to dispatch. Then find pen and ink and paper and write down every item you noted in Master Wroth's pack."

* * *

"The dead man had no mark of violence upon him." Robert paused to refill his goblet with a sharp white wine from Angulle.

He and Lord Benedick and their servants had been stopped on the way home from the hunt by the coroner, who had been called in as soon as the body was discovered. Robert had been asked if he could identify the deceased. He claimed he'd never seen the fellow before.

"No mark at all?" Susanna asked as she and Beatrice exchanged a worried glance. Had no one noticed the lump on his head? This was a complication they had not foreseen.

"The fish had nibbled him," Robert said.

"He must have drowned, then," Beatrice murmured. "Will your coroner declare the death an accident?"

"He is reluctant to do so without knowing the identity of the victim, and he has some suspicion that the fellow may have taken his own life. He cannot be buried in hallowed ground if that is the case."

"What's to be done then?"

"The coroner has persuaded the justices to look more deeply into the matter."

Susanna's fingers clasped her wine cup so tightly that her knuckles showed white. They suspected murder. She was sure of it.

Beatrice did not seem to share her fears. "Officials are wont to fuss and fume and make themselves look important," she declared with a little laugh. "This will all turn out to be much ado about nothing."

* * *

The next morning, after Robert and Lord Benedick left for a second day of hunting, Susanna, Beatrice, Jennet, and Ursula gathered in Susanna's study, a pleasant room full of books and maps, with windows that overlooked Leigh Abbey's fields and orchards to the east and the approach to the gatehouse on the north.

"The man's name was William Wroth," Susanna announced.

Ursula gasped, made the sign of the cross, and fumbled for her rosary.

"You know this man Wroth, good Ursula?" Susanna had not expected any reaction. She'd brought up Wroth's name as a preliminary to discussing how they could convince the authorities that his death was an accident.

The old woman's deeply-lined face crumpled further and her eyes, filmed with age, sought her mistress, but she did not speak.

Beatrice laid a hand on her arm. Her voice was gentle. "You must tell us if you know who this man was, Ursula."

"He was evil, mistress," Ursula answered.

Or, rather, that was what Beatrice told Susanna and Jennet Ursula had said. They had spoken in a language only they understand.

"Why does she think he was evil?" Susanna asked.

Their incomprehensible conversation resumed. Beatrice asked questions and paused now and again to translate when Ursula answered, but it seemed to Susanna that the waiting gentlewoman took a great many words to convey very little. She began to wonder how much Beatrice was holding back.

"She knows nothing of help to us," Beatrice said at last, "only that when she was in my mother's service here in England, there was a man by that name who was well known for his hatred of all things Spanish. This was many years ago, for I was still a small child when my parents died."

"Did she ever meet William Wroth?" He'd have been a young man in his twenties then.

"She knew him by reputation. She says he was wont to pick fights with the servants of Spanish merchant families in London. And their sons."

"And no one stopped him?"

"Why should they, once Queen Catherine had been set aside? I remember a little of that time myself, for all that I was so young. My mother would cry herself to sleep over what had happened to her mistress. Once King Henry divorced her, men who felt as Wroth did had few restraints on their behavior. It was a popular belief that the only good Spaniard was a dead Spaniard."

"That must have made things difficult for your parents."

A great sadness clouded Beatrice's countenance. "Since I have been back in England, I have felt their loss most deeply, but when they were alive they knew great happiness. My father loved my mother as much as Benedick loves me and she returned his feelings tenfold."

Through the north-facing window, Susanna caught sight of an approaching rider. She knew him by his bright green cloak and dappled horse. By the time her neighbor, old Sir Eustace Thornley, who had served as a justice of the peace since Susanna was a girl, had been shown to the study, all four women were seated in a circle, applying their needles to a large piece of tapestry work.

"I am sorry to trouble you," he apologized after he'd been presented to Beatrice, "but I seek information about a man seen in the area of late." He gave particulars of William Wroth's appearance but did not say he was dead. Susanna suspected that Sir Eustace, who had never married, clung to the quaint notion that women should not trouble their pretty little heads about such matters as sudden death and coroner's inquests.

"That is a passing general description, sir," she said with flutter of eyelashes and a pout. "Has he no distinguishing characteristic?"

Flustered, Sir Eustace mumbled, "A faint smell of mint clung to his clothing and beard." He cleared his throat and pressed on. "It is not, I think, a common perfume."

"Mint has many uses." Susanna's voice was level but her heart raced triple time. She could scarce deny knowledge of the herb. Every woman received some training in the stillroom. "I steep the leaves of garden mint to make an infusion. Drinking one to two cups of this daily, but not for more than one week at a time, is an excellent remedy for sleeplessness and helpful to the digestion, as well. Mayhap the gentleman spilled his medicine."

"I prefer to distill mint," Beatrice said. "One must use freshly cut, partially dried plant tops, cut just before the plants come into flower. An over-mature plant produces an oil with a sharp, bitter smell, but if the process is done right, it yields a hot, pungent aroma."

The justice's eyes began to glaze over.

Taking her cue from Beatrice, Susanna launched into a detailed description of the preparation of a stimulant using mint and other herbs. She gave up all pretense of stitching. She was not much of a needlewoman in the best of circumstances.

"Well done, Susanna," Beatrice said when Sir Eustace took his leave a few minutes later. "How quick men are to lose interest in domestic matters!"

"A pity. I so wanted to tell him that some mints are cultivated as an aid to love. Why pennyroyal, given to quarreling couples, is even supposed to induce them to make peace."

"It is also a protection against evil," Beatrice remarked.

"Well, then," Susanna said with a smile, "we have nothing to fear. With all the mint we have stored at Leigh Abbey, we are certain to be safe from further trouble."

* * *

The next day Susanna and Beatrice rode with their husbands to Canterbury to visit the cathedral. On the way back, Robert stopped at Sir Eustace's manor house, sending the others on ahead without him. Susanna had no opportunity for a private word with him until they retired to their bedchamber for the night.

"Do you hunt again tomorrow?" she asked.

"Aye." He sounded disconsolate. "Lord Benedick cares for naught but hunting, hawking, and dallying with his own wife. He has no intention of attaching himself to the court."

Concealing a smile, Susanna made a sympathetic sound and continued to take pins out of her hair.

"You are a clever woman, Susanna. Can you find a way to give Beatrice a dislike of you?"

She fought a sense of disappointment as she brushed her long, thick hair. Robert believed it was a waste of his time to entertain Lord Benedick any longer, but he did not want to be the one to offend him, just in case Benedick turned out to have some use, after all. Robert expected Susanna to do his dirty work for him.

"I see no reason to discourage her friendship. Beatrice is most pleasant company."

"What do you know of her family?"

The question surprised her. "Her mother was in the household of Queen Mary's mother. I'd think such a connection would be helpful to you."

"Any benefit is overshadowed by what happened afterward. Beatrice's mother killed her English husband, then took her own life."

Aghast, Susanna put down her hairbrush and demanded details.

"Their family seat was at Staines," Robert said. His voice was muffled as he settled himself for the night. "That is all Sir Eustace told me." Their neighbor was well known for his long memory and love of gossip. If he'd had more information, he'd have repeated it.

Susanna crossed to the bed and pulled aside the bright blue damask hangings to glower at her spouse. *Staines. The location could not be a coincidence.* "Did Wroth come here because of Lord Benedick and his wife?"

Just before his eyes shifted away from her unrelenting gaze, she read the truth in them. He recognized Wroth's name. Had he known all along who the dead man was?

The belligerent jut of Robert's jaw warned her he did not intend to answer questions, but two could play at that game. She did not intend to explain how she'd discovered Wroth's identity. She perched on the foot of the bed and deftly began to braid her hair.

"I am as anxious as you that you regain favor at court." How else could she hope to continue her rescue efforts? "But if I do not know as much as you do, Robert, then I may make some mistake or say the wrong thing. If this dead stranger, for example, is the same Wroth who had such a reputation for hating all things Spanish—"

"God save me from meddling females!"

"He sounds the worst sort of extremist." She could not regret that Wroth was dead, knowing the sort of man he had been, but neither could she continue to ignore the possibility that he had been murdered. "He brought no credit to the cause he claimed to espouse."

"Nor was he faithful to it."

"What do you mean?" Her hands stilled in her hair.

"When last I was in London, I heard a rumor that Wroth, who had been in prison under sentence of death, had agreed to do some service for Queen Mary in order to save his own skin."

The possibility that Wroth had come to Leigh Abbey as a spy made Susanna's blood run cold, but she did not dare ask Robert any more questions for fear of arousing *his* suspicions. Beatrice had been right. Susanna's husband would turn her in himself if he saw any profit in it.

* * *

Mark returned to Leigh Abbey the next day, bringing a reply to the message Susanna had sent to Sir Anthony Cooke's daughter. The verbal questions had been accompanied, as proof of the sender's identity, by a sprig of rosemary. Margaret Cooke's answers came back with a bit of rue. She sent word that no one in Staines should have known what went on at Leigh Abbey, but that Wroth himself owned property there. He'd bought the estate of a man—Margaret could not remember his name—who had been murdered by his wife.

"Good news," Mark added, unaware that his mistress had been obliged to take a tight grip on the arms of her favorite carved oak chair to quell the sudden trembling in her hands. "When I passed through the village, I heard that Sir Eustace took another look at the body and this time noticed the lump on the dead man's head. The death will be ruled an accident. No more questions will be asked."

"Good news, indeed." Susanna gave Mark a reward for his services and sent him back to his usual duties.

Sunk deep in thought, it was some little time before Susanna realized that Jennet, who had come into the study with Mark, had remained when he was dismissed. She had a talent for disappearing into the woodwork when she did not want to be noticed.

"What did Beatrice do with the dead man's pack?" Susanna asked.

"Cut it into small bits and burnt them."

Trust Jennet to know. The list she'd made had been helpful, too. Wroth's pack had contained only clothing. No papers. No key.

"Why do you think she did that, Jennet?"

"To protect you, madam?"

"I wonder."

"Madam?"

"Yes, Jennet?"

"It is possible I missed seeing a key in Master Wroth's pack." At Susanna's start of surprise, she rushed on. "I do not know how else she could have got hold of it."

"Beatrice?"

Jennet nodded. "She must have been the one who sent old Ursula to get rid of it, since metal will not burn. I saw it clear when I followed Ursula to the fish ponds. The key caught the sun as she threw it in."

***

Susanna found Beatrice and Ursula in the small parlor. Beatrice had pulled the Glastonbury chair close to the window in order to read by the light streaming in through the panes. Ursula sat close to the fire, mending a stocking.

"Did you arrange to meet Master Wroth here?" she asked. If Robert wanted her to give the other woman a dislike of them, an accusation of murder should suffice.

Beatrice's demeanor remained calm. She marked her place in *Liber de Arte Distillandi* and met Susanna's eyes before she answered. "No."

"But you recognized him when you saw him?"

"No," she said again.

Susanna believed her, but she felt certain Beatrice was hiding something. "If you sought to trap Wroth in the mint room, intending to hold him there until Lord Benedick could deal with him—"

"Why ask all these questions?" Beatrice interrupted. "I thought you deemed Wroth's death an accident, even if Sir Eustace does not."

It was on the tip of her tongue to correct Beatrice. At the last moment, she decided to keep the justice's most recent conclusion to herself. "Someone must have struck Wroth down, then locked him in the storeroom afterward," she said instead. "If he simply fell, I'd have found the key. Tell me, Beatrice, what is the connection between William Wroth and the death of your parents?"

With an abrupt movement, Beatrice rose from the chair and went to stand by the window and stare out at the bleak landscape. Her view encompassed the ornamental gardens, but at this time of year they showed no sign of life.

"You recognized Wroth," Susanna said in a voice she hoped conveyed her sympathy. "You locked him in, doubtless meaning to fetch Lord Benedick to deal with him, but by the time you returned, Wroth was dead."

"Benedick knows nothing of this!" As soon as the words were out she looked stricken, but it was too late to call them back.

If Benedick had seen the body, Susanna realized, it would have been long gone by morning, but if Wroth had not been locked in to await interrogation by Benedick, then Beatrice must have meant to kill him. Unless—

"Ursula," Susanna whispered. "Ursula was the one who recognized Wroth. *She* locked him in."

With obvious reluctance, Beatrice nodded. She returned to the chair. "I see I must tell you everything. Yes, she locked him in. Then she came to me. It took some time to sort matters out. It was the middle of the night. She had to extract me from my bed without waking Benedick, then explain who Wroth was and what she'd done and why. I had been told my parents were carried off by a fever. It was a great shock to learn that my mother had been accused of killing my father and of taking her own life. Ursula insisted that Wroth was to blame for both deaths."

"Has she any proof?"

"No. My mother took her aside one night at Staines, gave her money, and told her she must take me back to Spain without delay. Then she led Ursula to a window and pointed to a man—Wroth—and said we must avoid being seen by him when we left because he was dangerous. Within the hour, Ursula and I were on our way to Calais. It was there that word reached us that my parents were dead."

"And Ursula did nothing?"

"What could she do? She knew Wroth's reputation. She was sure he had killed them, but she feared for her own life and mine if she remained on English soil long enough to accuse him. But now—now she is old. She no longer fears death." She smiled faintly. "And because she is old, her bones ache, preventing sleep. She was up in the middle of the night and chanced to look out a window. She recognized Wroth at once, for the situation was much as it was when she saw him all those years ago. She went outside for a closer look, followed him into the storeroom, caught him by surprise, hit him on the head, and took the key to lock him in. She reasoned that, together, she and I might be able to persuade him to confess his crimes, but by the time I heard her explanation and dressed and went with her to the storeroom we were too late. He was dead."

"Why leave him there? You must have known he'd be found."

"It was too close to sunrise to do anything else. As it was, I scarce had time to lock the door again and return to my bed before Benedick woke. I meant to go back and dispose of him as soon as the men left for the hunt, but you were there ahead of me."

Susanna wanted to believe her. If Wroth's death had been an accident, the matter was closed.

She'd had a narrow escape. Had he lived to be accused, the existence of the inner room and its purpose would have been exposed. She'd have ended up in gaol alongside Will Wroth.

Although *he* might have been acquitted, *she'd* have been executed for treason. She swallowed hard.

"We will say no more of the matter."

Beatrice frowned. "Benedick and I plan to return to Padua soon, where we will be safe from English law, but the smell of mint made Sir Eustace suspicious of you, Susanna. What if he continues to investigate? What if he discovers that Wroth died in your storeroom?"

"I am confident he will not." Had the return of the hunting party not interrupted her at that moment, Susanna would have gone on to share the verdict on Wroth's death.

* * *

"I thought they meant to leave this morning," Robert complained the next day. "What is Beatrice doing in your storeroom?"

"Stillroom, Robert. She's preparing her secret recipe for *aqua vitae* as a parting gift, using pennyroyal to add protective properties to the distillation."

"Do we need protection?" He sounded suspicious.

Susanna smiled. "No, my dear, but Beatrice took note of the way Jennet carries on, fearful of evil in the wake of the star with the long—"

She broke off, beset by a vague sense of alarm as she remembered that, as far as Beatrice knew, what Susanna needed protection from was Sir Eustace's investigation of Wroth's death. In the bustle of preparations for Beatrice and Benedick's departure, her intention to tell Beatrice she no longer had any need to worry had completely slipped her mind.

Robert failed to notice Susanna's distraction. "She will not be at it much longer," he said after a few moments of consideration, "not with the goodly fire she had Benedick build for her in your storeroom."

"Stillroom." Susanna corrected him again, but she frowned. A stilling pot was heated over a *soft* fire.

"Storeroom," Robert insisted.

Susanna felt her face drain of color. *Aqua vitae* had another name. It was called "burning water" because it so easily turned into flame.

"Storeroom?" she whispered.

No one heard her. The explosion drowned out all other sounds. It blew the bricks and stones of the storeroom walls outward as the fire, in one bright flash, consumed the incriminating bales of mint. It did not spread, nor was Beatrice harmed. She'd taken care to avoid both consequences when she planned this parting gift for her hostess.

"The fire was too rash." Benedick's cheerful wink told Susanna that he was now in his wife's confidence. His generous offer to pay for the damage mollified Robert and prevented him from asking awkward questions.

Beatrice, Susanna thought, had also been too rash, but only because she'd believed she owed it to Susanna to protect her from Sir Eustace's suspicions.

* * *

"Will you rebuild your storeroom?" Robert asked a few hours later as they watched their guests ride away.

"There is no need." From now on, she'd hide escaping heretics in the stable with their horses.

"But where will you store pennyroyal?" Jennet asked. "Won't you need a great deal more of it to keep Leigh Abbey safe from the star with the long tail?"

"No, indeed," Susanna assured her, "for Beatrice had the right of it all along. Your ominous portent, Jennet, is in truth a dancing star, and a sure sign of good things to come."

A Note from the Author

The idea for this story came out of a visit to the Celestial Seasonings "mint room," a side trip during Historicon II in Boulder, Colorado. As many mystery writers before me have observed, the strangest things can inspire someone to say "What a great place to hide the body!"

Although Sir Anthony Cooke and his daughter Margaret were real people, there is nothing in history to indicate that Margaret was part of a conspiracy to smuggle heretics out of England. She married a London merchant in 1558 and died soon after. Her four sisters, Mildred (Lady Burghley), Anne (Lady Bacon), Elizabeth (Lady Hoby and later Lady John Russell), and Katherine (Lady Killigrew), were far more famous, in part because of the men they married and in part for their learning. The education they were given provided me with a model for Susanna's schooling.

Several contemporary descriptions survive of the "blazing star" seen three years before the events in *Face Down in the Marrow-Bone Pie*. Both Henry Machyn and John Stow described this comet, which could be seen over England in early March, 1555/6. This "double dating" stems from the fact that in those days the new year began on March 25.

As for Beatrice and Benedick, they are the protagonists of Shakespeare's *Much Ado About Nothing*. This story was originally written for an anthology of mystery stories using Shakespearean characters as sleuths (*Much Ado About Murder*, 2002, edited by Anne Perry). Since Shakespeare gave no specific dates for his tale, there is no reason it could not have taken place in the sixteenth century, and there is no textual evidence in the play to disprove the possibility that Beatrice's father might have been an Englishman.

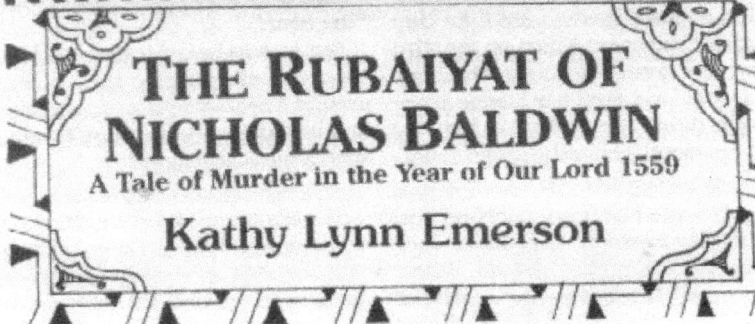

THE RUBAIYAT OF NICHOLAS BALDWIN
A Tale of Murder in the Year of Our Lord 1559

Kathy Lynn Emerson

The Rubaiyat of Nicholas Baldwin

Persia, 1559

A woman screamed.

A cat hissed.

Nick Baldwin forgot he was in a foreign land with strange customs and looked for a way over the wall that separated him from those sounds of alarm. Finding no convenient gate, he clambered up one side and dropped into a private garden lush with flowers and foliage, but he'd arrived too late. A crumpled female form lay no more than a foot away from the spot he'd landed. The blood pooling beneath her head was as vividly red as the roses on the bush beside her.

Nick surveyed the quiet, sun-drenched enclosure for some sign of the person who had attacked her. He caught a glimpse of white out of the corner of one eye, but it was only a small animal darting into a doorway. He turned back to the victim.

She was the first female he'd seen since arriving in Qazvin who had not been completely enveloped in the light-colored robes Persian women wore when they ventured out of their homes. The knife that had slashed her throat had cut right through the lacework veil meant to shield her face and neck from masculine eyes.

Moved to pity, Nick knelt beside her. He regretted that he'd not been in time to save her.

He heard no approaching footsteps before he was roughly seized and jerked to his feet. Exclaiming in horror and rage, apparently convinced Nick was the murderer, three men hauled him away from the body.

In the loudest voice he could manage, Nick bellowed a desperate demand for justice: "Let me plead my case before the Great Sophy!"

That he spoke their language gave his captors pause. Two released him and backed away. Nick glowered at the ruddy-faced young man who still clung to his arm. He repeated the demand. This was not how he'd envisioned obtaining a royal audience, but he felt certain Shah Tahmasp, known in other lands as the Great Sophy of Persia, would honor his plea. The only question was whether that powerful ruler would bestir himself to save a foreigner's life.

The young man did not loosen his grip.

A debate ensued. Nick stopped trying to break free and concentrated on translating the barrage of heated words exploding over his head. He'd begun to study the language four months earlier, when he'd resolved to journey to Qazvin and persuade the Persian king to open trade with England. Nick had a gift for foreign tongues, possessing the happy facility of learning to speak them with ease, but in the heat of strong emotion some of what he now heard was well nigh unintelligible. He comprehended only enough to know that Bihzad, the fellow with the terrier's hold on his arm, argued for his immediate dispatch.

"He must have killed her," Bihzad declared. "There is blood on his hands."

"And on your own." Nick pointed to the gore and noticed that a streak of red also marred the robe worn by another of his captors. "Where is the weapon? How did I slash that woman's throat without a knife?"

"Search him, Hamid," Bihzad ordered.

The man with the stained sleeve hastened to obey.

Concealed inside a series of hidden pockets in the elaborately slashed and puffed doublet that marked Nick as a foreigner, was a small fortune in gemstones—pearls, sapphires, and rubies—portable trade goods Nick had brought with him from Muscovy. He resisted Hamid's efforts until the third man rejoined the fray.

Their rough, inefficient probing missed the valuables, but Nick was relieved of his eating knife and his dagger. Neither showed any sign of recent use and both were free of bloodstains. It was only then, when he considered asking his captors to produce their own weapons for inspection, that he realized none of them seemed to be armed. A scar blemishing the third man's cheek might have been made by a blade, but Nick saw no other indication that they ever carried knives.

Hamid brought his face close to Nick's. "Are you a Portugee?" His breath was rich with the scent of cloves.

Nick grimaced at both the question and the overpowering aroma. "I am a London man." As far as he knew, he was the first from his homeland to set foot in this exotic and dangerous country.

All three stared at him, the blank looks on their faces making it plain they'd never heard of London. Nick doubted the word England would mean any more to them.

He tried to picture how he must appear to their eyes. He was nothing out of the ordinary at home, a short, sturdily-built man in his twenty-seventh year with broad shoulders, dark brown hair and eyes, and regular features behind a neatly-trimmed beard. Here, however, the paleness of his skin marked him as an outsider just as surely as his clothing did. His complexion had darkened from exposure to the sun during his travels, but it was still several shades lighter than what they were accustomed to seeing.

The scarred man's gaze shifted to the doorway of the house adjoining the garden. "Master!"

They turned as one to watch the newcomer, a man several decades older than themselves, inspect the body. When he had done so, he called to the scarred man, using the name Qadi, and spoke quietly to him. In short order, Qadi departed, several menservants arrived, and Nick was seized and stuffed into a small, windowless chamber. Left there under guard, he was unable to overhear further discussion of his fate.

Nick considered his surroundings. He was in a house typical of those he'd seen since coming to Qazvin. His prison occupied one corner of one of four large porch-like parlors surrounding a smaller private parlor at the center of the house. The door blocking his exit was no more than two thin, wooden leaves folded one over the other like window shutters. He could break through, overcome the guard, and escape into the street through the front of the house, which at best would be open and at worst shut with another fragile sash.

But then what?

Running would be seen as proof of his guilt. He'd be pursued. If they caught him before he could change from his English clothes into Eastern garments and darken his skin, he'd be dispatched without mercy. There would be no opportunity to plead his case before the shah, only a painful and ignominious death.

Nick leaned against the plain plaster wall, prepared to wait for the Master's decision. *Well, here I am*, he thought, *in the land the legendary Tamerlane conquered, and it is not at all like a play*. He felt his lips twist into a wry smile and the smile turn into a grin as he remembered how captivated he'd been as a boy to see scenes from "The Persian Knights" acted out on a makeshift wooden stage in an innyard. He'd longed to see the world even then, or at least to run off and join the troupe of traveling players.

Had he chosen the latter course and been in a situation like this, he'd have been able to call up a puff of smoke and a trap door to vanish through. Instead, after what seemed like hours, the old man's servants came for him. He'd been granted his wish. They were taking him to the palace.

* * *

The audience hall was redolent with rich fragrances—aloe, camphor, saffron, and frankincense. Large and sumptuous, its walls were colorfully painted and its floor covered with thick carpets. Impressively bearded royal guardsmen, armed with fearsome blades and wearing turbans wound around scarlet uprights, added an exotic overlay of menace to the splendor.

Shah Tahmasp did not match his surroundings. He was a small, wiry man with a pinched face and dark, haunted eyes. Nick had been told he was in his forty-fifth year. Although both his bushy whiskers and his hair had been dyed black, he looked far older.

Tahmasp regarded the captive Englishman with suspicion, then signaled the old man's servants to release him and dismissed them. Their master remained in the background to watch the shah solemnly stretch out one leg.

Nick took a deep breath, grateful he'd been coached in the proper way to greet the monarch. Dropping to his knees, he kissed the shah's extended foot with as much reverence as he could muster.

A little murmur of approval greeted the act and he was cautiously welcomed, even allowed to sit when the shah did. Praying the rest of the advice he'd been given was also accurate, Nick perched awkwardly, his buttocks resting on his heels and his knees close together. Such, he had been told, was the proper position to assume when one wished to show respect for one's betters. He was careful to keep his toes out of sight, since for a man to let them show when he sat was considered a great piece of rudeness in this culture.

Nick's mentor, Abd Allah Khan, a sensible, personable fellow Nick greatly admired, was also the shah's cousin and brother-by-marriage. As such, he had provided a letter of introduction, which Nick now produced, watching in anxious silence as Tahmasp examined the seals and read the contents.

After another considering look at Nick, the shah ordered rose water brought in a silver bowl. Nick duly washed his face and hands and, although the procedure seemed strange to him, dried off by bending over aloe smoke, which left its scent on his hair and beard.

The interrogation that followed was long, thorough, and, at times, difficult to follow. The Persian habit of choosing the most convoluted way to express a simple thought tested the limits of Nick's command of the language. In addition, the shah mumbled when he spoke. Some of his words were impossible to understand. Nick did not dare offer insult by asking him to repeat what he'd said. Instead he bluffed, giving the answers he thought Tahmasp expected.

On the matter of murder, the shah said little. After a search, a bloodstained knife had been found at the scene, but it had been identified as belonging to the victim. Tahmasp did not accuse Nick of killing the woman in the garden. He was more interested in London, a place he claimed never to have heard of, although he'd had dealings with Russia and seemed to understand that Nick had come to Persia from Moscow.

Nick decided against trying explain that he'd been there as a stipendiary with the English Muscovy Company, or how a joint-stock company operated, or even why he'd struck out on his own after traveling as far as Bokhara with his friend, Anthony Jenkinson. With luck, Jenkinson was halfway back to England by now. It had been his plan to return to Moscow, then sail home while Nick investigated opportunities in Persia for trade in silk, spices, and other luxury goods. God willing, in a year's time they would both be back in Moscow.

As chief merchant of Persia, Shah Tahmasp held the monopoly on raw silk. Nick presented him with a pistol inlaid with mother-of-pearl. It had been concealed in his boot. Next came the emerald pendant shaped like a grape, which he'd worn around his neck.

The shah accepted both and waited for more.

Nick hesitated. If he gave away all he had, he'd have naught to bargain with and no means to pay for lodging and food. He chose his next words with care. He wished to convey a complex notion—that he had more of value to offer, but not just yet. He mentioned rubies.

The shah looked momentarily intrigued. Encouraged, Nick asked what Tahmasp wished to acquire from the west. The answer surprised him—London clothes such as Nick wore and also chain mail and suits of armor.

Nick assured him that such things could be provided.

"And a marriage alliance," Tahmasp declared, going on to ask who reigned in Nick's homeland and if there were unwed females in his house.

Nick hesitated. At the time of his departure from Moscow, the last news from England had already been months out of date. Did Mary Tudor rule there with her consort, Philip of Spain? Or had her half sister Elizabeth succeeded her? Or was Elizabeth dead, executed for her refusal to give up the New Religion established by her father and accept the tenets of the church of Rome?

"There are princesses in England yet unmarried," Nick told the shah. That seemed a safe statement. After Elizabeth, unless Mary and Philip had produced a son, several other females stood in line to inherit the throne.

"Is London home to unbelievers?"

"Those who live there believe there is but one God."

It did not trouble Nick to call that God *Allah*. As far as he could see, Muslims and Christians worshiped the same deity. Abd Allah Khan had warned him, however, that Tahmasp was as extreme in his religious views as any supporter of the Inquisition. If he doubted Nick's expedient statement of faith, the mildest outcome was likely to be a demand that Nick prove he embraced all aspects of Islam by undergoing circumcision.

Abd Allah Khan had taken great delight in providing his honored guest with a detailed description of the process, one very painful for an adult. It was, he'd claimed, commonly a fortnight or three weeks before a man could walk again. The prospect did not bear thinking about.

Nick felt a rush of relief when Tahmasp once more changed the subject. He spoke at great length about a dream he'd had the previous night. Nick soon lost the sense of it, although he did catch the word *rubai,* which he himself had used when speaking of the gemstones he had to trade.

At the end of this oration, the shah fixed Nick with a steely gaze. "If you wish to become a merchant in Qazvin, you must first prove yourself innocent of murder."

Nick swallowed hard. He had no idea how to accomplish such a feat, yet he had no choice but to agree. Bowing low, he murmured, "My hand is on the skirt of the robe of the Shah Tahmasp," the standard phrase Abd Allah Khan had taught him. It meant he depended upon the shah for protection. That was no less than the literal truth.

* * *

A short time later, the shah's guardsmen returned Nick to the scene of the crime. The old man was already there. Once they were alone in one of the parlors, he approached Nick, for the first time coming close enough to the London man for Nick to get a good look at him.

"The woman in the garden," he said, "was nursemaid to my youngest daughter."

He spoke in Italian.

"God's blood!" Nick exclaimed, startled into replying in the same language. "You are no Persian." The fellow's eyes were a bright, sapphire blue.

The old man gestured for Nick to sit on the thick carpet covering the floor. A servant brought refreshments. "I have lived here more than forty years now," he said, "but I was born in Venice. My name is Lorenzo Zeno."

"Nick Baldwin of London, at your service."

"*Cherab*?" He offered a wine of a deep purple color. "It is similar in taste to Muscadine."

Nick shook his head.

"Very wise. The punishment for drinking wine, unless one has permission—" he displayed his, with its special seal "—is to have your belly ripped open on the spot. A long poniard is plunged into you on the left side and drawn round to the back. It is not a speedy death."

Servants offered Nick a choice between a cup of barley water and a drink called sherbet, but he was distracted by his desire to ask Zeno questions. The old man waved them aside.

"By the king's sacred head, you have no time for inquiries into my history. You've two tasks to perform, neither of them simple."

"Two?" Taken aback, Nick almost choked on a swallow of barley water. "I know I must find the real murderer in order to clear my name. What more?"

Zeno grinned. "Tell me, Englishman, what is the meaning of *rubai*?"

"Ruby. The gemstone."

"The ruby that comes from Egypt, a very fine stone, is called *yacut eeylani*. The rose-colored ruby is *balacchani*. The carbuncle, said to be bred in the head of a dragon, is called the *icheb chirac*, or flambeau of the night. Then there are the *cha mohore*, the royal stone, and the *cha devacran*, the king of jewels."

"And a *rubai*?" Nick was no longer sure he wanted to know.

"A poem of four lines only, of which the first, second, and fourth lines rhyme. It needs no connection to what comes before or after, but a collection of these poems is called a *rubaiyat*. That is what you agreed to give to the shah, after you find the person who killed my servant. An original composition. Verses. Have you any skill with poetry?"

Nick drank deeply of the iced barley water and helped himself to a handful of grapes from a platter that also contained dates and slices of melon. Grammar school Greek and Latin had introduced him to Petrarch and other classic poets, and as a young man he'd written his share of sonnets to a lady's eyebrows, but he'd long since abandoned such flights of fancy for life as a merchant.

"I appear to have overestimated my command of the spoken language of Persia," he admitted. "Poetry aside, I did not understand much of what the shah said when he spoke of dreams. Is it some superstitious belief on his part that dictates the tasks I am to perform?"

"Last night the shah, who sets great store by such things, dreamt of the coming of a poet who would make right a wrong and tell of it in verse."

Nick bit back a groan. He would not, it seemed, even have the freedom to choose his own subject. "Must these poems be written in the language of this land or may I compose in my native tongue?"

"You need not write them at all, only recite the verses."

"In Persian?"

"In Persian. And you must take care to avoid any suggestion of heresy in your words."

As he would in England, also, Nick thought.

"It is safest to begin with religious orthodoxy and a plea for forgiveness of any failings in the lines to come."

Nick contemplated his empty cup. "I cannot compose any poem until I know the identity of the murderer. First I must discover what befell that woman in your garden." Setting aside the drinking vessel, he rose and began to pace. "What alerted those inside the house to what had happened? It cannot have been the cry I heard. Had that been audible, those young men would have arrived before I did."

"A servant reported seeing someone climb over my wall."

"Who are the young men who seized me?"

"My students." A sweep of one hand indicated their surroundings.

Until that moment, Nick had been oblivious to the room's contents. Now he took note of gilded and burnished pages on which miniatures would be painted. Brushes, drawing boards, and a little shell full of silver paint gave further evidence of Zeno's profession. Nick lifted the brush a colorist would use to complete a painting-in-small that had been outlined but not yet filled in. It appeared to consist of a single hair tied into a quill handle.

"Kitten fur," said Zeno.

A memory flashed through Nick's mind at the comment—an animal in flight. "I saw a white cat in the garden just after the murder took place."

Frowning, Zeno rose from the rug. "There is no help for it. You must speak with Halima."

Nick had been in the East long enough to know that the women's quarters were forbidden to men outside the family. It was almost as unusual for a wealthy merchant or artisan's womenfolk to emerge from these private rooms to speak to a strange man. In a noble household, such activity would be strictly forbidden. Zeno's daughter Halima, however, was too young yet to be required to wear the veil.

She regarded Nick with undisguised curiosity through eyes as blue as her father's. Nick stared back, equally curious, noting that she wore a long shirt and a vest atop what appeared to be silk, ankle-length drawers. A small cap sat atop hair drawn back and woven into a great many thick wefts. The ends were trimmed with ribbons to make them long enough to reach her waist.

"Marta saw someone in the garden," Halima said in response to Zeno's questions. "One of your students, Father."

"Which one?"

"I do not know." When she shook her head, the fragrance of civet, which here was called *zabad*, wafted toward them. "Marta said only that he appeared to be hiding a small object. She feared he'd stolen something from the house and that when its loss was discovered, the servants would be blamed. She went to retrieve it. She never returned."

"Perhaps," Nick mused, "this Marta surprised the fellow when he came back for his prize. He must have murdered her to keep her from telling anyone what he'd done."

"But why kill over that?" Zeno asked. "A woman's word against a man's—"

"You would have believed her, Father," Halima interrupted. "He must have known that. And she told me what she knew. That's two."

Noticing Nick's puzzled expression, Zeno explained. "The Koran requires the evidence of two women to match the testimony of one man, and even that is not accepted unless a man corroborates it."

"And if it was accepted?"

"The punishment for thieving is amputation of a hand. It is chopped off by repeated blows of a mallet."

"That would surely end a man's career as an artist!" To be hanged for theft, England's punishment for stealing any item valued at more than a shilling, was less violent and less painful, but it was more final. "What is the penalty for murder?"

"Killing a man is a capital offense. Murdering a woman is a lesser crime. Although a Muslim man who murders a Muslim woman must be executed, this cannot be done until the woman's guardian pays half of his blood money. This is negotiated with and given to the murderer's family."

"Blood money?"

"The sum the man would be worth if he were to live a normal life."

"There was blood on Bala's fur after Marta was killed," Halima said. "I think he must have been with her in the garden."

"Bala?" Nick asked. "A white cat?"

"A kitten," Halima clarified. "He was accustomed to ride tucked inside the top of Marta's vest."

"A pity he cannot testify." And an even greater pity, Nick thought, that there was not some simple way to narrow their suspects from Zeno's three students down to one.

When Halima had returned to the women's quarters, Nick and Zeno went into the garden to search the area around the rose bushes. "Tell me about those young men," Nick urged him.

"Qadi is the youngest. Only seventeen. He chafes at being given the task of coloring in a whole miniature outlined by a master. He must toil for months illuminating works that will be credited to another artist who spent far less time on the piece."

"How did he get that scar on his face?" Nick was sympathetic to the universal plight of the apprentice but more interested in Qadi's propensity for violence.

"A scuffle with another child when he was ten. He fell against a sharp metal edge."

"Has he a quick temper?"

"No. Nor do the others. Hamid is frustrated by the requirement that he learn to paint the human form. He believes he will be happy as a gilder, only adding the arabesque ornaments—the designs of flowering vines which are necessary to any painting—and the framing rectangles that isolate text areas."

"And Bihzad? What of him?" The man's fingers had left impressions on Nick's neck.

"Bihzad has a sense of humor that may one day cause him difficulties. He likes to put the faces of prominent courtiers on his figures."

"Would Tahmasp punish him for that?"

"Who can say? Once our king was an artist himself. He appreciated all the pleasures of life."

Nick thought of the sour, stoop-shouldered old man in the palace. "What changed him?"

"Dreams. As you know, he takes his dreams most seriously. They make him moody. In good moods, he enjoys knowing others appreciate pleasures he denies to himself, but when the guilt and responsibility of his position are upon him, he suspects everyone, even those he loves. There are no more court artists. No more court musicians. One dream told Tahmasp to revoke all taxes not justified by religious law. The next day, he remitted all sales taxes and tolls." Zeno's lips twitched. "They have since been restored, but when he decided he would have all his subjects renounce wine and hashish and even sexual congress, since he equates any pleasure with sin, he closed down all the wine shops and brothels."

"Such eccentricity must be difficult for a subject to deal with year in and year out."

"Persia is more to my liking than any of the Italian states," Zeno averred. "I have been content here. Most Persians are open and friendly and would give their own lives before they would harm another."

Nick bent beneath a willow tree to examine a patch of earth in the failing light. It appeared to have been disturbed. "Someone did harm. What are the habits of your three students?"

"Their habits are like any other man's."

Which told Nick nothing. He brushed away a top layer of dirt and uncovered an odd-looking stone. "Bezoar?"

Zeno sighed. "So that is what was stolen. I'd hoped Halima was mistaken. In Persia it is called *padzuhr*."

"Stolen to sell?"

"Or because someone is ill."

Nick nodded. Westerners also knew of its powers. Taken internally or used externally, bezoar was popularly believed to be an antidote against most poisons, including the bites of snakes and other venomous creatures. Some credulous folk even thought it could cure the plague, falling sickness, fevers, and the pox.

"Where are your students now?" Nick asked as Zeno led the way inside. At this time of year, night fell with little twilight. Servants had already lit several tiny, odorless oil lamps.

"I sent them on errands so that we might talk uninterrupted, but they will return soon."

"What is their normal pattern?"

"Bed between nine and ten of the clock. Up at dawn."

"And if you were to give them a day of freedom?"

Zeno's eyes narrowed. "Do you think one of them may betray his guilt by running away?"

"That would be too much to hope for. I only intend to follow them to see where they go and with whom they speak. It may be that I will observe some behavior that will advance my quest. Even if no one does anything suspicious, I will be able to take the measure of each man."

Nodding and looking thoughtful, Zeno approved the plan.

* * *

In the morning, before the heat of the day came upon them, all three students set out for the *bazarga*. Nick, wearing Persian garments Zeno had found for him, trailed after them past houses of red brick and plaster and into the heart of the city. He moved with greater confidence as they neared the marketplace. Once there, he was certain he would go unnoticed by his quarry. There would be plenty of activity to hide his presence inside the vaulted-over gallery that contained the shops.

Qadi left the group when they came to the turning for the *hamam*. Nick hesitated. He doubted he could pass for a native in there. A pity, he thought with a wry twist of the lips. He'd have liked to bathe, but Moslem men did more than just cleanse themselves in the public baths. They also had all their body hair removed, usually with a lime and arsenic depilatory. He'd be noticeably hirsute in that company. The fact that the other men would all have had other bits removed, bits that did not grow back, would have made him even more conspicuous.

He continued on after Bihzad and Hamid. The former entered one of the shops. A quick glance inside showed Nick a customer accepting silver in exchange for goods he'd brought to sell. Nick frowned. He still had possession of the bezoar stone. Unless Bihzad had stolen something else from Zeno, he had nothing for the shopkeeper.

In order to keep Hamid in sight, Nick remained outside. He could not make out what was being said, but he was near enough to tell the shopkeeper was annoyed with Zeno's student. The young man's voice rose in anger. The other barked a sharp command. Then both adjourned behind a curtain that hid a back room.

In the distance, Hamid was accosted by a veiled woman. No, Nick corrected himself, not just a woman. A *cahbeha*. Her professional status was made clear by the broad embroidered border on her veil. Honest women, Nick had been told, displayed no borders.

But what was she doing out in broad daylight? Abd Allah Khan's instruction had been far-reaching. He'd explained to Nick that such women appeared in a certain place in Qazvin only after night fell.

"Many immoral women," he'd warned, "their faces concealed, stand in a long line and offer their shameful wares. Behind each is an old woman, known as the *dalal*, who carries a cushion and a cotton-filled blanket on her back and holds a lamp in her hand. When a man wishes to come to an arrangement with them, the *dalal* lights the lamp and with this the man sees each *cahbeha's* face and orders the one who pleases him most to follow him."

Shouts from within the shop drew Nick's attention back to Bihzad. The young man stormed out, nearly bowling Nick over as he made his escape. The shopkeeper hurled abuse in his wake, but made no attempt to follow. Nick caught only a few words, but they were sufficient to explain at least some of the animosity. The shopkeeper was Bihzad's father.

Nick remained in the marketplace several more hours, but learned little that seemed useful to him. He did not see any of Zeno's students again until supper, a strained meal filled with surreptitious looks in his direction. They alternated between suspicious and hostile.

After they'd eaten, he met with Zeno in private.

"The only way we can hope to discover the identity of Marta's murderer is to set a trap for the killer," Nick told him.

"How?"

"With a dream, and a trick I learned in the innyard playhouses I frequented in my youth, and the *rubaiyat* I have been commanded to compose. And with the help, I do think, of that kitten."

A scheme had begun to suggest itself when they'd questioned Halima. In the course of the day, Nick had come to realize that his foreign appearance and strangeness might be just the thing that could save him. He explained what he had in mind.

Zeno pointed out the flaw in his plan—that he must first compose his poem.

"I will work on it tonight," Nick said, "and have it ready by morning."

"It is as well, then," Zeno said, "that nights in this region and in this season are ten hours long."

* * *

The wind that came up every evening when the sun went down rattled the shutters and moaned like a tormented spirit. After the first hour, Nick wanted to wail along with it.

He had models to go by—*rubai* Zeno had provided that praised the beauty of a mole on a woman's cheek and the ugliness of having a nose as big as a gugglet—but he would indeed need every second of the darkness in order to complete his task.

The kitten, Bala, proved remarkable soothing to stroke when inspiration waned. The animal belonged to a breed Nick had first seen in Moscow. Highly valued for their long, silky coats, these cats were imported from Turkestan and Persia and sold to Russian noblemen, the only ones wealthy enough to buy them.

With Bala curled in his lap, Nick struggled through verse after verse. He wrote using the English alphabet and spelled Persian words by the way they sounded. He was rather proud of the figure of speech that proclaimed murder had as rank a smell as Muscovy leather, and of his use of the proverb "a black ox trod on my foot" to mean trouble had come upon him. On the whole, however, he knew his *rubaiyat* to be an awkward collection of verses in a flowery foreign tongue he had not yet mastered. Not a single one of the quatrains translated well into English.

By the time Nick finished, it was almost sunrise and the clove-scented candles had burned down to stubs. Persians did love that smell, he thought. Even the bezoar stone carried a trace of it.

* * *

As he'd promised, Zeno listened to Nick's composition. He declared it free of heresy, but found a few errors in meaning. After Nick corrected them, he committed his creation to memory. That done, Nick left Zeno's house to make several purchases in the marketplace. Powder of vernis, he discovered, was more readily available in Qazvin than in London.

By mid-morning, all was in readiness. Zeno had collected the three students in his private parlor to await Nick's grand entrance. The plan was simple—prey on what Nick hoped was a universal fear of the occult. Everyone he knew, whether Englishman, Muscovite, or Hollander, believed in the power of spells and curses. He counted on Zeno's apprentices to be every bit as superstitious as their English counterparts.

With as much dignity as he could counterfeit, he advanced into the room. Striking a pose, he began to recite his *rubaiyat,* the tale of a powerful western magician who called up the restless spirit of a murdered woman. There had been a witness, the verses claimed, to Marta's death, a kitten called Bala. With the help of Nick's spell, Bala would be the instrument of Marta's revenge.

He had concealed the small white feline in one of the hidden pockets of his doublet. With slight of hand with flint and steel and the powder of vernis, he produced a flash and a cloud of smoke at the moment when it would have the best dramatic effect. Seconds later, the haze cleared, revealing Bala in Nick's arms. Around the animal's neck hung the bezoar stone.

The theatrical trick startled all three students, but there was an added flicker of guilt in one pair of dark eyes. *Thank God!* Nick thought, and flung Bala directly at Hamid.

The young man scrambled backward with a cry of alarm. Covering his head with his arms to ward off attack, he began to babble. "Keep it away, master!" he begged. "Master Zeno, save me!"

"There was blood on your sleeve in the garden," Nick said, "and you had been chewing on cloves. Your breath reeked of them. The scent was on your hands, as well, and came off onto the bezoar stone."

Zeno reached out to his sobbing student, touching his shoulder. "Why, Hamid?"

"A woman," Nick murmured. "The woman in the marketplace."

"For Lilas," Hamid admitted. "She swore to refuse me if I did not bring her its magic."

"There was no need to steal the *padzuhr*," Zeno protested. "I would have loaned it to you, had you but asked."

"She did not wish to borrow it, master. She wants things for her own. She can command a great price, and most of her lovers give her rich gifts besides. She honored me with her favors. All she wanted was the *padzuhr*." At that, Hamid broke into loud lamentations.

Watching him, Nick felt a deep sense of sadness engulf him. He had succeeded in clearing his own name, but he could take no pleasure in this outcome. Nothing the authorities did to Hamid could change the senselessness of Marta's death.

* * *

At Nick's second audience with Shah Tahmasp he recited the collection of *rubai*. Afterward, he was required to witness Hamid's punishment. The shah had decided to be merciful. Marta's killer would not be executed. Instead, with his own knife, Tahmasp cut off Hamid's lips, nose, ears, and eyelids.

He turned next to Nick, running his icy gaze over the Englishman's Persian garb. "Do you adhere to the religious teachings of the Prophet?" he demanded.

Nick did not quibble over semantics. "I believe there is no God but God," he declared in ringing tones. "Muhammad is God's Prophet and Ali is God's Imam."

A long silence followed this avowal. Then, as if there had never been any question but that he would do so, Shah Tahmasp granted Nick permission to spend the next few months traveling throughout Persia. He would be allowed to negotiate the exportation of pepper, cinnamon, mace, jewels, silks, drugs, and alum. After that, Tahmasp declared, Nick would return to England to carry Tahmasp's royal gift to the English ruler. The shah produced a small, ornately carved ivory box. Within was a wondrous well-carved piece of jade of intense apple green, fashioned into the figure of a horse and measuring no more than six barleycorns high.

* * *

A week later, dawn found Nick Baldwin mounted on the good Arab horse Tahmasp had given him. Its trappings were of gold and turquoise. Behind him ranged twelve camels and five mules, also gifts from the shah. One of the mules carried yet another royal present, a large tent suitable for use when sleeping in the open.

Lorenzo Zeno, who had insisted Nick remain as a guest in his house during the remainder of his stay in Qazvin, came out to see him off. "I do not believe you will come this way again," he observed.

"It does not seem likely," Nick agreed.

"Halima sends you a parting present." Zeno offered up a basket. From within came feline sounds of protest.

"Bala?"

"Bala. To remember us by."

Nick thought it unlikely he would ever forget this sojourn in Persia, although he intended to try his best to block out the memory of Tahmasp's swift and merciless punishment of Hamid.

As soon as he left Qazvin, his heart felt lighter. True, he would be returning soon to a country where heretics were burnt to death and traitors were hanged, drawn, and quartered, but he understood the complexities of life in England. English law, English political factions, and English religion were familiar to him.

He felt a grin overspread his features as he rode on. At home, he knew how to stay out of trouble. He was, after all, a London man.

A Note from the Author

Nick's travels in Persia are loosely based on real events. By 1553, England had an interest in finding a northern route to the wealth of the Indies. This led to trade with Russia, which was then called Muscovy. In 1558, Anthony Jenkinson set out from Moscow on a journey that was intended to retrace the footsteps of Marco Polo. When it took Jenkinson nine months to reach Bokhara, however, and he was told it would take another nine to reach China, he returned to Moscow instead.

That is the point at which I depart from history and have Nick go off on his own. To reach Qazvin, then the capital of Persia, he follows the route Jenkinson would take two years later, crossing the Caspian to Derbent, meeting Abd Allah Khan, king of Shirvan and ruler of the Uzbeg people, and then going on to meet Shah Tahmasp. Unfortunately, Jenkinson and the official delegation did not succeed in opening trade between Persia and England. He so offended the shah with his arrogance that at one point Tahmasp threatened to cut off his head and send it to Suleyman the Magnificent.

"The Rubaiyat of Nicholas Baldwin" was originally published in the September 2001 issue of *Alfred Hitchcock Mystery Magazine*. Events in *Face Down in the Marrow-Bone Pie* and *Face Down Upon an Herbal* take place between this story and the next, in which Nick first meets Lady Appleton. He does not appear in a Face Down novel until *Face Down Beneath the Eleanor Cross*.

Lady Appleton and the London Man

"Folk hereabout call him the London Man." Jennet gestured toward the stranger at the far side of the gardens. "That is Master Baldwin."

Even as she wondered how Jennet could identify the fellow with such ease when this was his first visit to Leigh Abbey, Susanna Appleton had to smile at the sentiment behind the ekename. To country-dwellers who'd never traveled farther from their homes than Dover or Canterbury, London was as foreign a place as France or Spain. Wealthy city merchants like Master Baldwin aroused their darkest suspicions, especially when they purchased rural estates from the impoverished heirs of local gentry. Baldwin might now own a goodly parcel of land in Kent, but he was an outsider and would remain so.

"We will wait for him here," Susanna said, coming to a halt in the ornamental garden, a semi-circular space planted with shrubs, flowers, and a few fruit trees. Their visitor had not yet seen them, although it was plain one of the servants had told him where to look. The gardens on the south side of Leigh Abbey covered nearly an acre, far more extensive than the ones the monks had planted when the manor was, in truth, an abbey.

On this early August day, in the year of our Lord fifteen hundred and sixty-two, Susanna had suggested a mid-morning walk in pleasant surroundings in order to assure that Jennet, once her tiring maid, long her friend and companion, and now her housekeeper, did not wear herself out with work. Jennet would be delivered of her third child in a few months, several weeks before the second reached the one-year mark.

From a stone bench situated beneath an ancient oak planted on a little knoll, the two women had a splendid view. Susanna watched Baldwin pass through her herb garden and continue his advance between the long rows of parallel beds in the vegetable garden. He looked, she decided, like one of his own sturdy merchant ships under full sail.

Her new neighbor was stocky but not fat, with broad shoulders and surprisingly small feet. When he came closer, Susanna judged that he was a bit shorter than she was, but then she was tall for a woman, a legacy from her father. She'd also inherited his square jaw and his inquiring mind.

Baldwin appeared to be no more than thirty, although his brown hair had some white in it. He had regular features behind a fine beard, but at the moment, having spotted the two waiting women, they were much contorted by irritation.

She rose when he reached the base of the knoll, making her countenance as stern as a schoolmaster's. Why should a man she'd never met be so wroth with her? He seemed to be glowering at Jennet, too.

"Who are you, sir? And what business brings you to my home?"

Taken aback by her challenging stance, Baldwin hesitated, but only for a moment. "Good day to you, madam." He doffed his plumed bonnet, then replaced it with enough force to tell her he could barely contain some powerful emotion. "I am Nicholas Baldwin, your neighbor."

Had he been a dragon, Lady Appleton thought, he'd be breathing fire. She thought his scowling face and snapping eyes would look well on a carved wooden figurehead, but only if the piece graced the prow of a pirate's vessel.

"And your business here, Master Baldwin?"

He glanced at Jennet, then quickly back to Susanna. "It might be best if your husband were present."

"Impossible," Susanna informed him. "Sir Robert left five days ago on the queen's business. I do not expect to see him again for many months."

Gentleman, courtier, and sometime intelligence gatherer for the Crown, Sir Robert Appleton was often away for long periods of time. In his absence, Susanna ran his estates. In truth, she managed them even when he was in England. Although it galled Robert to admit it, she was better at such things than he was."

Again Baldwin looked in Jennet's direction, but this time his gaze remained fixed upon her. "I came here seeking this woman, Lady Appleton. I believe your servant stole something that belongs to me. Something of great value."

Deluded as one fit for Bedlam, Susanna thought, until she remembered that Jennet had been able to identify Master Baldwin before he introduced himself. The look now overspreading the housekeeper's face might indeed be guilt. Jennet's eyes were wide and her skin had lost all color. For a moment, Susanna feared the younger woman might faint.

She should have known better.

Servant she might be, but Jennet had never been backward about speaking her mind. Hands on her ample hips, she recovered in a trice from her shock at Baldwin's claim and returned his irate stare with one of her own. Her position atop the knoll allowed her to look down her nose at him.

"I never stole anything!" she declared. "I am innocent as a newborn babe."

Had the accusation not been so serious, Susanna would have applauded the show of bravado. Unfortunately, the law was clear. Theft of goods worth more than twelvepence was punishable by execution.

Baldwin looked unconvinced by the heartfelt protest. He shifted his attention to Susanna once more. "I must have my property back, madam. If it is returned to me without further ado, I will not bring charges against anyone in this household. Indeed, I will say nothing more of the incident to anyone."

If the claim that Jennet was a thief had been outrageous, this promise of leniency seemed more so. Master Baldwin, Susanna concluded, had something to hide.

"You are blunt, Master Baldwin," she told him.

"I am truthful, Lady Appleton."

"Why do you suspect Jennet?"

"She was seen in my house a week past, lurking in places where she had no business and creeping about in a furtive manner."

"I did but pay a visit to Master Baldwin's cook!"

Susanna motioned for Jennet to remain silent, fearing she might say too much. She was well known to have a habit of listening at keyholes, but that was a far cry from stealing.

"Why wait a week to accuse her?" She met his eyes without blinking.

Baldwin looked away first. "I did not discover my loss until this morning."

"What does Jennet stand accused of taking?"

"You have no need to know."

Susanna's eyebrows lifted. She had heard that excuse too often from Robert and been obliged to accept it. She owed Baldwin no such obedience.

Under her steady glare, her neighbor's uneasiness grew until it was almost palpable. There, she sensed, lay a weakness she could use to advantage.

"I see no constable at your heels," she said. "No justice of the peace."

"You cannot want me to take the matter to law. Think, madam of the consequences."

Beside her, Susanna felt Jennet tremble, vibrating with a mixture of outrage and fear at this reminder of her danger. A convicted felon great with child might delay execution until she delivered, but afterward the sentence would be duly carried out.

"I will not permit such an injustice," Susanna declared. She slipped a comforting arm around the other woman's shoulders. Jennet might be adept at spinning tales and be able to lie without a qualm when necessity demanded, but she was no thief.

Baldwin looked thoughtful. "All I have heard of you, madam, from the vicar and from my servants, indicates you are a practical woman. This matter is easily settled. Allow me to search here at Leigh Abbey for what I have lost. I am certain I can rely upon your common sense to tell you this is a happy solution."

Flattery did not sway her, but neither did Susanna have any logical reason not to allow Baldwin to scour the premises. In truth, she could think of one very good argument in favor of permitting him to search.

"I will make a bargain with you, Master Baldwin," she said. "You may go through the entire house and all the outbuildings, look in any place you think Jennet might have secreted this stolen item. But when you have done, and have found nothing, you must grant me a favor in return."

"What favor?"

"To be taken to the scene of the crime, where you will answer any question I pose about the theft."

Master Baldwin began to sputter a protest, but Susanna was spared the need to argue with him.

"Lady Appleton is the most skilled person in all England at reasoning out the truth of strange events," Jennet declared.

Baldwin did not look convinced, but he agreed to her proposal with a curt nod of assent. Likely he felt certain he'd find what he sought. Susanna was equally sure he would not.

"Shall we start with the stillroom?" She led him back through the gardens and up to the door of a separate building near the kitchen. "You may look, but not touch," she said.

Baldwin hesitated in the doorway, taking in the sight of drying herbs surrounded by all manner of equipment for distillation and dozens of jars, pots, and other vessels, all labeled and dated. Apparently, he knew of her reputation as an expert on herbal poisons. When, after a thorough examination of the rest of the stillroom, his gaze fell upon the black chest in the darkest corner of the room, he did no more than request that she lift the lid.

"The thing I seek is not here," Baldwin admitted when he saw that it was full of papers containing notes she had made over the course of many years of study.

In Susanna's company, Master Baldwin investigated every nook and cranny of Leigh Abbey, combing kitchen and bake house and snooping in the servants' quarters and the stables, too. He found nothing, and at length the only room left to be searched was the study.

"A pleasant chamber," he remarked, taking in the hearth with the marble chimney-piece, the east-facing window, and the small, carpet-draped table holding crystal flagons and Venetian glass goblets. Susanna did not offer him refreshment. She had no desire to encourage him to linger.

A second table was heavy-laden with leather-bound volumes. The presence of so many books seemed to intrigue Baldwin. One by one he examined them with something bordering on reverence. Susanna did not think he was still looking for the missing object. Simple curiosity drove him.

A copy of *Variorum planetarium historia*, written in Latin by a French physician and botanist, told him she was literate in more than one language. Then he found *A Cautionary Herbal, being a compendium of plants harmful to the health*. This small volume, printed by Master John Day of London two years earlier, bore only the initials S.A. to identify its author, but Baldwin, having just seen the papers in her stillroom, guessed the truth.

"You wrote this?" he asked.

She nodded. Remaining anonymous had been Robert's idea, not hers. It had allowed him to claim credit for her work.

Without comment, Baldwin abandoned the books and prowled the small room, stirring the rushes with every step to release the scent of the bayleaves strewn among them. He stopped in front of a large engraved map, mounted for hanging, which occupied a place of honor in the room.

Susanna felt herself tense. She forced herself to relax. "Mayhap you would care to look behind the *mappa mundi*?" she asked. "Doubtless there is a hidden panel in that wall."

"This, madam, may be a map of the world, but the term *mappa mundi* properly refers only to written descriptions."

"My husband calls it a *mappa mundi*."

"Sir Robert is a gentleman who dabbles in seafaring and exploration, but only in books and conversation." Baldwin's tone implied he himself was a participant in such things, and therefore an authority.

"Have you finished your search?" She heard the testiness in her voice and that annoyed her nearly as much as Baldwin's attitude.

"Aye, I have done what I set out to do."

"Good. I gave orders some time ago for my mare to be saddled."

A few minutes later, she was perched sideways on her horse, both feet resting on a velvet sling and supporting one knee in a hollow cut in the pommeled saddle, but there was a delay in setting out because Jennet insisted upon coming along and she required the help of two stout fellows to hoist her onto a pillion.

"You hate going anywhere on horseback," Susanna reminded her, "even when you are not great with child."

"The journey is short," Jennet argued, grasping the waist of the man in the saddle in front of her.

Plainly, she did not intend to be left behind, and Susanna had to admit that she had every right to accompany them. There was little likelihood now that Jennet would be arrested or tried, let alone convicted and executed, since Baldwin had found no proof of her guilt, but neither had he rescinded his accusation. Jennet's honor was at stake.

Baldwin's house was less than two miles distant if one went by way of a footpath that ran through Leigh Abbey's orchards and a small wood and led straight to his kitchen door. Master and servant alike had often taken this shortcut over the years. By the road, the distance was nearly double, and because there had been rain during the night, going was slow.

So was pulling information out of Master Baldwin. He still refused to reveal the exact nature of the missing item.

"It was something meant to be presented to the queen," he allowed after considerable badgering on Susanna's part, "to be given to her once certain diplomatic goals have been met. I hold it in trust for someone else."

With further encouragement, he was persuaded to talk about his travels. A merchant adventurer, he'd only lately returned from Muscovy and Persia. To hear him tell it, he'd been the first Englishman to visit the court of Shah Tahmasp, arriving there a full two years ahead of the merchants of the Muscovy Company. In all, Master Baldwin had spent six and a half years away from England and come home a wealthy man.

When they at last arrived at his house, Baldwin escorted Susanna and Jennet into a private chamber on an upper floor. From Jennet's look of surprise, and by the way she peered with such curiosity into every corner, Susanna concluded that her housekeeper had not had an opportunity to explore this part of the premises on her earlier visit.

There were many charts and maps on the walls, and the London Man kept other treasures in chests and on tables. On display were an odd collection of objects, some of which Susanna could not identify.

"Those are navigational instruments I brought back from my travels," he said, noticing the direction of her gaze. "Your husband found them as fascinating as you seem to."

She was about to ask what had occasioned Robert's visit when Jennet let out a shriek. Her face turned bright red with embarrassment. "I did not think it was alive," she stammered, pointing toward a creature perched atop a silk-covered cushion on the window seat. "Not until it opened one eye and stared at me."

"It" was a cat much larger that those Susanna was accustomed to. It was covered with long, white fur.

"His name is Bala," Master Baldwin said of the odd-looking beast. "I brought him back from Persia, too."

Bala continued to stare at them with baleful eyes while Master Baldwin retrieved a small, ornately carved ivory box from a chest and handed it to Lady Appleton. "The queen's gift was kept in this."

"Jewelry," she said. "Of what description?"

"What makes you think it was a jewel?"

"I watched you search Leigh Abbey, saw where and in what you looked. Together with the size of the box, I perceive the object you seek may be contained in a space no bigger than the palm of your hand. Add to that conclusion all you told us of your travels and my deduction is reasonable. Everyone knows that traders carry valuable jewels to exchange for other goods. The first Muscovy merchants took pearls and sapphires and rubies with them, and travelers to the East regularly bring back jasper and chalcedony."

"It is not a jewel, as it happens, but I cannot fault your logic. You are a most unusual woman."

"Unusual enough to convince you to tell me what was stolen?"

Baldwin came very near a smile. "It was a carved figure of great age and beauty. The like has never been seen in England."

"Why do you think Jennet took this bauble?"

"She was the only one with opportunity, unless you wish me to accuse your husband."

He smiled.

Susanna did not.

She'd known for years that her husband had flaws. It was possible, although it seemed unlikely, that he had removed something he should not have from Master Baldwin's house.

"I discovered the stone missing this morning," Baldwin continued. "The last time I lifted the lid of this box, Sir Robert stood beside me."

For a moment, Susanna thought she heard something in Baldwin's voice, a hint that he did, in truth, suspect Robert.

"How careless of you not to have checked to be certain it was still there as soon as he left, Master Baldwin." To avoid meeting his eyes, she crossed the room to the window seat to make a closer inspection of the odd-looking cat. His fur was passing soft to the touch.

Her mild sarcasm had Baldwin blustering. "I had been advised, by someone high in Her Majesty's favor, that the head of the household at Leigh Abbey could be trusted."

"Whoever told you that," Jennet muttered, "he's more likely to have meant Lady Appleton than Sir Robert."

Baldwin trained his intense gaze on the housekeeper. "You are a strange sort of servant."

Deciding he'd had enough of a stranger's attentions, Bala abruptly rose and leapt down from his cushion. A moment later, he began to play with a lightweight wooden disk. After a moment, Susanna recognized it as a checker.

"I have been looking for that," Baldwin said, stooping to retrieve it. "It is part of a set. This is yours," he said to the cat, and tossed a square of canvas, stuffed with catnip by the smell of it, toward the center of the room.

Bala ignored the offering.

Susanna smiled. If Master Baldwin was the sort to make toys for a pet, there was hope he might yet learn to appreciate the advantages of individuality in servants and to value intelligence in women. The best way to convince him was to solve the mystery of his missing carving.

"What does your stolen object look like?"

Still watching the cat, he answered her. "In color it is an intense apple green. No more than six barleycorns high, it is the image of a horse."

Jennet would have no interest in such a thing, Susanna thought, but Robert was uncommon fond of horses. After a moment's silence, she began to muse aloud. What was most important at the moment was to clear her housekeeper of suspicion.

"I see no sign that anyone broke into this room," she said, "but you must realize it is scarce secure. The window is an easy climb from the ground. The horse might have been taken at any time since you showed it to Robert. Tell me, was it in this chamber that he inspected the piece?"

"We took the box with us when we went down to the winter parlor near the kitchen, where my cook had set out a modest repast. It was there that your housekeeper was seen, Lady Appleton, although none of my servants thought to mention her presence to me until after I discovered the carving was missing and began to question them."

Master Baldwin led the way to the lower floor. Bala followed after them, but soon tired of their company and left the winter parlor by way of another open window.

"When is Jennet supposed to have had an opportunity to steal the carving?" Susanna asked. "When was the box out of your possession?"

"I left it on the table when I bade Sir Robert farewell. I saw him off, through the front of the house, then returned here to collect it."

To clear Jennet, Susanna thought, all she had to do was accuse Robert.

Instead she asked for a few days to consider the problem, hinting that local folk would confide in her, where to Master Baldwin they would plead ignorance. "You are a foreigner in their eyes," she explained.

"Aye," he agreed. "A London Man."

* * *

"Well, Jennet?" Lady Appleton asked when they were well on their way back to Leigh Abbey. They had sent the horses ahead with the groom and taken the footpath. No one was in the wood to overhear what they said to each other.

"I did not take the little horse."

"But you were at Master Baldwin's house the day Sir Robert visited him."

Reluctantly, Jennet nodded.

"And you were in the parlor."

"Aye. How could I not be curious when I heard Sir Robert's voice?"

"You crept out of the kitchen and hid yourself, so that you might listen to whatever he said to Master Baldwin." It was not a question and Jennet did not try to deny it. Susanna knew her ways too well.

"When they left the little box behind, I wanted to see what was in it. I dashed across the room and opened the lid to peep inside."

"And was the carving there?"

"Oh, aye, but I scarce had time to admire it before I heard Master Baldwin returning. I closed the lid again and hid myself in the alcove behind the wall hanging until he collected the box and carried it away. Then I left his house and came straight home."

That the carving had still been in the box when Robert left surprised Susanna. She did not like suspecting him, but she knew her husband well, and it was still within the realm of possibility that he had returned to Baldwin's house and stolen the queen's gift.

"What do we do now, madam? I find it passing unpleasant to be thought a thief."

"We will discover the truth." She was just not certain what she would do with it when she did.

* * *

Sir Robert Appleton had given his wife no reason to expect him to return to Leigh Abbey before he left the country on his latest mission for the Crown, but he was there when Susanna and Jennet reached home. Susanna found him in the study, just lifting down the *mappa mundi*.

"I thought you were to set sail from London," she said as he removed a panel in the wall behind it to reveal his accustomed hiding place for small valuables.

"I must cross the Narrow Seas to meet my ship off the coast of France."

Leigh Abbey was on the road between London and Dover. To break the journey here was not suspicious in itself, but Susanna could not like this new development.

"You had best make haste," she advised, "before you are arrested."

The glance he shot at her over his shoulder conveyed annoyance. Theirs had been an arranged marriage, and although they managed as well as most couples, nowadays there was little love between them and less liking. "Have you some particular reason to think I will be?"

In clipped sentences she told him of Master Baldwin's visit and his search of the house. She did not mention that it had been Jennet he'd accused of theft.

A furrow appeared in his high forehead, centered between an escaping lock of dark, wavy hair and equally dark brows. Something disturbed him in her report, but she was not certain that meant he had stolen the carving himself. Being accused was reason enough for worry.

"What was in that box was intended as a gift for the queen," Robert said after a moment. "It was to have been given to Her Majesty after the men of the Muscovy Company, with whom Baldwin was associated in his youth, return from their visit to the Shah. Baldwin's trip to Persia was not authorized."

Susanna waited, letting the silence lengthen until he was driven to fill it.

"The theft of that piece could thwart a political alliance between England and Persia."

"Who would want to do that?"

"You have no need to know."

"I have every need if blame falls on someone at Leigh Abbey. What was your business with Master Baldwin? Why did he show you the carving?"

"That is none of your concern."

As Susanna watched, unable to subdue the anger his attitude provoked, Robert removed a number of oilskin wrapped papers from the opening behind the panel and tucked them into the front of his dark green doublet. Then he reached in again for something smaller, which he likewise tucked away beneath the heavily embroidered velvet garment. She blinked. Had he just palmed the little horse?

She wished she'd looked behind the map before his return. No woman wanted proof her husband was a thief, but not knowing one way or the other was far worse. Perhaps she had been too clever earlier, diverting Master Baldwin's attention from the map with her sarcastic suggestion that he might find a hiding place behind it. She had not suspected then that Baldwin might have his own doubts about Robert's honesty. Now she realized that by accusing the servant rather than the master, he'd achieved the same end, a search of Leigh Abbey, with far less opposition.

When Sir Robert's hiding place was once more concealed, he approached his wife. "Farewell, my dear." He caught her to him for a rough parting kiss before she could evade him. "I have no time to deal with our new neighbor. You must take care of the matter as you see fit."

He knew she took seriously the vows she'd made when they wed. She had sworn to obey him. Echoes of his taunting laughter lingered in the room long after he'd gone.

Susanna did not follow her husband to see him on his way. The days were long past when she felt obliged to offer the traditional stirrup cup and blessing.

Instead she stared at the map. In her mind, she saw Robert reaching into the wall that second time. To take something small out? Or to put something in?

Master Baldwin had said the little carving was no more than six barleycorns high. She glanced down at her hand. Strong and work-hardened, the nails blunt, the skin stained with the residue of various herbal preparations, it was large enough to conceal a object that size. Robert's hand could easily have done so.

Susanna knew the nature of professional intelligence gatherers, her husband in particular. They tended to complicate matters. It would be just like him to put the carving back while trying to make her believe he'd removed it. Her mind full of possibilities, she took a step closer to the map.

* * *

Early the next morning, Susanna once again followed the footpath, this time walking from Leigh Abbey to Master Baldwin's property alone. She paused to examine several likely places along the way, the last just at the point where the path came out of the wood and plunged steeply downward toward the manor house.

Barely a quarter of an hour later, when Master Baldwin joined her in his winter parlor, she handed him the missing horse. With his fingers curled tight around the apple-green figure, he waited for her explanation.

"You said, did you not, Master Baldwin, that you left the box containing that object unattended while you escorted Sir Robert to the door?"

"Aye, I did."

"And the box was not locked?"

"No. I did not turn the key until I returned. You know already that I did not look inside."

"And Bala, I perceive, is a very clever cat."

"Bala?" He blinked at her in surprise.

"The cat took your carving."

"Bala?" he repeated, thunderstruck.

"I found it beside the footpath that runs between this house and Leigh Abbey," she explained. "It is small and lightweight—easy for a cat to carry off in its mouth. When Bala tired of it, he must have dropped it there, where it could not be easily seen for the twigs and leaves."

"I did not search along any path," Baldwin admitted. "I did not realize there was one connecting our two properties."

Baldwin abruptly crossed the room to where the large white feline slept atop a carpet-covered table and picked him up. There was no question in Susanna's mind that the cat could have done what she'd said. In common with all felines, he roamed far and wide in search of mice and other prey.

"This cat was well named," Baldwin said. "In the language of Persia, Bala means nuisance."

For a moment, Lady Appleton feared he might harm the animal. He held him at arm's length, but all he did was give him a hard stare. Then, shaking his head, he cuddled him in his arms and turned to face his neighbor.

The show of affection wrenched at Susanna's heart. She was suddenly very tired of letting Robert shift the blame for his less honorable actions to others. She had *never* liked to lie.

Did she dare tell Master Baldwin that the carving had been behind the map? That Robert had by stealth entered the upper room of his house and stolen it?

Her words came out in a rush: "Bala did not—"

"Mean to cause so much trouble," Baldwin finished for her. "I am well aware of that. Perhaps you will allow me to send a small gift to your housekeeper by way of apology?"

"She would appreciate that, but I—"

This time he held up a hand to stop her. "The end result is the same. Through your involvement, your desire to protect those close to you, the carving has been returned. It is best we say no more about it."

The look in his eyes brought to an abrupt end her need to confess. It was a curious mixture of triumph and compassion.

For that brief moment, Lady Appleton and the London Man shared a perfect understanding of the truth.

A Note from the Author

"Persian" cats originally came from Turkey. They did not yet have the flat-faced look associated with the breed today. In the sixteenth century they were a popular export from Persia and Turkey to Muscovy, and although I do not know of any that made the journey to England, there is no reason someone associated with the Muscovy Company could not have brought one back with him.

"Lady Appleton and the London Man" first appeared in *More Murder They Wrote* (1999). Events in *Face Down Among the Winchester Geese* take place between this story and the next.

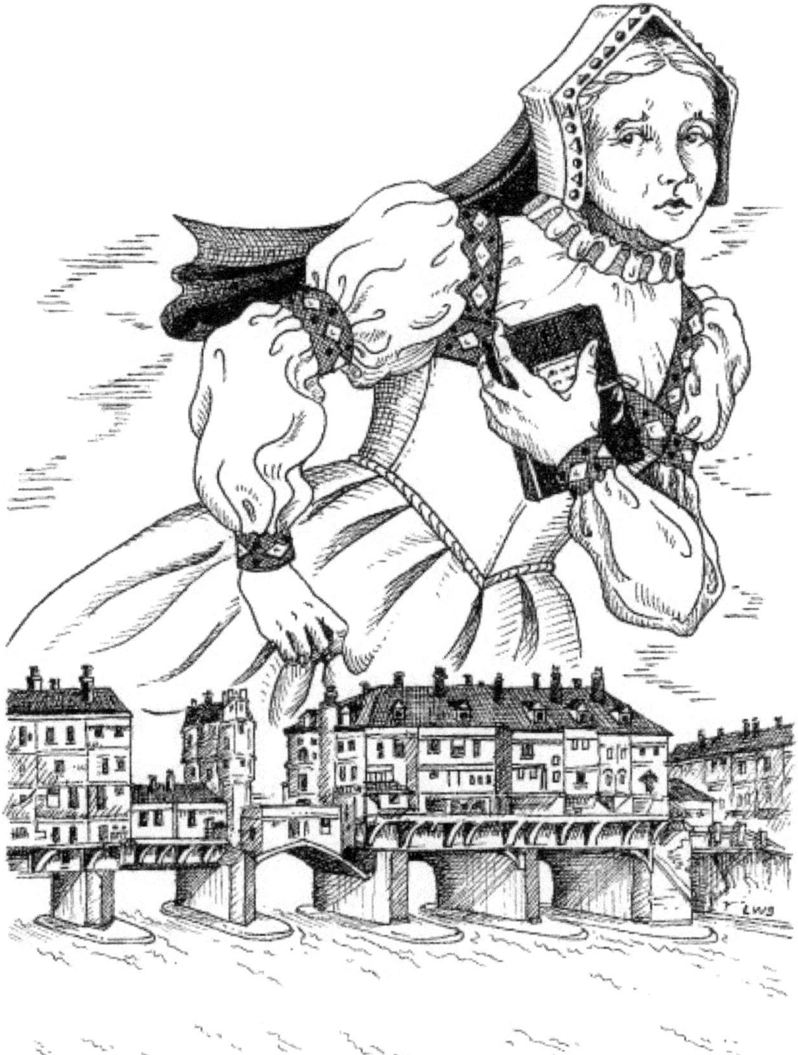

Lady Appleton and the Cautionary Herbal

A horn sounded to announce the arrival of a post boy at Leigh Abbey, a not uncommon occurrence since the manor house stood so near the main road from London to Dover, one of the most traveled highways in Elizabeth Tudor's England. He was gone again before Susanna, Lady Appleton, reached the gatehouse, but he had left a package. She eyed it with mild surprise. Although she was in regular correspondence with a goodly number of friends and acquaintances throughout the kingdom, they rarely exchanged anything but letters.

Puzzled, she hefted the parcel. Nothing on the outer wrapping, which was slightly torn, hinted at who might have sent it, but the size and shape left little doubt she'd find a book inside. Her fingers trembled as she undid the string that bound it. The world thought her a widow, but she knew in her heart that her deceitful, traitorous husband still lived. She feared this might be some sort of communication from him.

To her astonishment, the package contained an inexpensive folio copy of the volume she herself had written. *A Cautionary Herbal, being a compendium of plants harmful to the health* was the result of many years of research. Susanna had been motivated to compile it by her younger sister's untimely death following the consumption of some harmless-looking berries that had, in fact, been poisonous.

As she retraced her steps to the house, Susanna tried to think who might have sent the book to her and why. It had not, she concluded, come from Sir Robert Appleton, who had disappeared just a year earlier. If he'd wished to communicate, he'd have sent a quite different book. But her relief was tempered by perplexity. That she was the author of this little herbal was no great secret, but on the title page the work was attributed only to "S.A." and her identity, or so she'd always believed, was not widely known.

Since no note accompanied the volume, Susanna carried it into her study and began to turn the leaves, looking for anything written in the margins. She found not a single annotation but she did make another discovery—a jagged edge where a single page had been torn out.

The entries were alphabetical and each had a drawing opposite. The missing text had detailed the properties of hemlock, a particularly deadly poison. In ancient Athens it had been used for state executions.

"Most troubling," she murmured. Still carrying the book, she went to the window to stare out at fields where the summer ploughing had begun and at orchards filled with apple and cherry trees. She found no solace in the peaceful vista, nor did the sight provide any answers.

A jangle of keys warned Susanna that Jennet, her housekeeper, had entered the chamber. She stopped short when she caught sight of her mistress's expression, then crept closer. She had to peer upward to see Susanna's face clearly, for the lady of Leigh Abbey was uncommon tall. She had inherited that characteristic, along with her intelligence, her sturdy build, and the square set of her jaw, from her father. Jennet, although of middling height for a woman, stood somewhat shorter. She was a blue-eyed, pale-skinned, fair-haired, small-boned individual who had gone from slim to plump in the course of giving birth to three children. She had never, in all the years she had served Lady Appleton, been shy about asking questions or expressing her opinions.

"What is the matter, madam? What has happened?"

Before Susanna could answer, Jennet caught sight of the herbal. She had no difficulty recognizing it or perceiving, as anyone in the household would, that it was not one of the copies housed at Leigh Abbey. Those were all bound in expensive hand-tooled leather.

"Someone sent this to me," Susanna said.

"Who?"

"It could have been anyone. It is not difficult to purchase a copy."

Indeed, it had been Susanna's hope when she wrote the slim volume that it would be readily available to all those who needed it. She'd collected information on poisonous herbs for the benefit of housewives and cooks, those most likely to mistake one plant for another and accidentally poison an entire household.

"Madam, what is it?" Alarm made Jennet's voice sharp. "Your face has of a sudden gone white as a winding sheet."

Susanna felt for a stool and sat. "I feared this might come to pass," she whispered as a wave of dismay and guilt swept through her.

She'd realized soon after her book was published that in her effort to do good, she had also gathered together a collection of recipes that could be used by an evildoer intent upon harm. In the wrong hands, this herbal designed to protect the unwary became a manual for murder. Did the package she'd just received mean *A Cautionary Herbal*, compiled in order to save lives, had been used to take one?

Susanna lifted the folio and stared at it, seeking in vain for answers. When she at last put it aside, she was determined to reason out who had sent it to her and why.

The postboy had come from London. She knew that much. London was also the most likely place for her herbal to have been purchased, but was sending the book an announcement of a crime already committed or a challenge to her to prevent murder? If there was any chance she could do the latter, she knew she had to attempt it.

"We must go to London," she said. "At once."

***

John Day had printed Susanna's herbal. His premises in London were in Aldersgate, where his printing house was set against the city wall and his shop, warehouse, and lodgings in the churchyard were attached to the gate. From the outside, he did not appear to have much space to conduct business, but the buildings extended backward and Susanna knew, from a previous visit, that there was a fine garden hidden away behind them.

There were many such pleasant places in London, did one but know where to find them. On this bright mid-June morning, however, Susanna was only interested in answers. Accompanied by Jennet and one of Leigh Abbey's grooms of the stable, she entered Day's place of business.

The rattle and clash of presses assaulted their ears as soon as they stepped through the door. An inking ball stuffed with feathers brushed the top of Susanna's French hood. She wrinkled her nose at its pungent smell and took note of the location of several more of these offensive objects, which had been suspended from the ceiling in order to be in easy reach of Day's apprentices. A similar stench emanated from the freshly printed pages draped for drying over lines strung between the presses.

As Susanna searched the huge workroom for Master Day, her gaze took in piles of quartos and pamphlets, already assembled and stacked on tables, and shelves piled high with boxes of movable type. The printer himself, a tall, thin man with a face like a basset hound's, was at his hand press, so engrossed in producing an ornate title page from a finely engraved copper plate that he did not notice Susanna until she called his name.

At once, he abandoned his task. When she requested that they speak in private, he escorted her to a comfortable parlor in his lodgings and settled her in his best chair.

"I came here, Master Day," she said, "hoping you know what persons have of late bought copies of my book."

"I do not keep a record of the names of purchasers, Lady Appleton." With ink-stained fingers, he began to pleat the fabric of his long canvas apron. "Indeed, my stock for the most part goes to booksellers."

Her question had made him nervous and she had to wonder why. "You also sell a few individual copies. Do you remember if any recent customer behaved in an odd manner? Think, Master Day. Do you recall one who looked furtive, or guilty? Was there someone, mayhap, who asked you to identify the S.A. who wrote my book?"

"I print many books, madam, and have many customers." The fabric of his apron was now as goffered as a ruff, convincing Susanna that he knew more than he wished to admit.

"Well, then," she said with an exaggerated sigh, "there is no help for it. I must withdraw all remaining copies of my book."

As she'd anticipated, Day was horrified by the possibility of lost profit. "You cannot be serious, madam!"

"My work may have been used to do murder, Master Day."

Shock, but no surprise, showed in his features. "Surely the good your herbal may do far outweighs its potential to cause harm."

Although Susanna had reached that same conclusion during the two-day journey from rural Kent to London, she was not inclined to abandon her quest. "Someone sent a copy of the herbal to Leigh Abbey with one page missing," she said. "I believe that person intends to commit murder, or has done so already. Have you heard of any deaths by poisoning in London in recent days?"

"Indeed I have not!" Day sounded indignant, but he could not meet her eyes.

"Then mayhap I am in time to prevent one."

Susanna waited, saying nothing more, letting Day's conscience prick at him. The printer's nervousness increased visibly, causing him to abandon the stool on which he'd been perched and begin to pace. He paused by the window, through which drifted the scents of roses and honeysuckle from the garden below, before turning to glare at his unwelcome guest.

"What profit to save one life at the cost of another?"

"Explain yourself, good sir. I do not wish to bear responsibility for *any* death and I would think you'd feel the same."

"You ask me to vilify a person who has done naught but buy a copy of your herbal."

So he did suspect someone! Elated, Susanna had to struggle to keep her voice level. "If no crime has yet been committed, I would have that remain true, but you must see that I need to investigate. If my suspicions are correct, if that torn page means someone is contemplating murder, then how can I do nothing to stop it and still live with myself? Give me a name, Master Day. Let me pursue the matter. You have my word that I will be discreet."

Day looked everywhere but at her.

"The book was *sent* to me." Using her most persuasive voice, Susanna rose from her chair and crossed to him to place one hand on his forearm. When he reluctantly met her eyes, she added, "Someone *wanted* me to know, and to act."

Heaving a heavy-hearted sigh, Day capitulated. "You must speak to Mistress Drood, wife to Ralph Drood the merchant. You will find his house on London Bridge, near the sign of the Golden Key." In his misery, his resemblance to a basset hound increased. "She is his third wife, Lady Appleton. Her two predecessors died under most suspicious circumstances."

* * *

Once more accompanied by Jennet and the groom, Susanna went first to the church of St. Magnus, located near the north end of the Bridge. For some thirty years, all England had been required by law to register births, marriages, and deaths. Some did so more religiously than others but Susanna's luck was in. She found the entries she sought without difficulty. Day had been right. Drood had married his second wife only seven months after burying the first, and had wed the third within a month of the second's demise.

"A most unlucky fellow," said the rector who helped Susanna find the records.

"Do you know Ralph Drood?"

"Everyone knows Master Drood in this parish. He has given most generously to the church."

"Is he a rich man, then?"

"Oh, aye."

Further questioning elicited the information that Drood imported iron, wax, ginger, woad, Spanish asses, herring, beaver, and wine. He exported grain and cloth, and on occasion acted as a moneylender. He had a fine house on London Bridge, five stories high and filled with servants.

"Two maids and a cook among them," the rector bragged, "and Master Drood has property in the country, too."

"Why, then, do you say he is unlucky?"

"Two years ago, he had a wife and son. Then the boy was overlaid and so died."

Overlaid. Susanna winced. Someone had rolled on top of him and he'd suffocated. As a cause of death it was not uncommon, not when an entire family often slept in the same bed. She frowned. This family was wealthy. The child should have been sleeping in a cradle by himself.

"A few weeks after," the rector continued, "the bereaved mother died. Pining for her infant, or so it was said."

"Pining," Susanna recalled, had been written down as "cause of death" in the register. It was a useful term, sufficiently vague to account for all manner of symptoms.

"Master Drood remarried without the customary year of mourning," she remarked.

"Aye, that he did. Well, why not?" The rector's defensive tone of voice reminded Susanna that Drood was a generous contributor to the parish coffers.

"And the second Mistress Drood?"

"Stifled to death."

Another ambiguous term, Susanna thought. "Do you mean that someone held a pillow over her face?"

Taken aback by the suggestion, the rector made haste to clarify. "She fell asleep in a closed room after lighting a charcoal brazier to keep it warm. That was what the searchers determined."

The searchers were old women who examined bodies in order to report a cause of death to the authorities. They were untrained and ill-paid. Susanna put little faith in their skill. They could easily have made a mistake. More likely, she thought as she thanked the rector for his help and bade him farewell, they were bribed to accept Drood's version of his wife's death.

* * *

London Bridge was entirely covered with shops, taverns, and houses, nearly 200 buildings crammed together with room in the middle for carts, horses, and pedestrians to pass. At either end, one could see that a river flowed beneath the structures, but once upon the bridge it seemed to be just another long street.

For that Susanna was grateful. The mere sight of choppy water could make her queasy. She'd taken the precaution, en route from Day's premises to St. Magnus, of taking a preventative made of ginger root and peppermint.

An elderly maid answered the door at Master Drood's impressive dwelling. She led Susanna into a parlor, then took Jennet and the groom off to the kitchen. Jennet already had her instructions. She was to question the servants while her mistress spoke with Mistress Drood. Later, they would compare notes.

Left alone to wait for her hostess, Susanna took stock of her surroundings. The room was lushly furnished with turkey carpets and heavy, ornately carved furniture. One oak chest in particular attracted her attention. The front had been inlaid with other woods in a design meant to depict the exterior of some elaborate building, perhaps Nonsuch, the palace King Henry had built after destroying the village that had previously occupied the site.

She strode closer, curious to inspect the details. Too late, she realized that the open window above the chest looked directly down into the Thames. Swallowing hard, she backed away. It was foolish to become so overwrought at the mere sight of the river below, but she did not go near the casement again.

"Lady Appleton?" a meek voice inquired. Mistress Drood was a pale-faced mouse of a woman in rose-color taffeta too fine for her station. She was also rather older than Susanna had expected, and she looked frightened.

"Mistress Drood, I have come here to help you."

This comment seemed to surprise Mistress Drood. "I do not understand you."

"I believe you sent this to me." Susanna produced the herbal, which she'd brought with her in a pouch.

Mistress Drood's eyes widened, making it clear to Susanna that she recognized it. "Why would I do that?"

"Because I compiled this herbal. The initials S.A. represent Susanna Appleton."

"I did know that," Mistress Drood acknowledged.

"How?"

Flustered, the woman wrung her hands and kept her eyes downcast. "Master Baldwin told us. He supped with us one day last month and mentioned that his neighbor in Kent had written a book. He was mightily impressed by your scholarship, Lady Appleton."

One mystery solved, Susanna thought. Nicholas Baldwin, merchant of London, owned lands adjoining the Leigh Abbey demesne farm and knew she was the author of the herbal. She hastily repressed the small burst of pleasure she felt at learning he thought well of her for it. She was not here to garner praise.

"I believe you then bought a copy of my book," she said. "This copy."

Mistress Drood's head lifted. Her eyes were wide. "Oh, no, Lady Appleton! I did not do that."

"You did," Susanna insisted. John Day had identified her and he had no reason to lie. "Why?"

Tears welled up in Mistress Drood's eyes. "It was Master Drood's idea. He sent me to the printer to purchase a copy."

"Why?"

"Oh, Lady Appleton. He taunts me with it. He plans to kill me using one of the poisons you wrote about." Mistress Drood began to sob.

This was what she had feared, and yet something about Mistress Drood's tale did not ring true. "Who tore out the page?"

"He did! Oh, he did, and let me see that he'd done it, too. He torments me, making the last days of my life a misery before he acts."

Skeptical of such histrionics, Susanna studied Drood's wife. *Most peculiar behavior,* she thought, but she could not deny the woman's obvious distress. She led her to the window seat and made her sit, careful to avoid looking out as she did so.

Her words barely audible between sobs, Mistress Drood admitted to sending the herbal to Leigh Abbey and added that she'd done so because she wanted Susanna's help.

"But you sent no message with it. I had no idea who you were or what troubled you."

"I sent a note. It must have fallen out of the parcel."

Susanna frowned. Could a note have become detached? The wrapping *had* been torn.

"Why lie about it when I first asked? If you sent for me, you must have hoped I'd come."

With a lacy handkerchief she'd fished out of one sleeve, Mistress Drood patted her damp cheeks. "I was not thinking clearly. I feared my husband might recognize you. I did not precisely *send* for you, you see. I wrote to ask what that page contained and to request an antidote for the poison upon it. I thought you would reply by letter."

Susanna considered that. "You might have done better to go to Master Day and purchase another copy of my book."

The tears had ceased, but Mistress Drood's voice still hitched. "I did not dare. Master Drood might have heard of it. Then he'd have acted at once. As it is, I think he is waiting."

"Waiting for what?"

She made a fluttery gesture with one hand. "Midsummer's Eve is less than a week away."

Nonsense, Susanna thought, but she kept that reaction to herself.

"Ralph Drood killed his first two wives without any suspicion falling upon him," Mistress Drood said. "He believes he can do so again, and this time he means to employ poison."

Susanna had no difficulty accepting that Drood was a murderer. What troubled her was her suspicion that Mistress Drood had plans to strike first—to poison her husband before he could kill her.

She felt a reluctant sympathy for the woman. Mistress Drood clearly believed her life was at risk. Since Susanna herself had once contemplated an act that would have brought about another's death, she could understand the temptation.

Mistress Drood might be telling the simple truth and *had* sent to Leigh Abbey for an antidote. Perhaps that *was* all she wanted—the means to save herself. She did not look capable of harming a flea, but appearances *could* be deceiving.

"Let us discuss your husband," Susanna said. "What profit is there in your death?"

"Money."

"He is already wealthy."

"To Ralph Drood, there is no such thing as too much money. He always wants more. That is the only reason he married me. When I'm gone, he can wed yet again and collect another dowry from some poor unsuspecting father burdened with a spinster daughter."

"Can you go back to your father's house?" That might buy time to conduct a proper investigation into Drood's actions.

Mistress Drood shook her head. "My father is as great a brute and bully as Master Drood. He'll insist I return. And you need not suggest that I run away to friends. I have considered that. Master Drood would find me and force me to come back. He is wealthy and knows many powerful men. I am doomed, Lady Appleton, unless you can give me an antidote to keep always at hand."

Susanna had powerful friends of her own. If Drood was a murderer, one friend in particular might be able to help her prove it. "How can you be certain your husband killed his first two wives?" she asked. "Both cases were written down as accidents."

"I know they were murders." Mistress Drood spoke with convincing fervor. "He boasted to me of his deeds. He smothered one with a pillow. The other he starved to death."

"The law—"

"The law! Neither sheriff nor justice of the peace will act against him. He has the money to pay the most exorbitant bribe. Please, Lady Appleton, I beg of you—tell me how to keep myself from being poisoned. What was on that page?"

Susanna sighed. "Hemlock."

"How may I recognize it?"

"The seeds might be mistaken for anise, or the leaves for parsley. All parts of the plant are deadly, but the most powerful poison comes from juice extracted just as the fruit begins to form. This usually occurs toward the end of June."

"Around Midsummer Day?" Mistress Drood asked.

"Yes."

"He will no doubt try to give it to me in a drink."

"It has a bitter taste."

"Could that be disguised by herbs?"

"Perhaps. Hemlock also has a disagreeable odor—a mousy smell."

"And the antidote, should I notice these warning signs too late?"

"There is no sure antidote. There may be some small hope of survival if you empty your stomach at once. Some say that nettle seeds, taken inwardly, can counteract the poison, but I am not convinced they would be of any use. Hemlock is very potent and acts quickly. Few people, Mistress Drood, have ever cared to experiment, on themselves or others, to determine the efficacy of an antidote."

"Would my death look like an accident?" Drood's wife seemed to grow more calm with each bit of information Susanna provided.

"Aye. It well might."

Before Mistress Drood could ask any more questions, the slam of a door below and a series of sneezes alerted them to the return of her husband. "You must go," she whispered in obvious panic. "Hurry! Leave before he sees you or learns your name. It will go hard on me if he know you were here."

"Do nothing," Susanna warned as she was hustled out a back way. "Trust me to find a way to help you."

From the street outside, where she waited for Jennet and the groom to join her, Susanna heard Master Drood berating his wife. The words were indistinct, but there was no mistaking his foul temper. It seemed to get worse every time he was seized by a fit of sneezing.

"The cook says Master Drood sneezes for weeks at a time at this season of the year," Jennet remarked, appearing suddenly at her mistress's side.

Inhaling crushed basil might help, but Susanna felt no inclination to offer any suggestions. "Do the servants think he killed his first two wives?"

"Most of them do not seem to care if he did. They are well paid and have a roof over their heads and food in their bellies. Their loyalty is to Master Drood and not any of his wives." Jennet might have said more, but they had reached the end of the bridge. Nearby, boatmen waited to be hired and Susanna had to make a decision.

* * *

From the upriver side of London Bridge it was but a short ride in a wherry to reach the water stairs at Blackfriars. Throughout this brief journey, Susanna kept her eyes firmly fixed on the shore. Not even her ginger and peppermint mixture could completely quell the unquietness in her stomach, but at least she did not disgrace herself by being sick. It helped to keep her mind blank. Jennet, accustomed to her mistress's difficulty with travel on water, did not distract her with speech.

Sir Walter Pendennis had lodgings in Blackfriars, an enclosed precinct in the most westerly part of London. Once it had been a monastery, but in King Henry's reign it had been broken up into shops and dwellings. Near the north end of the former cloister was a door leading to the narrow stairs to Sir Walter's rooms. He lived above what had been the monks' buttery.

"My dear," Sir Walter greeted her when his manservant showed her in. "May I offer you some wine?" He insisted she sit in the comfortable Glastonbury chair he'd just vacated.

"Something restorative would be most welcome." As she remembered from a previous visit, a table by the window held a variety of drink.

Sir Walter looked well, she thought, as he filled a crystal goblet for her. If he was a few pounds heavier than when she'd last seen him, he was tall enough that his love of good food had not yet rendered him obese. He served her, then topped off a large, brown earthenware cup with ale for himself.

Revived by a few sips of fine Canary, calmed by the pleasant scent of marjoram flowers and woodruff leaves rising from the rushes underfoot, Susanna sketched out the bare bones of her tale.

"I know something of this man," Sir Walter remarked when Susanna completed a concise summary of the facts as Mistress Drood had presented them.

"That you have heard his name is ominous in itself. Is Drood a spy or a smuggler?"

He might well be both if Sir Walter took an interest in him. Her old friend was the most prominent of the queen's intelligence gatherers, a man with considerable influence at the royal court. Susanna had decided to speak to him for that very reason, and because she knew he would not mock her concerns, as a constable or a justice of the peace or one of London's sheriffs might.

"I have no proof against him. Only suspicions." Sir Walter absently smoothed one hand over his sand-colored beard, dislodging a crumb of bread. "We lack evidence."

"Evidence of what?"

To her surprise, he told her. "Clipping." At her blank expression, he clarified. "Clipping is a form of counterfeiting. For some men, there can never be enough wealth. They adulterate coin of the realm, scraping off some of the gold to sell, and then spend the clipped coins as if they had full value. In a case not long ago a woman clipped twenty half sovereigns, worth ten shillings each, by sixpence apiece."

"And Drood makes a practice of this?"

"Aye. He has done so for some time. Clipping was made a treasonous offense more than a century ago, but a loophole in the law has existed for the last ten years. It has only recently been closed and the Crown has been working ever since to apprehend those who profited in the interim."

Susanna did not need further explanation of Sir Walter's "loophole." She knew already that when the Catholic Queen Mary had come to the throne she'd nullified a great many laws as part of her attempt to overturn all that men of the New Religion had accomplished during the reigns of King Henry and his short-lived son, Edward. As a result, the baby had often been thrown out with the bathwater.

"He is clever, our Master Drood," Sir Walter continued, "but if I can persuade Mistress Drood to help us build a case, we may catch him yet." He gave a wry chuckle. "A pity I cannot simply encourage her to poison her husband before he gets a chance to poison her. That would solve any number of problems."

Susanna gripped the arm of her chair so tightly that she left little pock-marks in the swath of blue velvet flung across it for padding. "How can you joke about such a thing? Murder is never justified, and you know as well as I do that Mistress Drood would at once be suspected if her husband died. At the slightest hint of foul play, she would be arrested for his murder, and tried and executed, too."

With a courtly little bow, Sir Walter acknowledged her point, then resumed his former pose by the window, one shoulder negligently propped against the frame. "My apologies, my dear. You are right to admonish me. What, then, would you have me do?"

"Prove Drood guilty of clipping. Mistress Drood may be inclined to help you gather evidence against him if you explain the situation to her."

"I can offer her protection and a reward for her cooperation."

Encouraged, Susanna smiled at him. Clipping would be easier to prove than murder, and it carried the same penalty. "What can I do to help?"

"Go home."

When she started to protest, he held up a hand.

"Mistress Drood has already told you that her husband knows you wrote that herbal. To involve yourself further will only complicate matters, and possibly place you in danger. Besides, now that you have brought the situation to my attention, you may rely upon me to deal with it in the best manner possible."

Although his reassurances left her far from quiet in her mind, Susanna accepted the argument that she might impede an official investigation. She might even compromise it. "You will arrest Drood as soon as you can?"

"I swear it."

With that she had to be content, but she had no intention of going home until matters were settled. She returned to temporary lodgings at the Blossom Inn to await developments.

* * *

"Well, Jennet," Susanna said a short time later, kicking off her shoes and putting her feet up, "we have done a good day's work."

"Yes, madam," Jennet agreed. "Were you still wanting to know what the servants said?"

"We have not yet had the opportunity to compare notes, have we?"

Jennet had overheard Susanna's discussion with Sir Walter, but it was plain she was far from satisfied. In her effort to be brief and to the point, Susanna had left out a good many details. For Jennet's benefit, she now recounted her conversation with Mistress Drood in full. By the time she finished, Jennet was chewing industriously on her lower lip, a sure sign she was troubled.

"What?"

"Perhaps nothing, madam. Servants like to exaggerate their own importance." She had good reason to know, being a mistress of the art herself.

"Let me decide. What did you learn from the maids?"

"One of them is an elderly woman named Joan. She came to the household with the first Mistress Drood and stayed on."

Susanna nodded, remembering the servant who had admitted them. "There is nothing odd in that."

"She knew who you were. She said she'd been hoping you'd turn up. She said *she* was the one who sent the herbal to Leigh Abbey. She knew you wrote it because she overheard Master Baldwin say so to Master Drood. Then she was told you were clever at figuring things out."

"Did Master Baldwin say that?" Susanna thought it unlikely. He'd not have wanted to explain how he knew.

"Joan said she learned it from a certain person in Southwark."

"Oh," said Susanna. Her friends in Southwark were disreputable sorts.

"Joan said she does not know how to write, so she sent the herbal without any message. She asked the rector of St. Magnus to write your name and Leigh Abbey, Kent, on the wrapping. She told me to ask him if I did not believe her and said she hoped you would know what to do about Mistress Drood."

"Mistress Drood said *she* sent me the book, but at first she denied it."

"Joan said Mistress Drood bought the book, tore out a page, and discarded the rest. Joan found it. She cannot read, but she could see what it was about by the illustrations. She thinks Mistress Drood means to poison her husband. Joan is not pleased by that. She fears she'll be turned out once Mistress Drood is in charge of the household."

Susanna's feet hit the floor with a thump. Beset by a terrible sense of urgency, she donned her discarded shoes. "We must go back to Master Drood's house."

If Joan was telling the truth and Mistress Drood had planned all along to kill her husband, then Susanna's unexpected visit, followed so closely by the one Sir Walter would have paid by now, might provoke her to act precipitously.

If murder for gain was Mistress Drood's purpose, it would not suit her to have her husband executed. That would make her a widow, true enough, but in cases of treason the Crown seized all the traitor's property. Mistress Drood would be left penniless.

* * *

They had most of the city to cross and since it was now late afternoon, progress was slow. The streets were thronged with people hurrying home to sup.

The house on London Bridge was in an uproar by the time they arrived. "My wife! My poor stupid wife!" Ralph Drood danced a little jig as he bellowed the words. There was nothing grief-stricken in his expression.

Neither was he a great hulking brute, as Susanna had imagined. Ralph Drood was a scrawny little man whose most prominent features were a bushy red beard and a nose and eyes made nearly as red by fits of sneezing.

"We are too late," Susanna whispered to Jennet. "He has already killed her."

When she found no sign of Mistress Drood, alive or dead, in the rest of the house, Susanna returned to the parlor, this time taking note of obvious signs of a struggle. Broken crockery and scattered papers littered the floor. The ornate chest she had noticed earlier, which had been centered beneath the window, had been shoved to one side.

Frustrated beyond caution, Susanna marched up to Drood and took hold of the front of his doublet. "What happened to your wife?" she demanded. "Where is she?"

For an instant she thought he would not answer. Then he laughed—a wild, triumphant sound—and pointed to the window. "She fell into the river and is surely drowned. It was a terrible accident."

"How long ago did this happen?"

"Just now. Just before you came in."

Without another word, Susanna released Drood and ran from the house, calling to her groom to follow. No one had searched the water for Mistress Drood. Why should they? Her own husband clearly wanted her dead. He had, in all likelihood, pushed her out that window. But if she had survived the fall, and if she had managed to stay afloat, there might yet be time to save her.

Susanna forced her chronic fear of the water out of her mind. When she reached the end of the bridge, she signaled for a wherry. "Which way would the river carry someone who fell from up there?" She pointed toward the Drood house.

The waterman gestured downstream.

"Row that way, and quickly."

What followed was one of the most horrific journeys Susanna had ever endured. Her stomach in knots, her mind in equal turmoil, she scanned the choppy water for any sign of Mistress Drood. All manner of watercraft moved with the tide. Among the larger crafts were barges of the type noblemen used and a "shout" that carried timber.

With the tide going out, Mistress Drood had not been swept into the giant pilings that supported the bridge, but there was debris in the water that would have been just as deadly. There were also dead dogs and cats and even a dead mule.

Susanna had begun to doubt that anything could survive in this foul cesspit when she caught sight of a hand extending from a rose-colored sleeve and clinging to a piece of driftwood.

By the time they hauled Mistress Drood's limp form into the wherry, it was too late. She was no longer breathing and they could not revive her.

* * *

Sir Walter Pendennis was waiting at Drood's house when Susanna returned with the body.

"Can you find enough in a search to warrant his arrest for treason?" Tight-lipped, Susanna watched Walter's face as she waited for an answer.

"I *will* find proof."

His promise gave Susanna little satisfaction. She had failed to keep Ralph Drood from killing his wife. That he would be executed for other crimes would not bring back any of the unfortunate women who had been his spouses.

"Where is he?" she asked.

"In the room from which she fell. He has been drinking heavily since you left."

Drood looked up when they entered, never pausing in the act of broaching a new bottle and slopping wine into his goblet. He drank deeply, then waved the cup in Susanna's direction. "Most excellently spiced," he declared, and sneezed yet again.

Susanna's sense of smell was unimpaired. She had no difficulty identifying the contents of the goblet. Her heart began to beat a little faster.

Sir Walter Pendennis, royal intelligence gatherer, did not seem to notice anything amiss. His men had arrived and he was instructing two of them to guard Drood while he led the remainder in a search of the premises.

Drood continued to drink.

Susanna did nothing.

She estimated that a bit more than a quarter of an hour passed before Drood complained that his arm had gone numb. A little later, he began to feel pain in his muscles. Within an hour, he was barely able to move. He had lost all sensation in his limbs, as well as the ability to speak.

"Soon," Susanna told him, "you will also be blind, and yet your mind will continue to function perfectly well. You will know what is happening to you. You will retain full consciousness until the last."

Sir Walter came quietly into the room as she was speaking, alerted to what was happening by one of the guards he'd left behind. "Did he kill the first two wives?"

"I am convinced he did." Everything pointed to it. That the last Mistress Drood had lied about wanting Susanna's help did not change her opinion.

Sir Walter bent over the dying man. "We'll never know for certain. He cannot even move his head to nod or express denial."

"Mistress Drood was in no rush to kill him," Susanna murmured, "until you told her your plan to arrest him and charge him with treason."

Sir Walter did not seem unduly disturbed by that notion. "She provoked her husband's temper at the wrong moment."

"She had poisoned the wine before they quarreled and he pitched her out the window. Then he celebrated her death by drinking it."

"A fine irony." Sir Walter stared down at Drood's nearly lifeless body. "Such a death is just. A murderer should be forced to linger for many agonizing hours and giving him ample time to understand that the punishment was exacted for his crimes."

Susanna sighed. She felt remorse but no pity for the condemned man. "There will be an inquest. I must—"

Sir Walter held up a hand to silence her. "The searchers will give out that Drood died of a surfeit of drink, and you and I, my dear, were never here."

For just a moment, Susanna wondered if her old friend had done more than ask for Mistress Drood's cooperation. She decided she did not want to know. Neither did she have any desire to make public the fact that her book, written to save lives, could also be used to commit murder.

She had sought the truth. Belatedly, she had found it. Revealing it, she realized with a mixture of resignation and regret, would only make matters worse. Casting a last look at Master Drood before Sir Walter escorted her out of the room, out of the house, and out of London, Susanna consoled herself with the thought that even without truth, there had been justice.

A Note from the Author

John Day (1522 -1584) was a real person. This Elizabethan printer had a shop, house, and warehouse in the Aldersgate ward of London in the 1560s. Later he had a shop in Paul's Churchyard. The most famous of the books he printed was what was popularly called "the Book of Martyrs." John Foxe's *Acts and Monuments*, first published in 1563, was a runaway bestseller for those days. It detailed the persecution of Protestants by the Catholic Queen Mary.

In the 1570s, Day's stock of unbound works was valued at over £3000 and he had bound stock worth between £300 and £400. To give you an idea of relative wealth, it cost about £500 a year to run two presses, which could produce about two thousand pages. That includes the expense of ink, wages, and overhead. Paper for an edition of one thousand copies cost £350. A halfpence per sheet was the standard price of paper at retail. If Day sold all the copies at twenty-four shillings each, he made a substantial profit.

This story first appeared in *Alfred Hitchcock Mystery Magazine* in 2001. It takes place after the events in *Face Down Among the Winchester Geese* and before those in *Face Down Beneath the Eleanor Cross*.

The Riddle of the Woolsack

England 1569

"Ho, there!" called a harsh voice. "A word with you."

A rook, startled by the sound, gave a hoarse caw and took flight.

Mark Jaffrey, steward for Leigh Abbey in East Kent, murmured a quiet command to his mount, then turned in the saddle to survey the scene at his left hand. He looked west across fields that undulated gently. Their golden-brown hue was in harmony with the bright, coral-colored leaves of the cherry trees in a small orchard near at hand and the yellow, scarlet, and umber of the wood beyond it. The old woman in dusty black seemed out of place in the picture, and somehow ominous.

Mark patted the neck of his bay gelding, his fingers lingering on the smooth, warm horseflesh. Although he was as impatient as his horse to be off, he stayed put while the stooped, heavily-swathed figure trudged closer. There was nowhere he had to be in any rush. He had been bound for Eastwold, the nearest village, but without any pressing business to conduct there. What had driven him out of the house had been a sudden, fervent desire to escape the gloom that had eclipsed the manor since the departure of its owner, Lady Appleton, for foreign shores.

With Michaelmas just past and the harvest in, accounts had been rendered. It was a fallow time for fields and man alike. Mark knew he should be in the best of spirits. He and his family possessed good health. The estate had shown a profit. Instead, he had been discontent and sunk in a melancholy even the bracing, vaguely medicinal and bitter-sweet aroma of drying hops could not dispel.

An encounter with a stranger would at least break the monotony.

The figure limping his way appeared harmless enough, but he had the sense to be wary. He fingered the pommel of the good, sharp knife he wore at his belt and had a moment's regret that he had not strapped a stout cudgel to the back of the saddle before he left home.

Of late the roads had become infested with beggars and vagabonds. Many of them were tricksters who painted on their sores and pretended to be crippled in order to cozen the softhearted out of more alms. Some traveled in packs, sending the weakest of their number to distract a traveler so the others could attack him.

As steward, it was one of Mark's duties to offer aid to those in real need. He sent the other sort packing, and when sharp words were not sufficient to evict them from Leigh Abbey land, he used hard blows.

A faint odor of mint drifted up to him as the woman reached his side and pushed back the hood of her enveloping cloak. He stared down into narrowed eyes and a deeply-lined, scowling face.

"God save you, mother. What is your business here?"

"I came for to see Lady Appleton," the beldame declared.

"Then you made your journey to no purpose. She is gone from home and not like to return for some time."

Months, at the least, Mark reckoned, which was why his wife, Jennet, who was Leigh Abbey's housekeeper, had also been in a foul mood these last weeks. Jennet had not wanted to accompany their mistress, but she bitterly resented being left behind.

Mark started to ease his mount around the old woman.

"Hold!" The crone moved with slow and ponderous steps but spoke with such purpose that it never crossed his mind to disobey. "Who might you be?"

"I am Lady Appleton's steward. I am in charge here in her absence." He felt his face warm under the old woman's steady scrutiny and the rising breeze did naught to cool it. Wisps of mole-colored hair fluttered against ears that were too big for his head, tickling the rims in a most annoying fashion.

"May be you'll do."

Mark frowned. He'd *do*? He was not certain he liked the sound of that, but before he could turn away and ride off, a hand swollen with age and infirmity closed around the horn of his saddle.

"Three days past, there were murder done."

* * *

Jennet Jaffrey had just finished setting the maids to work making candles when a groom brought word that her husband had returned to Leigh Abbey and wished to speak with her. Jennet frowned. He'd left but an hour earlier. If he was back already, then something must be wrong.

Her first thought was that there had been word of Lady Appleton. Any journey by sea was perilous and after crossing to the Continent their mistress had meant to travel through the Netherlands, where England's enemies held sway. Heart racing, Jennet all but ran to the steward's office, where Mark had sent word he'd wait for her.

He was not alone. A stooped figure all in black stood next to him. Jennet blinked as she recognized the crone. At her sharp, indrawn breath, they both looked toward the doorway where she stood.

"You!" the old woman exclaimed.

She was called Mother Sparcheforde and was reputed to be a witch. The last time they'd met, she'd chased Jennet out of the grocer's shop she owned in Dover, hurling a curse after her. Now here she stood, bold as a Barbary pirate, just polishing off a cup of new-made perry.

"Why is she here?" Jennet demanded.

"Now, Jennet—"

"Blessings upon you, Goodwife Jaffrey." There was a malicious gleam in Mother Sparcheforde's eyes as she, too, recalled their previous meeting. On that occasion, Jennet had not revealed either her name or her purpose. She'd visited the old woman's shop hoping to glean information about her daughter, Alys Putney.

Jennet seized the pitcher from Mark before he could refill Mother Sparcheforde's cup and slammed it down hard on his writing table. The quills in their container rattled against the inkwell and a little of the perry splashed onto an account book, scenting the air with the aroma of pressed pears.

Mother Sparcheford tossed away her empty cup, drew herself up as straight as she could with her widow's hump, and clenched her misshapen fingers around the equally gnarled branch she used as a walking stick. She swung it upward, not to defend herself from Jennet or to strike her, but as if to cast a spell.

Mark stepped between the two women. "Never mind what happened in the past," he said to his wife. "Mother Sparcheforde seeks our help."

"I'd not give her the time of day. Nor to her daughter, neither." To show her utter disdain for both women, as well as her lack of fear—after all, Mother Sparcheforde's curse had come to naught—Jennet plopped down in the room's only chair, bouncing a bit as her bottom struck a cushion well-stuffed with wool.

"Jennet, Alys has been murdered."

At Mark's announcement, Jennet blinked in surprise, then voiced the first thought that came into her head. "No more than she deserved."

"She was beaten to death." Taking Mother Sparcheforde's arm, Mark guided her to a comfortable padded bench, eased her onto it, and retrieved her cup.

Alys Putney had been a venomous creature. Once, when Jennet had been great with child, Alys had given her a vicious shove that had sent her tumbling to the ground. It was a miracle young Rob had been born unmarked.

Mark knew that, but he propped one hip against the corner of the writing table, crossed his arms over his chest, and aimed a stern look at his wife. "Lady Appleton believes in justice, even for the unjust. Were she here, she would insist upon accompanying Mother Sparcheforde to Rye, where both Alys and Leonard Putney were slain."

"Alys *and* her husband?"

"Crowner got matters twisted," the old woman muttered. "Must have. Could not have happened the way he says."

"According to what Mother Sparcheforde has told me," Mark said, "the coroner's inquest ruled Alys's death a murder by persons unknown, and further declared that her husband took his own life out of grief."

Jennet frowned. Leonard Putney had been a violent man. People had said for years that he sent Alys out to whore for him, then beat her when she came home. It was not difficult to imagine that he might have gone too far and beaten Alys to death himself, but the rest of the explanation made no sense at all. "Even if Putney killed her, he'd never have taken his own life afterward."

"He'd have felt neither remorse nor guilt," Mother Sparcheforde agreed.

"He might have taken that course to cheat the hangman," Mark said.

"There are better ways to escape execution than self-murder." Jennet chewed thoughtfully on her lower lip as she considered the situation. A sympathetic jury might have ruled he'd acted upon provocation and should not be punished at all for an attempt to discipline his wife. Or he could have avoided trial altogether by hiding her body and saying she'd run off with a lover.

Mother Sparcheforde spoke into the silence. "Sir Robert Appleton abandoned my Alys at his wife's bidding." The old woman's smile was horrible to behold, revealing rotted teeth and blackened gums. "If he had not, my daughter would never have married Leonard Putney. She'd be alive today. I say Lady Appleton owes it to my girl to find out the truth."

Jennet marveled at her reasoning. Alys Sparcheforde, before her marriage to Leonard Putney, had been the late Sir Robert Appleton's long-time mistress. He'd set her up in a house in Dover, only seven miles from Leigh Abbey, all but flaunting his infidelity to his wife.

"She owes you nothing." Jennet glared at Alys's mother.

"I hear things, I do. They say Lady Appleton put herself at risk to help another woman who was her husband's mistress."

Jennet stifled a sigh. Although Lady Appleton had no obligation to those Sir Robert had wronged, she did seem to make a habit of involving herself in matters that affected their lives, helping those who needed her assistance. She would expect Jennet and Mark to look into Alys's death and do all they could to make certain justice had been served.

"What is it you think we can do?" she asked.

"Go to Rye on my behalf. Say I sent you to run Putney's inn there. Ask questions. Discover whether my Alys was killed by her husband or by someone else, someone who may yet be punished for what he did."

Jennet's eyes met Mark's. The spark of interest there reflected what she felt—the first tingle of excitement at the prospect of an adventure. Each time Lady Appleton encountered trouble, Jennet swore she wanted no part of it, but the sweet taste of a puzzle to solve and a wrong to be made right was as tempting as Xeres sack and twice as addictive.

When Mark rounded the writing table and took out paper, quill, and ink, Jennet knew he'd decided to do as Mother Sparcheforde asked. Whether or not he'd take her with him was another matter.

"Where was Alys's body found?" Mark asked.

"In the common room of an inn in Rye called the Woman and the Woolsack. Leonard Putney owned it. Bought it after he sold the Star with the Long Tail in Dover. It belongs to me now."

"How did you come to inherit?" Jennet asked before Mark could frame his next question.

"There are no other heirs. All that was my daughter's must come to me."

Jennet was not so sure of that. "Are you certain you want to prove Putney killed Alys? If he did, then all his goods and chattels are forfeit to the Crown. You will get nothing."

The old woman looked smug. "If that be the truth, I will not challenge the crowner's verdict. Why should I when my daughter's murderer is already dead? But if both were slain by someone else, I can demand justice for my murdered child and still keep all Alys and her husband owned."

The sound of laughter reached them from the inner courtyard where Jennet's two girls played with Lady Appleton's foster daughter. Jennet's chest tightened at the thought of what it must feel like to lose a child. It must be worse to suspect that the person responsible was still at large. Even though something besides maternal affection drove Mother Sparcheforde, Jennet's heart softened toward the other woman.

Mark cleared his throat. "You say that the coroner's inquest ruled Alys was beaten to death?"

Mother Sparcheforde nodded.

"How did Putney die?"

"They say he stabbed himself—a single wound to the chest."

"Were there any signs he'd been in a fight?"

Before Alys's mother could answer, Jennet interjected a question of her own. "Were his knuckles bruised?"

"I know not," the old woman replied. "You must question the crowner for yourself."

"There will be a record of the coroner's inquest," Mark mused, "but if there is aught irregular about it, they'll not show it to strangers." Of a sudden, his brow creased and his fingers tightened on the quill. "What do you know of your son-in-law's dealings with land pirates?"

Jennet leaned closer, beset by curiosity and trepidation in equal parts. Land pirates were those who disposed of goods illegally brought into the country. According to merchants with whom Leigh Abbey did business, their brethren in Rye provisioned the sea rovers who regularly preyed on Dover shipping.

Mother Sparcheforde seemed reluctant to answer, but at length admitted that Putney might have been involved in the distribution and sale of contraband when he'd owned his inn in Dover.

"Here in Kent, sugar and wine from pirate loot are bartered for powder, shot, salt beef, and bacon, and then sent by packhorse to London," Mark said. "It us a profitable business. No doubt a similar trade exists in Sussex."

"There's motive for murder, then." Jennet's excitement grew as she considered the possibilities. She envisioned a falling out among thieves, or a rival land pirate seeking to take over Putney's operation.

"There is also danger." Mark set the quill aside and addressed his wife. "Anyone who seeks to investigate a murder ends by threatening other secrets."

"It is too late to waver now. This riddle must have a solution." Before Mark could object further, out of worry for her safety, Jennet turned to Mother Sparcheforde and took over the interrogation. "What particular enemies did Leonard Putney have? Who hated him enough to kill him?"

"Everyone who knew him." Another rusty cackle issued from the black-swathed figure. "Even his own wife."

"Because he beat her?"

"Beat her. Bullied her. Belittled her. And you've only to look at the name of the inn to see how he regarded her. Go to a place called the Woman and the Woolsack," Mother Sparcheforde said with great bitterness, "and you expect the innkeeper's wife to be a whore."

Jennet's sympathy was once again engaged. The old, crude riddle was well known: When is a woman like a woolsack? When both are stuffed.

* * *

Two days later, Mark and Jennet stood staring up at the inn sign. He'd wondered what it would depict. A sack full of wool and a woman being tupped could not have escaped censure from the church, but there were more subtle ways to suggest the same ribald theme. Leonard Putney's sign showed a woman holding an empty woolsack in one hand and a chastity belt in the other. A large key dangled from the gold chain around her waist.

"Hmpf," was Jennet's only comment.

They went inside.

"Leonard Putney did well for himself." Jennet planted herself in the center of the common room and turned in a circle to survey the premises.

Mark had to agree with her assessment. It was a fine establishment.

"We'll need fresh rushes." Jennet stared hard at the spot where both Putneys had died—just by the door to the cellar, Mother Sparcheforde had said—then shrugged as if to say she'd scrub the floor later. There was only a small bloodstain. Putney had stabbed himself with suspicious neatness.

Apparently undaunted by the violence that had taken place in the inn, Jennet set out to inspect every nook and cranny. Seeing the return of her natural enthusiasm, conspicuously lacking since Lady Appleton's departure for the Continent, Mark put aside his remaining doubts about the wisdom of this venture. He'd already half convinced himself that Putney had killed Alys. A bully could also be a coward. Rather than face trial and hanging, he might well have committed suicide.

That explanation of events pleased him. If it was correct, Jennet was in no danger. Mark could look forward to watching his wife enjoy herself while she came to the same conclusion.

"The mattresses will want airing, and—" Jennet broke off with a squeak as a section of wall moved under her hand.

"What the devil?"

"It is the devil's work indeed! There is a hiding place here." Jennet poked her head inside, then sneezed.

When Mark brought a candle, they saw footprints in the dust of the narrow passageway beyond the opening. A ladder gave access to the chamber above.

Further exploration of the common room revealed a revolving cupboard, allowing for a rapid retreat into the street, and a door into the adjoining building, bolted from the other side. In addition, the Woolsack's back exit opened onto one of the estuaries that emptied into Rye's tidal bay.

"Convenient for unloading contraband," Mark said. "No doubt Putney dealt with free traders as well as freebooters."

Jennet chewed thoughtfully on her lower lip, as was her wont when she contemplated any perplexing matter. "I have heard the same tales as you—tubs full of smuggled goods buried on the cliffs above coastal towns and tunnels that run from certain houses into nearby woods."

"The sand and shingle coasts of Romney Marsh, near to Rye, are well suited to such activities," Mark said. "Local merchants can avoid export taxes by sending their wool abroad illegally, and the prospect of importing wine from France without paying duty on it would appeal to any innkeeper, even an honest one."

They continued their inspection of the Woman and the Woolsack. Leonard Putney's larder contained deep wooden meal-tubs, flour barrels, salting tubs, and earthenware preserving jars. In a storehouse separate from the main building of the inn were quantities of dried, preserved, pickled, and barreled food, and in the cellar, a cavernous space beneath the common room, they found roundlets of ale and several barrels of wine.

"The contents of the inn must have been inventoried at the time of Putney's death," Mark said thoughtfully. "If I ask for a copy from Rye's coroner, I may also discover more about how he died."

Jennet agreed this was a sound plan and sent him off in search of that official while she donned an apron and set about disposing of the old rushes.

Mark stopped first at another inn, the Mermaid. A merchant of his acquaintance had told him it was the finest hostelry in Rye. There, he thought, he would find men who knew the town—men who might be willing to set a newcomer straight.

A dozen customers occupied the common room, presided over by a prosperous-looking fellow with an enormous mustache and three gold teeth. "William Didsbury at your service," he greeted Mark. "I own this place."

"Then you are a man I am glad to meet." He introduced himself as a distant cousin to Alys Putney, sent by her mother to reopen the inn.

"This is a good town," Didsbury said as he poured Mark a mug of ale. "Our merchant shipping is on a par with that of Bristol and we average more sailings a month than Plymouth or Southampton. In addition, some twenty-five fishing vessels go daily to sea year round and twenty-four more set out in the season for conger and mackerel. Our fish are sent to London the same day they are caught, making them the freshest of any in England!"

During his short walk along the High Street to Mermaid Passage, Mark had seen one such packhorse train about to set out. Large baskets called dossers had been slung over the back of each beast. He took a long pull of ale, wondering if Didsbury wished to make some particular point.

"There is a forty shilling fine," Didsbury said when he returned from serving another customer, "for accommodating any light person, harlot, whore, or common woman."

Mark frowned. "I do not understand you, Didsbury."

"Your predecessor had a certain reputation."

"Ah, I see. Do not confuse me with Leonard Putney. I may share his profession, but I do not share my wife's favors with any man."

"Not a dutchman are you?" asked a patron with a shock of bushy white hair. He meant, Mark knew, not a man born in Holland but one with extreme religious views.

Mark considered his answer. If there were smugglers present, he did not want to alarm them. "I am just an ordinary innkeeper," he replied after a moment, "but I am curious about the death of the one who came before me."

Several more tankards of ale had to be emptied before the men in the common room began to talk freely, but every one of them seemed to be in agreement as to what had happened. Alys Putney had been killed by an unknown villain.

"A vagabond?" Mark asked. That was what Mother Sparcheforde had been told.

"Or a drunken mariner. It was during the time the ports were closed and the town was overrun with sailors."

"I am surprised her husband was not suspected of killing her."

"He might have been," Didsbury said, "had the circumstances been different, but her body was found before Putney appeared on the scene."

Mark wondered how they could be so certain. It would be an easy matter to slip out of the inn through one of the hidden exits and return by the main entrance.

"By the time the mayor's sergeant arrived, he found two bodies instead of one," Didsbury explained. "It seemed clear that when Putney saw his wife, he took his own life in a fit of grief."

Heads nodded throughout the common room. Mark tugged on his ear, thinking hard. No one seemed to be lying, but he had to wonder if any of these men had known Putney well. Mark remembered the fellow as the sort to keep to himself. "Who found Alys?"

"The ostler," Didsbury said. "Jack, he's called. No doubt he'll come looking for his old job back when he hears the inn's to reopen."

"My wife fears we'll be murdered in our bed," Mark said, knowing Jennet would forgive him the blatant lie, "by the same killer who attacked my cousin, or by some other vagabond." He drank deeply. "Are there many random killings here?"

There was a rush to reassure him. According to the stories he was told, there were few cases of murder in Rye. In every instance, an arrest had been made, although executions had been rare because the murderers could plead benefit of clergy. That meant Leonard Putney would not have had reason to fear the hangman's noose, unless he'd already borne a brand for some previous crime.

Mark's new friends provided the name of the coroner. Since John Breeds was also Rye's mayor, it was a simple matter to locate him and procure a copy of the inventory. On other matters, however, he was less forthcoming. He evaded Mark's carefully phrased questions about bruises on Putney's knuckles or brands on other parts of his body. Breeds was not about to admit that he might have made a mistake, and claimed that the town constable was still seeking the vagabond who'd killed Alys Putney.

"You are a stranger here," he reminded Mark. "Let Rye men tend to Rye business."

* * *

The next morning it was Jennet's turn to ask questions. She set off just past sunrise intending to buy fresh fish in the marketplace, make inquiries about the whereabouts of Leonard Putney's ostler, and keep both eyes and ears open for gossip.

When her purchase was wrapped and safe in her market basket, she strolled along quayside. The customs office was plainly marked and she wondered how the smugglers dealt with the royal customer. Bribery was the usual way.

She turned to walk back to the Woman and the Woolsack and let out a startled squeak when she all but ran into a dark-skinned man clad in fantastical garb. The cloth wound around his head and the evil-looking curved sword tucked into the sash at his waist had her eyes widening in alarm and her heart pounding faster. Unable to look away after he passed by, ignoring her, Jennet watched him until he was out of sight.

"Faith!" she murmured when she dared breathe again. "When did Rye turn Turk?"

A soft laugh drew her attention to a woman just letting down the shutter to form a counter at the front of her shop. "They are harmless enough in town," she said as she set out her wares, "but I'd not give odds for your life or your property if you met him at sea."

Jennet moved closer to a tray of fresh-baked pastries. "Do pirates walk the streets of Rye unchallenged? I vow that fellow must have sailed on a Sallee rover."

"If you've taken over Putney's inn," the shopkeeper said, "you must know already that customer, controller, and searcher alike know how to turn a blind eye."

Jennet had but a moment to decide between feigned innocence and a worldly acceptance of such matters. "Toward free trade, yes, but that fellow was surely a pirate."

"The local justices cannot try pirates. Even were they to catch one in the act of robbing a ship in the harbor, they'd be obliged to bind him over to the Admiralty Court." She grinned suddenly, showing a gap between her two front teeth. "Not that it is to anyone's advantage to curtail the activities of sea rovers, so long as they only prey on foreign ships."

Foreign, Jennet supposed, to a citizen of Rye, would include those setting sail from ports in Kent.

She lowered her voice, even though there was no one close enough to overhear. "The Woman and the Woolsack—was it popular with known pirates when Leonard Putney owned it?" That he'd done business with smugglers went without saying.

"It was popular with Frenchmen," the woman said.

Jennet frowned. "Religious exiles?" Was there a motive for murder in that? Politics? Intrigue? Intelligencers and secret messages in code? The ports had been closed when Putney died. Fear of invasion, she'd heard, but by whom and from where? Pray God, Jennet thought, that Alys and her husband had not been mixed up in that. She and Mark would never be able to sort out the truth if the Putneys had been involved in treason.

A woman came up to buy a loaf of bread, quickly followed by another goodwife. Jennet dug out a ha'penny and made her own purchase. Munching, she watched and waited until the shopkeeper was free, but by then she'd realized that any question she might ask would arouse too much suspicion. Better, she decided, to wait a bit.

"I must return to the inn," she said instead, hefting her basket. "Frenchmen you say? I hope they like fish."

Even more, she hoped they'd have coin to pay for it. If Rye's immigrant population bore any resemblance to the poverty-plagued exiles who'd settled in Kent, they had no extra income to spend on ale.

She had part of her answer as soon as she entered the Woman and the Woolsack. Putney's ostler had returned. He was a scrawny lad who had only enough English to understand orders related to tending guests' horses.

"Did you question him about finding Alys's body?" she asked Mark.

He sent her an exasperated look. "Unless your French is better than mine, I do not think we will learn anything useful from Jacques."

Jennet sighed, knowing he was right, and set about preparing food to serve their customers.

* * *

The first person through the door was a tall, broad-shouldered, big-bosomed female with lank yellow hair and a prominent mole on her cheek. She appeared just at noontide. In heavily accented English, she demanded the set meal.

"And that is?" Mark asked.

She looked down her nose at him. "A drink, a slice of boiled beef, and a portion of good wheaten bread for threepence."

"You'll have fish," Jennet informed her, and served up the fillets she'd cooked. A rich, steamy aroma, redolent of garlic and basil, filled the air.

The common room filled slowly. A man with a shock of bushy white hair was the second person to arrive.

"He was at the Mermaid," Mark whispered to Jennet.

Soon after a chapman came in. "Almeric Horsey," he introduced himself. "What is the price for a room?"

"Twopence for a feather bed," Mark said, "and another threepence a day if you need hay and litter for your horse."

Bushy-hair glanced up as a tall, thin man appeared in the doorway. "Rowland Weston, the resident undercollector," he muttered under his breath. With a grimace, he swallowed the last of his ale and left.

Mark studied the undercollector, not unduly surprised that he should come into the Woman and the Woolsack. He was taken aback, however, when Weston, after a single drink, produced a blank parchment with the seal of the port already affixed, and handed it over.

"My usual fee is thirteen shillings and fourpence," he said, "but as an introductory offer, I'm willing to exchange this one for a butt of your best imported sack."

When the two men adjourned to a back room, leaving Jennet to serve the inn's patrons, Weston boasted of the fact that he'd borrowed the authentic seal of the port long enough to have a cast made. With this seal, he'd set up his own private customs house to retail counterfeit cockets and customs clearances.

That night, after Mark blew out the candle and climbed into bed beside his wife, glad to be done with the day's work, he repeated his conversation with Master Weston. "I do not believe I have ever dealt with a villain so blatantly corrupt."

Jennet nestled close to him on the featherbed in the inn's best chamber. "We have too many lawbreakers to choose from, not only corrupt officials, smugglers, and pirates, but I begin to wonder if Mother Sparcheforde somehow managed to murder Leonard Putney, mayhap by witchcraft. It is certain she is the one who gained most from his death." She sighed. "How are we ever to discover the truth? Why, for all we know, there are *two* murderers."

Mark groaned.

Jennet was silent for a time, but he could almost feel her thinking. "If I'd killed someone in this inn, I'd have to take a close look at the new innkeepers to find out if they pose any threat. Living here, we might stumble upon something the coroner's men missed when they made their inventory of goods and chattel."

"If that is true, then, we have fewer suspects. The murderer is the chapman, or the undercollector, or one of the Frenchmen." At least a dozen exiles had come in, even Nicholas le Tellier, minister of the French Church of Rye.

"Or the old man with the bushy hair," Jennet murmured sleepily.

"I am most suspicious of the undercollector. Mayhap Putney did not pay his fees."

"You forgot to list the Frenchwoman," Jennet said with a yawn.

The only female to come into the inn, she'd made Mark wonder if he'd misunderstood Didsbury's comment about whores. He had not mentioned the innkeeper's remark to Jennet. Now he reached for his wife and planted a resounding kiss on her mouth. "I have not forgot the Frenchwoman," he whispered, "but a bit of effort on your part might make me do so."

"Poor creature," Jennet murmured as she obliged. "If her face were unblemished, she would be a handsome lass."

Mark did not answer. He had more pleasant matters on his mind.

* * *

The Frenchwoman came back the following day, again asking for the inn's set meal. As Jennet served her, she found it difficult not to stare at the mole. No doubt it was her imagination, but it seemed to have grown larger.

The woman lingered over her food until she was the only customer in the common room.

"A second cup of ale?" Jennet asked.

"I'd have a word with you instead, now that we are alone."

Jennet glanced into the small room behind the hidden panel. Mark looked back at her, lifting a brow. He was out of sight, having gone into the little chamber to investigate a sound they'd thought might be a mouse.

Jennet shut him in and turned back to the Frenchwoman, her heart pounding in anticipation. Whatever the woman wanted, there was no danger. Mark could open the panel from the other side if she screamed. Moreover, there was a knothole in the wainscoting. If he bent over and fixed one eye to the opening, he could keep watch over her.

The Frenchwoman moved closer, taking a stool that gave her a clear view of the entrance. The inn sign creaked as a breeze sprang up, but otherwise all was quiet.

"Will you hire chamberlains and laundresses?" she asked.

"With wages so high in Sussex, my husband and I must do all the work of running this inn ourselves," Jennet told her. "Just as the Putneys did."

"*Just* as they did?"

"What little I know of my husband's cousin tells me she did not rely upon selling food and ale for profit."

"Are you in favor of making a profit?" It seemed to Jennet that the woman's French accent grew less pronounced as the conversation continued.

"Not the way she did, and yet what sensible person is averse to becoming wealthy?" Jennet chose her words with care. She lowered her voice to add, "We came to Rye because we heard an inn situated here could thrive."

"My husband is an important man hereabout." The Frenchwoman now spoke with the familiar cadence of a native-born

Englishwoman, and one gently born, at that. "We will do business with you, as well, if you meet certain conditions."

"What conditions?" Jennet thought this a most peculiar conversation. By rights, this woman's husband should be having it with Mark.

Before she could answer, the chapman returned, ending any chance of further private discussion, but the woman promised to return after Jennet and Mark locked up for the night. As soon as she left, Mark opened the panel and came out, blinking against the sudden light.

The chapman sent him a hopeful look and pulled a slim volume out of his pack. "Will you accept a book of riddles in return for a pottle of ale?"

"Too few buyers, friend?" Mark asked, accepting the trade. He opened to the first page and chuckled at what he read. "What shines bright of day and at night is raked up in its own dirt?"

"The fire," Jennet answered, impatient with such foolishness.

"What runs but never walks?"

"A river."

"What turns without moving?"

"Milk. Enough!"

Laughing, Mark closed the book

"You are blessed with a clever wife," the chapman said.

A clever wife, Jennet thought, *would have looked to see which direction that false Frenchwoman took when she left the inn*. Although it was doubtless too late, she went out into the street.

The only creature in sight was an old yellow dog.

A sea breeze made Jennet's apron flap and caused the inn's sign to groan. She glanced up with a frown, wondering what they might do to stop that annoying sound. The board swung back and forth, but Jennet stood immobile, staring at the painting on the wood.

When is a woman like a woolsack? When she is used to smuggle contraband. The woman on the sign had a key, but it was too big to fit the lock of the chastity belt she held. Jennet's frown turned into a grin. How could she have missed something so obvious? That key unlocked the secrets of this inn, and the painted figure, by her dress a gentlewoman, had a mole on one cheek.

* * *

As soon as the Frenchwoman entered the common room that night, Mark closed and locked the door behind her.

She fixed him with a basilisk stare. "You have no call to hold me prisoner. My husband is prepared to offer you the same arrangement he had with Leonard Putney."

With a silent prayer that Jennet's solution to the riddle of the Woman and the Woolsack was correct, Mark went to stand at his wife's side. "I fear you have been deceived, madam. We did not come to Rye to take Putney's place."

"What do you want, then?" She sounded impatient but not alarmed.

"The truth about how Alys Putney died."

"Why?"

"For her old mother. She has doubts about the verdict of the coroner's inquest."

"Alys Putney's husband killed her."

"How do you know that?"

"I was here to witness it."

"And did not interfere?"

"Why should I?" She made herself comfortable on the bench beneath the window, regarded them steadily for a long moment before she shrugged. "If he had not killed her, I would have."

An icy finger crept up Mark's spine at her words. Jennet's fingers clenched painfully on his forearm.

"Leonard Putney sent his wife to seduce my husband," the woman continued. "I followed her from his bed back to this inn."

"Putney hoped for greater profits and thought that having his wife play the whore was the way to get them." Jennet's words exuded sympathy, but Mark's wariness increased.

"When Alys told him she'd failed, that her new lover was willing to enjoy her favors but would offer naught in return but bed sport, Putney flew into a rage. He beat her to death. I saw him do it. He came after me when he realized I was a witness."

"So you killed him?" There was no censure in Jennet's voice. Mark was not sure how he felt.

"I stabbed him," the other woman agreed, "and after Jacques sounded the hue and cry for Alys, I dragged his body out of hiding and left it by his dead wife's side, so that it would *appear* that he'd killed himself when he found her."

"If he beat her to death," Mark protested, "why hide his crime?"

The woman laughed. "Even if I had not had to strike him down to save myself, we could not allow a verdict of murder. If he'd been adjudged guilty, the Crown would have claimed this inn. We would have lost a valuable asset and provoked an unwelcome interest in the place."

At that moment, the connecting door to the next building, the one that had been bolted on the other side, swung open. The man with the shock of bushy white hair strode into the common room. It was a wig, Mark realized, as false as the woman's mole, which changed from day to day, not only in size but in location. The face beneath the hair was further obscured by a bristly beard. More ominous still, the man carried a pistol in his right hand, primed and ready to fire.

The woman rose from the bench, smiling at the intruder.

Mark exchanged a glance with Jennet. If her deductions were correct, this was the husband. Further, they were members of the gentry who engaged in smuggling and were willing to commit murder to hide their crimes.

An uneasy silence lengthened until Jennet broke it. "A second set of owners found dead in the same inn will also bring unwelcome attention to this place, and if I could solve the riddle of the inn sign, so can others."

Bushy-hair grinned. "That sign was painted by a previous owner, a fellow who much admired my lady's virtues."

Mark said nothing, wondering what fate Putney's predecessor had suffered. It would be all too easy to kill someone here and dispose of the body in Romney Marsh. Jennet thought they could count on the gentry's need for discretion to keep them safe, but Mark feared she misjudged the situation.

"Goodwife Jaffrey has a point, my dear," the woman said. All trace of a French accent had long since vanished.

"You told my wife you wanted the truth about how Alys Putney died. Now that you have it, what do you mean to do with it?"

"Leave," Mark said.

The man laughed.

"With your permission," Mark added, glancing at the pistol. He cleared his throat. "We will tell Alys Putney's mother, the owner of this inn, what we learned, but she will do naught to hamper your business. Why should she? She will not care that you killed Leonard Putney. Doubtless she will thank you for making it possible for her to inherit."

The couple exchanged a look Mark recognized. A husband and wife who knew each other well could communicate without words.

Bushy-hair lowered the pistol. His smile seemed a trifle less menacing. "Leave Jacques in place as ostler. I will provide a man to serve as tapster and keep the inn open."

Mark nodded his agreement. "We'll be off at first light." He managed a faint smile of his own. "Mother Sparcheforde will be well pleased."

Only after they left through the connecting door and Mark heard the bolt slide home on the far side did he dare breathe again.

"That went well." Jennet stepped into his arms, laughing up at him.

She was still well pleased with herself the next morning. As they left Rye behind them, she turned to him with a twinkle in her eyes. "Mayhap we should consider spending a few days away from home every year. I vow I feel most refreshed and invigorated and ready to take on my responsibilities at Leigh Abbey once more."

"A little less adventure would suit me better," Mark replied, but in his heart he knew she had the right of it. Thanks to their sojourn at the Woman and the Woolsack, his melancholy was well and truly cured.

A Note from the Author

In "Much Ado About Murder," Mark Jaffrey is a groom of the stable and Jennet a tiring maid. These fictional characters marry at the end of *Face Down in the Marrow-Bone Pie* and take on greater responsibilities in the household. By the sixteenth century, it was fairly common for upper level servants to be literate. Others were taught how to read but not necessarily how to write.

An estate's steward was the most important position in a sixteenth-century household. Among other things, he managed the demesne farm, bought grain and cattle, supplied the household with all the necessities of daily life, and received and disbursed monies. The housekeeper was in charge of baking, brewing, and overseeing the indoor servants.

Records from one sixteenth-century household of approximately the same size as Leigh Abbey list what its servants were paid per annum. The steward received fifty shillings, the housekeeper, twenty-six. The cook, usually a man, was paid twenty shillings a year. A head gardener earned ten shillings and sixpence. The maid of all work was paid six shillings and eightpence. The entire payroll totaled £50 per annum for some twenty-five servants. Food for that household came to £200 for the year.

"The Riddle of the Woolsack" was first published in *Murders and Other Confusions* (2004). Events in this story take place at the same time as some of those in *Face Down Before Rebel Hooves*. The ports were temporarily closed because of the Northern Rebellion of 1569.

LADY APPLETON'S WORLD

Lady Appleton and the Cripplegate Chrisoms

"Goodwife Billings is proved a widow." Nick Baldwin announced.

Susanna, Lady Appleton, looked up from the herbal she'd been reading, a smile of welcome and congratulation lighting up the pale oval of her face. "Excellent. I was certain you would be able to find the correct parish with no trouble."

He sent a rueful grin in her direction and advanced a few more steps into the room, a private parlor on an upper floor of fair, large house near London's Moorgate. It was furnished with considerable luxury—glass in all the windows, floors of Purbeck marble and glazed tile, and thick arras-work hangings.

"Aye. On the fifth try."

Light laughter eddied toward him as she rose from a high-backed elmwood chair inlaid with oak. "It might have been worse. There must be a hundred parishes in London." She went to the hearth, where a small pot sat keeping warm on a trivet near the flames, and ladled mulled wine into two goblets. She held one out to him.

"Gramercy," Nick murmured, closing the remaining distance between them. He took deep pleasure in his first sip of the hot, spiced liquid. After a long, cold day spent looking through parish records, both the drink and the heat from the crackling fire sent welcome warmth to his chilled bones.

"You found evidence, then, of the death of Mary Billings's runaway husband?"

Mary, the housekeeper at Nick's Northamptonshire manor, had been abandoned by her feckless spouse several years earlier. She'd heard rumors of his demise soon after, but she'd had no reason then to go to the trouble and expense of confirming them. Only when she'd expressed her wish to remarry and the vicar had refused to perform the rite until she could prove the new marriage would not be bigamous, had the question of when and where Billings died become important. Nick had offered to look into the matter. He'd been glad of the excuse to visit London while Susanna was in residence.

"Billings was buried on the sixth day of November in 1569, more than two years ago, in the parish of St. Giles without Cripplegate. The clerk there has made a fair and notarized copy of the entry in the parish records."

"All's well, then?" Susanna's sharp-sighted blue eyes fixed on his face, studying him with as much intensity as she'd been perusing the herbal when he arrived. She did not wait for him to answer. "There is something troubling you."

It did not surprise Nick overmuch that she could read his mood with such ease. They had known each other more than a dozen years and shared many adventures. If he'd had his way, she'd have long since become his wife, but Susanna refused to remarry and he had learned to content himself with what she would share—her affection, her friendship, her concern, and most of all, her clever, agile mind.

"Well?" Susanna prompted him.

Nick took another strengthening, warming, soothing sip of the mulled wine. "What Mary Billings knew of her husband's life led me to suspect he'd been buried in Cripplegate Ward, for we believed he died shortly after having been released from the Compter in Wood Street."

She nodded and drank from her own cup. The Compter, a prison, was used to hold those taken for offenses against city laws.

"Cripplegate contains five parishes. I started with the southernmost church, St. Mary Magdalen in Milk Street. I went on to St. Michael, and there came upon an entry in the register of burials that puzzled me. The cause of death was writ down 'overlaid.' Do you know what is meant by the term?"

Frowning, she set down her goblet. "I fear I do. It means to be suffocated, but in a very particular manner. You know that infants are wrapped in swaddling clothes, bound tightly in order to ensure that the limbs will grow straight?"

"Aye. I've always felt sorry for the children. They are unable to move."

"They are more helpless than you know. In theory a baby is unwrapped and washed two or three times a day, but far too many new mothers do not know how to care for their offspring, or else they do not wish to be bothered."

Nick considered that. Wealthy households employed nurses but poor women too busy to pay attention to their babies simply neglected them. "I fear you have the right of it. I have seen children hooked by the swaddling to a convenient wall or left in the cradle to cry all day."

"Either place is safer than being carelessly placed in a bed to share sleeping space with several older, larger bodies. An infant 'overlaid' has been smothered because a bedmate rolled over on top of him."

"Is this common?"

"Yes, more's the pity. A goodly number of infants die in their cradles for no apparent reason, but for those who sleep with others, when a cause is sought, it most often found that the mother or the nurse slept unnatural heavy due to drink or illness." She sighed. "Although I've never had any children myself, it is my belief such deaths could be avoided with a small amount of caution."

Nick drained his goblet and abandoned it on a round table made of walnut. "How easily could such deaths be arranged?"

Eyes narrowing at his words, Susanna caught her breath. "What have you discovered?"

"Mayhap naught but an odd coincidence."

"And mayhap more. Tell me."

"It was at St. Michael that I first saw the word 'overlaid,' and although I was curious as to what it might mean, I took little notice of it then."

Restless, Nick crossed the chamber to stand at a window, looking out over the garden toward the wall that shielded this property from the sprawling city beyond. He knew Susanna well enough to predict how she'd react when he told her what he'd found. He had debated with himself all the way here. Even if his suspicions were right, naught would be done about it under the law. Only once had he heard of a charge of murder being brought against someone for the death of an infant, and that had been the case of a mother who'd stuffed her newly delivered baby into a privy and left it to perish. Still, this was just the sort of wrong that Susanna relished righting. Besides, it went against all Nick himself believed in to do nothing, especially if by inaction he allowed more deaths to occur.

"I'd not have noticed the entry at all had it not been within the time period I'd resolved to search, but there was another oddity about the entry, too. Unlike most, only the name of the mother was given."

Susanna sank down atop the domed lid of a trussing-coffer, a chest designed for use while traveling and suitable for storing anything from clothing to muniments to books to grain and bread. "So, the dead child was a bastard."

"Aye."

Most records of burials in parish registers identified the deceased by his profession, or sometimes simply as householder. Dead women and children were almost always listed in terms of their relationship to a man. "John, infant son of John Smith, householder" or "stillborn son of John Smith, carpenter" would not have caught Nick's eye, but "John, base-got son of Jane Johnson" had been another matter.

"I went on to St. Alban," Nick continued, "then St. Mary Aldermanbury, and finally to St. Giles Cripplegate, which lies outside the city walls, since half of the parish is in the county of Middlesex. At two of the three I came upon similar entries. Three children in adjoining parishes were all dead by cause of being overlaid and all had been base-got upon the body of one Jane Johnson. I had not thought to do so in the other parishes, but at St. Giles I also inspected the records of baptisms. That child died during the first month of life."

"A chrisom," Susanna murmured, sorrow and pity coloring her tone of voice. The name given to such short-lived infants derived from the fact that the same white chrisom cloth laid over the baby at baptism was customarily used as a winding sheet when only a few weeks separated christening and burial.

"Do you think it possible the mother deliberately killed all three children?" he asked.

"Possible? Oh, yes." She'd gone pale, but her chin jutted out at a determined angle and her eyes blazed. "And who knows how many more we will find if we delve deeper?"

He nodded. Her thoughts followed his. "I mean to discover if there are more, and find out what happened to Jane Johnson. She may be dead."

"She may be about to give birth to another child and kill another infant." Spurred into action, Susanna hopped down from the chest and made her way to a writing table. "Tell me again the parishes where you found records and the dates given. We must determine what parishes border them and widen our search."

"There are, I believe, one hundred six churches in London, in some ninety parishes. Then there are the out-parishes."

"I do not care if there are a thousand! If what we suspect is true, it cannot be permitted to continue and it cannot go unpunished. We must find Jane Johnson, and if she is again with child, we must keep watch on her to prevent her from taking another life."

***

Three days later, Susanna's search brought her to the small church of St. Olave. Located in Silver Street, just where it turned to become the north end of Noble, St. Olave's was an unremarkable edifice, but the parish was adjacent to Cripplegate ward and worth the time to search. The clerk, who was the second most important figure in any parish and responsible for keeping the records, was even less impressive. A small, wiry fellow named Lawrence Whitney, he scowled over Nick's request that he remove the parish record book from its locked coffer to allow them to look at it.

"The register is taken out only on Sundays, when the week's new records are added."

"Must I roust a churchwarden?" Nick inquired. "I am certain one of them has the second key." This was regulated by law and had been since the time of old King Henry.

After three days of looking through records and asking for Jane Johnson by name, they were by now familiar with the way the system worked, but they had found no more entries.

Susanna hid a smile as Whitney buckled under Nick's steady regard. The clerk hovered as they went through the register, as if he feared they would criticize his diligence, or mayhap his penmanship, since he wrote a near illegible hand.

"There," Susanna said, pointing to an entry on the page of burials for 1568. Elizabeth, daughter of Jane Johnson, "base got," had been buried on the last day of March. No cause of death was given. Susanna turned to the clerk. "What do you know of this woman?" She tapped the page.

Whitney sidled closer and looked at the name above Susanna's gloved finger. "Jane Johnson? A vagabond."

"She does not live in this parish?"

"We do not want her sort here. She'd have been escorted to the boundary and sent on her way." Contempt laced his voice. Bastards were a charge on the parish—all expense and little reward. Those who bore them were held in low regard unless they would name the father and he could be forced to support the child.

"And the baby—how did she die?"

Whitney looked at her askance. "It was close to four years ago, madam. How am I to remember?"

Susanna turned to the record of baptisms and found that Elizabeth Johnson was another chrisom. She'd been buried three weeks after her christening.

Further questioning yielded nothing useful. Thanking the clerk, Susanna and Nick continued on to St. Mary Staining and St. John Zachary. They found no mention of Jane Johnson or her base-got offspring in either parish.

"Four children in four years." Nick shook his head. "Is that not enough?"

"But look at the dates," Susanna said, and produced the list she'd made.

St. Mary Aldermanbury—11 April, 1567
   St. Olive—31 March, 1568
   St. Giles without Cripplegate—5 November, 1569
   St. Michael—12 December, 1570

Nick frowned down at the page. "You think there is a fifth, more recent than the others?"

"Or Jane is even now with child." Susanna pondered what to do. She had already put out word among those few midwives she knew in the city, asking them to notify her if they encountered a woman named Jane Johnson, but it was a common name, the city was large, and midwives were numerous. Susanna was known to some of them because of the herbals she had written, but many others, who could neither read nor write, had no cause to do favors for a visiting country gentlewoman.

In the end, she could only think to revisit the parish where the most recent death had occurred. At St. Michael, the clerk could help them not at all, but he did give them the names of the parish searchers, two old women whose duty it was to repair to the place where a death had occurred and view the corpse, making enquiries and examining the deceased until they could determine what disease or casualty had caused the death. It was their report to the parish clerk that had resulted in "overlaid" being writ down in the register.

The searchers for St. Michael's were two elderly matrons, sisters who lived together in the garret of a sprawling tenement at the edge of the parish. Goodwife Mellon used a stick to help her walk, a slow, ponderous progress. Goodwife Frowley, all skin and bones, flitted birdlike throughout the interview, landing in one spot for a moment, then moving on. Her head bobbed and shifted as she spoke, not in a nod but rather as if she needed to twist it about in order to see everything at once.

"The death of a bastard is a blessing," she informed them when they'd explained their interest in Jane Johnson.

"Nay, sister," Goodwife Melon objected. "Say not so."

"What? Would you preserve the child as a charge on the parish?"

"No. No. But it is not such a great sin to procure an abortment. Better the mother prevent the birth of the child altogether."

"Better she do so by not lying with the father," her sister retorted.

Susanna listened to the debate with mixed emotions. She could not help but feel sympathy for a young woman who found herself pregnant and unwed. A clever lass would leave home and go to a parish where she was not known, where she might claim to be a widow, but most girls tried to conceal their plight by a judicious arrangement of aprons and skirts, only to be ejected from their place of employment when they were found out. Pregnant women were an all-too-common sight on the outskirts of villages and towns, where some gave birth alone in a field or hedge if they could not drag themselves to a church porch. Not all, however, were abandoned when they were "in the straw." Susanna had heard that even vagrant women banded together to help a birth proceed.

"Did she kill her own child?" Nick asked when the searchers gave him an opening.

"It was an accident," Goodwife Melon said.

"She was in a rare state by the time we got there," said her sister. "I am certain she did not mean the baby to die."

Susanna wondered whether she could trust what either searcher said. Neither dared admit she might have been wrong in declaring the cause of death, even though they disagreed about everything else.

"The woman was simple," Goodwife Frowley said. "That is the only reason I remember her at all."

"Nonsense, sister. She was a clever baggage. She pretended to be foolish so we would ask no more questions."

They glared at each other, but neither had more to add.

"Who is the local midwife?" Susanna asked. If she'd delivered the baby, she might remember Jane Johnson and confirm whether she was simpleminded or not. The possibility that she was added a new dimension to the situation, but either way, if Jane was with child again, that child was in danger.

The midwife lived nearby, two doors down from the apothecary's sign—a pill resting on a lolling pink tongue—but she was not at home.

"We will return tomorrow," Susanna decided.

"This is women's business," Nick said as they made their way back toward the house where Susanna was staying with friends.

She fought a smile. He was brave enough to slay dragons for her, but the possibility of encountering a woman in labor was enough to send him running for the hills. "I will talk to her alone if you wish."

He could not hide his relief.

The next morning, Susanna returned. The midwife was a plump, comfortable sort named Agnes Dane, and she remembered Jane Johnson.

"She has the mind of a child herself," Agnes confirmed, "and no sense about men."

"Is she a whore?" Most brothelkeepers took care that their women did not bear children.

"Not to judge by the rooms she had." Agnes described the chamber where the child had been born and had died. "It is long since vacated," she added. "A poet lives there now."

"Jane bore other children before the one you delivered. All of them were suffocated in their beds."

For a moment, Susanna thought the midwife unmoved, but then she stirred herself. "I passed Jane Johnson in the street not long ago."

"Is she breeding again?"

"She appeared to be."

"How far along is she?"

"The child should be due any time now."

"Did she name the father of the child you delivered?"

"Nay. She resisted all my efforts." Agnes made a dismissive gesture. "Likely she did not know."

"Or she is not as simple as she seemed."

Susanna left the midwife's lodgings more determined than ever to find Jane. It was too late to help the others, but she still had a chance to preserve this new life.

* * *

Just as the church bells tolled nine at night, signaling that lights and fires should be put out, one of midwives who'd heard of Susanna's interest in Jane Johnson sent word that a woman by that name was in labor in the parish of Allhallows, Honey Lane. With Nick's help Susanna found the house in a narrow, dark street.

Jane's screams reached them even before they entered. She lay on a thin pallet, her face contorted with the intensity of her labor. When the pain passed, her features resolved themselves into a vacant stare.

Simple? Mayhap she was, Susanna thought, but that did not mean she lacked the power to communicate. "Has she named the child's father?" she asked the midwife.

"Not yet." Her attention fixed on her patient, she paid little heed to Susanna, but when Nick made to enter the birthing chamber she sent him a look over her shoulder that could have turned the sun to ice.

In haste, he withdrew. Recalling that there was an alehouse two buildings along, Susanna suspected she'd find him there if she had need of him.

At hand was women's work.

Three tortuous hours passed. The midwife, relentless in her effort to discover who had fathered Joan's latest bastard, denied the straining woman a mother's caudle, the special drink made of spiced wine or ale and given to keep up her strength and spirits. She wanted Jane weak enough to betray her lover, but weakness was not what Susanna saw.

Jane's flailing hand caught the midwife's arm, causing her to yelp in pain. She needed Susanna's help to break the hold and Jane had gripped with so much force that she'd left red finger marks on the midwife's skin.

"I've known women in the straw to squeeze hard," the midwife muttered, "but this one's hands are as strong as a man's." Her face set with grim determination, she resumed her efforts to goad Jane into telling the truth about her child's father, but she kept her distance from those powerful fingers.

Another half hour passed.

"What if she does not know his name?" No matter what Jane might have done, Susanna pitied her for the suffering she endured in order to give birth. There were herbs that could take away much of the pain and others to ease delivery, but Susanna did not carry such remedies with her and the midwife, if she had them, held them back.

"She knows who he is, I warrant. Just because she is simple does not mean she lacks all sense." The midwife's face was set in a grim expression.

"What if he did not tell her his name?"

"Her lover will have given her some name to call him by, never doubt it."

Susanna had been watching the woman in the bed. Her eyes, open and glazed with pain, widened in fear at the midwife's words. Was she afraid of the penance for bearing a bastard? She would have endured that already, for each of the previous children.

"It may not be mere stubbornness that keeps her quiet," Susanna murmured. It was possible Jane was so stalwart in protecting her lover because she lived in terror of what he would do to her if she betrayed him.

Was he an important man in London, someone who could order her disposed of if she spoke? Or was he simply a bully who'd threatened her often enough that she dared not risk his wrath? Either way, Susanna thought, Jane would not tell them. If she had kept her secret throughout the torture of those previous births, she'd maintain her silence now.

The pains continued for another hour before Jane at last produced a healthy girl child. The midwife tied and cut the umbilical cord, washed the babe, and swaddled her in new linen bands until she was trussed from head to foot. These tasks complete, she handed the newborn child to her mother. Jane smiled at the downy head and cooed and petted the baby.

Concerned for the tiny girl's safety, Susanna moved closer to the pallet. "May I hold her?" she asked, tucking her hands under the small, squirming body.

With frightening ease, Jane resisted Susanna's attempt to take the child away from her. Surprised, Susanna's gaze flew to Jane's face, wondering if she knew her own strength. Mayhap she had been wrong. Such a powerful woman seemed unlikely to be cowed by a lover.

It was then that another explanation for the deaths occurred to Susanna. Jane *might* have killed her children by accident, if she had hugged each one with such an excess of affection that they'd suffocated.

Vowing to keep a watchful eye on mother and child, Susanna abandoned her attempt to remove the baby from Jane's arms. She'd just turned back to the midwife, meaning to offer to pay her to stay with Jane until other arrangements could be made, when the local vicar arrived.

"Did she give up the father's name during childbirth?" he asked the midwife.

"No. Silent as a monk, that one."

"You were charged with obtaining that information."

"Was I to torture her?" the midwife inquired. "If she did not speak when her time was upon her, she will not."

The vicar's disdain for both Jane and the midwife hardened Susanna's heart against him. He fell lower still in her estimation when he began to rant about the charge this child would be on the parish. "Even if it dies," he grumbled, "it will cost two shillings ninepence to bury."

"Enough, sir," Susanna protested. "I will support the child myself if money is all that concerns you."

The vicar, mollified, became effusive in his thanks. Then, duty done, he was about to take his leave when a cry from the baby drew his attention to Jane and for the first time he looked closely at her.

"I have seen this woman before," he said, "and in similar circumstances! Whore! How many bastards have you brought into the world?"

Susanna put her hand on his sleeve to prevent him from launching another diatribe. "There is more to this than you know, vicar. *Where* did you see her before?"

Her stern demand had as much effect as her obvious wealth and gentility. He swallowed his outrage and replied in measured tones. "I was previously the curate at St. Mary Aldermanbury."

That was where the earliest baby had died. "Will you tell me what you recall of the birth?"

The vicar frowned. "It was my clerk who called my attention to her," he said after a moment's thought. "Whitney showed a most unwarranted sympathy for this woman."

"Lawrence Whitney?"

"Aye. These days he is the clerk at St. Olave in Silver Street."

* * *

Susanna found Lawrence Whitney alone, and for a moment her steps faltered on the stone-flagged floor of the chancel. She'd had the remainder of the night to consider what she should say to him. In the wee hours of the morning, she had come to a conclusion that made sense to her, but now that the moment was upon her, she had second thoughts. Still, it was strange that he had remembered Jane as a vagabond, but not that she was simple.

He turned and, recognizing her, scowled.

"Good day to you, Clerk Whitney," Susanna said. "I am come to tell you that you have a new daughter."

His face blank with astonishment, he gawked at her. Then his expression changed to one of panic and he dropped the communion plate he'd been polishing.

"Do not trouble to deny it." She felt a grim sense of satisfaction that she had been right and went ahead with her plan. "This time Jane Johnson named her child's father." It was a lie, but a necessary one.

"She has not the wit to know whether she's had one man or twenty."

"If that is true, sirrah, your actions in taking advantage of her are even more foul. But tell me, if her children were not yours, why go to such pains to hide their mother?"

He started to speak, then appeared to change his mind. Sullen-faced, he settled for glaring at her. Only when the silence between them stretched to an unbearable length did he blurt out another accusation. "She's naught but a foolish woman and much to be pitied."

"Foolish? Is that any excuse to have overlaid four young children?"

"It was better so. She has not the wit to care for them. They'd have become a charge on the parish."

"Not if you married their mother."

"Impossible."

Susanna despised weaklings. The fellow was incapable of giving up his mistress, but unwilling to take responsibility for the children she bore him. He'd rather move her around in the same general area of London, each time into a different parish, so that no one noticed that she kept having bastard children who kept dying.

"You can be required to marry her," Susanna reminded him, "or do you prefer to sit in the stocks with a notice around your neck saying 'Lawrence Whitney hath got Jane Johnson with child,' and then be paraded through this church on three consecutive Sundays wearing a penitent's white sheet and a placard saying FORNICATOR"

"I am already wed." He spat out the admission.

"In that case, the placard will say ADULTERER, but having a wife will not spare you the obligation to support your child until she reaches her seventh year."

"Do you think you she will live that long? Such children do not thrive, not with such a mother."

"All the more reason for you to take steps to protect the babe."

He heaved a deep sigh. "You meddle in matters that are none of your business, Lady Appleton. What will be, will be. It is in God's hands." The pious glance he cast upward was so patently false that Susanna was surprised lightning did not streak out of the sky and strike him dead.

"The laws of God and man alike condemn you, sirrah, and I mean to do more than meddle."

"Why trouble yourself to report me to the church?"

There was no remorse in him, no doubt because he knew as well as she did that no dire punishment awaited him for seducing a simpleminded young woman and repeatedly getting her with child. He'd avoided embarrassment with his machinations, nothing more. It was Jane who would bear the brunt of the church's censure, not Whitney. After he did penance, he'd be forgiven.

In frustration, Susanna turned on her heel and stormed out of the church. She had powerful friends, but she could only hope one of them had enough influence to force Whitney to support the child.

Susanna meant to make certain Jane's newborn would thrive and that Jane herself was removed from her lover's influence. Her first plan was to fetch Jane and bring her to the house where she was at present a guest. Her hostess had no objection, but having birthed two children of her own, she suggested that it might be unwise to disturb a new mother so soon after she'd given birth. Instead, Susanna returned to Jane's lodgings accompanied by a maidservant, a quiet girl content to sit in a corner and sew. She also brought an ornate wooden cradle.

When the exhausted mother awoke, Susanna was at her side. After a moment of incomprehension, a smile blossomed on her pale face. "I remember you. You came with the midwife."

Susanna nodded. "Jane," she said in her gentlest voice, "how would you like to live in the country?"

Her confusion made Susanna wonder if she knew any place but the city existed.

"My friend Master Baldwin has a manor in Northamptonshire where he raises sheep to make wool."

"Sheep?" Jane sounded doubtful.

"You need not have anything to do with them if you do not want to. I am certain there is plenty of work for you in the dairy or in the house. You'll have livery to wear and good food to eat. Master Baldwin's housekeeper and the man she is about to marry, who is steward there, will take good care of you and your child."

Tears welled in Jane's eyes. "My babies die."

"Yes, my dear. I know." Susanna moved to sit on the pallet and placed her hand over Jane's cold one. "But this child is different. See—she has her own cradle to sleep in." She set it rocking with her foot. Inside, the swaddled child was awake but not yet restless. A series of knotted bands kept her secured to knobs on the sides of the cradle. Even if it tipped over, she could not fall out.

Jane turned her face into the pillow. "It is always the same," she whispered. "I wake up and find them dead. He says I roll over on them in the night. Then he goes away, and the searchers come, and I have to leave the parish."

"Do you speak of Lawrence Whitney?" Susanna asked.

At hearing the name, Jane looked afraid.

"Tell me about him, Jane. Do you love him?"

Jane said nothing.

The midwife had been right, Susanna thought. Jane might be simple, but she was not stupid. She had the mind of a child of eight or nine. She was capable of deceit, of stubbornly refusing to speak, and of great loyalty, no matter how little it was deserved.

"This time Lawrence Whitney will allow *me* to make the arrangements for your new lodgings," she said, "and it will be my privilege to keep your daughter safe from accidents. You see, Jane, when she sleeps in her own bed, no one can overlay her."

Still Jane said nothing.

"We must talk about what happened before," Susanna continued. "Four deaths in a row are more than mere accidents. It is possible your children had some physical aberration—a flaw in the lungs or heart, mayhap—that caused their deaths, but there is also a possibility that one or more of the babies was murdered."

Jane sniffled. "Will I be hanged?"

With an effort, Susanna kept her voice level. "No, Jane. You will be safe with me."

"Even if this baby dies too?" The child had begun to whimper. Susanna freed the infant from her cradle and handed her to Jane to nurse.

"No one will hang you," Susanna promised. She would remain with mother and child until they were safe in Northamptonshire. If the infant succumbed, it would not be from the actions of a murderous parent.

"He said I must hide. He said they'd think I done it apurpose."

"But you did not. You were asleep."

The beatific smile Jane wore as she looked down at her nursing babe vanished when she shifted her gaze to Susanna. Her face became a mask of horror. "The first one, I were suckling."

"In the bed?"

Jane nodded.

A few more questions elicited a clearer picture. Jane had fallen asleep with her breast still in the child's mouth. When she'd awakened hours later, the baby had no longer been breathing. Susanna ruled it a tragic accident.

"Did the same thing happen with the next child?"

Jane shook her head. "I were careful, but the baby died anyway."

"You slept soundly and awoke to find your child overlaid?"

Jane frowned. "Seems like I dreamed." She continued to nurse the new infant, stroking the downy head with an absent motion.

"Dreamed what, Jane?"

Her voice puzzled, she murmured, "Pillows."

"You thought there were extra pillows in the bed with you?"

She nodded.

Susanna leaned forward to take the sated girl child and place her in the cradle. It was closer than the bed to the charcoal brazier, the only source of warmth in the room. She did not take time to tie the strings. A new and troubling possibility had her turning back to Jane.

"Was Lawrence with you on those nights?"

Face clearing, Jane smiled, happy to be able to answer Susanna's question. "He said I needed looking after with the new baby."

"Was he with you *each time* a child died?"

Tears sprang into Jane's eyes as she nodded.

"Jane," Susanna asked in a tentative voice, "did Lawrence ever strike you?"

Jane bobbed her head. "He said I needed to know my place. He said it were his duty to punish me for what I done."

"For the deaths of your babies?"

"For being with child."

The words Whitney had spoken earlier came back to Susanna, rife with ominous meaning: *Such children do not thrive.* A chill ran through her. A man who would beat his pregnant mistress would dispose of a newborn without a qualm.

The risk that he might mean to do so again, and try to harm Jane as well, had her speaking in a sharp voice to the maidservant dozing in her chair. "Go at once to Billingsgate and fetch Master Baldwin. He must come without delay and bring with him a wagon so that we may take Jane and her child away."

"But madam, it is full dark!"

"Take a torch. Hire a link boy." Susanna thrust several coins at her. "Go quickly."

After the reluctant girl left, Susanna contemplated the chamber. She had miscalculated. Leaving Jane here once she'd told Whitney that she knew he was the child's father had been a mistake.

A pair of sewing scissors was the only potential weapon Susanna found in the room to use to defend Jane and the baby. She longed for a stout cudgel. Even more, she wished she'd asked Nick to stay here with her.

When she heard heavy footsteps on the stairs, she slipped behind the door before it opened. Unaware of her presence, Lawrence Whitney strode straight to Jane's pallet and seized her roughly by the shoulders. "Jezebel! You betrayed me."

Jane whimpered and cowered before his attack. "I said naught to midwife nor vicar."

"You talked to someone else."

Silently pleading for help, Jane looked past Whitney's shoulder and straight at Susanna.

He released her and whirled, an ugly look on his face. "I thought you'd gone."

"You saw my maidservant leave. She will return with Master Baldwin at any moment. You have time to flee before he arrives."

Whitney's features settled into a smile so false that no one but an infant could be deceived by it. "How can I go, Lady Appleton? I have a duty here."

"Do you mean to assume your parental responsibilities and make arrangements for quarterly payments?"

He glanced toward the cradle. "Ah, yes. The child."

Before Susanna could stop him, Whitney kicked the rocker hard enough to fling the tightly swaddled infant out of her nest. She fetched up against the brazier.

With a gasp of horror, Susanna rushed forward. Whitney tripped her before she'd taken a half dozen steps. The scissors she'd been holding flew out of her hand and skittered under the chair.

When the swaddling bands began to smoke, Jane lunged from her bed, wailing in distress. Using her bare hands, she beat at the first tiny flames.

The newborn screamed, indignant at having been ripped so precipitously from sleep. From the sound of those lusty yells, her wrappings had kept her from being harmed by her fall. Relieved, Susanna heaved herself upright.

Whitney stood with his hands clasped to his ears, staring at his daughter through eyes that were wide and frantic. "Make her be silent!" he bellowed. "Stop that noise!"

Jane stepped away from the baby and put her hands behind her back. Terrorized and confused, she seemed incapable of any action. The child, still on the floor, howled louder.

Whitney turned his wild-eyed gaze on Susanna. "This is all your fault. You meddled in matters that were none of your business."

With no more warning than that, he charged, striking Susanna across the face with the back of his hand. The blow sent her reeling into the wall. Pain lanced through her shoulder, joining the agony in her jaw, but she barely felt either injury when she realized that, in his rush to attack her, he had overturned the brazier. Within moments, the entire chamber would be ablaze.

In a panic, Whitney ran for the door.

Her steps unsteady, Susanna staggered to the bed, plucked off the heavy blanket, and flung it onto the glowing coals to smother the flames. Lifting her skirts out of the way, she used her sturdy boots to trample every spark she could find.

The wails of Jane's infant continued unabated. Mercifully, Jane had moved her far enough away from the brazier to avoid being burnt when it toppled over.

When the fire seemed to be out, Susanna gathered the baby into her arms, soothing her with awkward pats and murmurs. Only when the child quieted did she become aware of the scuffling sounds coming from the doorway.

Jane's hands, those strong hands that had bruised the midwife, were clamped tight around Whitney's throat. He flailed wildly, striking her repeatedly, but she did not seem to notice the blows. She did not loosen her grip.

Whitney's face, already red, turned purple. His struggles grew weaker. When he dropped to his knees, he took Jane with him, but she still would not let go.

Only when he was as limp and unresisting as a day-old fish did Jane heave herself off Whitney's body. Without a backward glance, she reached for her daughter.

Susanna relinquished the infant, wincing as Jane accidentally bumped against her. Her arm and face throbbed, but she forced herself to kneel beside the body. No life pounded in Whitney's veins, no breath escaped his dead white lips, and all emotion had gone from those bulging eyes.

"He escaped penance," she murmured, more to herself than to Jane. Nor would he have the burden of supporting his daughter for the first seven years of her life, but he *had* been served rough justice.

Belatedly, Jane seemed to realize what she had done. Her jaw went slack. "Will they hang me?"

"No." Susanna spoke with absolute certainty. "I will bear witness to everything that happened here. This man tried to kill us—you, me, and your child. You prevented that, Jane. You saved all our lives. You will not be punished. Indeed, I mean to see to it that you are richly rewarded. You will have your own little cottage in Northamptonshire," she added when she heard a door slam below stairs and the familiar sound of Nick's voice, "and a maid to help you with the baby, and a generous stipend."

Jane did not respond. Her attention had shifted to her child, a look of love and delight on her face.

A Note from the Author

The "bawdy courts" of the sixteenth century grew in importance as the Puritan influence in government increased. They concerned themselves not with criminal behavior but with offenses against the community standard of morality. These ranged from flirting in church to adultery. The ultimate punishment was excommunication, which could lead to imprisonment on the criminal charge of failing to attend church. Most punishments, however, required doing penance.

The churchwardens of each parish were responsible for detecting offenses and bringing them to the attention of courts set up in each deanery. Every diocese had several courts, each presided over by an archdeacon. They also heard "actions of defamation"—cases brought by those who felt themselves injured by gossip in the community or by charges unsuccessfully brought against them at an earlier church court.

This story first appeared in *Alfred Hitchcock Mystery Magazine* in 2003. Like the following story, it takes place in 1572, between events in *Face Down Across the Western Sea* and *Face Down Below the Banqueting House*.

Lady Appleton and the Bristol Crystals

July 1572

The stairs wound upward, narrow, steep, and uneven. Susanna, Lady Appleton had to brace one hand against a crumbling plaster wall to steady herself as she climbed. She was out of breath and her bad leg throbbed steadily by the time she reached the top floor of the George in Glastonbury. It smelt of disuse and mouse droppings.

"A moment," she said to Grace, her young tiring maid. The girl's pretty face was flushed and a strand of dark hair had come loose beneath her coif, but otherwise she showed no sign of exertion. The uncommon hot weather did not affect her as badly as it did her mistress.

The inn had been purpose-built more than a hundred years earlier to house pilgrims visiting Glastonbury Abbey. Susanna supposed those visitors had been more concerned with their spiritual well being than creature comforts, but for many years now, ever since the present queen's father, old King Henry, dissolved all the monasteries, the George had depended upon secular patrons for its custom. It seemed odd to Susanna that the innkeeper had undertaken so few repairs. True, Glastonbury was in a remote part of Somerset, but it was on one of the main routes westward from the midlands and what little she'd seen of it as they rode in had suggested a fair-sized market town.

The long, low room in which Susanna and her servant were to sleep, together with any other women spending the night at the George without a husband's company, was better swept but just as stifling as the landing. The shutters on narrow windows cut into thick walls, flung open to reveal the rooftops of the town, let in the only breath of air.

A tiny, tidily-dressed woman already occupied the chamber. She stood on tiptoe on a bench, looking out the far casement at the rapidly gathering dusk. Without turning her head, she spoke, her voice soft and melodious. "Lady Appleton, I have been waiting for you to arrive." She hopped down from her vantage point and pattered across the bare planks toward the newcomers.

Susanna was certain they'd never met before. The woman stood no higher than her shoulder and even though she was uncommon tall for a woman, that was surpassing small. Elfin features matched the stranger's stature—small chin and nose, narrow face, and ears that were just the slightest bit pointed.

"How is it, madam, that you know my name?"

"I am a seer." She made the absurd claim in a matter-of-fact voice as she met Susanna's gaze. Her eyes were an unusual clear gray in color.

Young Grace, only newly trained in her duties, abandoned unpacking her mistress's capcase. With the eagerness of a puppy, she tugged at the stranger's sleeve. "Can you see my future? Will I marry well?"

The seer spared Grace a quick, pitying glance. "You are not my concern. It is Lady Appleton I have come to warn."

Susanna felt both brows lift. *Ominous warnings from fortune tellers*, she thought. *What have I done to deserve this?*

"I see you doubt me." The woman seized Susanna's gloved hand in a surprisingly firm grip and closed her eyes. "You are on your way to Cornwall."

"It would be easy enough to learn that from the ostler." Susanna tried to pull free but the seer was not yet done with her.

"You go to visit young Rosamond, who lives with her mother and stepfather. It has been almost a year since you last saw her, but you have allowed only two weeks for the journey, two weeks to visit, and two weeks to return. You do not wish to be absent longer because you have a houseguest—someone recently bereaved."

"You are exceeding well informed, but you could glean all that by listening to servants' talk."

"A boy has been following your party since you left Leigh Abbey," the seer continued. "He is in grave danger of suffocating in an ill-chosen hiding place."

This ominous prediction set Susanna's heart racing. "Where?"

"In the cart with the furnishings you take to Lady Pendennis. He rolled himself into a tapestry. It shifted during transport, making it impossible for him to squirm free."

* * *

A quarter of an hour later, nine-year-old Rob Jaffrey stood before Susanna in the torchlit stable yard of the inn. Red-faced and disheveled, he kept his head down to avoid eye contact. He shifted his weight from foot to foot as he awaited her inquisition.

Thankful they'd been in time to rescue him, Susanna moderated her tone. "Account for yourself, my lad. Why did you stow away in that cart?"

She was annoyed with him but she was also very glad to have found him still alive. He was the child of two of her most loyal servants, her steward and her housekeeper. Jennet Jaffrey was also one of Susanna's oldest and dearest friends. She'd have been devastated by the death of her only son.

"I want to see Rosamond." Rob attempted to sound defiant but his high, piping voice defeated the effort.

So that was it. He'd followed them in secret because his mother did not approve of his friendship with Rosamond and would have forbidden it if he'd asked permission to go along on the trip to Cornwell.

Rob and Rosamond, together with Rob's two older sisters, had shared lessons at Leigh Abbey until Rob had been old enough to attend the village school. Rosamond, the girl Susanna had fostered for six years, had been a bad influence on Jennet's son, leading him into one scrape after another, but Rob had wept when Susanna broke the news to him that Rosamond would not be returning to Leigh Abbey to live.

At Susanna's side, Nick Baldwin, her neighbor in Kent and sometime lover, fixed the lad with a steely glare. "You deserve a good thrashing. You'd get it if either of your parents were here." Nick had business of his own in the West Country and had suggested making the journey together. Susanna had not needed much persuasion. Aside from her pleasure in his company, she appreciated the addition of his two stout henchmen, Toby and Simon, to her party.

By the way Rob's lower lip stuck out, Susanna judged he felt more put-upon than repentant. "Think of your poor mother," she admonished him. "Jennet must be frantic with worry."

"Mother thinks I've gone to visit cousins near Dover."

"When did you plan to reveal yourself?" Nick asked.

Rob dared peek at them through his lashes. Susanna fancied he was trying to gauge how much it was safe to tell them. "Soon."

"When you ran out of food?" By the mulberry-colored stain creeping up the back of Rob's neck, Susanna knew she'd guessed well. "Retrieve what you brought with you and go along with Master Baldwin's men. We will talk again in the morning." Simon and Toby would see to it that the lad had something to eat before the three of them bedded down in the stable.

Nick shook his head as he watched the boy walk away. "He is a resourceful lad, managing to follow us for so long without being seen." Reluctant admiration crept into his voice.

"We must send word to Jennet. I fear she may already have discovered he's not where he's supposed to be." She sent a sharp look in Nick's direction. "Do you intend to thrash him in *loco parentis*?"

"The lad is already suffering enough, since he is afflicted with a most painful ailment."

Alarm shot through her. "What did I miss?" With all her knowledge of herbal remedies, there was likely something she could do to help young Rob.

"There is no cure but time for unrequited love."

"Unrequit—! But he's only nine years old."

"As is Rosamond, but he's been her devoted slave since they first met at the age of three. Consider the situation from his point of view. He feels that if he is old enough to be sent away to school, he is old enough to undertake this journey."

"It is true he is to matriculate at the King's School in Canterbury at the beginning of the next term, but what has that to do with Rosamond?"

"To his mind, they've been separated by cruel fate. Now that he's to leave home himself, what chance will they ever have to meet again?" He took Susanna's arm to escort her back inside the inn.

"They can write each other letters. Indeed, they do already."

At sea with this mad notion of children so determined to be together that one would risk his life to reach the other, Susanna readily agreed to Nick's suggestion that they sup together in the common room before she retired for the night. By the time he secured a table, bespoke their meal, and gave orders for food to be sent to Susanna's chamber for her maid, Susanna had realized that they had no choice but to take Rob with them on the morrow. She could scarce send him home. They could not spare anyone to accompany him.

"You reward him for his bad behavior by giving him what he wants," Nick said when she told him her decision.

"What else am I to do with him? He and Rosamond can bid each other sad farewells and then we will return the grieving child to his parents. What a cheerful journey home that will be!"

When Nick produced paper, a portable ink pot, and a quill, Susanna scribbled a brief message to Jennet. Not for the first time, she was grateful her father had seen to it that all Leigh Abbey servants were taught to read. When she'd finished, she used her signet ring and the sealing wax Nick melted for her to secure the flaps of the thrice-folded paper.

He tucked the letter into the front of his doublet. "I will see this dispatched by messenger at first light," he promised. "Do you want to send word ahead to warn Pendennis or shall we surprise him?"

Susanna made a face at him. Warn Pendennis indeed! As if she did not know full well the real reason Nick's journey had so fortuitously coincided with her own. He wanted to see for himself that Sir Walter Pendennis and his wife, Rosamond's mother, had reconciled—visible proof Walter was no longer his rival for Susanna's affections. Men! She would never understand how they could continue a feud so long after all reason for it had lapsed.

The innkeeper brought bread and butter, eggs, boiled and roast mutton, pigeon pie, and a flask of wine. As they ate, Nick asked the question Susanna had been avoiding. "How did you guess Rob was hiding in that tapestry?"

She hesitated, aware of how he felt toward those he contemptuously referred to as "figure flingers," but after a moment she told him about the seer. His expression grew darker with every word she uttered.

Containing his anger with an effort, he drained his wine cup and set the vessel down with a resounding thump. "She wants something."

"No doubt."

"You cannot believe she has the sight."

"No more than I believe in love potions or using magic to find missing objects, but I confess I am most curious to hear how she'll explain her knowledge of Rob's presence."

"Have no more to do with her, Susanna."

"I can scarce avoid it when we must share a room."

"Then promise me you will be careful. Such people are dangerous."

* * *

Some time later, when Susanna returned to the bedchamber, she found her tiring maid deep in conversation with the seer. At her mistress's entrance, Grace flushed and sprang to her feet.

"Have you had your fortune told?" Susanna asked, "or have you been the one answering questions?"

The stranger laughed. "I have no need to ask. I simply know. You found young Rob Jaffrey hiding in the cart."

"I thank you for your timely warning."

"And yet you doubt my gift."

"There must be thousands of people who claim to tell fortunes. Some few of those predictions must come true."

"I see I must prove myself." She thought for a moment. "Do you recall the tales your grandmother was wont to tell of the time she spent at court?"

Surprised by what seemed to be a complete shift in subject, Susanna nodded. Her father's mother had been a waiting gentlewoman to the first of King Henry's six queens. In her later years, she'd loved to regale the household at Leigh Abbey with stories from those youthful days.

"She spoke of one Mistress Amadas, a woman with the gift of prophecy."

Susanna was blessed with an excellent memory. Although it had been almost thirty years since she'd last heard the tale, she recalled the story. "Mistress Amadas was also cursed with a sharp tongue. She spread tales about a courtier's scandalous behavior with a lord's wife and thus incurred the king's wrath."

"She had the gift of seeing what others could not, and I inherited it from her. I am Elizabeth Amadas."

"Well, Mistress Amadas, do you mean to predict more details of my future, or mayhap tell me what I am thinking, for you seem to combine more than one skill in this gift of yours."

Responding to Susanna's sarcasm with a glare, the little woman spoke with unexpected heat. "You do not deserve more warnings." Without another word, she disrobed, climbed into bed, and pulled the coverlet over her head to block out the candlelight.

* * *

In the morning, after Susanna had broken her fast with bread and ale, she called Rob Jaffrey to her. Since the others in their party were in the stable yard, preparing to resume their journey, they had the inn's common room to themselves.

"You will accompany us to Cornwall," she informed him.

"Thank you, madam. I will not be in the way. You'll see. I'll earn my keep."

"I expect you to do so." His delight made a mockery of her firm voice and fierce expression. "You may begin at once. Go and help Master Baldwin's men with the horses."

In his hurry to obey he nearly knocked Elizabeth Amadas off her feet.

"Slow down, lad," she cautioned him. "You will do yourself an injury." Ignoring his stammered apology, she entered the common room and addressed Susanna. "Will it convince you of my gift if I am able to tell you something known only to you and Mistress Rosamond?"

"What would that be?" Susanna asked.

"Your foster daughter does much admire certain stones called Bristol crystals. When she could not persuade her mother to share those she'd been given, she 'borrowed' two. She keeps them in the hidden drawer of the globe in her schoolroom."

Taken aback, Susanna stared at Mistress Amadas. "You know more than I do, mistress."

Rosamond had spoken of Bristol crystals in a letter. The glittering stones were transparent rock crystal of little value but were sometimes sold to the unwary as diamonds. Sir Walter Pendennis, Rosamond's stepfather, was a justice of the peace. A case had come before him the previous summer that concerned these baubles. He'd sent the malefactor off to gaol, charged with fraud, and made a present of the evidence to Eleanor, Rosamond's mother.

Susanna frowned, thinking of what else Rosamond had said in her letters. Rambling accounts of whatever struck the girl's fancy, they covered many close-written pages. She did not often refer to her mother, although she had provided Susanna with the details of Eleanor's attempts to find a suitable gentlewoman to employ as her companion.

The self-proclaimed seer gasped and clapped both hands over her mouth.

"What is it?" Susanna demanded. "What is wrong?"

Eyes squeezed tightly shut, the tiny woman swayed. Susanna grasped her upper arm to prevent her falling. At once her lids lifted, but her gaze was fixed, as if whatever she stared at lay beyond the ken of mere mortals.

"Elizabeth!" Susanna said sharply, giving her a shake. "Come back."

The gray eyes blinked. "We must help her," Elizabeth whispered, and rushed out of the common room.

Susanna hesitated, wondering if she should call for Nick. Then she remembered how Rob had nearly suffocated. If this situation was as dire as Elizabeth's behavior indicated, there was no time to lose. She hurried after the seer, reaching her side just as Elizabeth opened the door to an empty chamber and went in. She crossed directly to a wall hanging, twitched it aside, and began to descend the privy stair hidden behind it.

Again Susanna hesitated, but again she followed. The steps were steep and increasingly uneven as they neared the bottom. The only light was what filtered down through the hanging.

As she went, Susanna fumbled in the pouch suspended from her waist until her searching fingers located the candle stub, flint, and steel she kept there for emergencies. At the foot of the stair, she lit the candle, illuminating a narrow passage. Six cautious paces brought her into a larger space where a single rush dip burned in a wall sconce, casting eerie shadows. Had Elizabeth Amadas not seemed so agitated, Susanna would have balked at venturing farther into the murky underground room, but the other woman was already groping her way along one side of the cellar.

"Here," she whispered. "A servant sent down for supplies. A fall."

Someone *had* left the torch burning, but although Susanna listened for groans or whimpers, she heard nothing but her own breathing and that of the woman ahead of her.

"In there." Elizabeth pointed to a high stone step below an opening in the wall. It appeared to lead to a smaller room, mayhap used for storing wine, but the entrance was less than three feet high and the interior was unlit.

The hairs on the back of Susanna's neck prickled. She was already turning to retrace her steps, intending to go for help, when pain lanced through the back of her skull. Stars burst before her eyes. Then there was only blackness.

* * *

"Where is she, Cowdrey?" Nick Baldwin slammed the innkeeper against the wall and tightened his grip on the fellow's throat. "A gentlewoman does not vanish without a trace unless she's been helped on her way. Tell me what you know and quickly or it will be the worse for you."

Through a red haze, Nick saw the working of his host's contorted face. Denials were followed by protests of innocence and, finally, by a confession to watering the wine, but he could tell Nick nothing about Susanna's sudden disappearance. Half an hour since, when Nick had gone to fetch her from the common room, he'd discovered she was no longer anywhere in the inn. Neither was Rob Jaffrey. A frantic search of every room had roused one unhappy pair of newlyweds from their nuptial bed but otherwise had uncovered only inn servants and members of Nick's own party.

"Where is the woman who shared her chamber?" Nick's voice rose to a bellow and he gave Cowdrey another shake for good measure.

"I know naught of her!" he cried, but Nick saw a brief flash of guilt in his goggling eyes and tightened his grip. "A bribe! That is all it was. I swear it. She bribed me to say I had but one room suitable for female travelers."

"The one she already occupied?"

"Aye."

Nick barely had time to absorb that information before he heard a flurry of activity at the entrance to the stable yard. Rob burst through the gathered servants, eyes wild and chest heaving from the speed of his run. His face was dirt streaked and marred with several small cuts. His clothing was disheveled and likewise dirty, especially at the knees.

"They've taken her!" he shouted. "They've kidnapped Lady Appleton."

One of Nick's big hands settled on the lad's shoulder, but he kept hold of the innkeeper with the other. "Who has, boy?"

"The seer and some men. We must hurry. They have horses. They are taking Lady Appleton away."

Nick shoved Cowdrey aside. His men had been mounted and ready to go—with Grace on a pillion behind Simon—when they discovered Susanna's absence. It took only moments to reassemble.

"Leave the cart," he ordered. "Rob, take your mistress's mare." He pointed a finger at the guide he'd hired to help them find the quickest route to the main road into Cornwall. "Do you know *all* the territory around here?"

"As well as any, sir."

"Then come with us now. You will be well rewarded for your service. Which way?" he asked the boy.

Rob took the lead. "There were four men," he said as they forged a path through Glastonbury's early morning traffic.

"How did they get her away?"

"Through a tunnel."

By the time he'd explained that he'd stopped outside the common room to listen when he'd heard mention of Rosamond's name, they'd reached the gatehouse of an old abandoned abbey. The ruined buildings were not far distant from the inn but were well-concealed by walls and trees.

"The tunnel came out there," Rob said, pointing.

Stumbling over his words, he told Nick how Susanna had followed the fortune-teller down a flight of hidden stairs at the inn to enter a cellar where a man with a cudgel had been waiting. He'd used it to clout her on the head.

"Then he and the woman dragged her into the tunnel. I followed them. I was afraid I'd lose sight of her if I went for help." Rob slanted a nervous glance at Nick. He had to swallow hard before he could continue. "They had horses waiting, and three more men. That's when I left to get help."

"You did well, lad." Calling out would have made the villains aware they'd been seen. Most likely they'd have captured Rob, too, or killed him. "Was Lady Appleton still unconscious when they rode off?"

Rob nodded. "They placed her on a pillion, with her arms fastened to the rider so she'd not fall. Then they pulled her cloak around her to hide the ropes."

The image made Nick's blood boil but he contained his anger. There would be time enough to explode later. "Which way did they go?"

"The road to Meare," their guide said when Rob showed them the direction the riders had taken.

Nick dug his heels into his horse's flanks and set off with the others following after him. He hoped they'd shortly overtake Susanna and rescue her, but although he kept a sharp watch, he saw no sign of the party they pursued. They were well away from Glastonbury and into rough country before they came upon a man herding pigs. He had seen four men and two women pass by on horseback.

Encouraged by the sighting, they pushed on, following narrow, meandering lanes that seemed to be bearing north and east. Only once, far ahead, did Nick glimpse a plume of dust that might have been kicked up by riders.

"If those are the villains we seek," he asked the guide, "where are they headed?"

"Likely o'er Zomerzet levels into Mendip," he replied.

Further questions revealed that Mendip was a high, rough, rocky area, partially forested but full of cliffs, caves, swallets, and underground streams. It was, in short, a landscape containing an untold number of places in which a captive could be concealed.

* * *

Susanna's awareness of her surroundings returned in fits and starts. The back of her head throbbed. The sting of a dozen cuts and scrapes was so intense it brought tears to her eyes. That she was in constant motion, jiggled and jostled about, occasionally slipping sideways into an even more uncomfortable position, added to both her sense of unreality and to the aches from the battering her limp body had endured.

She tried to move and found she could not. The left side of her face pressed into a thick wool surface she belatedly identified as the hood of her cloak. Beneath that layer of cloth was something solid yet flexible that smelled of leather and sweat and horse. She concluded she was riding on a pillion with both arms secured to the man in the saddle in front of her. She could not think how she had come to be there.

"She be wakeful." Since she was pressed against him, Susanna felt as well as heard the deep rumble of the man's voice. The rope binding them together bit into her armpits as the horse, cursed with an uneven gait to begin with, began a steep ascent.

As her scattered thoughts slowly regrouped, Susanna assessed her situation. Her injuries seemed to be minor, if painful. She supposed that what she'd thought was a room in the cellar of the inn had been a tunnel. Judging by the bruises and scrapes she'd acquired, they'd dragged her along it for some distance.

Listening hard, Susanna heard naught but the clop of hooves, the whisper of leaves, and the occasional murmur of a nearby stream. There were no voices and no sounds of commerce. Wherever they were, they had left Glastonbury well behind them.

In an attempt to dislodge the hood that had been drawn over her face and tucked in so that she could see only a sliver of the passing countryside, Susanna turned her head. Pain speared through her skull.

"If you struggle, we will knock you senseless again," Elizabeth Amadas said in a deceptively pleasant voice.

Susanna went still, but since she had not been gagged, she risked speaking. "What do you want from me?" Her words were muffled by layers of wool.

"From you? Nothing. But you have value to your friends and they should be willing to ransom you."

Susanna digested that information, then asked, "Where are you taking me?"

"To a place where no one will ever find you."

Unenlightened, Susanna fell silent. If she could determine her location and judge how far they were from Glastonbury, she might be able to use that information to escape, but concentrate as she might, she gathered only scattered impressions of their route.

She knew when they crossed a stone bridge and when they forded a stream, and she could tell the difference between a rough uphill track and the path into a deep valley. Once she smelled wild garlic growing nearby. Another time she caught a glimpse of butterflies in a field, but by and large her senses were of little use.

It was dusk when they stopped. They'd spent the entire day in the saddle. It was impossible to guess how far they'd come, but the terrain had been so uneven that Susanna thought it unlikely they'd covered more than ten miles.

It might as well be a hundred if Nick had no idea where to look for her. She had no doubt that he would try to find her, but Elizabeth's plan had been a clever one. She had been spirited away without fuss. To those left behind, it must have seemed as if she'd vanished into thin air.

Susanna's feet had been bound to the footrest on the pillion and had lost all feeling during the long ride. Once she was untied and lifted down, she tried to stamp life back into them, covertly surveying her surroundings at the same time. The last of the sun dappled a stony, downward-sloping path with shades of gray. It appeared to descend into a narrow gorge.

For the first time, Susanna also saw her captors. Elizabeth Amadas had four men with her, all rough-looking brutes who'd been mounted on small, sturdy horses. One-by-one they led their animals toward an outcropping of rock. One-by-one, three of them disappeared. The fourth ruffian seized Susanna's arm to hustle her after the others into a hidden cave. The entrance was barely high enough to accommodate a riderless horse and the area just inside was narrow. The footrest scraped against rock as the horse with the pillion passed through.

They continued on for some two hundred paces in near blackness, descending a steep slope before emerging into the upper level of a cavern. The flickering light of a torch revealed what at first appeared to be an immense void. Susanna could not discern a roof above her head and a chasm lay at her feet. To her horror, a rope ladder led downward.

"Climb," Elizabeth ordered.

With long skirts to manage, it was slow going. If for no other reason than to keep her mind off the dark pit beneath her feet, Susanna tried to calculate how far she was descending. The rungs were set apart by the distance from her knee to her ankle and she reckoned there were seven to a fathom.

Some two fathoms down, the rocks abruptly sheered away from the rope ladder. Susanna froze. With nothing to touch for balance or guidance, she succumbed to panic. Certain she was about to fall, she would have launched herself back up the ladder if the way had not been blocked by the man directly above her.

Anxious to feel solid ground beneath her feet, even if it was the floor of an underground cavern, Susanna resumed her descent. She counted twelve more fathoms and could hear the rush of water from a hidden stream before her boot at last touched bottom.

Three of Elizabeth's henchmen brought light with them. She followed, leaving the fourtht man above with the horses. "Light a fire," she instructed, "and find the cookpot."

By the erratic beams of torches made of sheaves of reed sedge, Susanna saw piles of supplies stacked against the cavern wall—provisions sufficient to feed a small band of outlaws for several weeks. The tension in her shoulders eased slightly. At least they did not plan to leave her here alone.

The cooking fire flared up, spilling light into dark corners and revealing a subterranean river wider than Susanna had expected. Nearer at hand, the glitter of reflected light caught her attention. Curious, she stepped closer. Given its resemblance to a diamond, the source could be nothing else but rock crystal. All around it were egg-shaped balls of reddish stone. One broke off in her hand when Susanna touched it. It was so light and fragile that she wondered if it was hollow.

When Elizabeth called to her she kept hold of the "egg" and surreptitiously slid it into the pouch that held her flint and steel. With a sense of dismay, she realized that she must have lost her candle stub in the cellar of the George.

"You mocked my skill as a seer," Elizabeth taunted her, "and I readily admit that I cozened you, but some *are* born with special gifts. My husband was a jowser."

Her West Country pronunciation confused Susanna for a moment before she realized that Elizabeth meant her spouse had possessed the ability to locate things with the help of a dowsing rod. "He found water?"

"He found calamine. No one could equal his talent."

Susanna did not reply. She'd never seen anyone work a dowsing rod but she knew enough about the subject to realize that if a dowser grasped his hazel branch tightly in his fingers, held his arms close to his sides, and pressed his hands together, he could make the rod seem to move of its own volition.

She was no expert, but she was widely read, and Walter Pendennis had talked to her a bit about mining. Calamine stone could be mixed with copper to make latten, and latten—brass compounded in specific proportions—could be used in turn in the manufacture of ordnance. Deposits of calamine stone were rare in England and most latten was imported.

Susanna also knew one other thing about calamine—miners often found rock crystals near deposits. When she was allowed a few minutes of privacy in the secluded corner of the cavern set aside as a latrine, she examined the "egg" she'd found more closely. When she squeezed it, it cracked open to reveal a half dozen transparent crystals fixed around the cavity.

* * *

Susanna was given a pallet and fed. After the meal, Elizabeth produced pen, paper, and ink. All manner of supplies appeared to have been stockpiled in the cavern.

"The ransom is two hundred pounds, to be gathered and sent to the George in Glastonbury. Write that message. Say also that you are well and will remain so if they obey. Then make a copy."

When both missives had been sanded and sealed—Elizabeth had indeed thought of everything—Susanna sat on her pallet, leaned back against the cushions provided for her comfort, and considered what she knew about her captors.

Elizabeth was clearly the leader of this small band of villains. Her husband, by the way she spoke of him, was either dead or in prison. What Susanna could not understand was why the woman had chosen *her* to kidnap, or why the demand was for two hundred pounds. That amount was enough to keep a substantial household for a year, but she could have asked for much more.

Forcing a hint of admiration into her voice, she asked, "How did you learn so much about me? You presented most convincing details. I was halfway to believing that you *were* a seer."

Elizabeth was not immune to flattery. "Diligence, Lady Appleton."

Hoping Mistress Amadas, if that was indeed her name, would be unable to resist the temptation to boast of her cleverness, Susanna encouraged her to preen. "You must have intercepted the letter Rosamond wrote about the Bristol crystals, but how did you learn of my impending journey to Cornwall?"

"You are well known in your part of Kent," Elizabeth said, "and you are the subject of much speculation."

"Did you follow me when I left, hoping for a chance to arrange an accidental meeting?"

"Oh, no, madam. I left nothing to chance. I knew your itinerary in advance. I think of everything, even this foolish attempt to coax me into saying more than I should. Sleep well, Lady Appleton. I intend to." With that, as she had at the inn, Elizabeth turned her back on Susanna, curled up on her pallet, and pulled a coverlet over her head.

Susanna dozed fitfully. Although she knew she needed rest if she was to outwit her captors, she wanted to stay alert long enough to take note of their movements. Once she concluded that the guard set on the upper level was relieved at regular intervals, she gave herself permission to drift off.

For a long time sleep eluded her. Dampness pervaded the cavern, making her glad of her wool cloak. Her hand, if she let it stray off the straw pallet, touched stone rough with lichen, making her uncomfortably aware that she was deep beneath the earth. She had to fight the irrational sensation that she had been buried alive.

Morning came with the same degree of darkness as the night, harkened only by the stirring of one of Elizabeth's henchmen by the fire. Susanna stretched, winced, and levered herself to her feet, feeling as if she'd aged ten years in a night.

There was bread and ale with which to break their fast. While Susanna ate, Elizabeth dispatched two of her men with the ransom notes.

Susanna supposed one was being sent to Nick and the other to Walter Pendennis, assuming the Bristol crystals Walter had given to his wife had something to do with this affair. Elizabeth had known more about them than Rosamond had written in her letters.

She glanced at the rope ladder and blinked in surprise. No one was paying any attention to it, or to her. Elizabeth had retired to the makeshift privy. The remaining henchman was fully occupied in an attempt to dislodge crystal-bearing stones.

Susanna set aside her cup and eased to her feet. She might never have a better chance to escape.

* * *

Nick Baldwin studied the cliffs surrounding the gorge. They were pearly, pale grey rock for the most part, although there were occasional outcroppings of red sandstone. Just at dusk, they'd lost the trail and been forced to abandon their search for Susanna. Once a colony of bats had left on their nocturnal hunt for food, they'd spent the night in one of the area's numerous small caves.

A peregrine flew across his field of vision. The birds nested hereabout, as did ravens, and butterflies were as common as blue damsel flies, but of the kidnappers and their victim, Nick had seen not a trace. For all he knew, Susanna might be miles away.

It was at that moment that two men appeared on the track ahead. Rob's sharply indrawn breath was all the identification Nick needed.

"Pretend to give way," he ordered his men. "Then close in and take them prisoner as they try to ride past us."

There was a moment when all might have been lost. One of the villains recognized young Rob. He would have turned and fled had Nick not been so close to him, his sword already drawn.

The messages the men carried were enough to condemn them. Written in Susanna's own hand, the notes demanded payment of two hundred pounds. One was addressed to Nick and the other to his onetime rival for Susanna's affections, Sir Walter Pendennis.

"I have seen both of these men before," Rob said once the prisoners had been trussed up and deprived of their knives. "One I saw along the Harroway, and that second fellow and two others spent the night in the stable where I found shelter on the road to Glastonbury. They sat up late, drinking and dicing and telling tales, and he recounted the story of Cleopatra, who rolled herself in a carpet in order to meet Julius Caesar. I had heard of that trick at school, but I'd never have thought to hide myself inside Lady Pendennis's tapestry if he'd not reminded me of it."

Clever, Nick silently acknowledged, *and if Rob had not taken the suggestion, they'd no doubt have devised some other scheme to incline Susanna to trust the seer.* "Did he also roll the tapestry against the side of the cart so that you were trapped inside and near died?"

Rob frowned. "It was not until the cart stopped at the George that the tapestry shifted."

Nick drew the lad aside. "Tell me, Rob—were there others who endeavored to assist you along the way? People who helped you stay out of sight as you followed us westward?"

Rob's answer confirmed Nick's suspicions. It seemed likely the boy had been watched over all the way from Leigh Abbey.

"You are in a perilous position," Nick said, addressing his captives. "You could be sentenced to be hanged for holding a gentlewoman for ransom."

Sullen silence greeted this statement.

"Fortunately for you, I am not the sort to hold a grudge, and it is obvious you are only obeying the orders of the woman who employs you. So here is what I propose: you tell me all you know, including the location of your prisoner, and I will petition the queen for pardons on your behalf."

He'd not wager money that they'd be granted, but that scarce mattered. Time was of the essence. He needed directions and he needed them quickly, in case Mistress Amadas decided a living prisoner was more trouble than she was worth. Now that the ransom notes had been written, she might think she no longer needed Susanna in order to collect the money.

The bigger of the two prisoners turned to Nick's man Simon. "Is your master a magistrate?"

"Not yet," he replied, "but he'll be appointed a justice of the peace by the next quarter sessions. The letter about it arrived just before we left Kent."

For once Nick was glad there were no secrets from servants. The prisoner agreed to lead them to Susanna.

"How many more of you are there?" Nick asked a short time later, just after they started down a path with delicate scree on either side.

"Two men and the widow."

"Lady Appleton do you mean?"

"The other one—Jowser's widow. She's the one come up with this plan. She's the one to blame."

"What has she against Lady Appleton?"

"Summat to do with Jowser dying in gaol," the smaller man said.

For the first time, Susanna's maidservant, who had been hanging on every word, spoke up. "The woman at the inn was not named Jowser."

"Her husband called himself Jowser. That's all I know. He made us call the woman 'mistress.'" He hawked and spat, then grinned. "Had grand ideas, did Jowser, till he got himself sentenced for selling Bristol crystals for diamonds."

Nick frowned, remembering that Rob had mentioned overhearing a reference to Bristol crystals in connection with Rosamond. "The magistrate in the case, I warrant, was Sir Walter Pendennis."

"Aye."

Further questions yielded no useful information. Their employer gave orders without explanation and paid her men well to carry them out.

After a treacherous passage over on slippery rocks and through a stretch of anemone-filled woods, they reached the entrance to a cave. It opened out into a cavern of immense proportions, but it was empty of life. Even the horses that should have been there were missing.

Nick's fear that they'd killed Susanna and left her body behind was only allayed after he descended a rope ladder and searched the lower part of the cavern. "Was Lady Appleton bound?" he asked once he ascended.

The villains admitted that they'd untied her, thinking her naught but a woman, and one with a limp and getting on in years besides.

Nick strode back out into the sunlight with a grim expression on his face. That old injury to her leg would not slow her down if she was determined to get away. She had escaped. That much seemed clear. Her captors had doubtless gone in pursuit.

She'd go up, he thought, and stay out in the open rather than risk being trapped, and she'd attempt to return to Glastonbury, hoping to find him there.

A rocky prominence rose above him, whence one could see out over the gorge and across all the low-lying Somerset countryside to the south. Without hesitation, Nick headed that way.

At first they rode through mixed woodland. Oaks, alders, and willows were native to the Mendips. White banks of ransoms broke the green of the trees. Once, he caught sight of a hare, a sandy, black-pointed creature most unlike his reddish cousins in Kent. Of signs that Susanna had passed this way he found none.

It was not until they were climbing in the open again that Nick saw a flash of light ahead. As he watched, it was repeated at erratic intervals. He was no seer, but he knew with a certainty that Susanna was behind the signal.

* * *

Wary of remaining too close to the edge of the cliff, Susanna backed away with the Bristol crystals clutched in one hand. Many-faceted without being shaped by a jeweler, they were as brilliant as real diamonds.

She swayed a little in the hot sun. She needed to stay in the open so she could see anyone who approached, but lack of sleep and the injuries she'd sustained during the last twenty-four hours had left her weak and dizzy. She felt over-warm. It was only with difficulty that she kept her focus.

It had been a risk using the crystals in an attempt to catch Nick's attention. The flashes would also have been clearly visible to Elizabeth Amadas and her henchmen. Susanna had no doubt they were pursuing her. They'd have come after her as soon as the guard revived and lowered the ladder.

Susanna would have taken it away with her if she'd had the strength, but it had taken all her energy to haul it up after she'd dealt with the guard. Only the fact that he'd been intent on currying his horse, humming to the beast as he worked, had allowed her sneak up behind him and strike him on the head with a rock. She'd considered taking one of the horses, but given the terrain, she'd decided she'd make better time on foot. Belatedly, she'd realized she should have driven them off so that her pursuers could not use them either.

The climb to her present location had been fraught with difficulty. For the most part she'd tried to ignore the dramatic view of the gorge below and concentrate on placing her feet safely on a steep, narrow path that took her through trees and ferns, boulders and scree to the top of an escarpment. Pausing for breath, she'd looked off to the south, in the direction she supposed Glastonbury must lie. The only habitation she'd been able to make out were a smattering of pudding stone cottages. She'd been considering how to reach them when she'd looked back the way she'd come and there, far below, caught sight of a familiar green cloak. Nick was searching for her.

Of Elizabeth, she'd seen no sign, but she was certain the other woman was nearby. She wanted to stay out in the open and wait for Nick. He'd reach this point eventually, even if he had not seen her signal, but so might Elizabeth, in which case it would be exceeding foolish to remain where she was.

Susanna was tired and hurting. She lacked the stamina to reach the village she'd seen. Even though she was aware she was not thinking clearly, and might be making a fatal mistake, she chose to walk to the nearest tree, a spindly ash, and sit down in the small pool of shade beneath its branches.

She watched butterflies and grasshoppers, and once caught sight of a roe deer, while enjoying the profusion of herbs and flowers that grew in the meadow. In the woods, even in flight, she had recognized lily of the valley and Solomon's seal. Now she had time to appreciate others—saxifrage, self heal, blue groomwell, and ox-eye daisies. Birdsong soothed her. There were nests nearby—black-tailed godwit, lapwing, redshank, and bullfinches, who went by the local name of "whoops." Far overhead, a kestrel flew past.

With a start, Susanna realized she was close to drifting into sleep in the warmth of the summer day. She struggled upright, bracing her back against the bark, just as the first party of searchers appeared at the top of the prominence.

Face livid, Elizabeth Amadas drove her horse straight toward Susanna, clearly meaning to run her down. Susanna willed herself not to flinch. She moved only at the last possible moment, opening her hand so that the crystals concealed in her fist reflected the sun.

Blinded by the sudden glare, the horse reared in panic and threw its rider. Before Elizabeth could recover, Susanna seized hold of the smaller woman and used every bit of strength she possessed to jerk her erstwhile captor's arms behind her. Holding Elizabeth like a shield, Susanna faced the woman's henchmen, but by then they had lost interest in helping their employer.

Nick had arrived.

A few moments later, held close in her lover's embrace, Susanna felt a quiet elation fill her. Not only had she survived, she had triumphed.

"Let me take care of you," he whispered when she stirred in his arms. "I'll see to everything."

She smiled up at him but shook her head. She would need to sleep soon, and for a good long time, and she hoped he'd be beside her when she did, but there was something she had to settle first. It could not be delegated to anyone else.

Hands bound behind her, guarded by Nick's men, Elizabeth Amadas was not in a good mood. She cursed Susanna and spat at Nick. Standing out of range, they conferred. Nick told Susanna what he'd deduced. She shared with him what little Elizabeth had revealed in the cavern.

"I believe I know the rest." She spoke loudly enough for the prisoner to hear every word. "When Elizabeth's husband died in gaol, she vowed to take revenge on Walter Pendennis, who had sent him there. To carry out her scheme, she became part of his household."

"Undetected by him?" Nick asked in astonishment. Sir Walter Pendennis had once been one of Queen Elizabeth's most formidable intelligence gatherers—a master among spies.

"I doubt he knew anything about her, and she would have used an alias. One of Rosamond's recent letters included an account of her mother's ongoing search for a suitable waiting gentlewoman. Several of them have been taken on, but none lasted long. Rosamond gave no names, but she described one as being as tiny as one of the fairy folk."

"You can prove nothing," Elizabeth said.

Susanna met her fulminating gaze. "Shall we take you to Cornwall with us and see if Eleanor Pendennis recognizes you? I do not imagine you were there long, but you would have heard, from servants' gossip if not from observation, that Walter and his wife have a tempestuous relationship. You must have feared that if you kidnapped her, he might tell you to keep her and you'd get neither ransom nor the satisfaction of depriving him of a much-loved spouse."

Nick swore under his breath.

Susanna ignored him. There was little either of them could do about Walter's continued affection for her, nor about what the Pendennis household thought of Walter's reconciliation with Eleanor.

"You decided that Sir Walter would be more willing to pay for my release than for that of his wife, and that by killing me after you had collected the ransom, you could hurt him even more."

The angry expression on Elizabeth's face deteriorated into a sneer. "He'll suffer for a time," she hissed. "I dispatched one of my men to Cornwall with a ransom note."

"Did you indeed? Then I fear you will be disappointed. Despite appearances, Walter would be far more devastated to lose his wife than me."

A sly look came into Elizabeth's eyes. "A pity, then, that she is the one behind all that has transpired. Lady Pendennis wants you dead, Lady Appleton. It was her idea to demand you bring her that tapestry and the other household goods in the cart. We planned together how you could be obliged to return to Cornwall to deliver those things to her in person."

"I might believe you," Susanna said, "but you have forgotten Rosamond. She is the real reason for my visit, and Eleanor knows that better than anyone."

"I forget nothing." It was very nearly a snarl.

"Ah, yes. You are a seer. You know everything."

"Curious, then," Nick said, "that she does not know that both her messengers were captured. They are in a small cave along the trail, securely bound."

When they collected the prisoners, Susanna learned the answer to her one remaining question. The smaller of the two men admitted he'd lived near Leigh Abbey for several months, sent by his mistress to spy on the household. There he had been told some of the old stories Susanna's grandmother had been wont to share. It had been the tale of Mistress Amadas, the one at the court of King Henry, that had inspired Elizabeth Jowser to pose as a fortune teller in order to lure Susanna away from the rest of her party.

"If she has any true skill as a seer," Susanna remarked after they'd turned the villains over to the local authorities in Glastonbury, retrieved their cart, and made their way to another inn for the night, "mayhap she knows already whether she'll end her days in prison or at the end of a rope."

As dangerous as Elizabeth was, it disturbed Susanna to think that she might die for her crimes. She had not, after all, killed anyone.

"I do not pretend to have supernatural powers," Nick said with a rueful chuckle, "but I believe I can predict the outcome of her trial. She had control of her temper by the time she came before the justice of the peace. He took one look at her and saw a delicate little flower of a woman. In that instant, he felt pity for her. By the time she returns to court, she'll have him eating out of the palm of her hand."

"Never tell me you think he will let her go!"

"I would not be surprised," Nick said, "if he ends up marrying her."

A Note from the Author

I've stayed at the George and Pilgrims in Glastonbury. It is reputed to have had, in its early days, a tunnel that led onto Glastonbury Abbey grounds. Unfortunately, if it ever existed, there is no trace of it today.

Bristol crystals are also called Bristol diamonds, Bristol stones, Bristowes, St. Vincent's rocks, Cornish diamonds, and Irish diamonds, depending on where they were found. They are rock crystals, usually colorless quartz. In the sixteenth century they were described as being as brilliant as real diamonds but without their inner fire, and were frequently found "counterfeiting precious stones." The cavern I've described does not exist, but it could. The landscape north and west of Glastonbury is dotted with caverns, caves, cliffs, and old mines.

This story first appeared in *Murders and Other Confusions* (2004). The events in *Face Down Below the Banqueting House* and *Face Down Beside St. Ann's Well* take place between this story and the next.

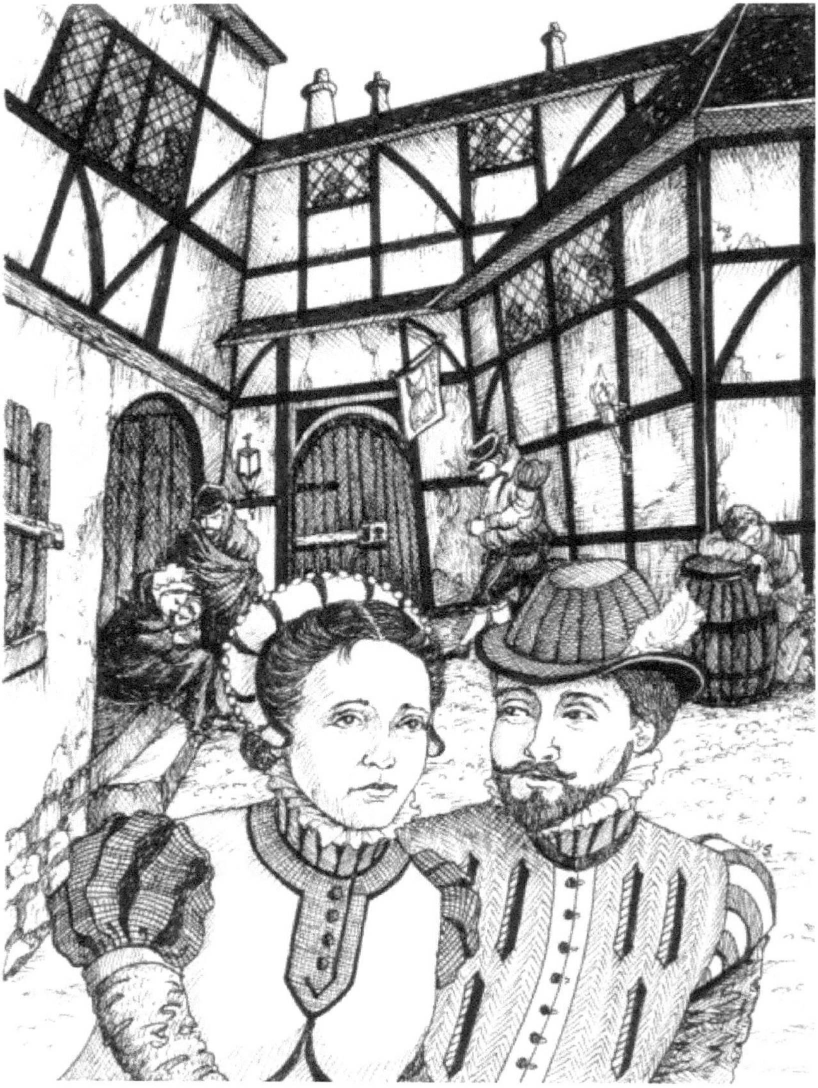

Encore for a Neck Verse

September 19, 1576

Alarmed by her companion's sudden stillness, Susanna, Lady Appleton, widowed gentlewoman of Leigh Abbey, Kent, looked up from a display of smallwares in front of a Dover haberdasher's shop. To her relief, the strongest emotion showing on Nick Baldwin's beloved face was bewilderment. Whatever had startled him did not present an immediate danger.

"Odd," Nick murmured. "The fellow coming out of that cookshop is the image of Stephen Bourne."

Susanna glanced in the direction of his gaze, although half her attention had already returned to the quill pens she was thinking of buying. A scarecrow-thin man all in gray, even to the feather in his bonnet, stopped to rotate his left shoulder, as if easing some old injury.

"Ho, there!" Nick shouted, advancing toward him.

"Do you address me, sir?" Spoken with a slight stammer, the words carried a suggestion of panic and Susanna thought she saw a flash of recognition in the fellow's wide-spaced brown eyes before he blanked his features.

Mayhap Nick did know him.

"Bourne?"

"Julius Woodward, at your service." Now stone-faced as a gargoyle, his stance was defiant.

"I crave your forgiveness. I mistook you for an Oundle man."

"Mappen the fellow looks like me, but Oundle means nowt, nor Bourne, neither. Good day to you, sir." With an abrupt nod, he continued on his way along Priory Road.

An expression of deep suspicion etched Nick's features as he watched Woodward pass the cemetery attached to the Maison Dieu, a hospital founded centuries earlier for the benefit of pilgrims passing through Dover, and disappear into the cross street by the little chapel dedicated to St. Edmund. "I warrant you will think me mad," he said to Susanna, "but I believe I have just seen a ghost."

"He looked passing solid for a spirit." She continued to contemplate the items set out on the haberdasher's pentice. Goodman Kelling offered a wide assortment of merchandise for sale, everything from pins and needles to mousetraps. The larger items—curtains, sheets, tablecloths, and even shifts and shirts and other bits of clothing—were displayed inside the shop.

"Aye." Nick did not sound convinced that he'd been wrong.

"It *is* possible for a man to have a double. Or a twin."

"One who denies he's ever heard of the market town of Oundle yet betrays with every word he speaks that he hails from Northamptonshire? Moreover, this Julius Woodward not only resembles Bourne in physical appearance, he favors the same colors, and he has, as Bourne did, what good Northamptonshire men call a maffle."

"The stammer?" She replaced the ornate little dagger she'd discovered between a lantern and a stack of almanacs and chapbooks and gave Nick her full attention.

"Aye. You're quick, as ever."

Nick's admiring smile warmed Susanna. They had been neighbors here in Kent for a long time, and friends, and sometimes more. She knew she was the only woman he had ever asked to marry him. She had turned him down, rejecting not his offer of love but the legal alliance that gave a husband complete control over both the person and the property of his wife. It was not that Susanna did not trust Nick. She simply saw no need to remarry. There were too many advantages to widowhood.

At times her adamant refusal to reconsider resulted in a certain strain between them, but she knew he had no doubt that she cared about him and she did not question his devotion to her. All in all, they muddled along well enough. She was not surprised when Nick escorted her into the cookshop Woodward had just left.

The proprietor sold meat pies and stews. There were several people waiting to buy. The air was redolent with garlic and onion.

"What reason would your Master Bourne have to hide his identity?" Susanna asked in a quiet voice.

"Bourne, alive, would have much to answer for, if the tale I heard at second hand from my housekeeper is true."

"Goodwife Billings?"

"Goodwife Chappell," Nick corrected her.

Susanna smiled. Through their combined efforts, she and Nick had made it possible for Mary Billings to remarry. Her second husband, Edward Chappell, served as steward at Candlethorpe, Nick's Northamptonshire estate.

"Time passes far too quickly," she murmured, performing rapid calculations.

It had been more than four and a half years since they'd found proof Goodman Billings was dead and, as an unexpected result of that investigation, sent a young woman and her newborn daughter to live at Candlethorpe. She had meant to visit Jane Johnson and her child long before this.

"Two of your best meat pies," Nick told the cookshop owner, proffering a rose noble, "and information."

The woman's eyes goggled at the value of the coin. A moment later it vanished beneath a none-too-clean apron.

Nick described Woodward, from his long, fitted rat's-color fustian doublet with its close-set buttons, to his scuffed leather boots, to the way he combed his hair forward at the front to form a short fringe over the forehead. "And he has a tuft of hair on the point of his chin," he finished. "Do you remember him?"

"Pencil beard and him all in dull gray? Aye, I know him. Woodward, his name is. He and his wife have a room at Molly Greene's victualing house." The woman grinned, showing a profusion of gaps where teeth had once been. "That's why he's been buying food from me. Molly's the worst cook in all of Kent."

"What does Woodward's wife look like?" Nick leaned a little forward as his interest quickened.

"No bulk to her. Dark-hair. Big eyes."

"Doe-like," Nick murmured.

At the description, Susanna sent a sharp look in his direction, but she refrained from asking questions until they left the cookshop. They took with them two savory meat pies and directions to the victualing house where Woodward and his wife had lodgings.

"This Bourne," Susanna said as they walked, munching. "I take it he is supposed to be dead?" The meat pie was very good indeed, containing tiny bits of shin of beef mixed with herbs and spices and generous chunks of carrot, white cabbage, celery, leeks, and parsnips.

"Murdered, according to Goodwife Chappell."

Susanna felt her eyebrows climb.

"In the same letter, which I received some months past, she also informed me that his killer had been caught. The Assizes are over for the year, Susanna. Those condemned for felonies have long since been hanged for their crimes. If Woodward *is* Bourne, an innocent man was executed."

"Might the man accused of killing Master Bourne have been allowed benefit of clergy?" Susanna was well aware that some convicted felons escaped hanging by reciting the so-called "neck verse."

"A man who steals may be branded on the hand and discharged if he has his books, as they say, but murder is excluded from the statutory qualifications for grants of clergy." Nick, a justice of the peace in Kent, had made a study of the current laws concerning such things.

Susanna, too, had reason to be familiar with the statutes on murder, but in her experience, a bribe could either subvert justice or secure it.

"There are exceptions," she reminded Nick, "and pardons." The latter were the only official recourse for women convicted of a felony, since women were specifically denied benefit of clergy.

He shook his head. "I cannot think of any reason why the two crown judges who ride the Midland Circuit would agree to free a convicted murderer."

"Then if Goodman Woodward is Goodman Bourne, a man died for a crime he could not have committed and there has been a great miscarriage of justice."

"Aye, and it seems all too possible Bourne *is* alive, for there was never any body found."

Susanna missed her footing on the cobblestones and stumbled. "How can that be? What other proof of murder would a jury accept?"

Nick caught her elbow to steady her. "Remains were discovered in Rockingham Forest. Some animal had been at them, leaving only a few bones and some scraps of clothing, but those bits were deemed sufficient to identify Stephen Bourne."

A passerby, overhearing, sent him a startled look before hurrying on.

Nick ignored him. "Having seen Julius Woodward, I must wonder if that judgment was warranted."

Susanna polished off the last of her meat pie. "Did Bourne have a wife?"

"Not his own. Stephen Bourne was a haberdasher in Oundle, the market town nearest Candlethorpe. He dealt in the same sort of smallwares Goodman Kelling stocks. As is not uncommon in rural towns, where the great livery companies that regulate such things in London are not so strong, a merchant may also offer goods not strictly within his province. Bourne had long been in competition with one Barnaby Morrison, a mercer by trade, selling shifts and shirts, cloth and clothing, and cheap bone lace. Morrison, although he styled himself a clothier and sneered at Bourne as naught but a petty chapman, himself sold smallwares in addition to woolen clothing and Italian silks and velvets."

Susanna wiped her mouth with a handkerchief and made a futile effort to remove all the grease from her hands. Nick was engaged in a similar exercise, also fruitless. "So the wife you spoke of was Morrison's?"

"Aye. They both courted her, or so I am told. Morrison married her. When Bourne vanished, so did Clementine Morrison. At first everyone assumed they'd run off together. Then a hogherd made his grisly discovery. Of the missing wife there was no trace. Her husband, to no one's surprise, was arrested and accused of killing them both."

They had reached Goodwife Greene's victualing house, one of more than two dozen such establishments in Dover. Like Dover's inns, they offered beds for travelers at a modest fee.

Goodwife Greene was in her garden, busy hauling wet sheets out of a wicker basket and draping them on bushes to dry. The color of Nick's money persuaded her to tell them all she knew about Julius Woodward and his wife. To Susanna's disappointment, it was very little.

"Pretty little thing, she is," Goodwife Greene said as Susanna helped her spread the last of the laundry over a clump of privet, "but sharp-tongued. Be dunked for a scold, she will, if she be not careful."

"And her husband?" Susanna asked.

"Dour, as the Scots say. They stayed at the Angel when they first arrived. That was late in April, as I recall. A few weeks later, they came to me."

Further questions elicited that Woodward had no visible means of support but no lack of ready money and that, at the moment, both husband and wife were abroad in the town. Another coin overcame any scruples Goodwife Greene might have about letting Nick and Susanna into her lodgers' chamber. Pocketing it, she led the way up a winding stair, smiling all the way.

When Susanna saw how small and bare the room was, she felt a reluctant twinge of sympathy for lovers forced to flee their homes in order to be together. She knew firsthand the difficulties of living in an unhappy marriage, as well as the painful joy of falling in love with someone she could not wed. On the other hand, she'd been faithful to her husband as long as he'd lived. She believed in keeping vows. If the two living here were Stephen Bourne and Clementine Morrison, they did not.

Nick had not said so, but the determined way he set about searching the lodgings made Susanna certain he believed Bourne had intended that Morrison be blamed for his death and executed. She doubted he'd find proof of his theory, but she helped him look. If he was right, what Bourne had done amounted to cold-blooded murder.

A chest contained changes of linen and a few other items of clothing, supporting the idea that the couple had fled their former lives in haste. Lifting each layer with great care, so that the disturbance would not be obvious, Nick came, at the very bottom, to a packet wrapped in cloth and fastened with a ribbon. When he untied it, a chapbook tumbled out. Nick examined it before passing it to Susanna.

"*A Warning to Wise Men*," she read aloud from the title page, "*being an account of unlucky days and what to avoid on them.*"

Well-thumbed pages indicated someone regularly consulted the cheaply-bound volume.

Goodwife Greene gave a derisive snort. "I am not surprised he'd have such a thing. Always gloom and doom with that one. Why only last week, when I broke a fingernail and he saw me clipping off the jagged edge, he told me I should have left it be. Bad luck to cut nails on a Friday, he said."

Susanna sent a questioning glance Nick's way, but he shook his head. "I did not know him well enough to say if Bourne was superstitious."

"Every almanac I've ever seen lists unlucky days, and always different ones. A man who believes in all of them would have difficulty finding a safe time to begin a new venture." Had Bourne consulted an astrologer, she wondered, to help him choose the best date on which to disappear?

They replaced the contents of the chest, careful to leave everything just as it had been. The rest of the room yielded nothing of interest.

They went next to the Angel, distinguished from other Dover inns by the fact that it lacked stabling for travelers' horses. No one there remembered anyone named Woodward, nor did a description of the couple spark recollections. Since Dover was the main stopping point for travelers to and from the Continent, hundreds of people had broken their journey at the Angel since April.

By the time Susanna and Nick left the inn, the afternoon was well advanced. They would have to leave Dover soon if they hoped to reach Susanna's home at Leigh Abbey and Nick's house, neighboring Whitethorn Manor, before dark. The distance was not great, only seven miles, but an uncommon wet summer and autumn had made a quagmire of the road and more water dogs now filled the sky. These small floating clouds reliably foretold rain.

"What now?" Susanna asked. "We've found no proof that Woodward and Bourne are the same man. Would you recognize Morrison's wife?"

Nick shook his head. "All I know of her appearance comes from hearsay. It was Mary Chappell's husband, Edward, who told me she had doe's eyes. He said she was the best looking woman in Oundle, but as far as I know I never met either Goodwife Morrison or her husband."

"Will you stay in Dover and confront them with your suspicions?"

"To what purpose? Even if I am right, it is far too late to save Morrison's life." Nick gave a bitter laugh. "Indeed, just think what the probable outcome will be if I tell Bourne that Morrison was charged with his murder, convicted, and executed. He will thank me, for I will have done him good service. He can express surprise and horror at the news, abandon his false identity, marry his mistress, and return to Oundle to lay claim to her first husband's estate."

At the inn where they'd stabled their horses, Susanna waited until Nick sent the ostler to saddle them before she asked him what he planned to do instead.

"I cannot ignore the possibility that the two of them, Stephen Bourne and Clementine Morrison, plotted to have her husband blamed for a crime he did not commit. It may be a futile effort on my part, but I will go to Northamptonshire and learn all I can about the case. At the least, I may be able to prevent them from profiting from Morrison's death."

"I believe," Susanna said after a long, thoughtful pause, "that I will go with you. I should like to visit Jane and her baby. I am, after all, the child's godmother."

* * *

A week later, at Stilton, accompanied by a few servants and a packhorse, Susanna and Nick abandoned the main road from London to Stamford and the safe numbers of a larger party for the less well-traveled track to Oundle. Since it was too late in the day to stop there, Susanna gleaned little more than an impression of houses, church, and market cross before they rode on into woodland thick with oak and beech. Nick identified it as the Forest of Cliffe, part of the Royal Forest of Rockingham.

"The queen came here once to hunt deer," he added.

"Fallow deer could not reduce a man to a few bones and bits of cloth."

"There are also badgers, foxes, wild boar, and herds of pigs left free to fatten on acorns and beechmast."

Susanna shuddered. Both the boar and its domestic cousin the pig would eat *anything*.

"If we are correct in our suppositions," Nick said, "the bones discovered in this forest did not belong to Stephen Bourne."

Susanna studied her surroundings. "In this terrain, those bones might never have been found."

"If the hogherd had not stumbled across them, a verderer, one of the judicial officers of the Royal Forests, would have, but by tradition, criminal or civil pleas are heard in common law courts even if they originate in the forest. The local justices of the peace are George Lynne of Southwick and Edmund Brudenell of Deene Park. Southwick lies yonaway, as they say in these parts—yonder, at a distance, with Bulwick and Candlethorpe beyond. Deene Park is a mile or so on the other side of Candlethorpe."

They reached Nick's manor in late afternoon and received an effusive welcome from Mary Chappell. Jane Johnson's greeting was quieter, but Susanna was delighted with the progress she and her daughter had made under Mary's care. Jane, who had the mind of a child herself, had learned to use a loom and had woven several beautiful pieces, which she insisted upon showing her benefactor within moments of Susanna's arrival. Little Susanna Johnson, when she was finally persuaded to come out from behind her mother's skirts, proved to be sweet-tempered and very bright. Susanna made a mental note to provide her with tutors as soon as she was old enough for schooling.

"A dimpsy lass and mild as a moon beam, but a handful all the same," Mary Chappell said of the girl when she'd shooed the others away and taken sole possession of Susanna to escort her to the well-appointed guest chamber where she would sleep. The windows overlooked fields full of grazing sheep. "You'll be wanting to refresh yourself while the master talks with my Yed'ard."

It took Susanna a moment to translate Yed'ard into Edward, Mary's husband and Nick's steward. Meanwhile, Mary bustled about, checking to be certain there was fresh water for washing and expressing her delight that the master planned to be at Candlethorpe for Pack Rag Day.

"Pack Rag Day?" Susanna echoed in a dubious voice.

"Michaelmas, you'd call it, when the year's service ends and servants who mean to move on pack up all their belongings to take away."

When a great racket broke out in the courtyard below, Mary rushed to the window and threw the shutters wide. "Stop that wouking!" she shouted. "Waffling cur! Belike he's after one of the cats." After the barking subsided into what Mary called a yaffle, she turned again to Susanna. "I'd fain have you ask if there be summat you're needing."

"I need answers to questions," Susanna confided. "A visit with Jane and her child was not the only reason we came here at this time."

"Twa'n't? Well, you may speak plain to me." Expectation writ large on her friendly countenance, she plunked herself down on the window seat. A moment later a sleek gray cat joined her to settle on her lap.

"We have come about the murder of Stephen Bourne. What can you tell me of Bourne and the Morrisons?"

Although startled—belatedly, Susanna realized the housekeeper had expected an inquiry of the sort a future mistress might conduct—Mary willingly recounted all she knew about Bourne's disappearance and that of Goodwife Morrison.

"Fig Sunday, it were. Palm Sunday, you'd say, but so called in these parts because it is the custom to eat figs on that day."

The more she talked, all the while stroking the cat, the easier it was for Susanna to translate her Northamptonshire dialect. The cat closed its bright topaz eyes and purred accompaniment while she revealed that when the bones were found in the wood, Goodman Morrison had sworn his wife killed Bourne and fled in panic.

"All the world and Little Billing knows Morrison did it," she said in a scornful voice. "He was a great gulshing fellow with a blob lip who always looked as if the black ox had trod on his toe."

The world and Little Billing, which Susanna presumed was a local village, also believed it likely that Morrison, enraged by his discovery that his wife had run off with Stephen Bourne, had followed them, caught them, and slain them both.

"They do say Bourne were her sprunny when they were young," Mary went on. "He courted her when he was yet an unlicked cub, but they quarreled over summat and when they'd burnt their writings, she married Barnaby Morrison, belike for spite. She were ever twea faced. Or mappen 'twas for money. He came here from away to take over a cousin's business, but he brought wealth with him."

"Did Morrison beat his wife or mistreat her in any other way?"

Mary shook her head. Gently she extracted the cat's claws from her apron. "Mind your manners, Greymalkin," she murmured.

"Then I am surprised no one took Morrison's claim more seriously," Susanna said. "Surely women are capable of murder."

"Clementine Morrison nettles up, no doubt of that, but why should she kill her lover and leave his body for the animals? A man's a good thing to have along on a journey."

Susanna could not argue with her logic. "So Morrison was arrested and taken off to trial in Northampton."

"Aye. Sir Edmund saw to that, for all that Morrison was distant kin to his steward at Deene Park."

"Sir Edmund Brudenell, the justice of the peace?"

"Aye. Married a rich heiress, he did, and was unfaithful to her from the start. Fine example that sets!"

Most assuredly, Susanna thought, *we must pay a visit to Sir Edmund Brudenell.* In the meantime, having changed her dusty traveling clothes for clean garments and washed her hands and face while Mary talked, she was ready to rejoin Nick.

"Master admires to go awalking," Mary said when Susanna asked where he might be found. "No doubt he's gone out adoors."

With Greymalkin following in her wake, Susanna located Nick and Yed'ard by the eastern wall, staring at a distant glow and haze of smoke. Nick smiled when he caught sight of her and bent to scratch the cat's head, receiving a nuzzle in return.

"What is burning?" Susanna asked. Nick's composure assured her it was not a house or, worse, an entire village.

"Stubble in the Fens. It is set alight every year at about this time. It may appear as if the marshes themselves are on fire, but there is no real danger."

He dismissed his steward after giving detailed instructions for repairs he wanted made. "Hire a carpenter from Bulwick if you need to for the work on the stable," he added, "and see that there are day men enough to do the plashing."

Susanna studied the hedges Nick meant to have the day men work on. Whitethorn, hazel, crab-apple, and holly would be carefully thinned of their wood and the remaining branches bent double and intertwined so that, in the spring, the growth would be twice as thick. Plashing was an effective way to control extensive flocks of sheep.

Nick slung an arm around Susanna's waist and pointed to the sky as the sun dropped below the horizon. "Watch just there and you'll soon see the shepherd's lamp."

As she waited for that first star to rise after sunset, Susanna summarized what Mary had told her.

"Chappell predicted his wife would be splatherdabbing, as he put it. She's a long-tongue of the first order, he says, and would do better to confine herself to her duties as my potwabbler."

Susanna fought a smile and lost. "Was there any detail Mary missed?"

"The location of the bones. Chappell says they were in a squeech—that's a wet, boggy place—just halfway between Oundle and Southwick and near the forest track. He also told me that Sir Edmund Brudenell is away from Deene Park at present."

"So we return to Oundle tomorrow?"

"Aye, and until then let us think of more pleasant things. Shall we go in and sup? Chappell tells me we are to have whispering pudding—that's plum pudding with many plums, as opposed to hooting pudding, in which plums are few and far between—and squab pie."

Susanna wrinkled her nose. "I am not fond of pigeons."

Nick laughed. "You will be pleased, then, to know that there are no birds in a Northamptonshire squab pie. It is made with apples, onions, and fat bacon."

* * *

On the way to Oundle the next day, Nick and Susanna stopped once, at the squeech Edward Chappell had described. There was nothing to see.

It was not yet noon when they crossed the north bridge over the Nene and entered the market town. Nick pointed out Morrison's house, now claimed by the Crown. It had been seized and its contents inventoried, but as yet no one had moved into the shop or the lodgings above. The windows were boarded up and the doors locked.

They located the constable, chosen from the citizens of the town to serve for one year, hard at work in his glover's shop. Josias Rutter continued cutting a piece of cheveril, the soft and flexible kid-skin used to make fine gloves, as he answered Nick's questions. His replies added nothing to their knowledge except the fact that the remains had been identified as Bourne's by the bits of rat's-color cloth found with them.

"He favored dull gray," Rutter said, shaking his head at Bourne's odd preference.

And still does, Susanna thought, recalling the man they'd met in Dover.

"There must have been more than that to prove the remnants belonged to Bourne."

"There were a bit of a glove too, one of mine own making. No other glover in the county makes stitches the way I do."

Faced with Rutter's unshakable conviction that the remains had been Stephen Bourne's, Nick offered Susanna his arm to escort her out of the shop.

"Han ye no desire to see the bones?" the glover asked.

"You have them here?"

"The cloth were ta'an to Northampton for the trial, but they did leave the bones with me." Rutter set aside his knife and rubbed his hands together, an avaricious gleam in his rheumy eyes. "Accounted a wonder, they bist. 'Twill cost ye ha'penny a peep to look at them."

The broken and discolored bones they were shown were not human.

"Cow?" Susanna speculated once they were away from the glover's shop.

"Or mayhap deer. Not Bourne. That much is certain."

It might have been a clumsy attempt to make Bourne appear dead, but it had worked. On the journey back to Candlethorpe, Susanna and Nick discussed what to do next.

"Bourne wanted to be certain no one would search for him," Susanna said.

"Yes," Nick agreed, "but was there another, more sinister motive? There was no love lost between them. It may have been his goal all along to have Morrison blamed and executed. Shall we travel to Northampton tomorrow and see what we can learn about the trial?"

Susanna readily agreed, but with the dawn came news that Stephen Bourne had returned to Oundle.

"Alive and well," Mary informed them while they broke their fast. She'd learned the details from a peddler who'd arrived from Oundle at sunrise to mend the pots. "He's admitted to leaving cow bones in the forest to be found. The searchers were supposed to think wild animals killed him and Morrison's wife so they could take theirsels off to London and beyond. She's come back with him, the brazen creature, claiming they're newly wed. By my life," she declared, "here be much wickedness!"

*　*　*

Morrison's house in Oundle was no longer boarded up, although the shop was still closed. Through an open door, Susanna studied Clementine Morrison, now Clementine Bourne, as she gave orders to two harried-looking servants. The woman had a striking appearance and was most forceful in her manner. The slaps she dispensed along with her commands did not appear to be necessary to hasten packing.

Bourne came out of the alley next to the shop just as Nick and Susanna were about to announce themselves.

"Are you Julius Woodward today?" Nick inquired in a polite voice, "or Stephen Bourne?"

Overhearing, Clementine dispensed with witnesses by sending the servants to the upper floor and drew Nick, Susanna, and Bourne inside. "Master Baldwin, I presume, and this would be Lady Appleton, your mistress. You are both well known in Dover. One might even say notorious."

Susanna caught Nick's arm to forestall an angry retort. Clementine's words cut too close to the truth.

"Why are you here?" Bourne asked.

"Curiosity," Susanna said before Nick could speak. "You did not want your true identity known when Nick recognized you in Dover."

"Not then. No. But a letter arrived soon after we met." Bourne's stammer intensified along with his nervousness.

"Do you meant to tell me that someone knew you were still alive and where to write to you?"

"Clementine had written to a cousin to ask him what happened after she left. She made no mention of me."

"A cousin in Oundle?"

"Peterborough," Clementine said. "You could ask him yourself, but he's just left on a long voyage."

Convenient, Susanna thought, *and difficult to disprove.*

"We did not know I was a widow until that letter arrived. When it did, we were at last free to marry, and did so before traveling to Northamptonshire."

"Where you hope to reclaim your late husband's estate," Susanna said.

"It was wrongfully confiscated by the Crown." Angered by the question, Clementine strode to the door and flung it open. "If your curiosity had been satisfied, madam, I'd fain have you leave. We have much to do before we depart again on the morrow."

A voice spoke from the street beyond. "I fear that will be impossible, madam, until you have answered certain charges laid against you."

While every bit of color drained from Bourne's face, Clementine confronted the speaker, her eyes narrowing to slits. "You are not the constable. What is it you want, sirrah? What charges do you speak of?"

The two men at the door were churchwardens, come to inform the newly married couple that because, before their nuptials, they had committed the sin of adultery, they must appear before the church court. They would be ordered to do penance before the entire congregation.

Susanna should have felt sympathy for the other woman, having once been threatened with similar charges before a church court herself, but she had never betrayed a husband, not by making a cuckold of him, or by devising a plot that would take his life.

Clementine showed no remorse or shame, only irritation that she would not be permitted to leave town as soon as she wished.

"You should not have insisted on beginning the packing, Clementine," Bourne whined as they were taken away. "I told you this was one of the unlucky days."

* * *

As Susanna expected, Clementine and Bourne appeared before the archdeacon and were sentenced to do penance on the seventh of October, the Sunday following their hearing.

"A generous bribe could not reduce their sentence," Nick informed her, "but no doubt it hastened the date of their public humiliation. Once their penance is completed, they will be on their way with Morrison's fortune. I wish I could think of some way, before they leave Oundle, to force them to confess to plotting to bring about his death."

"The seventh of October," Susanna repeated. "I seem to recall something about that date. Have you an almanac?"

Nick produced one and opened it to the list of unlucky days, but Susanna surprised him by thumbing through the little volume in search of something quite different. "As I thought," she murmured. "There is an eclipse of the moon that night. It should last from nine o'clock until just past one in the morning. I believe I know a way to trick Bourne into confessing what he and Clementine did to Morrison."

The sound of approaching riders interrupted her before she could explain. Nick glanced out a window into the courtyard below and announced that the newcomers were Sir Edmund Brudenell and a liveried servant. A few moments later, two cloaked and gloved men were shown into Candlethorpe's parlor and Brudenell was revealed to be a confident, prosperous looking fellow nearing his sixtieth year.

"I hear you have been asking questions about Stephen Bourne and Barnaby Morrison," he said after Nick presented him to Susanna.

Nick summarized what they'd discovered and their conclusions. Then, before Brudenell could comment, Susanna detailed the plan she'd been about to outline for Nick.

At first Brudenell looked skeptical, but by the time she'd finished a faint smile curved the corners of his thin mouth. He swiveled his head to locate his servant. "Morrison, come here!" At their startled looks, the smile broadened. "You will have heard my steward was kin to the accused?"

Susanna studied the thin, unhealthy looking man with Brudenell's sea-horse crest on his sleeve. He shambled forward at his master's command. Although he kept his head tucked in like a turtle, she could make out a lower lip so full it seemed to hang down over his chin—the "blob lip" Mary Chappell had spoken of. Apparently, like the big ears that ran in some families and the prominent teeth that descended through others, this was a Morrison trait.

"You heard what they told me," Brudenell said to his man. "It seems only right that you should help them avenge the wrong done to Barnaby Morrison."

"To play on Bourne's superstitious nature," Susanna said, "all you need do is let him think you are your cousin come back from the dead."

"I am nowhere near the fine figure of a man her husband was when Clementine left him," Morrison objected.

A great gulshing fellow, Mary Chappell had called him. In other words, he'd been fat.

"Well, then," Susanna said, "you must stuff your clothes with straw, for it is clear you are the best one here to impersonate Barnaby Morrison's ghost."

* * *

On Sunday, Susanna and Nick attended evening prayers at the church in Oundle. The penitents stood on two stools in the middle aisle near the pulpit, clad in white sheets. They were bareheaded and barefoot and held white rods. As they had at morning and afternoon services, Bourne and Clementine again confessed to the sin of adultery.

Susanna watched Bourne's face as he stammered out the intimate details and asked God's forgiveness. To judge by the dark circles under his eyes, he had not slept well. She wondered if he felt true remorse or simply regretted being caught.

Clementine maintained a haughty demeanor throughout her penance. Unbeaten, unbowed, unrepentant, she voiced her confession by rote, looking neither left nor right. She might be forced to endure humiliation, but she saw no reason to be humble about it.

The decision of the archdeacon's court required that they remain on their stools for the remainder of the service and stay in the church after the rest of the congregation had left. Sir Edmund's influence had been instrumental in arranging that. They would not be permitted to depart until just before nine, and then only to be taken to what they'd been told was the unmarked grave of the man they had wronged.

Susanna, Nick, and Morrison were in place in the boneyard well before Bourne and Clementine came out of the church. In truth, there was no grave. Those executed in Northampton were buried there as well, but Bourne and Clementine did not know that.

Susanna's plan was simple. Just as the eclipse of the moon began, Morrison's "ghost" would appear, accusing Bourne from beyond the grave. If the haberdasher was as superstitious as everyone seemed to think, he would panic and blurt out the truth.

The penitents, still in their white sheets, arrived on schedule, accompanied by Sir Edmund Brudenell, the vicar, and two churchwardens. At first everything went according to plan. Barnaby Morrison's kinsman appeared in the moonlight, convincingly rotund. Both Bourne and Clementine gasped when they caught sight of a face with a blob lip.

"Get you gone, Barnaby!" Clementine shrieked. "You are dead and must stay in the ground. Can you do nothing right?"

"You were never satisfied," Morrison shouted back, "not even when I tried my best to please you."

Susanna stiffened. That was not what he'd been told to say.

A moment later, he returned to the plan, accusing them of the crime and relating the details Nick and Susanna had worked out.

Bourne broke down, haunted by his own guilt. "Yes. Yes," he sobbed. "It is as you say."

"Be silent, you fool!" Clementine's shrill voice nearly drowned out Bourne's words. "You did nothing."

The "ghost" turned on her, advancing with gloved hands outstretched. "Aye. It was you, Clementine. Your plan. Your hatred. And you are the one who must suffer for it. Prison is bad, Clementine. Hanging is worse, but a woman who plots her husband's death will be burnt for it."

He was too close! Afraid Clementine would be able to tell this was no ghost, Susanna started forward, but before she could intervene, Clementine attacked. She rushed at Morrison with a cry of rage, clawing at his face.

He dodged the raking nails, bringing one arm up to protect himself. Flailing, her fingers caught his glove. When Sir Edmund seized her from behind and pulled her away, the soft leather slipped off Morrison's hand. The diminishing moonlight was still bright enough for Susanna to see the letter "M" branded on his thumb.

Stunned, she stared at it. This man was not Morrison's cousin the steward. He was Barnaby Morrison. Alive.

In heavy silence broken only by the distant hooting of an owl, the steady diminution of light continued, dissolving the brand into shadow. Then one of the churchwardens lit a lantern.

Clementine found her voice first. "How did you escape the gallows?"

It was Sir Edmund Brudenell who answered. "Murder may be excluded from the statutory qualifications for grants of clergy, but without a body, how can there be murder? A jury thought those bones sufficient evidence. The judges were not convinced, and Crown judges do not always feel obligated to respect the distinction between clergyable and non-clergyable felonies. Your husband was branded and freed rather than hanged because he could read the neck verse."

Rattled by this unexpected twist, Susanna struggled to make sense of it. She addressed Barnaby Morrison directly: "Why did you let everyone think you had been executed?"

"With my wife gone and all I owned forfeited to the Crown, I had no reason to return to Oundle." He glared at Clementine. "Then, too, I could guess who left the bones in the wood. I hoped Clementine would return one day and meant to avenge myself upon her when she did." He turned to Susanna. "I must thank you, Lady Appleton, for showing me the way."

"I knew he'd been freed," Brudenell admitted, "but I saw no need to tell anyone the outcome of the trial. Since he had lost so much weight in gaol and would scarce be recognized by his own mother, we deemed it safe for him to stay at Deene Park. Few people there have much to do with Oundle in any case. The market town of Kettering, which has more to offer, lies in the opposite direction."

Morrison continued to watch Clementine with an intensity Susanna found unnerving. "You failed, my love," he said in a chilling whisper, "and since Bourne plainly lives, that is proof I did not murder him. I can reclaim my property from the Crown. My suffering is over. Yours has just begun."

Some of her accustomed haughtiness returned. Standing straight in spite of Sir Edmund's restraining hand on her arm, she glared at her tormentor. "And yours will continue as long as you live. We are married, Barnaby. Tied together till death do us part. I swear to you now, before these witnesses, that I will make your life a living hell."

"I think not." He moved closer, until his face was only inches from hers, and spoke through gritted teeth. "You will be tried for attempting to arrange the death of your husband. That is petty treason. You will burn."

Still defiant, she sneered at him. "I will go free by reading the neck verse, just as you did."

In that she was mistaken. As Susanna had reason to know, the only circumstance under which a woman could plead benefit of clergy was if she had formerly been a nun.

Morrison did not share that knowledge. Believing his wife's claim and determined that the woman who had tried to kill him would not escape punishment, he seized her by the throat. Before anyone could react, let alone stop him, he had snapped her neck. Still holding her limp body, he turned to confront the horrified spectators.

"*That* for her neck verse!"

"Fool," Brudenell muttered. "She could not have used it, and now you cannot, either. Not a second time."

Brudenell and the constable led Morrison and Bourne away, leaving the churchwardens to deal with the body, but when Stephen Bourne reached the lych gate, he turned back to stare at Clementine's lifeless form. "This is not how it was meant to end."

"You are better off without her," Morrison said.

"Oh, I agree." Bourne's voice held no hint of a stammer, "but I meant to kill her myself as soon as we'd claimed her inheritance."

A Note from the Author

There were many laws regulating use of the "neck verse" (Psalm 50 in Susanna's day; Psalm 51 in the King James Version) and many felonies for which hanging was the accepted punishment. Both local officials and juries, however, tended to make exceptions to the law. Court records for Rye reveal the following crime statistics on hanging offenses for the years 1558-1603:

26 (including 3 accused of murder) fled to avoid arrest or had the charges dropped

24 were released when no one appeared to prosecute them in court

48 (including one accused of murder) were acquitted

2 were found guilty but received royal pardons

2 were found guilty but had their sentences reduced to whipping

11 were found guilty but claimed benefit of clergy

9 (including 5 who committed premeditated murder) were found guilty and sentenced to death by hanging

The eleven felons who made use of the neck verse included one case in which a plea of manslaughter was accepted and another in which the trial jury reduced the charge to "homicide by chance," since it took place during a duel with rapiers.

The use of animal bones as evidence of murder is not fiction. In early 1538, Philip Witherick of Bildeston, Suffolk was accused of killing his lodger, Ambrose Letyce, and burning his body. When bones were found in the kitchen ashes they were taken as proof of the crime, but after Witherick's execution, Letyce was located. He was alive and well and living in Essex.

An eclipse of the moon took place on October 7, 1576. Sixteenth-century almanacs also listed unlucky days. Most Elizabethans believed in signs and portents, ghosts and witches, and things that go bump in the night. They'd have considered Susanna

Appleton a bit odd, and somewhat foolish, for not taking these popular superstitions more seriously.

This story first appeared in *Murders and Other Confusions* (2004).

Confusions Most Monstrous

The wedding began in the usual way. The bride, Jocasta Dodderidge, was escorted to the Church of the Holy Cross in a procession that began its journey at her father's house. Led by a rosemary bearer carrying a silver bride cup, the bridal party walked from Dodderidge Manor to the village of Kyrton on a carpet of rushes strewn with roses.

Susanna Appleton, delayed by bad roads, arrived just ahead of them. As a guest invited to her kinswoman's nuptials, she had hoped to reach Devonshire days earlier. Instead, she almost missed the ceremony.

The bride was granddaughter to Susanna's mother's brother. A plain young woman of twenty-three, she looked uncomfortable decked out in a kirtle of cloth of silver mixed with blue and a gown of purple velvet embroidered with silver. Her flushed face and the determined gleam in her wide-spaced green eyes drew Susanna's attention. Palpable waves of some strong emotion seemed to radiate from her as she strode along, escorted by two bachelors selected by the groom. Susanna hoped it was suppressed excitement.

Jocasta had not left off any of the traditional bridal accessories. Silver ribbons, the so-called bride laces, had been loosely stitched to her bodice, sleeves, and skirt and tied in true-lover's knots. In her left hand, she carried a garland of gilded wheat ears. After the ceremony, she would place it on her head as a symbol of gladness and dignity, a crown signifying that the bride had steered a virtuous course against evil temptations before her marriage. As further proof of her virginity, Jocasta had combed her hair so that it hung down her back like a veil and she wore a brooch of innocence on her breast. Her only other jewelry was her betrothal ring.

There could be an alternative explanation for the bright color in her cheeks and the militant gleam in her eyes, Susanna thought.

She wondered if Cousin Arthur had coerced his daughter into this marriage. It was not uncommon for parents or guardians to arrange such matters for their children, but both parties had to consent.

Susanna studied the groom waiting on the church porch with the vicar. Henry Markland had good legs and a physique that looked well in the fashionable peascod-bellied doublet he wore. Shaped like a pea pod, its rigid and unwrinkled shell of crimson velvet extended well below his hips. Although it had decorative buttons down the front, it had been designed like armor and fastened at the sides. To preserve the correct shape, the back was lined with stiff canvas, the front with a triangular piece of wood, and the whole of it with stuffing.

The face above this finery sported a short brown beard. A slightly bulbous nose, narrowed grey eyes, and thin brows were shaded by an elaborate, broad-brimmed hat, but Susanna judged he was only a few years older than his betrothed. His expression, as he watched her approach, showed neither anticipation nor pleasure, but she could scarce fault his somber attitude. Marriage was a commitment for life.

A flash of memory had her hands clenching at her sides. At her own wedding many years earlier, Robert Appleton had smiled at his bride and she, foolish girl, had taken it for affection. In truth, what he'd felt was triumph. Her fortune had been about to become his. Taking her person as well had been the price he was willing to pay for wealth and position.

Jocasta acknowledged her groom's presence by slanting a quick glance at him from beneath lowered lids. She did not seem nervous or reluctant.

When Markland took Jocasta's hand to lead her inside the church, the bride maidens followed, but one of them, a snub-nosed, yellow-haired young woman, had a sour expression on her face. She clutched the chaplet she carried tight against the sprig of rosemary pinned to her ample breast and allowed the garland of gilded wheat she held in the other hand to droop alarmingly as she entered the church.

Arthur Dodderidge, the bride's father, came next in the procession, with household servants and friends of the family following close behind. Susanna joined them as they passed her. In their wake, those who had gathered to watch the procession set up a great clamor by beating hollow bones, saucepan lids, and tin kettles containing pebbles. Loud noise was supposed to be lucky at weddings. It drove out evil influences and brought good fortune to the marriage.

Inside the church, the formalities commenced as Jocasta bestowed a bag of pennies on a man chosen to represent the poor of the parish. He grinned and gave it a shake hard enough to make the contents jingle.

After the usual homily on the honorable estate of matrimony, an unexceptional service proceeded until the vicar asked, "Wilt thou take this man for your lawfully wedded husband?"

Jocasta spoke in a loud, clear voice. "I will *not*."

The yellow-haired bride maiden gasped, but an appalled silence engulfed the rest of the assembly. Only Susanna moved, prepared to lend Jocasta her support. She did not understand why the young woman had waited until this juncture to object to the marriage, but it did not matter. She had the right to refuse to wed.

Before Susanna could reach the front of the church, the groom seized Jocasta's hand, gripping it tight enough to make her wince. "Proceed," he said to the vicar. "You heard her say the necessary words."

The vicar cleared his throat and addressed Jocasta. "You *did* say 'I will.'"

Just as Susanna opened her mouth to object, Arthur Dodderidge caught her arm and hauled her roughly into the pew beside him. "Do not interfere," he warned.

The vicar resumed the ceremony, rattling through the words set out by the *Book of Common Prayer* at great speed. While Jocasta stood like a statue, white faced and wide eyed, Markland forced a ring onto her finger.

"I pronounce that they be man and wife together," the vicar declared, before droning on for another quarter of an hour to deliver a sermon on the duties of holy wedlock. After sharing his own deathly dull experience with the perils of marriage, he suggested superficial ways in which spouses could become tolerant of and remain faithful to one another.

In Susanna's opinion, blatant disregard of the bride's wishes did not bode well for a marriage. She had every intention of seeking out Jocasta during the wedding feast at Dodderidge Manor. If the bride's reluctance stemmed from more than sudden panic at the thought of giving herself to a man, then she would find a way help her kinswoman.

Additional rituals came first. The young men of the congregation had to pluck the bride laces from Jocasta's clothing. All the guests had to drink the health of the bride and groom from a bride cup passed from hand to hand. Then there was the procession from the church to the manor. This time the bride walked between two married men and hired musicians played joyous music. Susanna followed the crowd, resolved to bide her time. The entire afternoon and evening lay between the wedding and the bedding.

* * *

At the manor, the bride cake that had been carried to the church and back again was broken over Jocasta's head as she stepped through the door.

"Read the future in the pieces," someone called out.

"They are the broken bits of my life." Jocasta's words were so softly spoken that only Susanna, who had approached her cousin to present a bridal gift, heard the anguished whisper.

Retreating, she waited for a better opportunity and found one when Jocasta sought a moment's privacy in a sheltered corner of her father's great hall. Following her, she made her offering.

"These are a traditional symbol of the married state," she explained.

Jocasta fingered the blades of a pair of knives contained in a single sheath, each in turn. Her gaze flicked to her new husband. "They may prove most useful, cousin. I thank you."

Susanna caught her hands and spoke in an urgent whisper. "You must not do anything foolish. If your marriage is not yet consummated, it can still be set aside."

"It is too late. The die is cast." She, too, kept her voice low.

"If you were coerced into marriage, Jocasta, it can be undone."

"It scarce matters now."

"Jocasta—"

"It does not matter, I tell you."

All too aware that their intense conversation had drawn Markland's interest, Susanna moved to shield her cousin from his sight. "Was there someone else you hoped to marry?"

Tears glittered in Jocasta's eyes. "His name was Gawen Poole."

"Was? Is he dead, then?"

Jocasta had time to do no more than nod before her new husband appeared at her side and reclaimed her.

An hour later, when Jocasta slipped out to into the garden, Susanna once again followed her. Hidden by a pleached arbor, temporarily safe from prying eyes and stretched ears, she coaxed her cousin to explain herself.

"Gawen sailed on the *Squirrel* last summer. In October the ship put into port in Ireland. The crew was given the liberty of the town and in one of the taverns they discovered a supply of Spanish wine, sufficient proof to any good Englishman of Irish loyalties. A brawl broke out and several men were killed, including Gawen. We could not even bury him. His shipmates said the Irishmen disposed of the bodies to prevent being taken up for murder."

"Did you mean to marry him?"

"We—" She broke off, swallowed hard, and met Susanna's eyes. "What does it matter? He's gone!"

"I understand your grief, Jocasta, but you must have accepted Master Markland's suit. Why change your mind at the last moment?"

"Because I cannot bear the thought of spending the rest of my life with Hal Markland." She gave a bitter little laugh. "Not that he plans to spend much time with me. He has a mistress."

"Why did he marry you instead of her?"

"She has no dowry. Her parents are dead. She is the vicar's niece and serves as her uncle's housekeeper."

"Does the vicar know she's Markland's mistress?" In Susanna's opinion, that seemed an excellent reason to object to the marriage.

"He knows she wanted Hal for herself, but he did not approve. Not only would he lose an unpaid servant, but the community would suffer. The joining of my father's lands with Hal's is good for the village. That is why no one here in Kyrton opposed the marriage, not even Ticey. There is too much to be gained from it."

"Ticey?"

"Beatrice Atkinson, my yellow-haired bride maiden."

"Ah, there you are, my dear!" Arthur Dodderidge's booming voice made his daughter start. "Go inside at once. Your new husband is looking for you."

Since Susanna could see Hal Markland through a window, surrounded by his groomsmen and quaffing ale, this was patently untrue. Nevertheless, Jocasta hastened to obey her father.

When she'd gone, Arthur turned on Susanna with a glower. "Why does she have such a guilty look on her face? What have you been saying to her?"

"She told me she did not want to marry that man." Susanna glared back at him. "How could you force her into marriage?"

"I know what is best for my daughter."

Susanna had heard such reasoning before. Most of the time it meant a man saw financial or political advantages to coercing a woman into doing what he wanted.

Arthur sighed. "Try to look on him with unbiased eyes, Susanna. He is our nearest neighbor. He and Jocasta grew up together. They will manage well enough."

"What kind of marriage will it be when a man has forced an unwilling woman to tie herself to him for life?"

"She suffered a moment's panic in the church. It was no more than that, and it is none of your concern."

"She is my kinswoman."

"If you were so interested in her welfare, you should have visited Devon more often. It is too late now."

Susanna took the rebuke to heart. Arthur's wife had died several years before. As Jocasta's closest female relative, she could have asked that young woman to spend time with her in Kent.

* * *

It was during the masque after supper that Susanna noticed Jocasta's absence. The bride maidens were accounted for, which meant it was not yet time for the bedding ceremony. Although it was possible Jocasta had just slipped out to use the privy, Susanna did not think so. Heeding an unquiet heart, she made her way to her cousin's chamber.

The bride was there, but she had discarded her bridal finery. She had also hacked off her long hair. The knife she'd used was still in her hand.

"Do not look so shocked, cousin," Jocasta said. "Better this than that I use your gift to stab Hal on his wedding night."

The words were lightly spoken but Susanna feared she meant them. As she watched, trying to think what to say, Jocasta opened a chest and took out men's clothing. "These belonged to my brother."

Rowland Dodderidge, twenty when he'd died, had been a victim of a plague that had wiped out a quarter of the population of the parish and left Jocasta as Arthur's only heir.

"Being taken for a boy will not protect you from brigands."

"They'll have to catch me first. Besides, I have been practicing how to walk like a man, and swear like one, too. From now on, I will be John Rowland."

Once more bereft of words, Susanna simply stared at her cousin. Dressed in doublet and hose, bonnet and cape, her hair shorn, she made a passable young man, but the disguise would never stand up to close scrutiny.

"Travel in such garments if you must, but take women's clothing with you. When you are safely away—"

"I mean to live as a man," Jocasta repeated. "A woman has no freedom."

"Where will you go?"

"It will be better if you do not know."

"Make your way to Leigh Abbey and I will take you in."

She shook her head. "I intend to disappear."

"We will consult lawyers. Since the marriage has not yet been consummated—" Jocasta's expression stopped her. "Would an examination by midwives cast doubt on that?"

Jocasta's nod confirmed Susanna's guess. She had given herself to Gawen Poole, and since she could not prove herself a virgin, her marriage to Hal Markland would stand. Unless he repudiated her, she would be forced to live with him for the rest of her life.

Hefting a bulging capcase, Jocasta headed for the window. She had already tied a rope to the casement. With reluctant admiration, Susanna watched her cousin straddle the sill. Whether she'd thought this out well in advance or devised her plan at the last moment, it was clear she'd considered all the angles. It was equally obvious that she could not be dissuaded.

"Wait," Susanna called. From a pocket sewn into the underside of the heavily brocaded fabric of her skirt, she extracted a sum sufficient to pay Jocasta's way to Kent. "Come to Leigh Abbey when you can and we will talk again. You need not stay. I will help you reach any destination you choose."

* * *

Less than an hour after Jocasta's escape, the bride maidens came looking for her. Giggling, they tumbled into the chamber, ready to strip their friend naked—to show her husband and anyone else who cared to look that she had no flaws or deformities—and deposit her in the flower-strewn bridal bed to await the drunken revelers who'd bring Master Markland. Even in the most restrained version of the custom, wedding guests crowded into the bedchamber to throw stockings at the newlyweds and watch the bride share a sack posset with her new husband. Only after those rituals were complete would she be left alone with him.

"Where is she?" Ticey demanded when she saw that only Susanna occupied the room. Seated on a chest beneath the window, she'd been waiting for them, considering what she should say when they came.

"She needed a breath of fresh air." Rising, Susanna made a vague gesture toward the window. "She has gone out."

"Are you so anxious to see her in bed with Hal?" a second bride maiden taunted Ticey.

"She'll take any excuse to see him naked," quipped the third young woman, reminding Susanna that the groom was sometimes forcibly deprived of every scrap of his clothing before his friends thrust him into the bridal chamber.

Ticey glared at them both.

"Does she need a vial of pig's blood?" the fourth bride maiden asked. "He'll want to show off the sheets in the morning."

Susanna grimaced. Although she did not approve of young couples marrying without any of the traditional formalities—elopements were fraught with their own difficulties—she despised this sort of ribaldry. It was bad enough on the wedding night, but on the morning after the husband was expected to show proof he'd successfully deflowered his bride. She wondered how many unhappy arranged marriages might have succeeded if the newly joined couple had been allowed a little privacy in which to consummate their union.

"Jocasta," she began, "has—"

"Gone." Ticey's voice, high-pitched with astonishment, cut across Susanna's words. She'd opened the chest Susanna had been sitting on and found the rope Jocasta had used to escape.

The confusion this announcement caused continued for some time, and the noise of four young women all talking at once—and saying nothing—drowned out the sound of approaching footsteps. They were unprepared for the arrival of Hal Markland. When he flung open the door and came in, still fully clothed and, to Susanna's surprise, alone, he was greeted first by shrieks of dismay and then by an ominous silence.

Markland's gaze went to the empty bed. "Well? Where is she?"

Ticey Atkinson cleared her throat.

"Beatrice? Do you know where she is?"

"She fled." The suggestion of a smirk accompanied the announcement.

"What did you tell her to give her such a dislike of me?" Markland's roar reverberated through the chamber.

"She's known you all her life," Ticey shot back. "What could I possibly tell her that she does not already know?"

Hal Markland looked stricken and furious by turns. Seizing Ticey's arm, he hauled her into an alcove where they exchanged acrimonious words in a whisper. Susanna could not make out what they said, but the tone was unmistakable. Clearly he believed his wife had been driven away by something his mistress had done.

Before another hour passed, search parties were scouring the countryside in search of Jocasta. Since Susanna did not tell them how her cousin was dressed, they were looking for a woman.

With the sunrise, the men began to trickle back to the manor house, all but Hal Markland. They'd found no trace of the runaway and speculated on the groom's failure to return, wondering if he and Jocasta were together. It was somewhat later that morning before a servant discovered Markland's horse tied to a tree in Arthur's orchard.

Susanna accompanied the men to inspect the animal. She was uneasy in her mind about what might have happened. She was certain Hal was not with his bride, but he did not appear to be in the orchard either. While the others debated what to do next, she studied the ground near where the horse had been left. It did not take her long to locate an area where the grass was flattened. It appeared to her eyes that a man had lain there, asleep, unconscious, or dead, for some time. A short distance away, and every few feet thereafter, she discovered small tufts of fleece.

Remembering Hal Markland's peascod-bellied doublet, Susanna's concern deepened. If he'd torn it, or if someone had pierced the outer layer, it would leak stuffing. Shading her eyes, she inspected the terrain. The only potential hiding place she could see was a nearby thicket.

Markland lay, unconscious and curled into a tight ball, deep within a circle of raspberry bushes. Susanna called out for help even as she knelt to examine his injuries. He had a lump on his head and had been stabbed in three places with a small, sharp blade. The wooden triangle used to stiffen the front of his doublet had likely saved his life.

Susanna watched the unconscious man being borne away with a deep sense of foreboding, and when one of the groomsmen found a club stained at one end with blood, it was obvious Hal's injuries were the result of a deliberate attack. In a troubled state of mind, she followed the litter bearers back to Dodderidge Manor.

* * *

The song of a lark heralded the dawn, rousing Susanna from a restless doze. A moment later, a rock flew through her open window and landed on the floor with an ominous thump.

She scrambled out of bed and stumbled to the window but there was no one in sight. The paper tied to the rock proved to be a note from Jocasta. She wrote that she would wait for Susanna for an hour inside the village church.

Susanna dressed and walked the mile into Kyrton in less than half the allotted time. She passed few people on the way. None paid her any mind, but two caught her attention. Although they were some distance away, standing by the garden gate, Susanna recognized Ticey Atkinson. She was engaged in an animated discussion with the man to whom Jocasta had presented the bag of pennies at the wedding.

The church was quiet and seemed deserted, but as soon as Susanna closed the door and called Jocasta's name, her cousin appeared from behind the altar. She was still attired in her brother's clothes.

"Will Hal live?"

Susanna nodded. "Your father sent for a doctor from Exeter who bled him. Markland has drifted in and out of consciousness, but he says it was a woman who struck him, first on the back of the calves and then, when he fell, on the head. He cannot remember being stabbed."

"A woman?"

"He seems certain of that, although he claims he cannot put a name to her. Were you hiding in the orchard, Jocasta? Did you attack him when you feared discovery?"

"I heard nothing about what happened until late last night."

"Where have you been, then? I expected you'd be miles away by now." In her cousin's shoes, Susanna would already have crossed the Narrow Seas to France.

"I cannot tell you," Jocasta said.

Susanna felt like shaking her. "Can someone swear you were elsewhere than in the orchard? If they can, bring them forward Jocasta, for there is already talk of sending constables to look for you."

"I hid with old Mother Coombs. I was safe in her cottage by the time Hal was attacked."

Susanna would have felt relief had it not been for the expression on Jocasta's face. Before she could ask her what was wrong, the vicar arrived, closely followed by his niece.

Atkinson gaped at Jocasta in her male attire. "Have you no shame? How dare you come into the church in such apparel? You dishonor God by such dress."

Outrage made his face flame and his voice loud.

"Send for the constable," Ticey shrieked. "She is the one who attacked poor Hal Markland."

"She did not," Susanna said in a carrying voice. "Mother Coombs can tell you. Jocasta was with her."

This announcement did not have the effect she had hoped for. Two men, drawn into the church by the sound of loud voices, lost all the color in their faces. A third crossed himself. Ticey smirked.

"Mother Coombs lives alone in the woods and never comes into the village," Jocasta said in a subdued voice. "Most people think she is a witch and many fear her."

"A hermit?" Susanna asked.

"A cunning woman skilled with herbs. She knows how to cure ailments and make healing brews."

"A monstrous woman." The man who'd crossed himself stepped forward to take Jocasta into custody. "She hath a great horn, ten inches long, growing out of the center of her forehead."

* * *

Susanna found the cottage in the woods without difficulty, and she had no trouble at all recognizing Mother Coombs. The "horn" was a dark, elongated growth that looked as tough as leather. It hung over the poor old woman's face like a grotesque lock of hair.

To Susanna's shame, her first reaction was revulsion and her second curiosity. Only when she'd mastered herself did she step closer. "I am told you are skilled with herbs. I have some ability in that direction myself."

Mother Coombs mumbled an incomprehensible answer. She kept her head down, and in the murky interior of the house, filled as it was with smoke from the cooking fire, Susanna could not make out much of her face besides the horn.

"I am here on behalf of my cousin, Jocasta Dodderidge," Susanna said. "She has been taken to Exeter by the constable and charged with the attempted murder of her husband." If he died, she would burn for it. "I have come to ask you to step forward and confirm that she was with you at the time he was struck down. She says she came straight to this cottage from Dodderidge Manor and stayed here until she heard of the attack on Hal Markland." Susanna wondered who had brought word to Mother Coombs, but that question was less important than persuading the old woman to cooperate.

The hermit turned bloodshot eyes on her visitor. "Constable?" she croaked.

Susanna nodded and explained again. "She needs your help."

"A good girl," Mother Coombs said, but to Susanna's dismay, she began to gather her belongings into a sack, clearly intending to flee rather than deal with the authorities.

"Wait," Susanna begged. "Stay and help Jocasta and I will consult with the finest surgeons in England on your behalf. No doubt one of them can find a way to remove the growth on your head. You can live a normal life once—"

Mother Coombs's suddenly fierce expression cut short Susanna's promises. "Begone!" she bellowed, pointing at the door, and Susanna belatedly understood that Mother Coombs believed she would die if anyone attempted to remove her deformity.

Weighed down by a sense of failure, Susanna returned to Dodderidge Manor. She tried to persuade Arthur to send someone to the cottage and take Mother Coombs into custody, but no one would go. They were afraid the old woman would bewitch them. By the next morning, when Susanna herself returned, the herbalist was no longer there.

That afternoon, she traveled to Exeter, eight miles distant from Kyrton, and was permitted to visit Jocasta in gaol.

"You are still wearing your brother's clothing," she said in surprise. She had expected that the vicar would insist she assume women's garb.

Jocasta attempted a smile but only managed a grimace. "These garments are warmer than my skirts." Given the dampness and draftiness in the cell, Susanna saw the logic in her decision.

"Hal Markland has been brought to Exeter to recover in his own house," she informed Jocasta, "but he has not remembered any more about what happened to him." She hesitated before adding, "I am told the vicar's niece has moved in to nurse him."

Jocasta frowned. "I am surprised the vicar allowed it."

"He came with her. Markland's house provides a convenient lodging while he pursues his charges against you for wearing such monstrous apparel."

"That is a minor charge compared to attempted murder."

"Markland has not confirmed that you were the one who attacked him."

"But that is what everyone believes. That is why I am being held."

"There is another woman who might have been angry with him, and on several occasions I noticed odd behavior on the part of the vicar's niece."

"Ticey? She loves him. She'd never hurt him."

"Are you certain of that? Jealousy can lead to muddled thinking. If she could not wed him herself, she may have decided no one should have him."

"But I'd already fled."

"She could not be certain you'd stay away."

"It would have made more sense if she'd tried to kill me. She had ample opportunity in the days before the wedding."

"Mayhap that was her true goal," Susanna said. "If you are found guilty of the attack and executed for it, she'll have free rein to marry your widower. All she has to do while she nurses him back to health is convince him to accuse you."

* * *

Susanna spent the journey back to Dodderidge Manor pondering how they might prove Ticey was the culprit. She arrived just in time to join Arthur for the evening meal. He appeared to have imbibed a goodly quantity of sherry sack while she'd been gone.

"You could have prevented Jocasta from running away," he complained when they had been served.

"Only if I had tied her to the bedpost." Susanna bit into a chicken leg, although she had little appetite.

"The girl's an unnatural daughter. She did this to spite me."

"You forced her into an unwanted marriage."

"A proper child would be willing to sacrifice herself to save her family's estates."

Susanna studied him as she forced herself to eat. He was cup shot, but still capable of giving her answers. When the servants returned to the kitchen wing, leaving them alone, she abandoned tact.

"How close are you to losing Doddington Manor?"

His expression descended from lugubrious into morose and he sounded like a sulky child when he answered. "I invested everything I had in a shipping venture. The ships were lost at sea and their cargo with them. Markland promised to pay all my debts if I gave him Jocasta. What choice did I have?"

"You might have asked me for a loan."

"What reason had I to think you would give me money? It has been years since I last saw you."

"We are kin."

That would have been enough, but Arthur had the right of it—there was no way for him to know that she would be generous. Since the one delightful summer she had spent here as a child, she had seen him only a handful of times. She had little idea of what either his life or Jocasta's had been like.

"It is too late now." Maudlin, he reached for the sack and refilled his goblet. "She's ruined me. Ruined herself. A woman trying to pass herself off as a man is immoral."

Susanna blinked, surprised that the charge before the church courts appeared to upset Arthur more than the accusation of attempted murder. "In Persia," she informed him, "the women wear breeches and the men are attired in long robes. In that country it is a woman's *face* that must be hidden from men's eyes."

Arthur looked affronted.

"Besides, it is not as if Jocasta prefers to dress as a man."

"Do not be so certain of that. She is always prattling about such unnatural desires. She tells tales of women who lived as men for years without being found out. One, a soldier, was not discovered to be a woman until she was wounded in battle."

Susanna had heard similar stories. In a case that had recently come before the courts in London, a woman had been made to stand in the pillory in her men's attire. She had been committed to Bridewell afterward, since she was a prostitute. She had dressed herself as a boy as a means to entice clientele.

"What did I do to deserve such monstrous child?" Arthur lamented.

Annoyed by his attitude, Susanna spoke without thinking. "If it is acceptable for a woman to dress in men's clothing in order to travel long distances, then why not all the time?" Arthur looked horrified and, in truth, she had shocked herself with the suggestion.

"It is *never* right," her cousin insisted, "nor is it ever acceptable for a man to dress as a woman!"

"But they do so all the time, on the stage and for May Day revels."

"Never tell me you approve of plays and players."

"I have naught against them."

"Anyone who defies morality should be forced to do penance. That is the only way to stop such pernicious behavior."

"Penance is of little use as a deterrent to those who are truly wicked," Susanna argued, "and requiring penance of good people who have the misfortune to long for some condition beyond the narrow boundaries of convention does little more than create unhappiness and frustration."

Their exchange might have grown even more heated had Arthur's steward not interrupted to tell him a man named Tom Bickford was at the door and demanding to speak with him.

"Bickford? What does he want?"

"He says he has important information about the attack on Master Markland."

"We'd better see him, then," Susanna said. "Who is Tom Bickford?"

"Bickford is the fellow who accepted the bag of pennies from Jocasta at the wedding."

"Is he?" That meant Tom Bickford was also the man she'd seen talking to Ticey Atkinson just before the vicar found Jocasta in the church.

Bickford entered with a shuffling gait and held his cap in his hand, but his grin stretched from ear to ear. He should have been made to wait longer, Susanna thought. His prompt admission had betrayed how desperate they were to find a way to help Jocasta.

He wasted no time coming to the point. "Your daughter bought a club from me," Bickford said. "I did not know it at the time, but I sold her the very weapon she used to strike down Master Markland. For five gold angels, I'll keep silent about what I know."

The accusation, or mayhap the demand for money, restored Arthur to sobriety. "You are a runagate and a scoundrel. Why would anyone believe you?"

"Because it would cost me dear to lie." Still grinning, he turned to Susanna, offering a far-from-humble bow. "Anyone in Kyrton will tell you I have a long history of petty crime. The first charge was living out of service in my home village, but I escaped that by absconding. Later, I was taken up as a vagrant and imprisoned on suspicion of felony, but there was no indictment and I was released. Then a few years later, I was accused of stealing grain but acquitted, and next it was a charge at the quarter sessions for stirring up dissension by my evil tongue."

"Minor offenses." Susanna attempted to hide her distaste for the fellow, suspecting that his boasting might lead somewhere relevant.

"Then I was indicted for the theft of two skins worth two shillings, but the jury reduced the value of the goods."

"That is not uncommon." If the value of stolen goods was more than a shilling, a man could be hanged for the crime.

"After that the charge was petty larceny and I was whipped. Last year I was indicted for petty larceny a second time, found guilty, and whipped again, and at the next assizes I was indicted for taking some hose and petticoats valued at two shillings. That time the valuation was not reduced. When I was found guilty, I had to plead benefit of clergy and was branded with a T on one thumb."

Susanna doubted the fellow could read, but it was not difficult to memorize the neck verse—*Have mercy upon me, O God,* and so forth. "You will not get off so lightly again," she said.

The grin widened. "And that is why I will be believed. Another conviction, say for perjury, and I'd be hanged."

"Whatever possessed you to sell Jocasta a cudgel?" she asked.

"When a fine gentlewoman asks a poor man to do something for her, and offers to pay him, how can he refuse?"

"When did she approach you?"

"The very night of her wedding day, while she was escaping by moonlight in all her finery."

"She was running away, but she stopped to buy a weapon?"

"Why not?" he asked, all innocence. "A woman traveling alone must have some protection."

Susanna's eyes narrowed. Something he'd just said was wrong. Jocasta had not been wearing her wedding gown that night. She'd been dressed in her brother's clothing. "I suppose she feared her rich garments might attract footpads."

Bickford nodded vigorously.

"You, sirrah, are a knight of the post, willing to lie in court."

"Nay, madam. I tell you true."

"Then how could you have sold a weapon to Jocasta and not have noticed that she was dressed as a man?"

His astonished look would have been comical if matters had not been so serious.

"Who really bought your club?"

When he failed to answer, Arthur rose from table and seized him by the collar. A good shake was all it took to convince him to talk.

"I did not sell a cudgel. She offered me money to say I had, and I thought to earn more by promising my silence."

"You took a bribe to lie about my daughter in court?" Arthur gave him another shake, this one hard enough to make his teeth clatter.

Bickford nodded.

"Who paid you?"

"The vicar's niece, and not even in coin. She promised to give me the gloves Mistress Jocasta gave her for being a bride maiden."

"Release him, Arthur. Have your servants lock him in a convenient cupboard until the constable can take charge of him."

As soon as that was done, she told her cousin what she suspected Ticey Atkinson had done.

"I cannot imagine that delicate, sweet-faced girl striking down a sturdy fellow like Hal Markland," Arthur protested. "And then to stab him? No one will believe that she could do such a thing."

"You cannot believe *Jocasta* is guilty!"

He hesitated before denying it, making Susanna despair of ever reconciling father and daughter.

"She was with Mother Coombs, but fear of the constables made the old woman run away."

"It is well known that Mother Coombs shuns all company. No one will believe she allowed Jocasta to stay with her."

"Who is more to be despised," Susanna wondered aloud, "an old woman with a growth on her forehead, a woman who wears men's clothing, or a woman who tries to kill a man and would connive to see someone else burn for it?"

"All three are monstrous." This time there was no hesitation in Arthur's reply. "But how can a horned woman be anything but evil?"

"True monsters can lurk beneath the most pleasing countenance." Susanna knew full well that, of the three, Ticey Atkinson was most likely go unpunished. For her monstrous behavior, she might even receive the reward of a rich husband.

* * *

The following day, Susanna returned to Exeter. When she had arranged for mainprise, promising to pay an exorbitant fine if Jocasta did not appear at the next assizes, she went to the gaol. To her surprise, Jocasta already had a visitor. Through the bars of her cell, she was kissing a bearded and unkempt stranger who, by his manner of dress, had recently been at sea.

"Gawen Poole, I presume," Susanna said.

The couple sprang apart.

"Susanna, is it not a wonder?" Jocasta asked. "Gawen was injured but not killed in that brawl, but it was some time before he found another English ship to bring him home."

"A wonder indeed," Susanna agreed, "and we may see another such if you come with me now to Hal Markland's house."

"I will go with you," Gawen Poole said. "I've something to say to that blackguard."

Susanna sent him a quelling glare. "You will do nothing but watch and listen. At present he claims he cannot remember what happened to him, but since it is clear that he's not likely to die of his stab wounds, he may be inclined to listen to reason. I hope to convince him that Jocasta was not the woman who attacked him."

"By now he will have been told that I was responsible," Jocasta said. "He'll have no reason to doubt it."

"I am hopeful that is *all* he's been told."

When they reached Markland's town house, it was to discover that Ticey Atkinson and her uncle had gone out. No one stood guard in Hal Markland's bedchamber to prevent Susanna from entering that room, followed by Gawen and Jocasta.

Markland had been dozing. His eyes flew open at the sound of the closing door. "Lady Appleton," he murmured, recognizing her. His gaze skimmed over the pair behind her without showing any sign that he knew either of them.

"Master Markland, I trust you are recovering well?"

"As well as can be expected." His lips twisted into a wry grimace. "What brings you to my sickbed?"

"The hope that you will listen to reason." She motioned Jocasta forward, into the light streaming through the window. "You have said that a woman struck you with a cudgel. How could you tell?"

"I fear I do not remember." With an absent gesture, he touched the bandage on his head.

"If you have no memory of what person attacked you, it would be wrong to let the authorities charge your wife with the crime."

"I've no intention of pursuing the matter," Markland said in an irritable voice, "but neither do I wish to let someone who tried to kill me into my house."

"It is too late for that," Jocasta said. She removed her bonnet, revealing her cropped hair.

"Jocasta?" He gawked at her. "Why are you dressed in men's clothing?"

Exasperation writ large on her features, she stalked toward the bed. "Is that all you can say to me? At least do me the courtesy of cowering in fear. For all you know, I've come here to complete the job of murdering you."

Markland frowned, once again examining Jocasta's garments. "Is that what you were wearing when you ran away?"

"Yes."

"No one told me." He closed his eyes and massaged his temples. For a moment he said nothing. "It was a woman who attacked me. I remember the brush of her skirts against my arm after I fell, and I could smell rosemary."

"The bride maidens wore sprigs of rosemary pinned to their bosoms." Susanna said. Behind her, she heard the creak of the bedchamber door.

When Markland's eyes opened he stared in slowly dawning horror at one of the two people framed in the doorway. "Why?" he asked.

"Why what?" The vicar glared at Jocasta. "What is this monstrous woman doing here?"

"She is no monster," Susanna said. "It is your niece who clubbed and stabbed her lover."

Markland had not taken his eyes off Ticey. "It *was* you."

"You deserved to suffer! You do not love me as much as I love you."

"What is this? What are you saying?" The vicar's agitation had him hopping from one foot to the other as he fired questions at his niece.

She ignored him. "I love you, Hal, but you married *her*. Tell them she attacked you. Let them burn her for trying to kill her husband."

Gawen Poole chose that moment to clear his throat and step forward.

"Poole?" Markland exclaimed in astonishment. "You've grown a beard." And then, inexplicably, he burst into laughter.

"I confessed the truth to Hal when we were betrothed," Jocasta said. "It scarce mattered, since we thought Gawen was dead."

"Confessed what?" Susanna asked.

Gawen slid one arm around Jocasta's waist. "We went through a binding form of betrothal before I left on the *Squirrel*, and since I am not dead, she is *still* wed to me. The marriage to Markland is invalid."

"Well," Susanna said in relief, "that solves one problem." She turned to the vicar. "Do you still intend to bring charges against Jocasta?"

He did not seem to hear her. His gaze was fixed on the bed, where Ticey and Hal were locked in an embrace. After a moment he spoke in a choked voice. "It is clear to me now that my poor sweet niece grew deranged with grief when Maitland abandoned her."

"She tried to kill him," Gawen objected.

"No one will believe that to be true if Master Markland marries her." A sly look came into his eyes. "I will not pursue the matter of Mistress Dodderidge's monstrous garb so long as she swears never to wear wear men's clothing again."

"Jocasta Dodderidge never will," Susanna's cousin assured him.

Satisfied, the vicar turned back to his niece, thereby missing the look that passed between Jocasta *Poole* and her spouse.

"We will never be parted again," Jocasta said.

"Never," Gawen agreed.

Of a sudden, Susanna was reminded of another woman who'd dressed as a man. She'd gone to sea with her husband, so the story went, and lived a long and happy life as his ship mate.

Despite her suspicions, Susanna said nothing. She had meddled enough. If Markland and the vicar were willing to accept an act of violence as proof of love, it was none of her concern. As for Jocasta's future, that, too, was out of her hands.

It was time to go home and tend to her own affairs.

A Note from the Author

The laws on marriage in England were as complex and confusing as those on benefit of clergy and became more so after Henry the Eighth broke with the Roman Catholic church in order to obtain his divorce. His New Religion actually provided fewer ways to escape an unhappy marriage. Not only was there no specific provision for divorce, but annulments were harder to arrange. A pre-contract with someone else, however, could invalidate a marriage, and an informal exchange of vows, even without witnesses, could be as binding as a church wedding.

In sixteenth-century England, most women did not have a legal existence other than "daughter" or "wife." There were two exceptions. A woman could control her own fate if she was a childless widow or if she had reached the age of thirteen before her father died and she had not yet been betrothed to anyone. Economic pressures, however, usually made it impossible for such a woman to keep her freedom. The moment she married, her husband took control of everything.

There were no feminists, in the modern sense of the word, in sixteenth-century England, but many Elizabethan women enjoyed a great deal of personal freedom. As so often happens, this created backlash. Pamphlets attacked what they called "the man-woman." Some of these women chose to dress in men's clothing. Others imitated men in other ways, such as working in men's professions. Aspiring to higher education was also criticized. When the Puritans took control of the government during the seventeenth century, they set out to discourage any kind of independent thought in females. It would be the late nineteenth century before women again achieved the same degree of literacy they had in the 1570s.

The third "monstrous" woman in this story, Mother Coombs, is a fictional creation, but the "horn" is real. A display at the Mutter

Museum in Philadelphia features a woman who had just such an appendage growing out of the middle of her forehead.

This story first appeared in *Murders and Other Confusions* (2004).

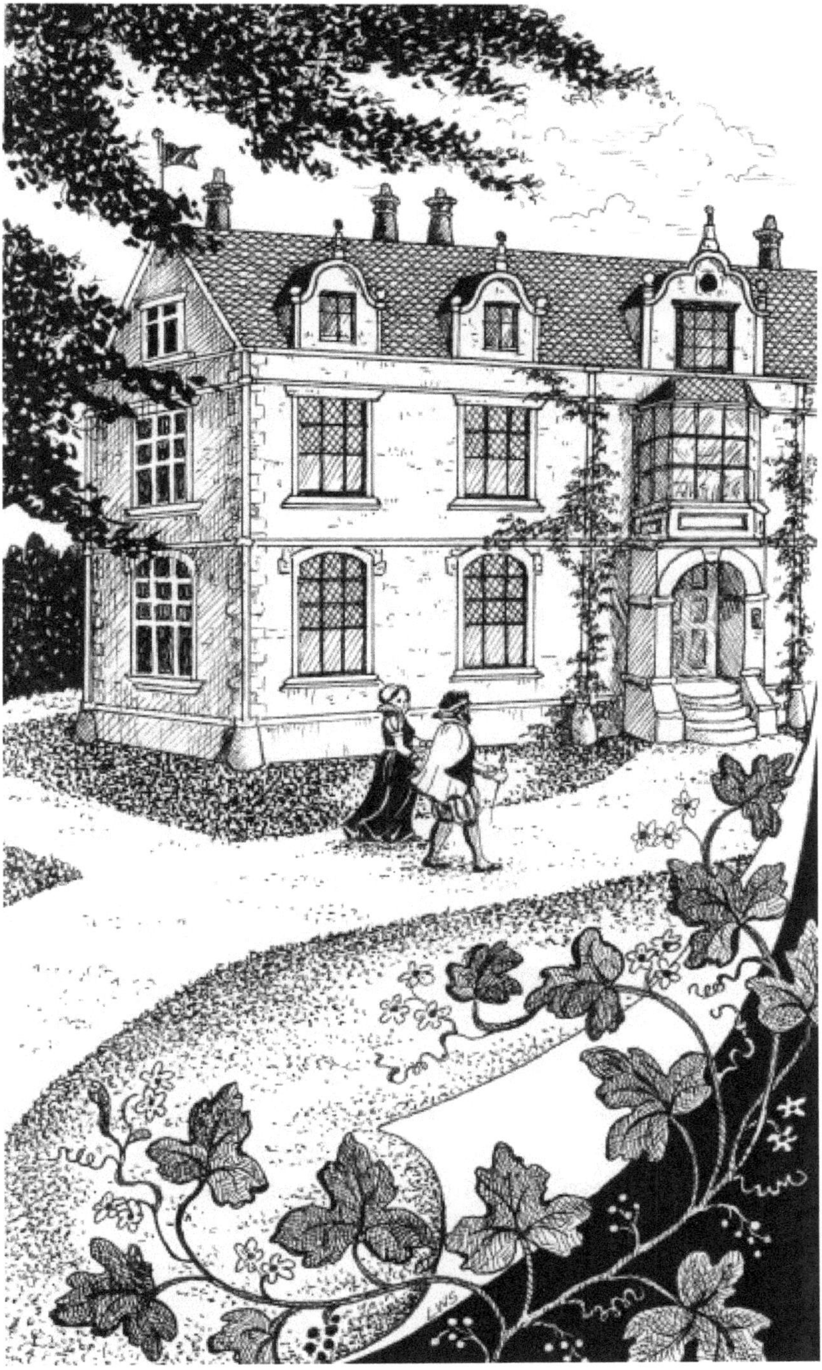

Death by Devil's Turnips

Northamptonshire, June 1577

"Good day to you, Sir Edmund," said Susanna, Lady Appleton.

"Not good at all, Lady Appleton," Sir Edmund Brudenell replied. "Three women are dead and I fear I am to blame."

Susanna exchanged a quick, startled glance with Nick Baldwin, whose houseguest she was, before her assessing gaze returned to Sir Edmund. The slump of his shoulders and a bleak expression accentuated the careworn look in his eyes.

"Is this a confession of murder, Sir Edmund?"

Her blunt question surprised him into a bark of rueful laughter. "What a to-do that would cause!"

"Because you have for so long been a justice of the peace in these parts?"

"Not only that. This year I am also high sheriff."

Nick gestured toward the Glastonbury chair he'd vacated when Brudenell arrived. "Sit, Sir Edmund, and tell us what you want of us."

"Are we private here?"

"As you see." The upper parlor at Candlethorpe was a bright, open room comfortably furnished and well-warmed by the morning sun streaming in through east-facing windows. As Brudenell, reassured, lowered himself into the chair, Nick pulled a bench closer for himself. Susanna remained where she was on the cushioned window seat, the book on her lap forgotten. With one hand she idly stroked Greymalkin, the cat curled up at her side.

She had first met Sir Edmund Brudenell the previous autumn on her last visit to Northamptonshire. He was a well-to-do country gentleman and Nick's neighbor at Deene Park. An active life with plenty to eat and no chance encounters with deadly diseases or unsheathed blades had left him with the appearance of rough good health. Only the presence of deep creases in his ruddy face and a slight paunch betrayed that he had passed the middle of his sixth decade.

"May we offer you ale?" Susanna asked. "Barley water? Wine?"

"Nothing but your indulgence while I tell my tale. You impressed me last year, madam, with your ability to solve puzzles and sort out truth from lies. I have need of those skills in this present crisis."

"You said three women are dead?"

The fingers of his right hand curled around the arm of the chair, gripping the knob at the end so tightly that his knuckles turned white. "Aye, and fool that I am, I did not see the connection until the third death. Early this morning the body of a young woman named Maud Hertford, a servant in my household, was found in Prior's Coppice, a remote section of my estate."

"What killed her?" Nick asked.

"She was found lying next to a flowering vine, a few berries still clutched in her hand and more in her mouth. I am reliably informed, by Dr. Roydon of Gretton, that the plant is called the devil's turnip and is surpassing poisonous."

Susanna felt her whole body tense. No wonder Sir Edmund had come to her. He wanted to tap into her extensive knowledge of deadly herbs. She would help him if she could, but she more than anyone knew how little accurate information anyone possessed about the properties of plants. The herbals she'd studied were full of contradictions.

"I have ruled her death an accident." Brudenell continued, the ironic twist of his lips giving the lie to that verdict. "I had no choice."

"The plant's proper name is bryony and just one berry would have burned her mouth. More would have blistered her throat and brought on nausea and vomiting. They are filled with bitter-tasting juice that has an acrid, unpleasant odor."

"Not self-murder, then," Nick said. Like Brudenell, he was a justice of the peace and accustomed to presiding over cases of unexplained death.

"No," Susanna agreed, "and to ingest a fatal dose she must have eaten a great many of the berries. Forty, perhaps fifty." She could not contain a shudder. "Were the other victims also poisoned?"

"They may have been, although there was no clear sign of it. A woman named Faintnot Blaisdell, the baker's wife, died in Rockingham six days ago. The cause was writ down as planetstruck because her death was believed to be the result of a seizure. Two weeks before that, Mistress Barbara Ratsey died alone in her lodgings in Kettering. By the time her body was discovered, no one could say what caused her death."

"Does something link these three women together, Sir Edmund?" Susanna had a suspicion but wanted it confirmed.

"I do. Two were former mistresses. The third shared my bed the night before she died." He sounded defensive, as well he should.

Susanna had to fight not to betray her distaste. If a man had to commit adultery, the least he could do was keep his light-o'-loves at a distance from his wife.

Sir Edmund glanced at Nick but found no support there. He returned his gaze to Susanna. "I believe the murderer's intent is to cause me pain and loss. If I have the right of it, he will kill Lady Brudenell next to strike the hardest blow. Lady Appleton, I need your help to protect her."

Incredulous, Susanna stared at him. From what Nick's housekeeper had told her about the Brudenells, Sir Edmund and Dame Agnes had been estranged for years. This sudden concern for his neglected spouse did not ring true.

"What about other previous mistresses?" Nick asked. "Have you no fear for their safety?"

"The three who are now dead were the most recent. No others need concern you."

"How recent?" Involuntarily, Susanna's hand clenched in the cat's fur. Offended, Greymalkin freed herself and stalked away.

"The woman in Rockingham was my mistress five years ago. I'd not seen the one in Kettering for months, although she still lived there at my expense. Maud Hertford was a milkmaid at Deene Park. She had warmed my bed, on and off, since mid-winter."

"A means to scratch the occasional itch?" Disapproval writ large on his face, Nick failed to keep the contempt out of his voice.

A defiant undercurrent flowed through Brudenell's reply. "I was fond of all of them and treated them well."

"It is generally known that you are not particularly fond of Dame Agnes," Susanna said. "Why suppose anyone would seek to strike at you by harming her?"

For a moment, before he regained control of his emotions, Sir Edmund's eyes blazed with the heat of anger but the words that followed were cold. "If I lose her, Lady Appleton, I lose half my wealth. She has given me no heir. When she dies, her male relatives will challenge my claim to the estates that came to me when we wed—seven fine manors in Lincolnshire, Derbyshire, and Rutland. That being the case, I have every reason to hope Agnes lives a long, long life."

"Assuming your conclusion that Dame Agnes is in danger is correct, what do you think I can do to keep her safe?"

"You know poisons."

"I know how easily they can be slipped into an innocent dish. You need a food taster, Sir Edmund, not an herbalist."

"You might notice something others would miss—a distinctive smell or a wrong texture."

Susanna could feel herself weakening. If a life was at risk, how could she not try to help? "In order to be of any use, I would have to stay at Deene Park."

"As it happens, Agnes has invited a troupe of strolling players to perform for us tomorrow evening. If you will both join us as my guests, it will be late before the entertainment is done. What more natural than to offer you a night's lodging?"

"A journey of less than two miles separates Candlethorpe and Deene Park," Nick reminded him.

"A gentlewoman cannot be expected to travel even that distance after midnight." He bestowed a smug smile on Susanna. "After that, Lady Appleton, I am certain I can trust you to contrive a way to extend your visit."

* * *

Dame Agnes, accompanied by a maidservant, was walking in the gardens at Deene Park when Susanna and Nick arrived at mid-afternoon. They had made a brief detour to inspect Prior's Coppice, the scene of Maud Hertford's demise, and the bryony that had caused her death.

Dame Agnes turned at the sound of voices, but the sour expression on her face offered neither warmth nor welcome. A wizened little woman a few years younger than her husband, she used a walking stick to get about. From the way she moved, Susanna guessed that her knees pained her. The maid, by contrast, was a sturdily built countrywoman, plain and pale of face with a wealth of thick black hair stuffed under her cap. She paused a few steps behind her mistress and kept her eyes lowered, but Susanna had the sense that her ears were stretched to catch every word uttered by her betters.

"We will leave you ladies to your flowers," Sir Edmund declared when he had performed introductions, whereupon he and Nick beat a hasty retreat.

An uneasy silence descended. Dame Agnes seemed to be waiting for Susanna to speak first, but Susanna had not the slightest idea what to say to her. The bald announcement that Dame Agnes's life was in danger would entail too many explanations.

Susanna assumed the woman was aware of her husband's infidelities and would prefer not to have them pointed out to her. She remembered well the agony of knowing that her own husband, the late Sir Robert Appleton, had repeatedly betrayed his marriage vows. Like most women in that situation, Susanna had, for the most part, pretended ignorance.

As Dame Agnes slowly resumed her perambulation of the garden, Susanna realized something else—Sir Edmund had overlooked one obvious suspect. A wife who had finally had enough of his unfaithfulness might well be capable of taking revenge by killing her husband's mistresses.

Pausing beside a plant Susanna recognized as cowslip, even though its flowering time was already past, Dame Agnes said, "Some women sprinkle the blossoms with white wine and afterward distill the mixture to make a wash for their faces." Her pursed lips and narrowed eyes made clear her distaste for this practice. "Cowslip wine is said 'to drive wrinkles away, and to make them fair in the eyes of the world rather than in the eyes of God, whom they are not afraid to offend with the sluttishness, filthiness, and foulness of the soul.' Do you hold with such vanity, Lady Appleton?"

For one slow blink, Susanna maintained her silence. She recognized both the words and the sentiment, but was uncertain why Dame Agnes chose to quote that particular passage from Master William Turner's *Herbal*. Was she expressing her religious beliefs or testing Susanna's? She would not be the first to judge Susanna and Nick for their decision never to marry.

"I would use a distillation of cowslips merely to cleanse unhealthy eruptions from the skin."

"You give a wise answer." Dame Agnes squinted at Susanna. After a long, careful scrutiny, both her voice and her manner softened. "You are older than I expected."

Too old, she meant, to be a rival for Sir Edmund's attentions.

"I have spent many of those years in the study of herbs," Susanna said, "and had the great good fortune, as a young woman, to be acquainted with Master Turner."

Dame Agnes mellowed visibly, her thin lips very nearly curving into a smile. "He was a godly man. I own other herbals, but I suspect those written by Papists."

"The ancients are worthy teachers. *De Materia Medica* is more than fifteen hundred years old but it lists over five hundred plants, with illustrations. I find it most useful."

"You read Latin?" At Susanna's nod, Dame Agnes beamed. "I have acquired a copy of Master Mathias de L'Obel's *Stirpium adversaria nova*, but when I wish to consult it I am obliged to wait until my husband, or my chaplain, or my cousin Richard, has time to translate for me."

"I am at your service, Dame Agnes. Is there some particular herb you wished to study?"

"Indeed there is." Limping noticeably now, she led the way into the house. "It is called the devil's turnip."

Susanna scurried after her. "Bryony? Why that one?"

Her hostess began a slow ascent of the main staircase, painful knees obliging her to climb sideways, settling the upper leg firmly on the tread before she brought the other up to join it. "One of the servants, a foolish girl, poisoned herself by eating the berries. I wish to avoid future accidents."

It was reasonable she would know what had caused Maud Hertford's death, Susanna supposed. The dead woman *had* been part of her household. Dame Agnes's interest in the plant was also natural enough, for in rural areas where physicians were a rarity, it was left to the lady of the manor to maintain a stillroom and provide remedies to those who were sick or injured.

When they reached her bedchamber, Dame Agnes sent her maidservant to fetch the herbals. "Before Judith returns," she said to Susanna, "I have a question for you. Do you mean to set things right by marrying Master Baldwin?"

Her grimace rueful, Susanna settled herself in a welter of skirts on a low, wide stool. "I have no plan to remarry at all, but set your fears at rest. Master Baldwin's housekeeper is in residence at Candlethorpe and there is nothing improper about my presence there. I came to Northamptonshire to visit my goddaughter."

"Goddaughter?" Dame Agnes could hide neither her surprise nor her curiosity. She inched her own stool closer to that of her guest.

"Susanna Johnson is five years old and has a lively intelligence. I have long had an interest in education for girls. I hope to provide her with a tutor before I return to Kent."

"Where is her mother?"

"She lives in a cottage on the Candlethorpe estate. Alas, the poor creature is simpleminded, but she has a good heart. Indeed, she once saved my life."

Dame Agnes looked thoughtful. "So, you are not Nick Baldwin's mistress?"

"We are neighbors in Kent, and friends. I do not share his bed." That he, now and again, shared hers was no one's business but their own.

"Tongues will wag as long as you remain at Candlethorpe, housekeeper or no," Dame Agnes said.

"It is human nature to believe the worst of others."

"I'll not have it," Dame Agnes declared with the air of a woman coming to a momentous decision, "not when there is a simple way to silence the gossips. You will stay here for the remainder of your visit to Northamptonshire. It will be easy enough for you to visit young Susanna from Deene Park and the child may come to you, as well. I like children and I share your interest in educating them. I have taken in any number of young cousins over the years."

"If you are certain it will be no trouble—"

"None at all." A pleased expression on her wrinkled face, Dame Agnes turned at the sound of heavy footsteps. Weighed down by massive tomes, Judith had returned.

While Susanna perused Master L'Obel's work, Dame Agnes consulted Master Turner's *Herbal*, which was written in English. "He says that bryony, when laid to with salt, does much relieve old, festering, rotten, and consuming sores of the legs because its properties scour away and dry moist humours, but he makes no mention of the fact that the berries can kill."

Engrossed in L'Obel's book, which had been published nearly ten years after her own little volume on poisonous plants, Susanna acknowledged Dame Agnes's information with an absent nod.

"My cousin Richard was good enough to put into English a part of Master L'Obel's explanation of his system for the classification of plants," Dame Agnes said after a moment. "I found it passing clever."

"To develop some means of grouping flora is an excellent notion," Susanna agreed, "although I am not convinced that arranging plants according to the characteristics of their leaves is the best method." L'Obel lumped together clover, wood-sorrel, and herb trinity, three plants that had little in common but the number and shape of their leaves.

"What does he say of bryony?"

"That there are at least two distinct varieties. Both black and white bryony are rampant twining and climbing plants. They send forth long tender branches with rough vine-like leaves and greenish-white flowers. The berries form in clusters and are red in color when ripe."

"Are these berries sweet, to tempt the unwary?"

"No. They have a foul scent and a loathsome taste."

"Then how could that foolish girl have eaten so many of them that she died?"

Susanna had no answer for her, nor did she understand why Maud Hertford had been found right next to the plant. The last resting place of the body was a mere indentation in the forest floor, in appearance as peaceful as the hollow left by a sleeping fawn. There had been no signs of illness or violent death throes and there should have been, since it would have taken her several long, agonizing hours to die.

"How do herbalists know how a poison tastes?" Dame Agnes asked. "I should think that to experiment would prove fatal."

"They rely upon hearsay." And often, she silently acknowledged, hearsay was wrong. She had herself once believed all forms of bryony had black roots, thus providing a simple way to tell them apart them from turnips, which they resembled in shape. Now she knew better. Only the root of black bryony was black. That of white bryony was white, making the devil's turnips much harder to distinguish from their benign cousins.

"Can all parts of the plant kill?" Dame Agnes asked.

Judith, who had made herself all but invisible in a corner, stirred uneasily at the question.

"Yes," Susanna said, "and neither cooking nor drying kills the poison."

"Is there an antidote?"

"No certain one. Some say galls counteract the effects, and others that if the victim can be made to vomit up what was eaten, there is a chance of survival."

"Did you read all that in there?" Dame Agnes indicated L'Obel's book.

Susanna did not hesitate to lie. "Yes." Closing the volume with a snap, she added, "If your wish is to avoid a repetition of your maid's fatal accident, then take your entire household out to Prior's Coppice and show them the plant."

Once again she heard a rustle of fabric from Judith's direction.

"Pull it up and display the roots," Susanna added, "that all may know what they look like, but have a care to wear gloves. The whitish liquid that seeps out of the stem is a most terrible irritant and can cause a rash."

* * *

Supper provided an opportunity for Susanna to meet the rest of the household. She went prepared with names and backgrounds Nick had supplied and began by considering all of them suspects in the poisonings.

Dame Agnes seated her mother, Lady Neville, on one side of Susanna and put Nick on the other. An older, stouter, healthier version of her daughter, Lady Neville regarded Susanna with skepticism when Dame Agnes informed her that they shared a number of common interests, the study of herbs and the education of girls among them.

"I would like to found a school one day," Dame Agnes added.

"Waste of money," Sir Edmund grumbled, but he subsided when all three women glared at him.

Lady Neville was twice a widow. By her first husband, John Bussy, she'd had but one child, Agnes. She'd given Sir Anthony Neville no children, and had been left dependent upon the good graces of her son-in-law when Neville died.

Two of Lady Brudenell's cousins were also present. Anthony Mears was a sour-faced individual considerably younger than the rest of the company. The other was Richard Topcliffe of Somerby—the Richard, Susanna assumed, who had translated parts of L'Obel's book for his cousin. He was doubly connected to the family, since his sister had married Sir Edmund's younger brother.

The final guest was Dr. Roydon of Gretton, the physician who had examined Maud Hertford's body. A gaunt individual relegated to the far end of the high table, he was long-winded and opinionated and seemed determined to deliver a lecture on the four humours as they related to diet. "Too much red meat can produce a harmful superfluity of gross blood in those of a sanguine disposition," he declared, "and you would do well to avoid raw fruit and raw herbs, whatsoever they be, as well as those that be roasted, boiled, or parboiled."

"What is safe to eat, then?" Lady Neville asked in an irritated voice.

"A little marmalade can comfort the stomach, and warm and moist foods, such as chicken and almonds, are closely akin to the ideal humoral state. You may also eat stewed capon and broth made from its bones, and other types of poultry, but fish, because they live in water, are naturally phlegmatic and hard to digest unless your cook takes great pains to dry them out."

"That man should not be allowed in a sickroom," Lady Neville muttered as she selected a succulent bit of trout from her trencher.

"Is he the only trained medical man hereabout?" Susanna asked.

"Trained? Hah! My daughter may swear by him, but I say he's no better than the most uneducated quack."

"He did not study at a university?"

"If he did it must have been one of those foreign places. Terrible, they are, turning out naught but Papists."

"Is the doctor a recusant?"

This was dangerous ground and Susanna was reluctant to pursue it, but she could not discount the possibility that religion might be at the root of the three deaths. She prayed it was not. Dealing with jealousy, greed, or revenge was much simpler.

Overhearing the words Papist and recusant, Master Topcliffe, who was seated on the other side of Lady Neville, let loose a stream of venom condemning all Catholics as traitors to the realm.

"Moderation, Richard," Sir Edmund Brudenell warned him.

Roydon abruptly fell silent and applied himself to his meal.

Topcliffe's glare suggested he believed anyone, even his host, might have Papist sympathies. "The queen's loyal servants cannot sit back and do nothing. The Pope is like a great spider, spinning his web in every corner."

Susanna suppressed a sigh. This household, like so many others in the Midlands and North, appeared to be divided by religious differences. Ever since Pope Pius the Fifth had excommunicated Queen Elizabeth several years earlier, the Catholics among her subjects had been encouraged to rebel against her. There were many who were not averse to freeing Mary of Scotland from captivity in Derbyshire and putting her on the throne of England in Elizabeth's place. As a result, there was also increasing pressure among the more radical Protestants to report anyone who refused to conform to the New Religion to the authorities.

As Topcliffe railed on, she studied the others. Only one face betrayed wholehearted agreement with his extreme views—Lady Neville's companion. Seated at the table just below the dais, this tall, angular, middle-aged female, Ursula Ratsey by name, listened with rapt attention, nodding at each point Topcliffe made.

Susanna frowned. The dead woman in Kettering had been a Mistress Barbara Ratsey. She made a mental note to ask Sir Edmund if she had been kin to Ursula.

It came as a relief when supper was finally over and the players were called in. Lord Derby's Men performed *The Wandering Knight*, a play that proved moderately amusing. It had little substance and a fair amount of bawdy humor, and it featured a dragon made of brown paper.

"I've seen better at a fair." Anthony Mears's words were slurred, betraying an inordinate consumption of wine.

Lady Neville gave a contemptuous snort. "Young lout! Mark my words, he'll come to a bad end. It is in the blood." At Susanna's lifted brow, the older woman leaned closer and lowered her voice. "His grandmother was a murderer."

Susanna doubted the solution to the recent poisonings could be that simple, but she encouraged Lady Neville's garrulous confidences all the same.

"Jane Bussy was my late husband's aunt. He told me she killed a man and had to be pardoned by old King Henry."

When pressed for details, Lady Neville admitted she knew nothing more of the matter. Susanna was inclined to consider her comments naught but mean-spirited rambling, but she resolved to keep an eye on Anthony Mears.

"These cousins," Susanna whispered to Nick, who was seated behind her to watch the play, "are they the male relatives Sir Edmund spoke of, the ones who stand to inherit if Dame Agnes dies?"

He nodded. "They and one other, John Bussy by name."

When their eyes met, Susanna knew he was thinking the same thing she was—that the three deaths might have been naught but preparation for the murder of the real target. Was Richard Topcliffe capable of such vileness? Was Anthony Mears? Near the end of the performance, when the hero of the piece would have slain the dragon, Mears staggered forward, now much the worse for drink, and ran his dagger through the paper, very nearly skewering the player beneath.

"Sit down, Anthony!" Sir Edmund bellowed. "Damned spooney."

Susanna glanced at Nick for a translation.

"A man so drunk as to be disgusting," Nick said.

Mears was most assuredly that! She watched him stumble out, no doubt in search of the privy. Dr. Roydon went after him and neither returned.

* * *

The next morning Nick and Susanna left Deene Park with the excuse that Susanna must return to Candlethorpe to fetch her belongings and assure her goddaughter that she had not abandoned her. In truth they rode to Rockingham, a distance of some three miles through woodlands in which oaks and beeches predominated.

They found Baker Blaisdell in the shop next to his bakehouse. Nick spun a convoluted tale for his benefit, pretending to be investigating the possibility that Goodwife Blaisdell's death had been caused by venison obtained in violation of forest law. No one but the king was allowed to hunt animals "of the chase" unless he had purchased a special license, although in practice the inhabitants of forest villages had special privileges and liberties within the wooded areas. Still, a local landowner's right to make inquiries was something not to be questioned.

The suggestion that the baker's wife had eaten the tainted meat of a red deer from the forest had Blaisdell's eyes narrowing. "*Red* deer? There be nowt but fallow deer in Rockingham."

Nick covered his blunder with arrogance. "Meat is meat. Had she eaten any?"

"Faintnot were ta'en in a planet," Blaisdell insisted. As Brudenell had said, the official cause of death was a sudden, unexplained fit.

The woman's given name suggested that her parents had been advocates of a pure church—plain vestments, no music, and the abolishment of bells. So, it seemed, was Blaisdell. When he launched into a diatribe on the will of God, Susanna slipped outside to inspect the immediate area, but she found no bryony growing nearby.

It occurred to her that bryony could be ingested in a number of ways. Women sometimes drank the expressed juice of the fresh root mixed with white wine to bring down their courses, although most midwives knew that too much could kill and were careful to dispense only tiny amounts. In addition, both the fresh and dried roots were used in medicine. In a posset, bryony was said to cure shortness of breath. According to the herbals Susanna had studied, fresh roots were collected in autumn and powdered. In that form, she suspected that bryony lost some of its odor, possibly enough to allow it to be added to food or baked into a loaf of bread.

That thought led her to inspect the bakehouse, where a gangly, bored-looking apprentice stood in a clean corner to shake flour through a piece of course canvas to remove the bran. As soon as an appreciable amount had collected, another lad swept it up with small broom and a goosewing and took it to be mixed with salt, yeast, and water in a wooden trough large enough for two more apprentices to knead the dough with their feet.

A journeyman baker stood at a long table, weighing dough that had already been worked into loaves. He sent Susanna a questioning look but did not stop work. By law, bread had to weigh a certain amount both going into and coming out of the oven. Bakers who failed to comply faced public humiliation as well as fines. When he'd finished weighing the loaves, he marked each one with a skewer and left them to rise, then strode to the large, bee-hive-shaped oven, broke open the oven door, which had been sealed in place with daub, and used a long wooden peel to remove freshly baked bread through the small rectangular opening.

"Is all your bread the same?" Susanna asked when the hot loaves had been safely deposited in racks to cool. "Do you always use the same ingredients, or do you sometimes add herbs like rosemary, basil, or garlic for flavor?"

"Yarbs?" he repeated, giving the word the local pronunciation. "Aye. Mistress were fond of such." He looked away, as if he did not want his emotions to show. "Master weredn't to know."

"Did you bake a special loaf for her that last day?"

He nodded and under Susanna's gentle questioning admitted that Goodwife Blaisdell had given him a dried, powdered root to knead into the dough. She'd not told him what it was and he hadn't questioned her. Neither had he noticed any odd odor.

The apprentice who had kneaded the bread had not noticed anything unusual either, and since his feet were swathed, the bryony would not have touched his skin to cause a rash.

More questions, subtle and not so subtle, yielded no further information. Susanna could see for herself that the apprentices would not have noticed much beyond their own exhaustion. They were kept too busy heaving sacks of flour, feeding the fire in one oven, clearing the ashes out of the other, kneading dough, and scouring the trough after each batch.

Susanna returned to Blaisdell's shop convinced that someone had provided Goodwife Blaisdell with powdered bryony root and persuaded her it would cure some ailment that afflicted her if she ate it baked in bread, but when she tried to question the widower about the state of his late wife's health, she discovered that Nick's interrogation had already exhausted his patience.

"'Twere her time to be ta'en!" he insisted, and threw them out of his shop.

* * *

"Do you suppose he knows he was cuckolded?" Susanna asked as she and Nick rode away from Rockingham. "Could he have exacted vengeance upon his wife and then set out to punish Brudenell by killing the others?"

"The timing's wrong," Nick said. "The woman in Kettering died two weeks *before* Blaisdell's wife."

He went on to repeat everything the baker had told him about Goodwife Blaisdell's final hours. Susanna sat up a little straighter in her saddle when she heard that the woman had suffered from shortness of breath.

"The local cunning woman told her there was naught she could do to relieve the condition," Nick reported, "or so Blaisdell claims."

"Do you suppose she consulted Dr. Roydon. Is Gretton nearby?"

"A mile or so from Rockingham."

"A pity I had no opportunity to speak with Roydon last night. He seized upon his earliest opportunity to escape Richard Topcliffe and his sermonizing. *Is* he sympathetic to Rome?"

"Who can say?" Nick leveled a warning look in her direction. "In these troubled times, it is best not to ask."

They met Sir Edmund Brudenell by arrangement beside the Eleanor Cross in Geddington, a village two miles north of Kettering. As they continued on to the place where the first victim died, Nick gave him an account of their visit to Rockingham.

"This is a waste of time," Brudenell said. "My wife is in danger. You, madam, should be at her side."

"I cannot help Dame Agnes if I do not discover all there is to know about the earlier deaths. Was Barbara Ratsey kin to Lady Neville's companion?"

"She was a distant cousin by marriage. Barbara was a widow."

"Was Ursula Ratsey aware that Barbara was your mistress?"

"I do much doubt it. They did not speak. They had a difference of opinion on matters of religion."

Religion again! Susanna dearly hoped that was not the motivation for these murders, but she could not discount the possibility. "Richard Topcliffe supports radical reform. Does your wife?"

"All her family does. That was part of the reason I stopped visiting Barbara. To have Topcliffe find out about her—" Suddenly he gave a bark of laughter. "I suppose it is too much to hope for that *he* is our murderer! Still, there would be a nice symmetry to it. If my wife is the next victim, he'd have eliminated one or two Catholic sympathizers and claimed the Bussy inheritance in one fell swoop."

* * *

Since Brudenell had paid for Mistress Ratsey's lodgings for the entire year, no one had disturbed anything in the three upstairs rooms after the body was removed.

"Her personal belongings should have gone to a nephew, but he is currently abroad." Brudenell hesitated, then admitted that the young man's present location was the English college at Douai.

Another Catholic! Susanna exchanged a worried glance with Nick. Douai-trained missionaries were sent back to their native land to encourage recusants to celebrate mass in defiance of the law.

Nick threw open the window shutters, letting in light and fresh air. It had been three weeks since Mistress Ratsey's death and no attempt had been made to clean the place afterward. Wrinkling her nose against sour smells, Susanna studied an abundance of furniture, luxuriously appointed. Atop an oaken table, she found the remains of a poultice. The wrappings still smelled faintly of bryony.

"There is your murder weapon, Sir Edmund. Bryony poultices are beneficial to remove a thorn or mend a broken bone, but if this was applied to a wound or an open sore it would release a deadly poison into the body."

At the other end of the table, she found a bit of spilled candlewax. Within it was the impression of a thumb, two long, thick fingers, and the heel of a large hand. Someone had leaned on that spot when the wax was still warm.

"Did Mistress Ratsey have large hands?" she asked.

"They were passing small."

She pointed to the spilled wax.

After Sir Edmund squinted at it, he held his own hand above the impression. "They were much smaller than this."

"Then this imprint may have been left by her murderer. A killer intent upon instructing Mistress Ratsey in the preparation of the poultice may not have realized he'd left evidence of his presence behind."

Susanna's gaze returned to the thumbprint. Thoughtfully, she studied the pattern of whorls and lines preserved in the wax. When she lifted her own hand and studied her fingers, she saw both similarities and differences, making her wonder if it was possible the ridges, spirals, and loops could be analyzed and categorized like L'Obel's leaves.

"Nick, show me your thumb."

His markings were not the same as her own, nor did they match those in the wax. Once again her thoughts leapt to L'Obel's theory about families of plants. If certain characteristic patterns ran in families, they might be able to narrow down their list of possible murderers.

Taking her little eating knife, Susanna carefully pried up the wax and wrapped it in a cloth Nick found in one of Mistress Ratsey's chests. As she worked, she shared her thoughts. "If I make wax impressions of the thumbs of all those we think could have killed these women, I may be able to match one of them to the one we found here."

"How will that prove anyone a murderer? More than one person must have the same pattern, and no doubt the lines in fingers change with time, as those in faces do."

"I am not so certain of that, Sir Edmund," Nick interjected. "You know that I traveled to Persia some years ago. Persian documents are impressed with thumbprints. I assumed the practice was based on superstition, since the Persians believe personal contact with the paper it is written on makes a contract more binding, but now I wonder if officials use the thumbprints to verify identity."

"Do you mean to say no two people's fingerprints are exactly alike? Such a thing seems impossible."

Susanna had to agree, and yet she was intrigued by the notion.

Impatient to return to Deene Park and begin making wax impressions, she had to force herself to stay in Kettering long enough to conduct a thorough examination of the dead woman's rooms. She found nothing more to indicate how Barbara Ratsey had died or who had killed her, but she did discover a rosary hidden behind a panel in the wainscoted wall.

* * *

They arrived back at Deene Park to find the place in an uproar.

Her eyes wide with panic and her voice hoarse, Judith burst into the stable yard just as Susanna dismounted and seized her arm with bruising force. "You must come at once, Lady Appleton. Summat is wrong with my mistress."

With Nick and Sir Edmund following close behind, Lady Brudenell's maidservant all but dragged Susanna into the house and up the stairs. They had reached Dame Agnes's bedchamber before Susanna was able to free herself from the other woman's ham-handed grip.

She was relieved to find Dame Agnes upright and in apparent good health. Anger, not fear, flamed in her eyes when she caught sight of her husband in the doorway.

"Murderer!" she cried. "You knew I'd find that packet of gingerbread. You thought I'd eat it all, to deprive you of your favorite sweet. You tried to kill me!"

His face blanched at the accusation. Acting swiftly, Susanna closed the door, shutting out both Brudenell and Nick.

"What has happened?" she asked Dame Agnes.

Brudenell's wife thrust a small box full of thin, crisp, gingerbread wafers into her hands. "You saved my life, Lady Appleton. If I had not gone to take a look at the bryony plant in Prior's Coppice, I'd never have recognized the scent."

Susanna lifted a wafer to her nose. The smell of the devil's turnips was unmistakable.

"My husband tried to kill me," Dame Agnes said.

Susanna regarded the box in her hands, then slowly lifted her head and let her gaze linger on the closed door, recalling the look on Brudenell's face. "I am not so certain of that. Where did this come from?"

"It was in the parlor. I assumed Edmund bought it on one of his trips to Kettering. We are both fond of—" She broke off, swaying. Judith caught her shoulders and eased her toward the bed.

"You had best lie down," Susanna said. "You've had a shock."

Bitter words tinged with sarcasm issued from beyond the bed hangings. "Oh, yes. A shock. That mine own husband should want me dead—that is a shock indeed. He hates me. He has for years. Now he has doubtless found someone else he wants to marry. He wants me dead so he can take a new wife."

"You have no proof of that."

"He has never been a faithful husband to me."

"That would be a reason for you to kill him, not the other way around." Susanna stopped herself on the verge of telling Dame Agnes that three of his former mistresses had recently been poisoned.

Agnes shoved Judith aside—no mean feat with a lass a strong as that one!—and sat up against the bolster. "He wants me dead," she repeated.

"Does he profit if you die?"

Dame Agnes paused to take stock, as Susanna had hoped she would. "Edmund would be free to remarry, but he stands to lose a fortune in the estates that came to him when we wed. I have three male cousins. Once I am dead, any one of them might take him to court to challenge his right to keep the manors I inherited from my father."

Two of those cousins were presently in residence at Deene Park. Susanna considered them in turn. Anthony Mears was a bold, boasting fellow, loud and lewd, thoughtless and impulsive. She doubted he would have the patience to poison three women in the hope of making Dame Agnes's death look like just one more in a series of crimes, but there was proof he had violent tendencies. He had stabbed the paper dragon with total disregard for the life of the man who wore that disguise.

Then there was Richard Topcliffe. He had never said precisely what it was he did in royal service, but Susanna suspected he might be an intelligence gatherer, as own her late, unlamented husband had been. Topcliffe had a fiery temper and an obvious intolerance toward Catholics who refused to compromise their faith by attending worship services conducted according to the *Book of Common Prayer*, but that did not make him the sort of man who would kill for an inheritance.

When Dame Agnes finally submitted to Judith's ministrations and allowed herself to be put to bed, Susanna took the box of gingerbread and went in search of Nick and Sir Edmund. She located them in Brudenell's closet, the room he used for private study and meditation. He stood with one hand braced against an elaborately carved and painted mantelpiece. As she approached him, Susanna saw that it bore the date 1571 and the motto *Amicus Fidelis Protexio Fortis*—a faithful friend is a strong bulwark.

"I knew this would happen if you went haring off and left my wife alone," Brudenell complained. "I brought you here to protect her."

"You overlook one crucial fact, Sir Edmund. There was so much bryony in the gingerbread that no one could have missed the smell. Someone wanted to frighten you, or mayhap hoped you would be charged with murder and attempted murder. *You* are the only person with ties to all three dead women and your estrangement from your wife is no secret. Should someone reveal those facts, there would be cause to arrest you."

"If conviction and execution followed," Nick mused, "whoever is behind this would have brought about your death."

Sir Edmund scowled, fingering the seahorse crest on his signet ring. "Who would go to so much trouble?"

"Unless this is a diabolical plot by one of Dame Agnes's cousins, it must be someone who does not know you'd lose financially by her death. The answer must lie in your past. Have you enemies, Sir Edmund? Men who would like to see you dead? What of those you've dealt with in the law? You have been a justice of the peace for many years. You have sent men to their deaths. A kinsman seeking revenge may be the one behind this."

"It takes two justices to condemn someone to die, and a trip to the Quarter Sessions or Assizes. I have not been solely responsible for any man's—" He broke off, a bemused look on his face. "There *was* a case, perhaps six years ago, after which a member of the condemned man's family threatened my life."

"What were the circumstances?"

"A vagabond, Jasper Redborne by name, stole several horses and was hanged for it. He swore he had a twin who would avenge him. A few days after his execution, I found a beheaded cock in the center of my great hall. I suspected Redborne's brother had left it. Shortly afterward, I was accosted in an alley in Northampton. I'd have had my throat slit had the watch not come along and forced the fellow to flee."

"You're certain your attacker was Redborne's twin?" Nick asked.

"Oh, yes. He told me so. He said 'This is for Jasper' just as he was about to slice me with his knife."

"Would you recognize him if you saw him again?" Susanna asked.

Sir Edmund shook his head. "I never saw his face and I would not recognize his voice. He was muffled in a hooded cloak and spoke in a harsh whisper. Since he did not trouble me again, I had quite forgot the incident until now."

"It he was a twin, he'd look like Jasper Redborne," Nick said.

"Not necessarily," Susanna said. "Not all twins are identical."

"After all this time, I cannot even remember what Redborne looked like," Sir Edmund admitted. "Besides, even a familiar face can be disguised if a man grows a beard or shaves one off."

"If this Redborne is responsible for the poisonings," Susanna said, "then he has been at Deene for some time. A stranger would not have been able to leave a box of gingerbread in the house without someone noticing, nor would he know that Sir Edmund favored the sweet."

"How are we to unmask him?" Sir Edmund asked.

"There is a way," Susanna said, "if you have faith in that thumbprint we found in Mistress Ratsey's lodgings."

* * *

The next day, after Nick left for Northampton to search the court records of the trial of Jasper Redborne, Susanna busied herself making wax impressions. She did not explain why she wanted them, but since she started with the servants, no one questioned her until she'd worked her way up to Ursula Ratsey. After Lady Neville's companion refused to let Susanna anywhere near her, Judith followed suit, as did Topcliffe. He looked at her askance and stalked out of the room. Doctor Roydon backed away muttering about witch's tricks and wax poppets.

"What ails him?" she wondered aloud as she pressed Lady Neville's thumb into warm wax.

"He learned about witchcraft while traveling on the Continent." Her eyes were avid with curiosity, contradicting the air of disinterest she had been trying to convey.

"When was he out of England?" Susanna asked.

"I do not know, but he only settled in Gretton two years ago."

Armed with that knowledge and a new theory, Susanna sought Sir Edmund. "You have not yet had your thumb impressed in wax," she reminded him.

"You might be wise to stop what you are doing," he said, "before someone takes Roydon seriously."

"I thought you wanted a killer brought to justice."

"I want to prevent more deaths, but this is not the way."

The desperate expression on his face gave Susanna pause and made her wonder just how determined he was to keep his secrets.

"Every print I've made has been different, Sir Edmund. That bodes well for our chances of identifying the poisoner. All I need do is match the lines on his thumb to those in the wax from Mistress Ratsey's lodgings. Two men have refused to cooperate. One is your wife's cousin, Topcliffe."

"He has influence with those who advise the queen. A word from him could cause me all manner of trouble. He already suspects me of sympathizing with recusants. In the last two years, the queen's policy on dealing with recusancy has changed. Where once local officials were in charge of enforcing attendance at church and fining those who missed Anglican services a shilling a week, now everyone is required to attend church or risk imprisonment. A census of recusants in each diocese has been ordered by the Privy Council. Those who continue to resist face ever-increasing restrictions. If they are not put in gaol, they are made to post bonds to appear in court when summoned and they are forbidden to have guests in their homes, lest they foment rebellion. Accusations, legitimate or otherwise, about my conformity could cause me untold harm."

"I think it more likely Dr. Roydon is the culprit," Susanna said in a soothing voice. "Could he be the twin who threatened you?"

Her suggestion startled Brudenell, but a pensive frown quickly replaced his initial look of surprise. "Do you truly believe the killer's thumbprint will match the impression you found?"

"I do, and if you will let me make an impression of *your* thumb, that should persuade everyone else that there is no harm in it. Let them think it a game. No one needs to know why we are engaged in it."

* * *

When the entire household gathered to sup, Susanna made thumb prints of Sir Edmund, Topcliffe, and Dr. Roydon. She covertly compared each one to the carefully preserved wax she'd brought back from Kettering, but none of them matched.

It was only when she pressed Ursula's thumb into warm wax that she belatedly realized Redbourne's twin *could* be a woman. Ursula's family history was well known and her print did not match, but she had overlooked another person in the household.

"Where is Judith?" she asked.

"Go on, girl." Impatient, Dame Agnes gave her sturdily-built maidservant a shove toward the small table where Susanna had set out her dabs of wax.

Judith balked. Turning, she tried to flee, but Nick, who had entered the hall while Susanna was busy with Topcliffe and Roydon, stepped in to prevent her escape.

"Redborne's twin was female," he said in a voice too low for anyone but Susanna to hear. "She'd be five and twenty now."

"I've done naught!" Judith wailed.

"Then place your thumb on the wax and prove it." Susanna spoke as softly as Nick had.

Judith thrust both hands behind her back.

"She is doubtless a recusant," Topcliffe said from the other side of the room. "It is her superstitious nature that makes her think the devil will rise up and take her soul if she presses her thumb into the wax."

Judith turned to stare at him, her eyes wide with terror. "I am no Papist."

"Then what are you, Judith?" Susanna asked. "It is not your place to seek vengeance. Such things must be left to God." She caught hold of the woman's hand and pressed her thumb into the wax.

Apparently convinced by Dr. Roydon's raving and Topcliffe's taunts that some occult power was at work, Judith began to sob uncontrollably. "He killed my brother!" she whispered. "I wanted him to suffer."

With Nick's help, Sir Edmund hustled Judith away, taking her into his closet. Susanna joined them a few minutes later, bringing with her the wax impressions.

"Her thumbprint matches," she said. "This woman killed Barbara Ratsey."

Judith rallied sufficiently to make a confession that left Susanna feeling stunned and sick. She had been in service in a wealthy household in London when she received word of her brother's arrest. She'd stolen a goodly sum of money from her employers and run away, intending to bribe her brother's jailers to set him free, but she'd arrived in Northampton too late. In her pain and anger, she'd struck ineffectually at Sir Edmund. When she'd nearly been caught, she'd devised a new plan, one that would take years to come to fruition. She'd settled in Rockingham and befriended the baker's wife. When Brudenell tired of her and took up with Barbara Ratsey, Judith had found a way to become Barbara's friend, as well. In time, she found employment at Deene Park, close to Dame Agnes, and was ready to take her revenge. The first two deaths had been simple to arrange. Both women had trusted Judith when she recommended remedies for their ailments.

"You are a fool!" she spat, rounding on Sir Edmund. "You did not even realize there had been murder done. I had to kill that poor cow, Maud Hertford, move her body to Prior's Coppice, and stuff more poison berries into her mouth before you noticed."

"Did you mean Sir Edmund to be blamed?" Susanna asked.

"I wanted him tried and executed, as my brother was, but I wanted him to suffer first. Dame Agnes was never in any danger. Her death would not have troubled him at all."

"Save for the loss of income," Susanna reminded her.

"I did not know about that, not until after she took the gingerbread meant for him." Judith's eyes went to the box Susanna had left on a table during her last visit to Sir Edmund's closet.

"What's to be done with her?" Nick asked.

Sir Edmund looked unhappy. "She must be tried at the next Assizes, but I am loath to reveal all the sordid details of the case."

"They need not come out," Nick said. "A charge of attempting to poison you is enough to condemn her."

From Judith's reaction to his words, she understood that she'd have no further opportunity to cause Brudenell harm. She'd be held in isolation until her trial, and because Sir Edmund had power in these parts, she would be prevented from speaking out in court. Her execution was inevitable. When she snaked out a hand to pluck up the box of gingerbread. Susanna made no attempt to stop her.

She was already dying by the time she had consumed the last wafer. She breathed her last several painful hours later.

The suicide of Judith Redborne, maidservant to Dame Agnes Brudenell, was writ down in the parish register as "death by devil's turnips."

A Note from the Author

This story came about because I realized Susanna had made a mistake in enumerating the properties of devil's turnips in *Face Down Before Rebel Hooves*. It isn't surprising that she'd be confused. The "experts" of the sixteenth century often were. I wrote a short piece called "Death by Devil's Turnips" for the now defunct Lady Appleton Newsletter, *Face Down Update*, in which I explained the error she'd made and why she'd made it. Then I took copies of that newsletter to the annual Bouchercon mystery conference. When people started asking me if "Death by Devil's Turnips" was a new Lady Appleton story, I realized it *should* be. The title was too good to waste.

The Brudenells and their kin were real people. After Agnes's death, her estate was tied up by the claims of her cousins. Richard Topcliffe, one of the claimants, is best known to history as the queen's torturer.

As for Susanna's discovery of fingerprints, this story contains much of the true history of that science prior to the sixteenth century. I'm certain there were others who made the same observations Susanna did. Some of them may even have been English gentlewomen with an extensive knowledge of poisonous herbs.

This story first appeared in *Alfred Hitchcock Mystery Magazine* in December 2003. The events in it are followed by those in *Face Down O'er the Border*.

Any Means Short of Murder

"The aim is to send the ball into the opponent's goal by any means short of murder," Bancroft said, slinging an arm around Rob Jaffrey's shoulders.

"Aye," Needham agreed. "The honor of Cambridge is at stake. We cannot let the townsmen of Chesterton defeat us."

"But there must be rules," Rob objected. "Every game has rules."

In company with more than two dozen other young scholars from the university, the three of them swaggered along the Huntingdon Way. The frost-hardened land, some of it still covered in white from recent heavy snowfalls, was almost level. Rob had a clear view of the open fields and fenlands ahead and of the village itself near the river. He'd been told it contained fewer than a hundred hearths, but every man, woman, and child seemed to have turned out for the football match. Most waited at a distance, bundled in woolen cloaks against the cold, but a few had ventured ahead to gawk at the competition.

"There are no rules," Bancroft said. "When the first team reaches the goal, the game ends."

"That one is ours—the gravel pit by the castle." Needham pointed to an ancient structure in the distance, then swung around to gesture the other way. "They will be trying for that stand of trees on the road to Histon."

The two points were widely separated—more than a mile apart. "That means our players will have to take the ball straight through the village."

At Rob's look of consternation, Needham grinned. "Have no fear. The good folk of Chesterton will have prudently barricaded their houses and shops."

"They'd have done better to lock up their daughters," Bancroft muttered.

Rob followed his gaze to a small group of villagers standing by the roadside. Among them were several pretty young women, one of them great with child. She stared back at him before turning to whisper to her companions. Rob had a feeling her comments were not complimentary.

Needham guffawed. "About to whelp, that one is. She'll not be playing today."

"Do you mean to say that *women* join in?" Rob could not hide his astonishment.

There were no football matches between parishes in the part of Kent where he'd been raised, but he could well imagine that if there were, his sisters and Rosamond and the other girls in Lady Appleton's care at Leigh Abbey would clamor to participate. Rosamond in particular did not like to be left out of anything.

"Not here," Needham said, "but I have heard they do so in some of the northern parishes. I vow I'd like to see that. Where we throw off our gowns and doublets at the start of a match, I warrant females would be wont to dispense with petticoats and kilt up their skirts, as well!"

When they reached the crowd of villagers, one man produced the ball—a bladder covered with leather. He identified himself as Thomas Prescott, the village constable. He duly warned one and all against the use of excessive violence but he accompanied the words with a knowing wink.

Rob expected the game to be vicious. He knew he'd suffer repeated kicks to his shins, likely making it difficult to walk on the morrow. He'd be exhausted, too. The midday sun was high above them now, but his fellows had warned that it might well be dark before anyone achieved victory. Still, it did not appear that more than brute strength and determination would be needed to win and he had both in abundance.

In the last year, he had grown into his feet. He was tall for his age and well-muscled, and there was little that frightened him. With his scholarship, he'd earned the right to matriculate at Cambridge. Now he meant to secure the good will of his fellow students by a show of physical prowess.

Prescott threw the ball high. As it fell, both teams scrambled for possession. Long minutes passed before it reappeared from beneath the writhing mass of bodies in Cambridge hands.

Rob lost all track of time after that. He was soon covered in mud and snow, his clothes dripping. His leather-soled shoes slipped repeatedly on the icy, uneven ground. He lost count of the number of times he was kicked.

None of the aches or pains or bruises mattered when Cambridge players entered the high street of Chesterton. Rob was dimly aware of passing a church and a manor house, but his attention was fixed on the castle ahead. He could almost taste victory. It would be celebrated with loud hurrahs and guns firing, or so Needham and Bancroft had assured him. Both were still beside him. The three of them had bowled over countless opposing players, clearing the way for the Cambridge man with the ball.

Without warning, several Chesterton men slipped out of a side street and came at them from behind. *No rules*, Rob remembered, and turned to meet the ambush with gleeful enthusiasm. The excitement of impending victory made him cocky. Too late, he saw that one of the newcomers wielded a cudgel.

The first blow struck the side of Rob's head. He was conscious long enough to know that his two friends had also been attacked. Then more blows landed, from both fists and solid English oak, and blackness descended.

* * *

"Because I do not want to!"

The voice was petulant, annoyed, and very familiar—Rosamond. She was the light of Rob's life and the bane of his existence. He'd adored her ever since she'd come to Leigh Abbey as a child to be fostered by Lady Appleton.

He tried to turn his head toward her but a shaft of pain forced him to lie still. It required too much effort to open his eyes and even hurt to think, but he knew that if Rosamond was nearby, he must be at Leigh Abbey, and that was not where he was supposed to be. He'd been at Cambridge. Hadn't he?

Struggling to recall made the throbbing in his head worse. Through the pain, he caught the glimmer of a memory.

"Who won the match?" he asked.

* * *

The next time he woke, his mind was clear and his hurts were less painful. He knew that the room—a sumptuous bedchamber once occupied by Lady Appleton's titled sister-in-law—was full of familiar faces. His mother, Jennet Jaffrey, Lady Appleton's housekeeper and long-time friend, hovered at the head of the bed. Lady Appleton herself was busy with mortar and pestle at a nearby table. She was an expert herbalist. No matter how bad her elixirs might taste or smell, Rob would trust her remedies over those of any physician in the land.

And there, standing by the window, was Rosamond. As if she felt his eyes upon her, she turned his way, a scowl marring otherwise pleasant features.

"He is awake."

"Oh, my poor, dear boy," his mother murmured, taking his hand. "You have been sore injured."

"We feared for your life," Lady Appleton informed him in her brusque, no-nonsense way. "It is good to have you back."

Rosamond said nothing, nor did she come near. It was not until much later, after the two older women had left the chamber, that she spoke to him.

"Fool!"

"Good day to you, too, Mistress Rosamond."

"What were you thinking to take part in such a fray?"

"It is a game, Rosamond. My injury was an accident." In truth, he did not remember being hurt. He could not even recall playing in the match. The last clear memory he had was of walking toward Chesterton.

"Indeed, it was not. You were set upon by louts from the town. They almost killed you."

"Bancroft? Needham?"

"Your friends? They fared better than you did!" Reaching his bedside, she stood with her hands on her hips to glare down at him. "They yelled for help and ran off the ruffians who did this to you, for all the good it would have done had you died."

"Well, I did not." He felt as peevish as she sounded. "How did I come to be here?"

"We brought you by cart. Insensible." Of a sudden, she burst into tears.

Rob gaped at her. Rosamond did not cry. She ranted. She raved. Sometimes she even screamed. He did not think he had ever seen her weep.

"You have been lying here for nigh unto two months, Rob Jaffrey. We began to despair that you would ever wake."

"Two months!" No wonder he felt weak! He looked down at himself. He was naught but skin and bones. They'd forced liquids down his throat, he supposed, enough to keep him alive.

When he tried to sit up, his head spun, but he managed after Rosamond came to his assistance. She smelled sweet. Gillyflowers, he thought. If two months had passed, it was already spring.

The football match had been played on Shrove Tuesday, the traditional time for feasts, masques, cockfights, and football matches before the beginning of Lent. This year it had fallen on the third day of March. That made it May.

He looked past Rosamond's shoulder and out through the window. "Why is there still snow on the ground?"

His mother, returning with a bowl of thick broth, overheard the question. Rosamond quickly stepped aside to let her through. The rich aromas of onions and stewed beef made Rob's mouth water.

"It has been a year of omens." She spooned the first portion into her son's mouth. "Signs and portents."

He swallowed ambrosia. "What signs and portents?"

"You must have seen some of them for yourself, even at Cambridge." Another spoonful prevented any reply. "There was a solar eclipse. Most frightening it was. And before that, the Thames flooded. Back in February that was. They say fishes were left behind on the floor of Westminster Hall when the waters receded. Then, the very next night, there was an eclipse of the moon, and after that a four-day snowfall that left deep drifts throughout the land. Many people and cattle were lost."

"I recall a storm a week or two before Shrovetide, but the same snow cannot still be on the ground." He gestured toward the window, wincing when pain lanced through his arm and ribs.

"Indeed it is not." Jennet pressed another portion of broth upon him. "What you see there fell but two days past. Most unnatural it was—a five-hour fall that left drifts a foot deep all the way from here to London."

"Mayhap it is a good omen." Rob quickly pressed his lips together, lest he eat too much and become ill.

When his mother sniffed back tears, he realized that there were more lines in her face than he remembered, and feared worry over him had been the cause.

"I am better now, Mother." He reached out and patted her hand. "Soon I will be completely well."

"You were sore hurt." She set the bowl of broth aside and brushed a lock of hair off his brow. "Your head was broken and bones, as well. Bringing you here was a risk in itself, but the physician who tended you in Cambridge had already given you up for dead."

"I do not remember what happened."

"That is just as well."

"It is not unusual for fights to break out during football matches."

"The game should be banned! Let young men take up archery instead, which may at least be used for the defense of the realm."

"The Vice Chancellor has restricted future play to university grounds," Rosamond interjected. "Your mother thinks he should have forbidden the sport entirely."

"It is scarce the game's fault!"

"Then why were you attacked? You had never set foot in Chesterton before."

Rob sank back against the bolster and closed his eyes, the pounding in his head worse that it had been earlier. "I have no notion, Mother. Perhaps you are right and the eclipse was to blame."

* * *

During the succeeding days, Rob slowly regained his strength. Daily visits from his mother, his father—Mark Jaffrey, steward at Leigh Abbey—and Rosamond helped. Especially Rosamond.

She was the only one who wanted to know about his time at Cambridge before the match. He'd entered Christ College the previous Michaelmas as a sizar, the lowest of the scholars, performing menial tasks like bed making, chamber sweeping, water carrying, and serving at table in return for his tuition, room, and board. He had been glad to exchange work for the chance to study. It was not every day that the son of two servants had such an opportunity.

"I am envious." Rosamond sat tailor-fashion on the foot of his bed, her skirts tucked under her knees.

"You'd hate sweeping chambers!"

She stuck her tongue out at him.

Rob thought Rosamond was the best medicine he could have had. When she was with him, he forgot his remaining aches and pains, but something was troubling her. He could see it in her face when she left off teasing him. He thought she might voluntarily unburden herself, but for once she seemed intent on putting him first. She so skillfully deflected any question that touched on her problems that several days passed before Rob realized what she was doing.

Finally, he'd had enough of her selflessness. "What is it you do not want to do?"

She heaved a deep sigh that thrust her bosom forward. Rob had to force himself to focus on her words.

"My mother and step-father have selected a husband for me."

Ice gripped Rob's vitals. He did not want to imagine Rosamond married. "Who?"

"His name scarce matters. He is wealthy and heir to a title."

"Have you taken a dislike to him?"

"I have not met him, nor do I intend to."

He breathed again. "Then why are you so gloom-ridden?"

"They will not stop. I have reminded them that I must agree to any marriage and told them that I will not, but they persist in sending letters. Before you know it, they will descend upon me in person."

"Lady Appleton told you years ago that you could not be forced to wed."

Rob knew most of the story. Rosamond was a merrybegot, the illegitimate daughter of Lady Appleton's late husband, Sir Robert, after whom Rob himself had been named. Lady Appleton had never held that against her. In fact, Rosamond was Lady Appleton's heir. Furthermore, when she married, she would come into a small fortune set aside from her father's estate.

"It is all very well to say I will not wed," Rosamond grumbled, "but as long as no one believes me, they will keep at me to fall in with their plans. I am tired of the lectures on my duties as a daughter. They will not stop. They will only get worse." A calculating look came into her eyes. "Unless . . . "

* * *

"Are you sure about this, Rosamond?"

Rob had doubts enough for them both. In truth, he was not quite sure how he had come to be in a strange church in front of a curate he had never met before, except that Rosamond, as always, had twisted him around her little finger.

"I know what I am doing," she whispered. "Just as I did last night."

Rob felt heat rise in his cheeks. She had come to his bed. They had exchanged private vows and sealed them with consummation. By some lights, they were already wed.

He lowered his voice. "If we go through with this and become legally bound, I will have complete control of your fortune. Are you certain you trust me?"

"You love me." There was utter confidence in her tone. "You will always strive to make me happy."

In other words, she was sure he'd let her make all the decisions. Rob sighed. She likely had the right of it. What did it matter that he was simply the best alternative she could think of to a man her mother had selected? He had always loved her. This way they would be together. They'd be bound to each other for the rest of their lives.

He scarce heard the mumbled words of the marriage ceremony. His heart pounded too loudly. He made the required replies and heard Rosamond do the same, and then they were out in the sunlight, standing on the church porch with the beaming curate beside them.

The sound of approaching hoof beats brought a smug smile to Rosamond's face. "They are too late to stop us."

Dreading the confrontation to come, Rob squared his shoulders and turned to face the riders. He expected Lady Appleton and his parents, but would not have surprised him to see Rosamond's mother and step-father, all the way from Cornwall. Instead, two unfamiliar horsemen hove into view. They wore wide-brimmed hats, pulled low, and had wrapped scarves around the lower part of their faces, making it impossible to recognize them. Rob's eyes widened as one of them raised a pistol.

He reacted instinctively, wrapping his arms around Rosamond and bearing her to the floor of the porch to shield her body with his own. He landed hard and had the breath knocked out of him and when his left elbow struck stone, he lost all sensation in that arm.

An instant later, he heard the gun fire and horses thundering past the church. He did not move until the sound of hooves against hard-packed road had faded away. Then, with a silent prayer of thanks, he opened his eyes.

The first thing he saw was Rosamond's face, turned slightly to the side. The second was the pulse at her throat, fluttering rapidly. He could feel the rise and fall of her breathing beneath him and knew she was safe, but her gaze was fixed, her expression one of horror, as she stared at her outflung arm. The sleeve was spattered with red.

Dreading what he would find, Rob levered himself upright, wincing at the pain in his newly healed ribs. A few feet away, the curate lay motionless, his sightless eyes open and staring.

A wave of panic shot through Rob when he heard more horses approaching. Fearing that the men were returning, he hauled Rosamond to her feet, meaning to take her inside the church. He had some notion it would provide sanctuary, although he had no faith that the curate's killers would honor that tradition.

Rosamond resisted, pulling free and running toward the riders when she recognized Rob's father and Master Nick Baldwin in company with her foster mother. "Murder!" she cried, grasping the bridle of Lady Appleton's mount. "There has been murder done!"

"They went that way." Rob pointed. "Two men in plain clothing mounted on bays. One had a pistol."

"How long ago?" Baldwin asked. As well as being Lady Appleton's neighbor and dear friend, he was the local justice of the peace.

"A few minutes. No more."

"They are armed and you are not," Lady Appleton called after Master Baldwin as he rode off. "Have a care for yourself!"

Rob's father caught his eye. "Are you wed, lad?"

"Aye."

"And consummated, too," Rosamond announced, "so it is no good trying to undo what is done."

"Rob is too young to wed without permission," his father informed her. "A girl may marry at fourteen, but a boy does not reach the age of consent until he is twenty-one."

Rosamond's scowl was formidable. "It is done, I tell you. We are married and I could even now be increasing."

Embarrassed by her brazen words, Rob dropped his gaze and once again found himself staring at the dead man. "The curate was shot before our very eyes. Why would anyone want to kill a churchman?"

"I can think of one or two I'd gladly dispose of," Lady Appleton quipped, but she urged her horse up to the church steps and dismounted directly from her sidesaddle onto the porch. After she circled the body, inspecting it from every angle, she declared that he was, indeed, quite dead.

***

"You cannot keep me prisoner here!" Rosamond shouted the moment the door opened to admit Lady Appleton, the woman she had called "Mama" for more than a decade.

As soon as they had returned to Leigh Abbey, Rosamond had been whisked into her bedchamber and Rob had been confined to his parents' lodgings on the other side of the courtyard.

"That is true," Lady Appleton said. "I can, however, demand your respect. I have things to tell you, Rosamond. Do me the courtesy of listening."

"Oh, very well. Speak your piece." Rosamond flounced across the bedchamber and flung herself down on her stomach on the bed, burying her head in her arms."

"You have entered into what most people would call a misalliance."

Rosamond bit back a retort. Everyone at Leigh Abbey seemed to agree that the daughter of a knight, even an illegitimate daughter, should not lower herself to marry the son of a mere steward.

"In the old days, your union would have been forbidden by the laws of spiritual affinity."

Still silent, Rosamond frowned. It took her a moment to work out that her father had been Rob's godfather, but that connection did not matter in Queen Elizabeth's England.

"You have succeeded in thwarting your mother's plans," Lady Appleton continued. "You cannot be forced to marry her choice for you."

Her face still safely hidden, Rosamond smiled.

"You have also succeeded in making Rob's mother, my dearest, oldest friend, gravely ill. The news that her son had eloped with the daughter of the house caused her heart to fail her. Does that please you, I wonder? You two have always been at odds."

Rosamond's smile faded. "I never meant her any harm,"

"No, I suppose not. It was simple thoughtlessness on your part. I do not know why I should be surprised by your actions. You have always been headstrong and impulsive."

"If I am such a disappointment to you, I will take myself off. Rob and I can make our own way in the world, now that I have control of my fortune."

"As to that, I fear you are mistaken."

Rosamond sat up. "I know that under the law it is *Rob* who controls my goods and chattels, but—"

"Matters are a bit more complicated." Lady Appleton's tone was rueful. "Rob is not yet of legal age to manage his own affairs. If you were married in truth, his father would take charge of your inheritance."

Eyes narrowing, Rosamond stared at her. "What do you mean, *if* we were married? We *are* married. We were duly wed by the curate before he was killed. It is wrong for man to put asunder those God has joined together," she added, assuming an attitude of prim piety.

"Therein lies the problem. At my request, our local vicar made inquiries about this curate of yours and discovered that he was not a clergyman at all, nor did he have the authority to perform marriages. There will no doubt be a great scandal over the matter, since you were not the only couple he deceived."

"Why would anyone do such a thing?"

"You paid him, did you not, to perform the ceremony?"

"An angel." The gold coin had a value of ten shillings.

"That is much more than any honest preacher would ask for."

Chagrin at being duped had Rosamond springing off the bed to pace. "Private vows are just as binding. Rob and I said those as well."

"So you did, more's the pity."

Rosamond turned to stare at her. "Our marriage cannot be dissolved."

"And that leaves you in an awkward position." Lady Appleton sighed deeply. "The marriage cannot be dissolved, as you say, but under the law you are not wed, and thus your inheritance remains under my control."

"No!"

"Do you love him, Rosamond? Is that why you wed?"

"I wished to be free!" She shouted the words.

"You *were* free."

"Not to live as I pleased. Not free of Mother's nagging or your rules."

"As a wife you are no better than your husband's chattel. Only widows control their own property."

"Rob loves me. He will never make me do anything I do not want to do."

"Do you love *him*?" she asked again.

"I am fond of him."

Lady Appleton's eyes locked on Rosamond's in a long, hard stare. "Rob must return to Cambridge. He is a promising scholar. He should be allowed to complete his studies."

"If that is what he wants, I have no objection." Rosamond told herself she did not care where he went as long as she was allowed to go her own way.

Lady Appleton gave a curt nod. "I will speak with the vicar. To regularize your private vows, he can marry you in St. Cuthburga in Eastwold. After that, Rob must go straight back to Christ College."

Lady Appleton was halfway to the door before Rosamond remembered another question that had been preying on her mind. "Wait! That curate—have the authorities discovered who killed him?" Master Baldwin's pursuit had been futile. He had not caught so much as a glimpse of the fleeing men.

"Doubtless it was someone else he'd duped. The fellow performed at least a dozen false marriages in that church, and others before that in different places. I cannot say that the death of a fraud and swindler is a matter that concerns me overmuch."

* * *

After the ceremony at St. Cuthberga's, Rob duly returned to Cambridge. He seemed glad to go.

Rosamond sulked. Rob's sisters were no longer speaking to her, even though their mother was back on her feet again. Another of Rosamond's long time companions had left Leigh Abbey shortly before her runaway marriage, and the family of the fourth girl Lady Appleton had been educating had demanded that she return to London as soon as they heard of Rosamond's elopement. She was to leave in two days' time.

"I will be alone and friendless once she's gone," Rosamond complained.

Lady Appleton did not even look up from the herbal she was reading. "I do not lack sympathy, Rosamond, but you brought this on yourself."

Dissatisfied with that response, Rosamond left the house and walked to the village of Eastwold, a mile and a half way. As she'd hoped, the vicar's wife was more than willing to listen to her woes.

"You have aroused interest far and wide," she confided in return. "My maid tells me that a stranger was in Eastwold only yesterday, asking about your new husband." She gave Rosamond an encouraging smile, clearly hoping to become the recipient of more confidences.

Rosamond frowned. She had no idea why anyone would be curious about Rob. Even if they were, why come to Eastwold? They should be looking for him at Cambridge. Still mulling over this small mystery, she left the vicar's house to walk back to Leigh Abbey.

The village of Eastwold was a tiny place, consisting of the church, a smithy, two water mills, an alehouse, a petty school funded by Lady

Appleton, and a dozen houses with gardens. The two hundred or so residents, most of them yeomen farmers, went to Dover if they needed anything other than the services provided by a blacksmith, brewer, miller, carpenter, schoolmaster, or vicar.

Rosamond had just passed the forge when she heard the rush of footsteps behind her. She turned expecting to see Rob's aunt, the blacksmith's wife. Panic gripped her at the sight of a man with a cudgel. His dark eyes burning with hatred, he swung it at her.

Rosamond threw herself sideways into a field, narrowly escaping a blow that could have cracked her skull. Panting, she scrambled to her feet and ran toward the smithy, stumbling over the uneven ground. As she drew in breath to scream, she glanced over her shoulder, only to discover that the man was not chasing her. He was stalking off in the opposite direction, toward a horse tethered to a tree.

Rosamond stopped in her tracks. Her attacker's horse was a bay, just like the horses ridden by the men who'd killed the curate. She shaded her eyes, trying to get a better look at the man, but all she could see with certainty was that he had a lantern jaw.

Hurrying back into the village, Rosamond hired two stout lads to escort her home. If the stranger had planned to ambush her a second time, he thought better of it. The only person she encountered was a farmer driving a herd of milch cows.

When Lady Appleton heard of the incident, she announced that it would be best if Rosamond paid a visit to her mother and stepfather in Cornwall. "How fortunate," she added, "that you will be able to travel as far as London in the company of a friend."

* * *

A week later, with the maid she had hired in London to lend her respectability, Rosamond bespoke a room at the best inn in Cambridge and sent word to Rob that she'd arrived. He lost no time obeying her summons, but he brought along two friends, Bancroft and Needham, and he did not seem pleased to see her.

He was even less happy when she told him about the attack on her and her conclusion that the man with the lantern jaw and burning black eyes had also killed the curate who married them.

"Since he was asking questions about you in Eastwold," she added, "he must know by now that you are a scholar at Christ Church."

For a long moment the three young men just stared at her. They looked much alike in their identical black robes and caps. The idea, she supposed, was to make them all fit into the same dull mold.

"These events cannot be connected," Rob said. "Why would anyone wish to harm either one of us?"

"The man rode a bay horse," she reiterated.

"Bays are not uncommon," Bancroft said.

Rosamond frowned at him. He did not look well. Mayhap hearing about murder upset him. Dismissing the fellow as a person of no account, she concentrated on Rob. She had to make him understand that he might be in danger.

"You have been at the center of three violent events in the last few months," she said in what she hoped was a reasonable tone of voice. "First you were attacked and beaten *with a cudgel* during a sporting event. Second you were standing next to a man who was shot by a villain riding a bay. Third, a man, *with a cudgel*, riding a bay horse, attacked me after he had been asking questions about you. These three things are connected, Rob. You cannot deny it."

Bancroft's skin color had gone from pasty white to an interesting shade of green, but Needham watched their debate as if he were a spectator at a tennis match. His head swiveled back and forth between them, his eyes alight with interest.

"That is all the more reason for you to go straight back to Leigh Abbey, or on to Cornwall." Rob's face was set in a mulish expression. "It is not safe for you here."

"Nor is it safe for you."

"You were the one attacked."

"You were attacked first!" With their faces only inches apart and their hands fisted on their hips, they were mirror images of each other.

"I am your husband, Rosamond. You will do as I say!"

"Hah! You have no power over me. I have my own money." She had been given a generous allowance for the trip to Cornwall and had jewelry she could sell if she needed to. "I intend to stay in Cambridge until I find the answers I am looking for. I will hire henchmen to guard me, but I will not go away."

Their staring match continued for a full minute longer before Rob abruptly capitulated. "You will need four henchmen, two to be posted outside this door at night and all four to accompany you when you venture outside."

"Agreed. I am not so foolish as to put my own life at risk." Impulsively, she caught his face in her hands and pulled him close enough to deliver a smacking kiss. "Now tell me—what will *you* do to protect yourself?"

"I have friends to look out for me."

Rosamond snorted. With that weak stomach, Bancroft would be useless. Needham was a strapping fellow, but he seemed too easy-going to be much help.

"They rescued me during that first attack," Rob reminded her.

"Then let us hope they remember more of it than you do." She gestured toward a bench. "Sit down, gentlemen, and tell me everything you can recall. In particular, I wish to know the appearance of the fellow with the cudgel."

"We were too busy fighting for our lives to pay attention," Bancroft said.

"Not so," Needham objected. "She may be right, Jaffrey. The fellow had a lantern jaw, just like the knave who tried to harm her."

"I am certain you are wrong," Bancroft said. "I'd have remembered."

"I will discover the truth soon enough," Rosamond said. "As soon as I have hired my henchmen, I mean to pay a visit to Chesterton." She cut short Rob's objections by touching her finger to his lips and holding his gaze. "It is safer for me to go than you. Most people hesitate to attack a woman. Besides, I will to go directly to the constable with my complaint."

"You do not know the name of the man with the cudgel," Bancroft pointed out. "How do you expect to identify him?"

"I anticipate no difficulty." Rosamond sent him a confident smile to underscore her words. "After all, how many lantern-jawed men with black eyes and bay horses can there possibly be in one small village?"

* * *

"Half the men in Chesterton ride bays," Constable Thomas Prescott said.

Even worse, during the brief time Rosamond had been in the village, she had already caught sight of a half dozen men with lantern-shaped jaws. She'd ridden close enough to two of them to see that they also had dark eyes, although neither one had stared back at her with anything beyond mild curiosity.

"The man I seek would have been absent from the village on two occasions."

She gave Prescott the dates of the curate's death and the attack on her in Eastwold and had the satisfaction of seeing his expression harden.

"A name if you please, constable."

"Glover by name and glover by trade."

"Will you escort me to him?"

"I cannot tell which Glover you seek, mistress. There are a father and four sons in the family."

"I believe I will know the villain when I see him."

Reluctantly, Prescott led her to shop on a street beside the river. "They live above the business. It would be best to speak with them there."

When Rosamond agreed, Prescott left her standing outside with her henchmen while he made arrangements. He returned a few minutes later to escort her indoors, but when her guards started to follow them, Prescott held up a hand to stop them.

"There is not enough room inside for everyone. Remain here."

Over Rosamond's objections, Prescott whisked her into the Glovers' living quarters, bringing her face-to-face with five lantern-jawed stalwarts. She swallowed hard and turned her gaze on each one in turn. Her breath caught when she recognized the hate-filled black eyes she'd last seen in Eastwold.

* * *

"A more self-reliant female than your lady wife I have never seen." Bancroft sprawled on the window seat, idly watching the ostlers come and go in the courtyard below. "You need have no fear on her account."

"I should have insisted she let me to go instead." Rob stopped pacing long enough to scowl at his friend. Rosamond had left the inn early that morning and had not returned by the time he and his friends arrived to meet her, as they'd arranged the previous day, at three of the clock. "I dare delay no longer. I must go to Chesterton and find her. Are you with me?"

"That would be foolish," Bancroft objected.

"Why?" Suddenly beset by a terrible suspicion, Rob caught his fellow scholar by the neck of his gown and hauled him to his feet. "What haven't you told me? Do you know something more about the lantern-jawed man?"

Bancroft tried to deny it, but Rob saw through the lie. In disgust, he shoved him away. "I am going."

"Wait," Needham called after him. "We'll come with you."

"I cannot!"

Slowly, Rob turned to fix Bancroft with a steely gaze. "What are you afraid of, Bancroft?" His tone warned of dire retribution should he detect another lie.

"They'll kill you if you go there, Jaffrey, and if they do not, they will kill me!"

This time it was Needham who grabbed their companion and shook him. "A woman's life is at stake. Speak, or I will kill you myself."

"He cannot speak if you do not loosen your grip." So great was Rob's desire to strangle the truth out of Bancroft that his hands clenched and unclenched of their own volition, but even greater was his need to find out what the other scholar knew.

"Do you remember the girl we saw that day?" Bancroft's voice was a hoarse croak. "The one great with child?"

"On Shrove Tuesday?" Rob frowned as a vague recollection came to him. He *had* seen such a young woman in the crowd.

"She was not married. She'd coupled with a Cambridge scholar and everyone in the village knew it, including her brothers."

"She was staring at Rob," Needham said.

Rob's innards twisted. "Do you mean to say that was enough to make them think I was the father?"

"She was trying to protect her lover by casting the blame elsewhere," Bancroft said.

"You?"

A picture of misery, he nodded.

"Then let us find the girl and have the truth out of her. Since she *knows* I am not the one who—"

"She died in childbed, and it appears she never told anyone that she lied when she identified you as the child's father. The men who attacked us on Shrove Tuesday might have been content to maim you, but after her death—"

"They meant to kill me and shot the curate by mistake."

"If your wife is right about the bay horses, I fear so. Two of the brothers ride bays. One of them must have decided to seek revenge for the death of their sister by killing the woman you wed."

Rob felt every bit of warmth leech from his body. Without waiting to see if either Bancroft or Needham followed, he raced out of the inn and along the Huntingdon Way toward Chesterton.

* * *

When Rob and his friends burst into the glover's upstairs room they found Rosamond sitting at ease with the women of the family, a mug of ale at her elbow and a baby in her lap. She seemed unsurprised by their abrupt arrival. At a gesture from her, her four hired henchmen sheathed their knives and stepped back.

"You will be pleased to know that the matter of the false clergyman's death has been resolved." Rosamond spoke in a low voice so as not to wake the sleeping child. "One of the glover's sons has confessed to the crime, although I believe the shooting may yet be ruled an accident. After all, he did not intend to kill the curate."

"He *meant* to kill me, and later tried to murder you."

Rosamond ignored Rob's protest, her attention shifting to his two companions. "Henry Glover has acknowledged his guilt, but he would never have sought revenge at all had someone not meddled with his sister. Which one of you fathered this child and what do you intend to do about it?"

Her gaze flicked from Bancroft to Needham and back again. It skipped over Rob. He could not be sure if she'd have been so quick to exclude him if she had not known that the child was conceived before he matriculated at Cambridge.

Under her intense scrutiny, Bancroft began to sweat. "The child is mine," he whispered. "Let me live and I will provide for him."

"You will provide for *her*."

"I will, but I must be alive to do so."

"Not necessarily, Master Bancroft, but the child's kinsmen have already agreed that you will remain in good health as long as you make a settlement on her, in writing and witnessed by the constable and your two friends."

"But—"

"No arguments, Master Bancroft." Rosamond smiled sweetly. "To persuade you to do the right thing by a merrybegot like myself, I am prepared to use any means short of murder."

A Note from the Author

A football match much like the one described in the story and played according to those rules led Cambridge University to institute new rules about town-gown competition.

Some of the details of Rosamond's elopement are based on the story of Dorothy Devereux's runaway marriage to Sir Thomas Perrott in July of 1583. Dorothy was the stepdaughter of one of Queen Elizabeth's favorites (Robert Dudley, earl of Leicester) and the sister of another (Robert Devereux, earl of Essex). Her mother was the notorious Lettice Knollys, countess of Essex and Leicester, and her sister was Penelope Devereux, Lady Rich, who inspired the poetry of Sir Philip Sidney and later scandalized England by bearing numerous children to her lover, Lord Mountjoy, while still married to Lord Rich. In March 1583, according to a rumor reported by the Spanish ambassador, Leicester was negotiating a marriage between Dorothy and King James of Scotland. The queen did not approve. Neither, apparently, did Dorothy. She took matters into her own hands by eloping. Her mother sent men to try to stop the wedding but they galloped up to the church just a little too late. When the queen found out about the marriage, Perrott was imprisoned in the Fleet for a month and denied access to Dorothy's dowry of £2000.

"Any Means Short of Murder" was first published in *Alfred Hitchcock Mystery Magazine* in January 2009. It takes place almost two years after the events in *Face Down O'er the Border*, the last novel in the Face Down Mystery Series.

References to Rosamond's age in the novels and short stories may occasionally seem contradictory. I attribute this to the fact that Elizabethans did not pay much attention to birthdays. According to my timeline for the series, however, she was born in December 1562, making her seventeen when Rob is injured and brought home to Leigh Abbey to recover.

A Wondrous Violent Motion

Susanna, Lady Appleton had just sat down to sup on the sixth day of April in the year of our Lord 1580 when the walls began to shake. The chair beneath her bucked, nearly unseating her. Her favorite clock fell off the sideboard and broke, its hands stopped at quarter past five. Goblets clattered and plate clashed. Smaller objects took flight. A chunk of the plaster frieze that decorated one wall fell to the floor, sending up a small cloud of white dust.

On the other side of the door, a servant shrieked and dropped, by the sound of it, an entire platter of food. Jennet Jaffrey, Susanna's long-time friend and housekeeper, gave a little cry of distress and threw herself into her husband's arms, clinging to him for all she was worth. Mark Jaffrey shielded her with his body, but his attention remained fixed on the ceiling. Susanna followed his gaze, dreading what she would see, but although a long crack had appeared across the design of flowers and leaves, nothing came loose or fell.

As suddenly as it had begun, the tremor stopped. An eerie stillness hung in the air. No one quite dared breathe, but every dog on the estate began to howl at once.

Susanna stood, gripping the table for balance when she realized that her lower limbs were trembling. "Well," she said, striving to sound calm, "what a wondrous violent motion that was!"

Jennet moaned, still hiding her face on Mark's shoulder. "We are doomed. Doomed! It is a sign. A portent of terrible things to come."

"It was an earthquake. I cannot remember hearing of such a thing happening in Kent before, but there was one in Derbyshire several years ago."

Jennet continued to mutter about omens. There had been rains and floods the previous September, and a blazing star in the sky in October.

The dust had scarce settled before a servant burst into the room. "Madam, come quickly. A chimney has collapsed."

"Is anyone hurt?"

"No, madam, but—"

"Has the collapse spread the fire in the hearth?"

"No, madam, but—"

Taking the girl by the arm, Susanna set out to inspect the damage. She had to step around a manservant who was attempting to pick up the food that had spilled from his serving tray. His face was ghost white and his hands shook so badly that he dropped as much as he retrieved.

"Good man," Susanna said, pausing long enough to pat his shoulder. "There is naught to fear. The worst is past."

In the room with the collapsed chimney, acrid smoke made her eyes smart, but there did not seem to be any other damage. Mark, who was the estate steward, joined her there and brought a lantern. He agreed with her assessment.

More trembling servants were gathered in the kitchen. Susanna spoke to each of them before she and Mark moved on to make certain everyone at Leigh Abbey was accounted for and to check for damage to the house itself. Along the way, she collected one of the soothing possets she kept on hand and instructed a maidservant warm it and take it to Jennet.

She left the great hall until last, since no one had been in that room when the earthquake hit, and discovered that a pile of rubble covered the table on the dais. When she looked up, she expected to see a gaping hole in the wall, a fissure that would go clear through to the outside. Instead, at first, she could not even tell where the debris had come from.

She squinted. Something was different about that area, but she could not tell what it was.

A mild aftershock distracted her. The servants needed calming once more. By the time she was free to contemplate the damage done by the earthquake, Mark had lit the candles in the wall sconces. With their help, she was able to pick out what appeared to be a shelf hanging in mid-air. Slowly it dawned on her that she was looking at the interior of a small room that should not have been there.

Susanna's gaze shifted to the fallen masonry. Approaching the dais, she held the lantern high, using its light to inspect the broken bits of local sandstone and mortar. Amid the debris lay something else that should not have been there. She studied it for a long moment before picking it up. It was a bone—a human bone—and where there was one, there were likely to be more.

Mark fetched a ladder, but Susanna insisted upon making the climb herself. This was not a task she could delegate to a servant. She had a good idea what she would find in the remains of the newly-revealed room. As soon as she stood upright, lantern in hand, she saw that she had been correct. A skeleton, minus one leg bone, it lay in a heap just beyond the rim of the partially collapsed section of floor.

Ahead of her, she could make out the outline of a door, but it had been filled in with bricks and doubtless plastered over on the other side. In all the years she had lived at Leigh Abbey, Susanna had never suspected the existence of this room or what lay concealed within it.

* * *

Morning shed no clearer light on the mystery, but it did bring Nick Baldwin do the scene. He was Susanna's neighbor and, most conveniently, the local justice of the peace. While they waited for the coroner to arrive, Nick searched the hidden chamber with a thoroughness she could not fault, even tapping on the walls to check for hollow places behind the wainscoting. He found nothing but the droppings of small animals, dead flies, dust, and the remains of a large rat. When he was satisfied that there was nothing else to see, he ordered his men to break through the bricked-up door.

Together they turned their attention to the skeleton. There was no weapon present to show how he had met his end, nor did he have any obvious wounds, although some of the bones showed evidence of having been chewed on. Well versed in the effects of toxic herbs, Susanna did not believe it was fanciful to suspect that the rat had died because it had chewed on a man who had been poisoned.

She wondered if he had still been alive when he was sealed in, but surely someone would have heard him if he had shouted for help. The bones lay in such a way that he appeared to have fallen to the floor and curled himself into a ball, clutching his belly. She hoped he'd died quickly.

"He has been here a long time." Nick stooped to pick up a metal button and a buckle. Together with tiny bits of cloth and leather, the rest of his clothing had rotted away.

"From the time this house was built, I imagine."

"When was that?"

"Forty years and more. I was a small child at the time, but I can remember watching the walls go up."

"Are there written records—lists of workmen and the like?"

"If there are, they will be in one of the iron-bound chests in my study."

Nick helped Susanna step through the new-made opening. It gave onto a familiar upstairs passageway only a short distance from the room where she kept accounts and wrote letters. Once there, she went straight to the oldest of her storage chests.

While she rummaged, he stood at the window, staring out across the fields with his hands clasped behind his back—a sure sign that he was deep in thought. Rather than disturb him, Susanna seated herself at her coffin desk and unrolled the papers she'd found. They were mostly letters and receipts, but there were also lists of payments to those employed by her grandfather during each year of building. Included were both household servants and day laborers. She also found a rough sketch of the rooms in the house.

The floor plan was difficult to decipher. Notations, mostly numbers, ran around the edges. Susanna supposed they indicated the amounts of various building materials that were needed. They were much overwritten, and elevations were marked, too.

The original Leigh Abbey had been a monastery. Susanna's family, the Leighs, had lived nearby. After the Dissolution, her grandfather had bought the property and remodeled some of the original buildings into a dwelling house. As near as she could tell, the room they'd found had been intended as a private closet—a small study to which he could retire when he wished to read his Bible or catch up on his correspondence.

When Nick came up behind her, she handed him this rough rendering of the manor house.

"The date at the bottom of this drawing is 1536. How long did your grandfather spend building it?"

"Four years, as I recall."

Nick's eyes twinkled. "*Do* you recall? You must still have been on leading strings when work began."

"True enough. I was born in October of 1534, but I can well remember that in the summer of 1540, my grandmother, who raised us after our mother died, took me and my sister to visit Mother's brother, Matthew Dodderidge, in Devonshire. My cousin Arthur, who is a few years older than I am, taught me how to swim."

"Is there anyone at Leigh Abbey older than you are—someone who can better recollect those years?"

"No one I can think of. My grandfather died when I was eight, and my grandmother two years later. My father drowned, and you know about my sister." Joanna had eaten of poisonous berries, mistaking them for edible fruit. Her tragic death had been the impetus for Susanna to become an expert on dangerous herbs.

"What of servants? Is there no old retainer, long pensioned off?"

Susanna's brow furrowed. "There was a nursemaid who accompanied us to Devonshire, but I cannot recall her name."

Nick shuffled through the other papers she'd taken from the trunk. "Can you find it here?" He handed her the list of wages and payments.

Susanna ran her finger down the list, stopping when she came to the name Gittens. There were two maidservants by that name, Maud and Emma. "Emma," she said aloud. "Emma Gittens. I cannot picture her in my mind, but I remember that she did not return with us to Leigh Abbey. She married a man she met in Exeter and stayed there. My grandmother was most put out about it at the time."

* * *

The coroner's inquest came to the conclusion that the death of the unknown man was never likely to be explained. The remains were duly buried in the churchyard of St. Cuthberga in the nearby village of Eastwold, earthquake damage to Leigh Abbey was repaired, and the matter might have been forgotten altogether except for one thing.

Susanna Appleton had an aversion to leaving any mystery unsolved. That there had been a crime—a murder—seemed likely. Otherwise, why hide the body? It troubled her to think that her grandfather must have known of it, but that, too, was a conclusion she could not escape. No one else could have ordered that room sealed off. She worried that Sir Anthony Leigh might have been responsible for the man's death. Distressing as that possibility was, it was not in her nature to leave a question unanswered.

"There is no one left to ask," Nick reminded her when she shared her concerns with him.

"We must make certain of that. It is true that few people survive past their sixtieth year, but some do. You said yourself that there might be a servant, long since pensioned off, who is still alive, or mayhap one of the workmen survives. My grandfather could not have bricked up and plastered over that door by himself. Someone must have helped him, and more than one person at the time must have known that the room existed."

"Are you certain you want to know the truth? It is not as if I can order an arrest, no matter what evidence you gather."

"The man we buried had a name. He had a family, one that never knew what became of him." The more Nick objected, the more determined Susanna became to do all she could on behalf of the unknown victim.

Starting with the list she had found, Susanna inquired first within her own household. Kinfolk of many former servants still worked at Leigh Abbey. One by one, she crossed out the names of those who were no longer living until only a handful were left. When she extended her search into the nearby village of Eastwold, she eliminated a few more. It began to seem unlikely she would ever locate anyone who had been at Leigh Abbey in her grandfather's time.

On succeeding days, she ventured farther afield. Finally, halfway to Canterbury, her luck changed. "Gittens?" she repeated.

"Aye." The aged farmer leaned on his hoe.

"Not Emma Gittens?"

The old man laughed. "Nay, Lady Appleton. Maud Gittens, sister to Emma."

As it turned out, Maud Gittens was Emma's older sister and a very old lady indeed. Toothless and blind in one eye, she lived in a surpassing fine house on the outskirts of Canterbury with her daughter, a woman a little younger than Susanna who provided them with refreshments and then left them to talk in private.

Maud made a cackling sound once or twice as Susanna told her tale, but offered no comment.

"Well?" Susanna prompted her. "Do you recall the days when Leigh Abbey was being built? Do you remember that your sister journeyed to Devonshire with my grandmother and did not return?"

"Oh, aye. There is nothing wrong with my memory." She took a healthy slurp from a cup of sweetened barley water and smacked her lips. "I was one of your grandmother's maidservants for nigh onto five years. She trained me to speak like the gentry and appreciate all the good things money can buy."

Elated, Susanna leaned closer. "Have you any notion who the man we found might be?"

"I warrant your pile of bones is the lad who ran out on Emma."

"This fellow did not run anywhere. Emma's suitor—did he have a name?"

"Ask Emma. I never cared to know."

Susanna's elation dimmed. "Is she still in Exeter?" To reach Devonshire from Kent would take more than a week of traveling, but if that was the only way to solve the mystery of the sealed-up room, then she would gladly make the journey.

"She married a man named Oswyn. Daniel Oswyn. A joiner by trade." Maud shifted in her chair, bones creaking.

"Are you certain Emma is still living?"

Maud's laughter grated on Susanna's nerves, but when the old woman assured her she'd have the answers she sought when she and her former nursemaid were reunited, she made her decision. She would leave for Devonshire as soon as she could arrange for horses to be posted along the route.

* * *

Ten days later, Susanna's coach thundered through the Great Gate into Exeter. She bespoke a room at the New Inn in the High Street and, with a sigh of relief, closed the chamber door on her henchmen. Once she'd eaten the light meal she'd ordered brought to the room, she intended to go straight to bed.

Every muscle in her body ached. She had felt every shake and rattle of her coach as it caromed over mile after mile of uneven road. She did not even want to think about how many bruises she'd acquired on the journey.

Even worse, she'd had far too much time to think. Worrisome questions had gnawed at her. Why had her grandfather sealed that chamber at Leigh Abbey, pretending that it never existed at all? Even supposing he had killed the man they'd found there, why would he keep the body in his own house? Why not simply bury it in the nearby woods?

Only one reason made any sense—he'd not dared risk the accidental discovery of the remains while it was still possible to put a name to them. Somehow, knowing the identity of the victim would have led to trouble for those at Leigh Abbey.

She was hopeful that Emma would have the answers she sought. Throughout the long journey, just out of reach, some detail she'd once known about Emma Gittens kept nagging at the back of her mind, but her attempts to force herself to remember produced nothing but a pounding headache.

She supposed she must have been close to her nursemaid when she was a young child, and even as a little girl, she had possessed an inquiring mind. The more she thought about it, the more certain she became that Emma was the key to solving the murder.

* * *

The next morning, Susanna made inquiries about a joiner named Daniel Oswyn. To her dismay, she learned from the innkeeper that both Oswyn and his wife had been dead for several years.

That Maud did not know her sister was dead seemed strange to Susanna, but the alternative, that she had deliberately misled her, did not make sense, either. She wondered if, despite Maud's appearance of lucidity, her age had caught up with her, leaving her confused about what was real and what was not. She might have been told of her sister's death and forgotten, as the elderly were sometimes wont to do.

Then Susanna remembered Maud's cackle and shivered. Something was very wrong, but she could not put her finger on what it might be.

Piers Oswyn had inherited his father's house and workshop in Frog Street. Susanna made her way there from the inn, although she had little hope of learning anything useful. Her spirits sank even lower when she saw what a shabby place it was. The stools Oswyn made were poor and plain and he had but one apprentice. Emma's son himself was a tall, stoop-shouldered fellow with a taciturn disposition. He grunted but made no comment when Susanna mentioned Maud's name.

"How is it that your aunt knew nothing of your mother's death?" she asked.

"Is that what she told you? Lying old beldam. She knew. She came here for the funeral."

"Did your mother ever speak about her time at Leigh Abbey?"

"She was never one for talking."

"Did she leave any papers behind?" All Leigh Abbey servants, both men and women, were taught to read and write. Both her father and her grandfather had held radical beliefs concerning education.

"If she did, Maud has them now."

Since the joiner's demeanor grew increasingly surly, as if he resented being asked questions, Susanna saw no reason to explain why she was interested in Emma. It seemed obvious that he knew nothing of use to her.

She thanked him, returned to the inn, and left Exeter that same afternoon, but she traveled only as far as her cousin Arthur's house, Dodderidge Manor, eight miles distant. Arthur's welcome was reserved, since they had not parted on the best of terms on her last visit, but courtesy required that he invite her to spend the night.

Over supper, she reminded him of their first meeting.

"I taught you to swim." Arthur's voice was gruff, but his lips twitched at the memory. "Father called me a fool for doing so. He said there was no need for a girl to learn such a thing."

"Years later, those lessons saved my life."

"Did they?" He looked pleased.

"Do you recall anything else from that time? I am trying to find out more about my nursemaid, Emma Gittens. Rather than return to Leigh Abbey with us, she remained behind to marry a man called Daniel Oswyn, a joiner she met in Exeter."

Arthur chuckled. "Oh, I remember her right enough. It would have been hard to miss that enormous belly."

Susanna stared at him. "She was great with child?"

"She was, and well before she wed, too."

And that, Susanna realized, was the detail she'd been struggling to recall.

Her grandmother had been angry with Emma because Emma had been about to bear an illegitimate child. What Susanna's memory failed to reveal was why the child's father, obviously someone left behind in Kent, had not been made to marry her. If he was the man in the sealed-up room, he might already have been dead, but that possibility created other questions. Had Amata Leigh, Susanna's grandmother, known what happened to him? Had Emma?

* * *

The next day, Susanna and her escort began the return journey to Kent. She intended to confront Maud Gittens again, but she had no idea if a second meeting would yield answers that were any more honest than those she'd been given during their first encounter.

The coach and outriders had traveled no more than three miles when the party was set upon by masked brigands. Hearing shouts and the clash of steel, Susanna armed herself with the little pistol Nick Baldwin had given her. It was largely useless, since it took so long to prime and held but one shot, but it was better than nothing. When one of the would-be robbers flung open the coach door, she fired. With a cry of pain he fell back, clutching his shoulder.

The brigands had cudgels and knives but Leigh Abbey's men were armed with swords. By the time Susanna reloaded her pistol and stepped out of the coach, two of the attackers lay dead, the one she had wounded was a prisoner, and the rest had fled.

"Unmask them," Susanna ordered.

She had never seen the first dead man before, but the second was Piers Oswyn. The surviving brigand was his apprentice. He looked barely old enough to grow a beard and she felt a pang of regret that she'd injured him. It passed quickly.

She addressed him in a stern voice. "A man can be hanged for a far less serious crime than the one you just committed."

The lad began to babble, pleading for his life.

"I have no intention of harming you further, or turning you over to the law. I will even tend your wound, so long as you answer my questions honestly."

"Anything, mistress. Anything!" Tears stained his cheeks, as much from fear as from pain. He readily admitted that it was his master, Piers Oswyn, who had conceived the mad plan to rob a wealthy traveler, but he had no idea why.

"As his apprentice, you had to obey, but why did the other men join him?"

"For money," the boy said. "A bill of exchange came with the letter and Master Oswyn took it to the goldsmith to trade for coins."

"What letter? Where is it now?" Her henchmen, who had searched both bodies, had found no writings.

"Burnt," the lad said.

Further questions revealed that the letter had been delivered only hours after Susanna's visit to the joiner's shop. As soon as Piers read it, he had begun making plans to attack her coach.

"He sent me to the New Inn to see if you were still there. You had already gone, but Will Bindoff, the ostler, overheard your men talk of a visit to Dodderidge Manor." He gestured toward the other body. "That's him there."

It had to have been Maud who wrote to Piers, Susanna thought. She could think of no one else who could have convinced him to act as he had, but she did not understand why she would want her nephew to kill an innocent stranger.

* * *

By the time Susanna returned to Maud Gitten's house, three weeks had passed since their last conversation. As before, Maud's daughter admitted her, but this time Susanna did not give the younger woman any opportunity to warn her mother that a visitor had arrived. She pushed past her into the inner room and found Maud standing by the hearth.

"Who was at the door, Joanna?" Maud's voice was querulous. Her gaze remained on the fitful flames licking at the wood in the fireplace as she stirred them with an iron poker.

Susanna checked at hearing the familiar name. Her younger sister had been called Joanna.

That momentary delay gave Maud time to turn toward the door. Her one good eye widened, showing first shock and then fury. Before Susanna could draw breath to speak, the old woman ran toward her, the poker raised to deliver a killing blow.

Susanna deflected the weapon with her left arm, preventing the poker from striking her head. Reacting without forethought, she aimed her right fist at her attacker's jaw. Maud staggered and clutched at her chest. All color draining from her sunken cheeks, she crumpled to the floor.

* * *

Some hours later, Susanna stood with Maud's daughter at the dying woman's bedside. She knew the signs. In her rage, Maud had driven her frail old body too far. It was doubtful she would survive the night. Even if Susanna had been inclined to help her, she knew of no herbal remedy that could cure someone so aged and infirm.

"Do you know why she wanted me dead?" she asked. "I have discovered nothing to tie her to the murder I was investigating."

Joanna Gittens spoke in a whisper. "You have a reputation for finding things out, Lady Appleton."

"So she saw me as a threat, even though I might never have been one, and her irrational fear cost Piers Oswyn his life."

While Joanna wept for her cousin, Susanna absently rubbed her arm. For a time it had been rendered numb by Maud's blow, but as soon as sensation returned, it had begun to throb. Nothing was broken, but she would have spectacular bruises by morning. The pain made her less sympathetic than she might otherwise have been.

A whisper of sound issued from the woman in the bed. Maud, conscious for the first time since she'd collapsed, glared up at the woman who had felled her.

"Can you speak?" Susanna asked. "Can you answer my questions? If I were you," she added, "I would want to clear my conscience before I meet my maker."

"I'd rather confess to a priest than to you, Lady Appleton." Maud's voice was stronger than Susanna had expected.

"Do you still cling to the old religion?" Almost half a century had passed since Queen Elizabeth's father had broken with Rome to establish the Church of England. "Tell me what I want to know and I will find a priest to give you last rites."

One of her neighbors continued to hear mass every Sunday in the privacy of her own home. The service was conducted by a gentleman who lived in her household in the guise of her children's tutor.

"It is too late for that." Maud stared up at the bed's ceiler, a lovely thing of silk patterned with roses.

Susanna could not tell if she meant that a priest would be of no use, or that there was no time to wait for one. "What do you want, then?"

A gleam came into the old woman's eye. "I want my alabaster effigy on a tomb in the church. Swear to me that you will erect one."

Such things were expensive, but Susanna was a wealthy widow. "Answer me true and I promise you that you will have such a monument."

"What does she want you to say?" Joanna wailed, twisting her hands together in distress. "What have you done?"

Maud spared her daughter one brief glance. "I want an annuity for my girl, too—a hundred pounds per annum."

Susanna winced but agreed. Since time was of the essence, what choice did she have? It was a miracle Maud could still speak. She had already lost the ability to control the movements of her extremities. Her arms lay useless at her sides. At any moment, she could release her tenuous grasp on life.

"Who was the man who died at Leigh Abbey?" Susanna asked.

"He was the son of one of Lady Leigh's old friends from court."

"Do you mean my grandmother, Amata Leigh?"

Maud made a sound of assent.

Amata had been a chamberer to Queen Catherine of Aragon in the early days of King Henry's reign. Prompted by that thought, a memory popped into Susanna's mind. During the trip to Devonshire, her grandmother had spent many hours in prayer. Although she'd tried to keep it hidden, she had used a rosary, a beautiful creation of black gemstones and gold, to aid in her devotions. Even that long ago, such things were supposed to have been put aside, along with statues of saints in the churches and other trappings of the Church of Rome.

The Leighs had been prompt to embrace the New Religion, or so Susanna had always believed. Her grandfather, Sir Anthony, had acquired Leigh Abbey as a result of the dissolution of the monasteries. During the brief reign of Catholic Queen Mary, when everyone in England had been expected to conform to the old faith, Susanna herself had been part of a secret network of loyal co-religionists who smuggled radical reformers out of England before they could be arrested and burnt for heresy.

When Maud coughed and gasped for breath, Susanna helped her take a sip of barley water from the jug at the bedside. "Who was he, Maud? What was his name?"

"David Botolph," she said, her voice growing fainter with every word. "He was on his way to Calais. His brother, Gregory, was plotting to seize control of the English Pale and turn it over to England's enemies. They called it the Botolph Conspiracy at the time and it came close to succeeding."

Susanna frowned. She could not recall ever hearing of such a scheme, but she had no doubt it had been real. Vivid in her own memory were details of numerous other failed plots, each more ill-conceived than the last and all of them treasonous. They had been foiled by a careless word, or by the betrayal of a disenchanted conspirator, or through the work of the queen's intelligencers.

"Was that why he was killed?" she asked Maud. "Because he was a traitor?"

A cackle that ended in a violent fit of coughing answered her. "Never think it," she choked out after the worst of the fit subsided.

Susanna fumbled in the pouch she wore at her waist. She was accustomed to carry a few common remedies with her. Some of the healthful infusion she made Jennet drink daily to strengthen the housekeeper's heart would have been of more use, but failing that she had fennel root, which was good for easing a rasping cough. She mixed it with some wine she found on a sideboard and helped Maud take several swallows.

"Who killed him, Maud?"

"I did. With rat poison." If she felt any remorse, it did not show.

"Aconite," Susanna murmured. That fit with what she had observed. All Maud had needed to do was sprinkle the powdered root of the plant commonly known as monkshood onto David Botolph's food. First he would have felt dizzy. Then he'd have experienced palpitations and a tingling sensation in his skin, followed by numbness. His heart would have beaten slower and slower. Movement would have become impossible, and he'd have known he was dying long before he drew his last breath.

"Why, Maud?"

"He preferred Emma to me. He was going to abandon his brother's cause and follow her to Devonshire just because she was carrying his child."

Susanna sighed deeply. Jealousy was not an uncommon reason to commit murder, but it did not explain why the body had been left where it was. "How did David come to be sealed up in a hidden room?"

With a visible effort, Maud gathered what remained of her strength. "That was where he died. He'd cozened Lady Leigh into letting him stay in the new house while it was still being built and he liked that room because it was private—an ideal place to convince young serving maids to give up their virtue. Sir Anthony had no idea he was there, or even in Kent. He'd not have approved, and that was even before the details of the Botolph Conspiracy came out." She paused to gasp for air.

Susanna raised her head to give her another drink of the wine and fennel. "When did my grandfather find the body?"

"Right after the treason plot was discovered and made public."

Maud's voice had begun to fade in and out. Susanna leaned closer, anxious to catch every word.

"It was a few days after Lady Leigh and Emma and you two girls left for Devonshire. If the local coroner had been called in and learned who David was, Sir Anthony would have been sent straight to the Tower and Lady Leigh with him. The Crown arrested anyone who had anything to do with Gregory Boltolph, especially if there was a stench of the old religion about them. Some ended up hanged, drawn, and quartered."

As if she relished that image, Maud smiled, but telling her tale had exhausted her. She sagged against the bolster, weak as a newborn kitten.

"There must have been clear signs of poison," Susanna murmured, more to herself than to Maud. "My grandfather was no fool. Who did *he* think killed Botolph?"

A faint but recognizable cackle preceded Maud's answer. "He thought it was your grandmother."

Susanna tried to recall how her grandparents had behaved toward each other, both before and after the trip to Devonshire, but she had been very young and ignorant of all but childish concerns.

As an adult, she knew much more about gentlemen's households. Although the gentry could keep few secrets from their servants, Maud knew far more than she should have.

"How is it that you were privy to what my grandfather believed?"

"Before David Botolph came along," Maud whispered, "and after, too, I was as privy as any woman could be with Sir Anthony Leigh. I was your grandfather's mistress. How else do you think Joanna and I came to live in this fine house?"

Susanna sprang to her feet. "No!"

She glanced at Joanna. Maud's daughter looked as shocked as Susanna felt.

Maud was clever with words, she reminded herself. She'd led her to believe she'd meet Emma in Exeter when she'd clearly meant them to meet in the hereafter. Even then, she'd been plotting Susanna's death to protect her secret.

"Anthony named her in memory of your sister," Maud rasped. "That first Joanna died the year before my Joanna was born."

"No," Susanna said again, but the protest was weak. There were few things more convincing than a deathbed confession.

Maud's thin, cracked lips curved into a smug smile, delighted that she'd been able to strike one final painful blow at Sir Anthony Leigh's remaining legitimate descendant. Her last breath was a sigh of malevolent pleasure.

A Note from the Author

Both the earthquake in 1580 and the earlier one Susanna mentions were real. This one was centered in the English Channel and caused destruction as far away as London. Since natural disasters of all sorts were prime fodder for chapbooks in sixteenth-century England, there are detailed written records of the event.

The Botolph Conspiracy was also real. I dealt with in more detail in *Between Two Queens*, one of six novels I wrote as Kate Emerson. David Botolph, however, is a fictional character.

This story first appeared in the December 2013 issue of *Alfred Hitchcock Mystery Magazine*.

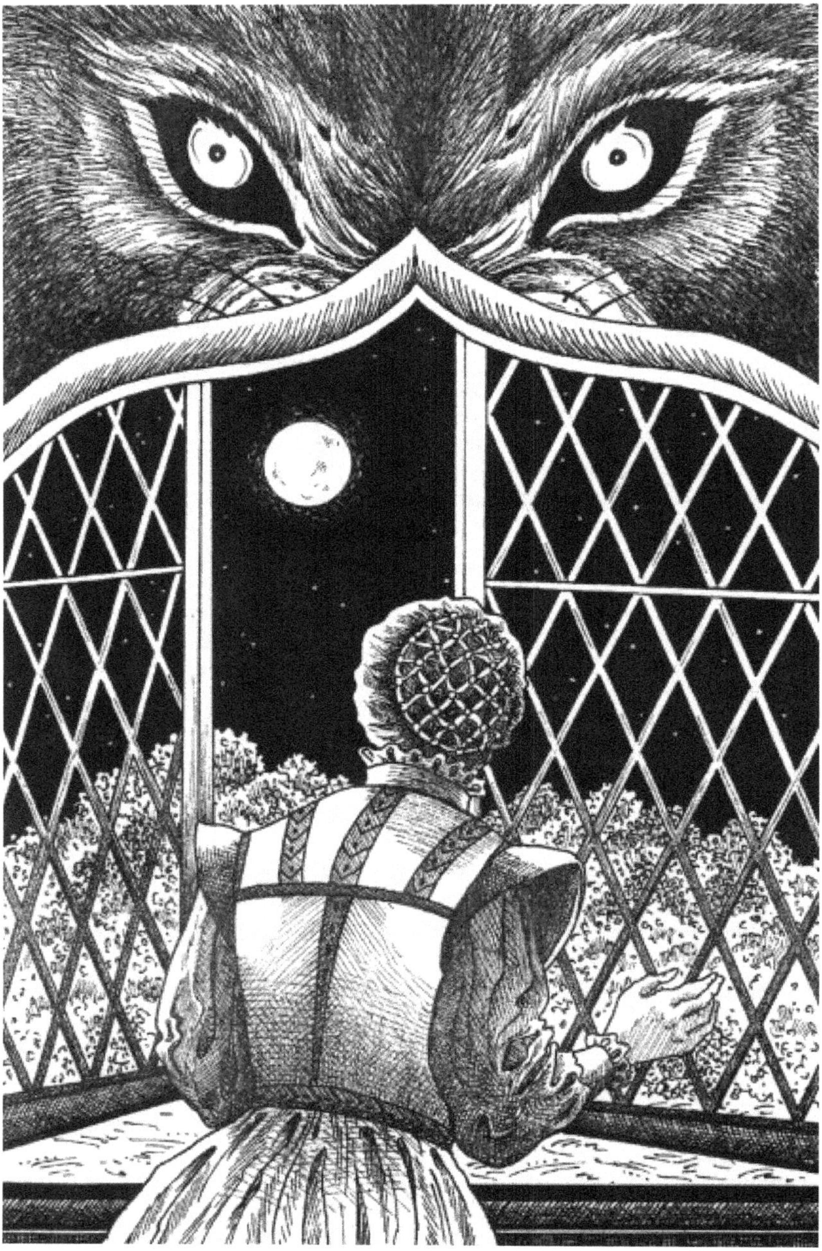

Lady Appleton and the Creature of the Night

1581

The vicar came to dine with Susanna, Lady Appleton only as often as she could tolerate his company. As the leading landowner in the parish, she had an obligation to support him and his church. Indeed, she had been the one to appoint him to his living and he was, furthermore, a distant relative, but she did not much care for Nathaniel Lonsdale or his diatribes against sin.

"It is most alarming," he insisted between bites of succulent roast beef. "This very morning there were seven reports of chickens and pigs gone missing, and the mauled and partially eaten carcass of a calf was found just the other side of Whitethorn Manor."

His wife nodded in agreement. Once she'd been a bright young thing, full of enthusiasm for life and fresh ideas. Years of living with her husband had turned her into a stodgy matron without an original thought in her head. She parroted back Lonsdale's opinions as if they were Gospel.

"Sightings of a strange and diabolical beast in the forest?" Susanna let her skepticism show. "Surely it is just some creature that has strayed from its usual haunts. I have heard that there are still wildcats in Scotland, and wolves, and a breed of lions, too."

"Scotland is a great distance from Kent." Lonsdale drank deeply of the fine wine Susanna served at table. "I fear this is the devil's work. There is an old beldam living by herself near the woods—"

"Stop right there, Nathaniel. I will not have you persecuting innocents."

"Scarce that! She keeps a cat. A black cat."

"I keep a cat. Several. And the notion that a domestic animal, one that earns its keep by catching mice and rats, can be turned into a beast by magic is as nonsensical as the idea that witches can fly."

If he'd been a Catholic instead of a Puritan, Nathaniel Lonsdale would no doubt have crossed himself. As it was, he goggled at her and began to sputter. "You must let me tend to the spiritual needs of my parishioners, cousin."

"I have no intention of preventing you, but the physical needs of those who live on my land are my concern. The old woman you mention is Mary Cresswell. She was once a servant at Leigh Abbey. She was pensioned off when she grew too old to work and lives on that small annuity. I allow she has grown feeble in both mind and body, and no doubt the local children are afraid of her, but she harms no one. Leave her be, Nathaniel."

Susanna promised herself she'd visit the old woman herself in the next day or two and make sure she was still able to manage on her own. If not, she would send someone to serve as her caretaker for as long as was necessary. Loyal service deserved to be rewarded and Susanna had been taught from a young age to take care of every member of the household. Leigh Abbey was prosperous enough to support any number of aged former retainers.

She set out the next morning on foot, a basket containing bread, fresh eggs, cheese, and cold roast beef over her arm. It was a pleasant walk, taking her through Leigh Abbey's orchard before the trail entered the woods. If she'd continued on the main path, she'd soon reach the back of Whitethorn Manor. Instead, she turned off on a way less well-traveled, coming out of the trees again in a clearing near the southern edge of the forest. The cottage old Mother Cresswell had been given, nestled among apple trees and rosebushes, was a pleasing sight, but as Susanna approached her steps slowed.

There was no smoke rising from the chimney and the door was ajar.

The smells reached her before she saw what lay within—the sharp, acrid tang of spilled blood and the even more distinctive stench of a body releasing its fluids at the moment of death.

Steeling herself for what she would find, Susanna set down her basket and stepped inside the cottage. The black cat streaked past her into the forest.

The old woman lay on the rush-covered floor, her back to the door. Susanna frowned as she took in the spatters of blood, thinking they made no sense. Then she circled the body and looked down.

At first her mind refused to believe what she was seeing. Could the black cat have done all this? She'd heard that cats would sample a dead master or mistress's body. After all, dead meat was dead meat. But Mary Cresswell's throat had been torn open and there were bite marks on her face and arms that were too large to have been made by the small black animal Susanna had just seen.

When she had made a thorough examination of the body and concluded that the old woman had most likely died sometime during the night, Susanna retreated the way she'd come, closing the door behind her.

As she made her way back to Leigh Abbey, she tried to find a logical explanation for what she had found. This was not a case of murder and yet it felt like one. What kind of animal left its kill to rot? She considered mastiffs, trained to attack bulls for entertainment at Paris Gardens in London. She supposed a large dog could have done this, but one such would have been as alien to this small forest in southeastern Kent as the wolves and lions and wildcats she had spoken of to Nathaniel.

Every odd sound from among the trees had her walking faster. The possibility of a ravening beast on the prowl made it unwise for anyone to be alone and unarmed in this place. She did not take an easy breath until she was out in the open again.

As soon as she reached Leigh Abbey, she gathered the household together and told them what she had found, adding the admonition that no one was to go outside alone until they discovered the cause of Mother Cresswell's death. When she sent her steward, accompanied by two grooms of the stable and the second gardener, to fetch the body, the grooms carried loaded pistols and the gardener took a scythe.

Susanna sent her horse master and the gardener's boy, similarly armed, into the nearby village of Eastwold to gather a party of searchers. The sooner they scoured the woods, the better.

She thought it a great pity that Nick Baldwin, her neighbor at Whitethorn Manor, was away from home. He was a good man in a crisis, but he was in London and there was no point in sending for him when it would take two days for a message to reach there and another two for him to make the journey home.

"Back to your duties, now," Susanna ordered the rest of her household. "There is nothing to fear so long as you stay indoors."

Her housekeeper and friend, Jennet Jaffrey, remained behind, her face a mask of disapproval. "How can you say that? I heard what the vicar said at dinner. It was no ordinary creature that killed Mother Cresswell."

"I do not believe in demons conjured up by witchcraft." In the usual way of things, Susanna found Jennet's superstitious nature amusing, but today was different. "And do not tell me that witches can shift their shapes and become animals. Mother Cresswell did not turn herself into a black cat."

"Then what happened to her?"

"Something killed her. Something of the *natural* world, albeit something that should not be living in our woods. A large, well-armed party composed of men from Leigh Abbey and Eastwold will hunt it down and kill it and that will be the end of the matter."

Jennet did not look convinced.

The vicar put in an appearance shortly after Mother Cresswell's body had been wrapped in its winding sheet. Sounding even more pompous than usual, he announced that she could not be buried in holy ground.

Susanna looked up from her chair in the small parlor adjacent to the great hall, the room where she was wont to pass many a winter's afternoon reading to her maidservants while they sat and sewed. "Why not? She was not a heretic or a witch and she did not kill herself."

"Nonetheless, to assure the safety of the rest of my parishioners, she must be buried at the crossroads with a stake through her heart. The ritual will allay the fears of the good people of my congregation."

"Do you mean to drive the stake through her heart yourself?" Susanna's voice was deceptively sweet, making it clear she thought her cousin was a fool.

A tick appeared beneath Lonsdale's right eye. "It is my duty."

"Will you bury her there at the traditional time between the hours of nine and midnight, in the dark when hellhounds are on the prowl? What if the beast meant to return to finish devouring its kill? Do you suppose it can track a corpse by smell? If so, I would not want to be the one caught burying it at a deserted crossroads."

The vicar had gone as pale as Mother Cresswell's winding sheet, but he knew his duty. "I will take armed men with me." Then he brightened. "It will not be all that dark. The moon is at the full."

"How fortunate. You will be able to see this creature of the night before it reaches you."

Nathaniel Lonsdale was still sputtering when the search party returned from the woods.

"We found no sign of any creature bigger than a hare," Susanna's steward reported, "but we did discover this in that old abandoned hut by the stone wall." He produced a leather sack. "Mayhap some vagabond took shelter there and has since moved on."

"Unless he, too, was killed by the beast," the vicar muttered.

"There would have been signs if he'd been attacked. We found none."

Taking the sack, Susanna peered inside. It was empty, but the interior had a faint odor that made her nostrils twitch. That she could not identify the whiff of scent surprised her. She possessed an extensive knowledge of herbs, spices, and flowers and it was rare she encountered a smell unfamiliar to her.

Jennet appeared in the doorway before Susanna could sniff again. "There is a Mistress Catsby at the gate, madam, seeking shelter for the night."

Susanna did not know the name, but that scarce mattered. It was an old and accepted custom for country landowners to offer hospitality to travelers. "For her own safety, she should continue on. If she is headed north, she has time to reach Canterbury before dark. If her destination lies to the south, Dover is no farther away. Both towns are well supplied with inns."

"Her coach has lost a wheel."

"Then make her welcome, Jennet. Nathaniel, go home. If you will not bury Mother Cresswell in the churchyard, she can be interred in Leigh Abbey's chapel."

A short time later, after Susanna had made certain the searchers had been given food and drink and rewarded for their efforts, she returned to the small parlor to greet her unexpected guest. A woman stood before the fire. She held the leather sack the searchers had found. Unaware that she was being observed, she lifted it to her nose and inhaled deeply.

"It is a peculiar scent," Susanna said. "Do you recognize it?"

Mistress Catsby lowered the sack and turned, revealing a youthful face dominated by large, oddly slanted green eyes. She wore costly silk and soft velvet, an indication that she came from a family possessed of both status and wealth. Her smile was tinged with embarrassment.

"It is unfamiliar to me. I am known for my keen sense of smell and when I detected that one, I was curious enough to seek its source. I am grateful for your hospitality, Lady Appleton. I will try not to be a burden to you."

Susanna cocked her head. "You are from the north, I think, by your manner of speaking."

"Northumberland. You have a good ear."

"What brings you so far south, if I may ask?" She waved Mistress Catsby toward the window seat and took her own usual place in the Glastonbury chair.

"I have been searching for my cousin. A family matter demands his attention at home, but no one has heard from him for some time. His name is Edward Catsby and he looks a good deal like me." She hesitated, then reached up to remove her French hood. "He has my eyes and his hair is the same as mine."

"How unusual," Susanna murmured. For the most part, Mistress Catsby's hair was an attractive red-gold—a shade that would make her most popular at court—but on the right side there was a distinctive streak of pure white at least two inches wide. "I would have remembered him if I had seen him."

They passed the evening in casual conversation, supping together and later adjourning to Susanna's study, where she kept chests full of books and other treasures. She could not help but notice when Mistress Catsby's gaze kept drifting to the window that looked out over the orchards to the woods beyond. She wondered if her guest had heard of Mother Cresswell's death, but she did not see how that could be, given that she was a stranger to these parts. She did not broach the subject herself. She saw no reason to frighten the other woman.

When the hour grew late, they parted on friendly terms and Mistress Catsby retired to her bedchamber. Susanna remained in her study, where she drew out a sheet of paper, dipped her quill into the inkpot, and began to write.

What manner of beast attacked Mother Cresswell?
  Why did she open her door when there was a beast outside?
  Are others in danger from this creature of the night?

The animal killings the vicar had mentioned had taken place at during the hours of darkness. So had Mother Cresswell's death. Susanna feared they would make another terrible discovery on the morrow.

Abandoning her list, she left the desk for the window seat. With the moon at the full, as it had been for the past two nights, she could see all the way to the point where the path entered the woods. Nothing stirred, not even a field mouse, and yet Nathaniel Lonsdale's foolish talk of witchcraft niggled at the back of her mind. She had read several accounts of witch trials where the accused was said to have turned herself into a a cat or a dog or a toad, but she had never heard of a case where a witch became a wolf or a lion or a bear.

What she did remember was a story her grandmother had told her many years ago. In the tale of Bisclavret, a noble knight was transformed by magic into the shape of a wolf. He did not, however, behave like a predatory animal. He retained his sense of honor and his intelligence and was eventually restored to human form with the help of the king—Henry the Second of England, if her recollection was correct. Mayhap she should ask Queen Elizabeth to come to Kent and charm the beast out of the forest.

Susanna smiled to herself. If virgins were able to entice unicorns, then surely—

Her thoughts scattered when something moved in the moonlit landscape beyond her window. She leaned out, squinting to see better. There! She caught a glimpse of long, bright hair and a female form clothed all in white. It drifted like a ghost toward the small footbridge that crossed the stream separating the field from the orchard.

In the next moment, she recognized Mistress Catsby. Tendrils of fog had created the otherworldly illusion. The figure below was real, and she might be in danger.

Susanna had not thought her guest needed to be warned not to go out at night. It was rare anyone wanted to. Most people believed the night air was unhealthy to breathe, and even more were convinced that spirits walked in the midnight hour.

She did not take the time to rouse anyone else in her sleeping household. Instead, she descended the stairs at a fast clip, hurried through the chapel, and left Leigh Abbey by a little-used side door, determined to stop Mistress Catsby before she reached the woods. Once outside, she followed a well-worn path to the footbridge.

Although she did not find Mistress Catsby there, the bright moonlight picked out the garment she had been wearing. A night rail of the finest white lawn had been carelessly tossed onto the planking.

Alarmed, Susanna peered down into the murky depths on both sides of the bridge. Nothing stirred and she heard no splashing. The quiet murmur of water passing over rocks was the only sound in the stillness of the night.

That stillness was abruptly broken by a low growl coming from the orchard. Susanna caught sight of something moving among the apple trees, but the moonlight did not penetrate far enough for her to make out more than a vague shape the size of a large dog.

Without warning, a second beast appeared. With a horrific screech, it attacked the first animal. Her heart in her throat, Susanna watched the two thrash and roll as they fought. Shrieks more feline than canine filled the night, so loud that the very air seemed to vibrate.

Susanna stood frozen, her hands clapped over her ears. She was unable to look away until the battle shifted in her direction and she realized she would be in mortal danger if the creatures caught her scent. Slowly, she backed off the footbridge.

Once on solid ground, she turned and fled toward Leigh Abbey. She stumbled and nearly fell more than once before she reached the house.

Her entire household had gathered in the great hall, roused from sleep by the unholy racket in the orchard.

Susanna fought for calm. It was up to her to reassure her dependents, and she must also organize a search for Mistress Catsby. If her men armed themselves, they should be able to drive off the creatures of the night.

As suddenly as it had begun, the caterwauling stopped. Susanna sent the grooms to the stables to see to the horses, knowing they would have been as frightened as the servants. She dispatched the cook to the kitchen to heat a calming posset everyone could share.

It did not take long for the questions to begin. Since Susanna did not know how to explain what she had seen, at first she said only that the sounds they'd heard had been made by wild animals. She was about to reveal that Mistress Catsby was still outside when Jennet demanded to know if one of those beasts had killed Mother Cresswell.

"It may have."

Before she could say more, Mistress Catsby appeared in the great hall. Yawning, she regarded the assembled company with wide, innocent eyes. "What is all this to-do about?" she asked.

"Did you not hear the shrieking and howling?" Jennet asked.

"I sleep most soundly." She yawned again. "It was the light of flickering torches in the stable yard that woke me."

Susanna stared at the young woman with narrowed eyes. She did not believe anyone could have slept through those loud, eerie sounds, and she had not imagined seeing a figure in white and finding a night rail. She wished she had not left it on the footbridge, but picking it up had been the last thing on her mind when she was running for her life.

"There was a disturbance, Mistress Catsby," she said in the calmest voice she could manage, "but there is no more we can do about it until morning." She turned to address the members of her household. "Go back to bed, all of you. We will investigate further once the sun has risen."

* * *

The next day, when Susanna accompanied her men to the orchard and Mistress Catsby came with them. It was easy to find a place where the ground had been disturbed. Blood stained the grass, although there was less of it than Susanna expected.

When Mistress Catsby bent double and drew in a deep breath, Susanna feared she was about to be sick, but when she straightened, she was smiling. "Can you smell it?" she asked. "It is the same scent that clung to that leather bag. Where did you find it?"

After sending most of her men to search elsewhere, Susanna took two others with them and led her guest to the abandoned hut. One wall had collapsed. What was left offered shelter from the elements but no protection from wild animals. It had not, it appeared, saved Mistress Catsby's missing cousin from harm.

They found him curled into a ball on the dirt floor with one arm shielding his face. His clothing was in shreds. The bare skin showing through was covered with scratches and bites that reminded Susanna of those on Mother Cresswell's body.

Mistress Catsby ran to him, calling his name. Susanna followed her into the ruins of the hut, amazed to discover that Edward Catsby was still alive. She needed only a moment to determine that he burned with fever.

"Fashion a litter to carry him to Leigh Abbey," she ordered.

Once there, she and Mistress Catsby tended his injuries while searchers continued to comb the woods for the wild animal that had killed Mother Cresswell and mauled the young man. After a few hours, he awoke, still weak but capable of speech.

"What manner of beast attacked you?" Susanna asked him.

"Wolf," he whispered.

"*Wolf?*"

Seeming to sense her skepticism, he wavered. "Mayhap it was a feral dog."

Having examined the scratches and bites on his body, Susanna was puzzled. "Could it have been some kind of big cat?"

There were lions in the royal menagerie in the Tower of London, but none nearer than that. For some reason a lynx came to mind, although Susanna had never heard of any living in England. Their fur was imported and used to line cloaks and trim collars.

For a moment, the injured man's voice gained both strength and certainty. "It was not a cat."

"How did you survive?"

His eyes, so like his cousin's, searched for Mistress Catsby before he answered. "I had a knife. I struck a fatal blow. I am certain of it."

Then where, Susanna wondered, was the predator's body?

* * *

The searchers found no sign of a wild animal, living or dead, large enough to prey on humans. Throughout the day, tales of supernatural creatures of the night grew apace.

Early that evening, Susanna entered the sickroom just as Mistress Catsby was reaching across the bed to apply a cool cloth to her cousin's forehead. For an instant, the bulky shape of a bandage showed beneath her sleeve.

At the sight of it, a foolish thought crossed Susanna's mind. She dismissed it at once, but that night, by the light of the waning moon, she once again watched the path to the woods from her window. Nothing disturbed the stillness. Near dawn, when she looked in on her patient and his cousin, she found them both sleeping peacefully.

Nothing untoward happened the next night, either, or on the ones that followed. By the end of the week, Mistress Catsby's coach had been repaired and Edward Catsby was deemed fit to travel.

"I am most grateful for your hospitality, Lady Appleton," Mistress Catsby said, "and for your care of my cousin. I am sure Edward succeeded in killing the beast that attacked him. You will have no more trouble from that cause."

As Susanna wished the travelers a safe, swift journey home, she too felt certain they had heard the last of the creature of the night. She would admit to no one save herself that she put any stock in legends of humans who turned into animals, but she knew what she had seen.

She understood why her guests were in such a hurry to depart. They wished to be well away from Leigh Abbey before the next full moon.

A Note from the Author

The sixteenth century was a superstitious time. Even a rational woman like Lady Appleton sensed that there were more things in nature than she could understand. Although she was adamant that those accused of witchcraft were simply women unfortunate enough to incur the dislike of their neighbors, and was certain that ghosts did not exist, she was not immune to the fears that come to all of us in the dark of night.

This story first appeared in the December 2016 issue of *Alfred Hitchcock Mystery Magazine*. Since I had long wanted to write a story about a werewolf (or maybe a were-lynx), I took this opportunity to do so. For those who prefer their mysteries to be firmly based in the real world, I ask your indulgence for my flight of fancy.

It is at this point in the chronology of Face Down novels and short stories that three full-length mysteries featuring Rosamond Jaffrey (née Appleton) as the amateur detective take place. Many characters from the original series, including Lady Appleton, reappear in Rosamond's adventures. *Murder in the Queen's Wardrobe, Murder in the Merchant's Hall,* and *Murder in a Cornish Alehouse* are set in the years 1582-1584.

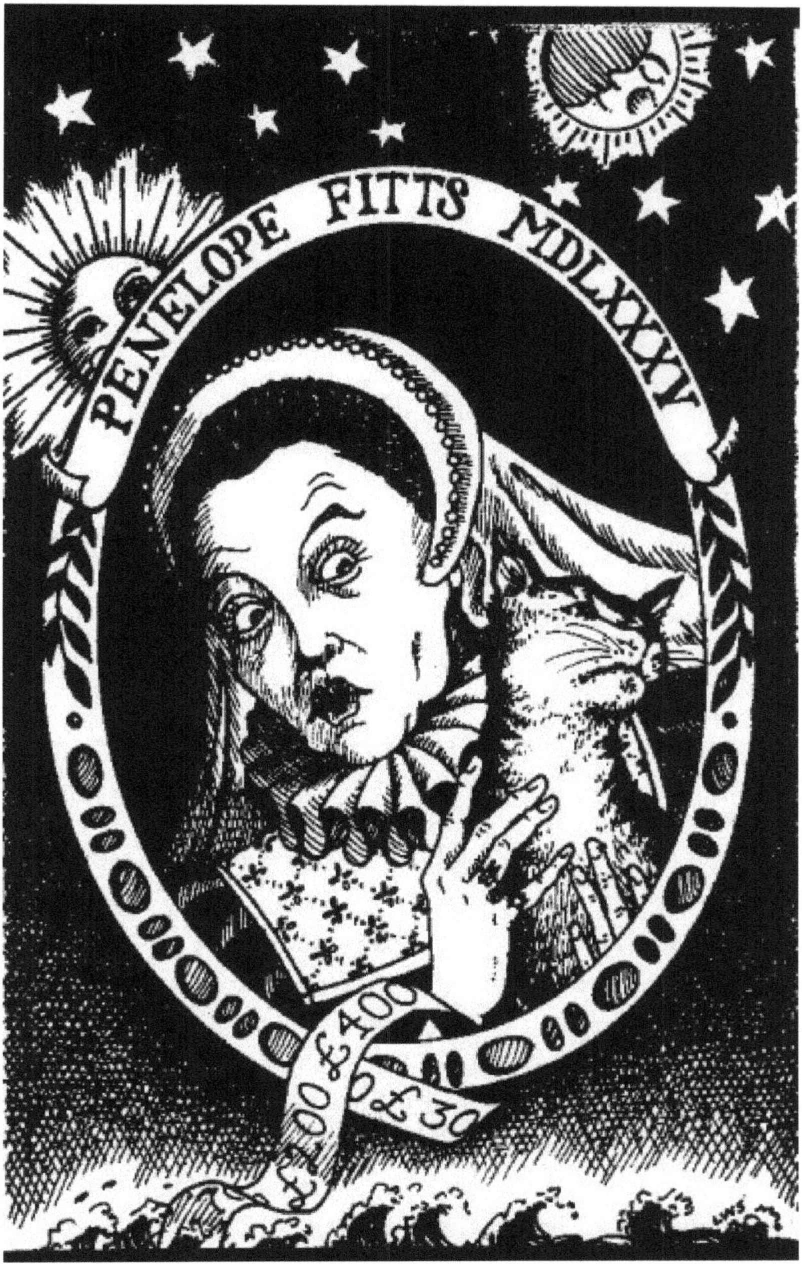
PENELOPE FITTS MDLXXXV
£400

The Curse of the Figure Flinger

Among the merchants of London in the year 1585—a year heralded by prophesies of doom on a scale not seen since old King Henry died—there lived a wadwife who called herself Mistress Fitts. I doubt it was her real name any more than Dame Starkey, the one I go by, is mine. Reputed to be a rich man's widow, she used her inheritance to become more wealthy still. Through connivance, she loaned out money at a rate forbidden by law. Some would say she reaped the reward she deserved.

In other words, one fine spring day she was murdered.

Now the law of England is a peculiar entity. At times it works, but at others, well, then there is a need to find out the truth by other means.

I am a figure flinger. For most of the sixty years I have been on this earth, I have made my living finding lost objects and charting the future in the stars. In truth, those are no more than clever tricks learned at my father's knee. If I'd been an able prognosticator I would have seen the constable coming in time to avoid both him and his questions.

Caught in my garret chamber, I thought I was being sued again. Londoners go to court at the drop of a hat. If flight would not serve, I reasoned, a bribe would have to do to keep me from arrest. I grimaced at the thought, but there seemed no help for it. When Constable Timmons, a bold youth with a shock of yellow hair, asked when I'd last seen Mistress Fitts, I made the mistake of assuming he asked because she'd brought suit against me for fraud.

"Yester e'en," I replied, honest for a change.

"When you cursed her soundly and threatened her with bodily harm if she pursued her case in court?"

Foolish enough to grin at the memory, I nodded. There had been other shouting matches between us and I anticipated there would be more. Penelope Fitts had always been a most disagreeable person.

"Dame Starkey," the constable said, "you must come with me."

"Now, Timmons. I have no time for this. Go back and tell Mistress Fitts I will draw up a new horoscope to replace the one she does not like." I was reaching into my purse for something to encourage his cooperation when he laid hands on me.

"You are under arrest for murder, Dame Starkey. Mistress Fitts is dead."

* * *

London's gaols are none of them pleasant. I'd been in Ludgate before, for debt, but felons are taken to Newgate, the worst of the lot. All that saved me from being thrown in the darkest, deepest hole in the place, a dungeon called "the Limboes" that is lit only by a single candle set on a black stone, is the fact that I am a woman. Female prisoners at Newgate are kept in a single stone tower.

A generous bribe assured me of a private cell with a bedstead, warm blankets, and a charcoal brazier—it is cold even in spring behind the stone walls of a prison. Once I'd paid for these "luxuries" and for food to be brought on a regular basis, the heavy door slammed shut with a solid thunk and the key rasped in the lock, leaving me alone with my whirling thoughts.

The prognosis was not good. I did not have unlimited funds. I'd already had to pay an exorbitant admission fee in addition to the rental and expenses for this "special apartment." I'd also given the keeper £5 for "exemption from ironing." Well worth it, I suppose. Otherwise manacles at my wrists, or fetters or shackles on my ankles, or perhaps an iron collar around my neck, would be chained to the ring in the middle of the floor.

I anticipated daily expenses would continue to mount as long as I was held in Newgate. I'd even be charged a fee for washing water. That commodity flowed freely into the prison through leaden pipes, but the person who brought it to my cell would have to be paid.

When my money ran out, I'd be sent to the common side. There I'd still have to find a way to buy food. In addition, the prisoners themselves collect garnish to finance the occasional evening of drunken debauchery. Those who refuse to donate to the cause have been known to end up naked and shivering, their very clothes confiscated to make up for their lack of funds.

It did not take me long to reach a conclusion—I needs must discover who killed Mistress Fitts. The only other way out of this place required doing the hempen jig at Tyburn.

After some thought, I sent a carefully worded note, containing just the hint of a threat, to someone who owed me a very great favor.

* * *

Nicholas Baldwin, prosperous merchant of London, stormed into my cell just as I was about to partake of a simple repast, exorbitantly priced, consisting of rye bread, porridge, and cheese.

"I see, Griselda," he said, "that you have at last met the fate you so richly deserve."

I winced at his use of my real name. I hadn't thought of myself as Griselda Ferrers in years. "Good day to you, Nick. So kind of you to visit."

Nick does not approve of the way I earn my living, but that he turned up at all meant he intended to help. Otherwise, he'd have ignored my letter and left me to rot.

In a cause as good as saving my own skin, I was willing to endure a certain amount of preaching. I continued to munch on the bread as he surveyed my cell. All the luxury I'd paid for was revealed by candles a cellarman sold for twice what they cost outside Newgate.

"I suppose you want money," Nick said.

His nose wrinkled in distaste as he spoke. Small wonder! The two large angular stone towers of the old Roman gate at Newgate straddle a broad market street that is dominated, just inside the city walls, by the Shambles. This long row of butchers' stalls extending toward Cheap accounts for Newgate's nickname, "the Stink," and for the pervasive odor that infects the entire prison.

"I can earn my own coin," I snapped. "There is always some fool ready to pay for a glimpse of his future, even in prison."

He snorted. "How long will that last? You are trapped here. If someone decides you're a fraud, if your prediction doesn't turn out the way you promised, your victim will know right where to find you."

"I suppose you think there's poetic justice in that?"

"Delicious irony at the least. I am told it was because of a horoscope you devised for Mistress Fitts that she intended to take you to court."

"She claimed the prognostication was false."

"Is that why the authorities think you killed her?"

I took heart from his choice of words. "There is more," I admitted. "I confronted her. I cursed her, in fact, and naturally insisted, in a loud and carrying voice, that every word in her star chart was Gospel."

"And so you were arrested for her murder when she turned up dead the very next morning."

"It seems I was the last person to see her alive, saving only the one who killed her."

"And that was not you?"

"No. I do not even know how she died, since I was not present at the inquest."

"She was drowned," Nick said.

I could not contain my surprise and that reaction convinced him I was innocent of the crime.

"Someone pushed her face into a basin of water and held it there."

I shuddered. "I knew this was not destined to be a good year."

There had been a partial eclipse on the nineteenth—the day before I quarreled with Mistress Fitts, a warning of disaster I should have heeded even if I discounted malevolent conjunctions shown by the planets and disturbing signs revealed by the moon.

Nick sat down beside me on the low camp bed. "Easter term begins in less than a week. They'll try you at the Sessions House in Old Bailey Street."

"I know." The quarter sessions were held hard by Newgate, convenient for transporting prisoners.

"Trial to execution is generally only a matter of days, and it is a rare trial indeed that lasts more than a quarter of an hour."

"If I cannot leave this place, I do not know how I can hope to discover who really did kill Mistress Fitts. It was likely one of her clients, someone who defaulted on a loan, or was about to."

After a long, contemplative silence, he said, "The keeper of Newgate will allow you out on furlough if you pay the wages of a guard."

"More expenses," I complained.

Nick almost smiled. "And not yet the end of them. Even if you manage to prove your innocence, you will have to return to Newgate to await a royal pardon. Another two months might pass before one arrives, and then, to add insult to injury, you'll be charged a release fee."

"Only if I am alive to pay it."

"At least there need be no lawyer involved. None is permitted in criminal cases."

"Small mercy," I agreed. Even moneylenders and fortune tellers are more honest than the average man of law.

* * *

Nick went off to speak to the keeper of Newgate. When he returned a few hours later, he was accompanied by a man of about my own years. This fellow, Bates by name, was short and brick-shaped, but he had the biggest head I'd ever seen on a man. An unkempt gray beard and lank hair cut just below his ears exaggerated its size and only partly concealed the pockmarks that mottled an otherwise plain face. Dark, deep-set eyes regarded me with a blank stare.

"You're not allowed to leave London," he said.

"Why would anyone want to?" I'd been born within the sound of Bow bells and had never felt any desire to travel farther beyond the city walls than Westminster or Southwark.

Bates slanted his eyes toward Nick. "Had a prisoner once who went all the way to Lancashire on her furlough," he said. "Turned out she was innocent."

"As I am," I assured him.

"So say they all."

* * *

The stench of the Shambles and a profusion of sights and sounds engulfed us the moment we left Newgate.

"Ass's milk! Two shillings a pint!" a boy cried, offering up his product for inspection.

A porter with a trunk on his back pushed past without apology, nearly shoving me into the path of a lady carried in a chair. For a moment, she looked alarmed, but she was quickly transported out of harm's way by her two sturdy chairmen. There were horses in the street as well, and a few coaches. These awkward vehicles had proliferated in the past few years, to the point of causing traffic jams on the narrower thoroughfares.

I reveled in every bit of the confusion, delighted to be free again.

"It is clear you do not intend to return to your lodgings just yet," Nick remarked when we'd passed several streets leading toward the Thames without turning south. "What is your plan?"

"Penelope Fitts did business through an agent, one Hornsby. He styles himself a scrivener." He'd arranged loans for her, drawn up the bonds, and shared in the profits.

As we walked, I thought over what I knew of the moneylender's sharp practices. By law, interest on loans is limited to 10% per annum. A typical bond for £100 might say that the borrower would pay the lender's agent £105 in six months time. Mistress Fitts thwarted the law by falsifying the amount of the loan. Her bond would say the borrower owed £200, and therefore she charged twice as much in interest. This was naught but a convenient fiction as long as the borrower repaid the £100, with the double interest, within six months, but if he defaulted on the loan, the bond became enforceable for the higher amount. Mistress Fitts had never hesitated to proceed against deadbeats at the common law, or to settle out of court if she received a good offer. She'd made an excellent living from penalties alone.

Such a one as she made enemies.

One of them, I felt certain, had killed her.

While I ruminated, we walked as far as the city cross, a small, highly decorated stone tower set upon stone steps. A few years back, religious vandals destroyed most of the lower sculptures—scenes from the life of Christ—even removing the Christ child from His mother's arms.

"The bonding of borrowers to lenders is a flourishing business in London," I said, "and the center of the industry is that church." I gestured toward an impressive edifice on the south side of Cheap, bracketed by Hosier Lane and Cordwainer Street. Just beyond stood the Conduit, surrounded by groceries and apothecary shops. I fancied I could smell the spices even this far away.

Nick stood aside to let pass two water carriers burdened with wooden containers that looked more like butter churns than barrels. Then he bade me farewell and God speed. As he walked away, bound for his lodgings and warehouse in Billingsgate, I almost called him back. If Mistress Fitts had begun litigation against someone who'd defaulted on a loan, the Court of Common Pleas would have the records, but a clerk would need bribing before he would release information on any civil suit arising from non-payment of debt.

With a sigh, I let Nick go. He had already done more on my behalf than I'd expected. That left me on my own with Bates. I sent my warder a baleful look. I did not need to consult the stars to predict that he would prove more hindrance than help.

***

The vaults beneath St. Mary Le Bow have long been the principal meeting place for brokers, moneylenders' agents, and clerks who specialize in drawing up bonds. It was no great feat to locate my quarry there. Hornsby wanted borrowers to find him and made himself easy to spot by wearing a brightly colored doublet and a bonnet with a large, drooping feather. He'd just finished signing papers with a nervous little man in country clothes when I accosted him.

"There you are, Hornsby," I declared in a loud, carrying voice. "Just as I foresaw!"

He turned, a cheerful smile on his cherubic face. It faltered only slightly when he recognized me. The bushy brows over his bright blue eyes lifted in an unspoken question. Since he had been her tenant as well as her agent, he'd undoubtedly heard I had been arrested for murdering Mistress Fitts.

"I have read the stars," I informed him, "and they told me to come to you for answers."

His normally ruddy complexion paled a bit at that but he recovered with alacrity. "What can I do to serve you, Dame Starkey?"

"You can help me find the real culprit before they hang me for something I did not do. I need names—all those who defaulted on loans from Mistress Fitts and were about to be sued, and all those from whom she cozened larger penalties than she was due."

"Do you think one of them killed her?"

"Have you any better suggestion?" I gave him the look I'd practiced on countless clients, the one that convinced them I could unleash the dark forces of the occult should I choose to do so.

Hornsby whisked me into a secluded area in the crypt of St. Mary Le Bow where we were not likely to be overheard. His answers yielded two names worth investigating. Weems the weaver had defaulted on a loan of five pounds. I knew him. He had a quick temper and a chronic shortage of funds. I had never met Mistress Gamage of Soper Lane, but she apparently had a problem with gambling. She had failed to repay the somewhat greater sum of seventy-five pounds. If Mistress Fitts had sued, Master Gamage would have learned what his wife had been up to. He had, Hornsby told me, a reputation as a pinch penny.

"Is there anyone else?"

"No one, and chances are Mistress Gamage would have repaid her loan before the case came to court. She always has before. I fear, dear madam, that you were the only one who threatened Mistress Fitts. I heard you cursing her myself. Some might say the curse of a figure flinger alone is enough to kill."

"Faugh! I am no witch, Hornsby, and you know full well that when I left her she was hale and hearty."

Bates cleared his throat. I had almost forgotten his presence, but when he spoke, I found myself regarding him with new interest.

"You were the one who found her, were you not?" he asked Hornsby. "Are you also the one who told the coroner about Dame Starkey's curse?"

One look at Hornsby's face was answer enough. "Villain!" I cried, rounding on him. "How dare you accuse me of such a heinous crime?"

"I made no accusation. I meant you no harm!" He was all but babbling. "I did but tell them what I knew."

I conquered a compelling urge to strike him and settled for the most formidable glower I could produce. When he was suitably cowed, I peppered him with more questions. By the time I was done, he'd provided me with every detail he could remember about his discovery of the body, and agreed to let me search her house. She had left everything she owned to endow the grammar school associated with St. Mary Le Bow, but Hornsby was executor of her will as well as her lodger.

"Well," I said to Bates as we set off for St. Helen's, Bishopgate, where Mistress Fitts had lived for many years, "that went well."

"I wonder why he was so cooperative."

"He's afraid of me. Many people fear fortune tellers. At times, that is passing convenient. My father was an astrologer," I added. He had not been a very good one, but I saw no reason to share that information, or to tell him that my mother, a gentlewoman, had abandoned us when I was a baby. "I learned my craft at his knee. This is a bad year for any man who must make a journey by land or water. Violence frowns upon travelers." That forecast came straight from the pages of Master Porter's almanac.

"I plan to stay in London," Bates said.

"Even traveling the distance from one street to another can be dangerous," I said in my best doom-laden tones. "Where do you lodge, Bates?"

"I rent a room from Mistress Clover in Cow Lane."

I permitted myself a small smile. Cow Lane was located in Faringdon Without, a ward on the west side of Smithfield. It was hard by Newgate but a goodly walk from my abode. Bates would be looking over his shoulder the entire way home.

"I will not be returning there until you are back in prison," he informed me.

"Do you mean to tell me I must house and feed you as well as pay your wages?" I'd intended to give him the slip once I got out of Newgate, but so far he'd stuck to me like a burr.

Bates gave a negligent shrug. "That is what Master Baldwin agreed to on your behalf."

"Pestilence and pestilent fevers will sweep cities and scour towns," I sputtered, too indignant to make sense.

"Perhaps they will," Bates said with equanimity, "but that does not change my charge."

I narrowed my eyes at him. "I do not suppose you suffer from the French Pox?"

Bates grinned, showing a great many big yellow teeth. "I am prodigious healthy and always have been, and particular what females I sport with."

Master Lloyd's almanac, which supported all the claims in Porter's, additionally warned that this would be a bad year for those who suffered from venereal diseases. *No help there*! Also in danger were effeminate men, but Bates most assuredly did not fit into that category. Now that I looked more closely at him, I saw that, for his age, he was a fine figure of a man.

"I give up," I conceded. "For my sins, it seems I am to be cursed with your company for the nonce." Touching my throat and imagining a noose cutting into it, I hoped it was not also to be for the rest of my life.

* * *

The key Hornsby had given me fit smoothly into the lock and we entered the quiet screens passage. The servants had been let go after Mistress Fitts died. Only her cat, a large, surly, gray and white striped beast, remained to greet us. He made a brief appearance, then vanished.

I gave the rooms on the lower floor only a cursory examination. Over the years the furnishings had changed, becoming more costly and more comfortable, but otherwise little had altered since the first time I visited the premises to pledge my best cloak in return for a loan.

I'd heard of Mistress Fitts by word of mouth and approached her privately. No agent had been involved. That is sometimes done among women, but is not always wise. Such private loans lack the protection of law.

The line between pawnbroker and moneylender is exceeding thin. Mrs. Fitts acted as both. Knowing that, although I meant to pursue the two names Hornsby had given me, I also wanted another look at something I'd noticed on my last visit, just before our fatal final quarrel.

A woman's gown of cloth of silver had been laid out in Mrs. Fitts's private chamber. When I'd remarked upon the workmanship and cost of the garment, she'd boasted that someone had just borrowed £600 from her, pledging not only the gown but a number of pieces of good jewelry. She'd shown me pearl and gold garnishings—earrings good for at least 500 marks.

The gown had not been moved. Nor had anyone bothered to clean up the mess where Mistress Fitts had died. That stopped me for a moment. I could envision all too clearly her final struggles as someone held her face in that basin of water. She'd been a small woman, half my size. It would not have taken great strength to kill her, only cold-blooded determination.

The basin, Hornsby had said, had fallen next to her. Her face and hair had been soaked.

Squaring my shoulders, I set about searching the chamber for records of transactions. Penelope Fitts had been the sort to keep written accounts. She'd hide them, but in an easily accessible spot.

First I looked under the featherbed. Then I tried to find an uneven floorboard. Finally I surveyed the wainscoted walls hung with tapestry. I located the hidden panel behind the first hanging I lifted. It opened at a touch and proved to be stuffed full of record books. I removed the one on top, which proved to be the most recent.

Bates came to look over my shoulder. "That does not look like regular writing," he observed.

I glanced at him, guessing from his expression that he could not read. It would not have done him any good if he had he possessed that skill. The records were in code.

Fortunately, I am familiar with the tricks of secret writing. My father employed many codes and ciphers. Indeed, half the art of casting a horoscope is using archaic symbols. I handed the volume to Bates.

"Make yourself useful. If you must follow me everywhere, carry this."

"Carry it where?"

"I am going home. We will decipher it there."

I expected him to protest at this blatant theft, but he simply tucked the volume under his arm and opened the door for me.

I hesitated, wondering if anything else had changed since my last visit to this room. I eyed the bed, the dress, and the plain wooden box containing the rest of the pledge. Striding back into the chamber, I opened the latter. It contained two gold pieces and some gold buttons but no earrings.

* * *

I live in a garret and have done for more than a dozen years. The premises, located in Bread Street just beyond the turn into Five Foot Lane, are broken into three tenements. Two are divided vertically so that both the compass maker and the pulley maker have a shop on the ground floor with a parlor and kitchen behind and two chambers above. My garret, reached by a stair alongside a compass-maker's shop, is the third lodging. It is a good location, save for its proximity to the fish wharf.

My front room is designed to give my clients what they expect. Black cloth covers the windows in the dormers so that the only light in the room comes from a single candle and the coals glowing in the brazier. The furnishings consist of a large, black, curved-top storage chest and a long table covered with charts and the instruments for making them. Scattered about are rolls of parchment tied with velvet ribbon, an irregularly shaped black stone I use as a paperweight, a crystal ball, and several packs of colorfully painted cards.

The long academic robe that belonged to my father hangs on a peg in the corner. When I wear it with the hood pulled up to hide my face, it gives me an added aura of mystery, but for the most part I dress like any other female of the merchant class, in fabrics and fashions as rich and new as I can afford.

Bates's expression of distaste at the sight of my outer chamber changed to approval as soon as he entered the second room. There, where I live, light and color abound. I possess a fine, high, comfortable bed and even have a mirror.

I glanced into it as I passed and frowned. I do not see myself as that stout woman of indeterminate age. In my mind I am still a slender, healthy eighteen, ready to take on the world. I needed all my self-confidence just then. Bates's very presence was a constant reminder of the dire fate that awaited me if I did not succeed in my quest to find the person who murdered Penelope Fitts.

"I will go to a cookshop and buy two set meals," Bates offered, "if you will promise not to disappear while I am gone."

I blinked at him in surprise. "You'd trust my word?"

He thought about it for a moment. "I trust your desire to clear your name. For that you must stay in London."

"Be off with you then. I'll study the record book while you're gone."

I tried every cipher I knew, but none revealed any comprehensible text. I began to have a bad feeling that this was the sort of code that depended upon a key.

"Why did the moneylender go to so much trouble?" Bates asked when he returned with ale, two meat pies, and a wedge of cheese.

It was a good question, and a great pity that I had no answer.

We went to bed unsatisfied, I in my fine high bed and Bates on the floor of the outer room. I did not sleep well. Thoughts of what would happen to me if I did not find the killer kept me from my rest. When I did doze, I dreamed I was being prodded up the steps of a ladder, a noose around my neck. Once I reached the top, I was expected to jump off, hanging myself. If I did not, I'd be "turned off" by the executioner. What a choice!

In my nightmare, I'd have none of it. I reversed direction, backing down the ladder until I stood on firm ground again. I turned to face the hangman, staring at him in an attempt to see who was behind the mask. Only the eyes were visible, but there was something familiar about them.

I awoke disoriented and wondering if I had gone about things backwards. I reached for the record book, said a brief prayer, and tried a new tactic.

Read from right to left, every word Mistress Fitts had written made sense. That simple ruse had successfully hidden the name of the woman who had pawned her gown and earrings.

* * *

Lady Dorothy's home, when she was not at Queen Elizabeth's court, was a grand London mansion only a short distance from where Mistress Fitts had lived. Later that morning, when Bates and I paid her a visit, I was not surprised to be ushered into a private parlor. I had met Lady Dorothy on several occasions. Her last consultation with me, more than a year earlier, had been to inquire whether or not her husband would survive a sea journey. She'd seemed disappointed when I predicted a safe voyage.

Rumors are wonderful sources of information. I'd long been aware that Lady Dorothy had married to a wealthy, titled man who kept her on a short leash, but whether or not he knew she was addicted to wagering, like the merchant's wife Mistress Fitts planned to sue, was anyone's guess.

"I did not send for you," Lady Dorothy said by way of greeting. "What do you want?"

"I've come to discuss your dealings with Mistress Fitts. The pearl and gold garnishings you pawned are missing. Did you kill her to get them back?"

With Bates beside me, I felt safe making such a bold accusation. I theorized that the earrings were not Lady Dorothy's to dispose of and that, desperate to retrieve them, she had paid a late night visit to the moneylender's house. When Mistress Fitts refused to part with them until the loan was repaid, Lady Dorothy could have taken them by force and murdered the wadwife to cover up the theft.

Lady Dorothy's eyes widened as she sputtered in indignation. "What arrant nonsense!" Then she drew breath, calmed herself, and revealed the flaw in my logic. "If I had retrieved my jewelry, I'd have taken back my gown as well."

She had a point. I sighed and conceded it. "Ah, well. It was worth a try."

"How do you know my earrings are gone?"

"I searched Mistress Fitts's rooms and I read the entries in her account book."

"She kept records?" Lady Dorothy looked as if she'd just bitten into a sour grape.

"Aye. I'll destroy the ledger, for a price."

While we negotiated my fee for this service, a part of my mind continued to work on the matter of the missing earrings. *Had* Mistress Fitts surprised a thief in the middle of a robbery? That might explain why she'd been killed, but not the manner of her death. A common thief would have fled. If she'd attacked him, he might have struck her, stabbed her, or snapped her neck, but I could not picture him resorting to drowning.

* * *

Having eliminated Lady Dorothy as a suspect, Bates and I visited the two people Hornsby had named. Either they were both accomplished liars or they were innocent of the crime. Weems the weaver claimed he'd had the money to repay his loan and his wife swore he'd never left her side on the night of the murder. Mistress Gamage, upon hearing her moneylender had been murdered, had confessed her indebtedness to her husband and been forgiven. When I confronted him, he confirmed his wife's story.

"St. Winifred's wimple," I muttered as we left Soper Lane. "At this rate I'll be dead in a fortnight."

"Talk to Hornsby again," Bates suggested.

"Why are you so helpful?" For some reason, his sympathy irritated me.

"I like you, Dame Starkey." His face turned an interesting shade of red.

At a loss how to react, I kept walking. "Hornsby was passing cooperative yesterday. I wonder why."

"He found the body," Bates said. "Mayhap he was in the house when she was murdered."

My steps faltered. "Could he have murdered her?" I shook my head in disbelief. "If he killed her, why help me?"

"Why not?" Bates countered. "You have only a few days of freedom. Then you will no longer be a threat to anyone. He gave you the names of clients who defaulted on their loans and were about to be sued—clients who had nothing to do with the murder. That wasted your time by sending you off in the wrong direction."

"I have difficulty imagining Hornsby turning on his long-time employer. He profited mightily from his association with her."

"How did he know she died by drowning?" Bates asked.

"From her wet face and hair, or so he said." I frowned. "That means he found her soon after she died. Is there any way you can find out when Hornsby set up the hue and cry? If it was morning and her face and hair were still wet, then I could not have killed her. Our quarrel took place the previous evening."

"I will find the local constable and ask." Bates nodded toward the nearest building and, to my surprise, I realized we had returned to Mistress Fitts's house. "You can search Hornsby's chamber while I'm gone."

Using the key Hornsby had given me, I let myself inside. The door to the scrivener's chamber was locked, but that did not deter me. Another of the skills my father taught me was how to pick locks.

I found the missing earrings within a quarter hour of starting my search, proving Hornsby was a thief, but was he also a murderer? Did he take the jewelry and kill to cover up his crime, or did he kill first, then steal from the dead woman? Or, to be fair, did he simply palm the most valuable object in the room after he found his employer already dead?

Pondering the possibilities, I continued my search, turning up a veritable treasure trove of documents in a padlocked chest. I carried a handful to the window seat and made myself comfortable. It did not take long to realize two things. The first was that Mistress Fitts was not the only wadwife Hornsby had dealings with. The second was that he seemed to have kept bonds for a great many loans that had already come due. The possibility that they had been paid intrigued me, for Mistress Fitts had recently complained that one of her competitors had been accused of "keeping bonds." When a borrower and his seconds sign such a document, the lender keeps possession of it, but only until the borrower repays his debt. This unscrupulous lender would claim to have lost the bond. A year later, when no one could quite recall the details of the loan, the bond would turn up and the lender would claim the debt had never been repaid. The ensuing lawsuit demanded not only the original sum, but also the penalty specified in the bond.

For all her conniving ways, Penelope Fitts had some scruples. She might, on occasion, cheat her clients, but she did not rob them blind. If Hornsby had been keeping bonds and Mistress Fitts had discovered it, she'd have been furious. She'd have threatened him with the loss of his position as her agent, and possibly with jail.

Just as I resolved to take the documents I'd found to the authorities, I heard a door slam and the sound of footfalls on the stairs. A moment later, Hornsby appeared in the doorway.

"What are you doing here?" Fury made his eyes glitter with a dangerous light. He snatched the papers out of my grasp.

The door, which had not latched behind him, swung partway open again. On the far side, I saw a flutter of movement. The possibility that it was Bates brought me to my feet to face my foe.

My voice steady and my outward demeanor unruffled, I looked him right in the eyes and lied through my teeth.

"Lady Dorothy wants her earrings back." I held out the glittering baubles, jiggling them to catch the light. "I agreed to search for them. No doubt you were keeping them here for safety's sake. Did you find them when you discovered the body?"

His anger faded, replaced by a calculating look.

The door creaked, opening another few inches and making us both jump, but it was only Mrs. Fitts's striped cat. It stalked into the room, sneered at me, twitched its tail, and went out again.

My heart, already in my throat, threatened to lodge there permanently. That movement had been the cat. Bates was not lurking nearby, listening to what we said and poised to rush in if Hornsby tried to kill me.

I felt sick inside as Hornsby took the earrings from my nerveless fingers and glanced once more at the papers. When he looked up, his eyes were as cold and deadly as a viper's.

"You are a clever woman. Penelope Fitts always said so. She praised your good brain and excellent memory. You notice details, she said. I should have remembered that, but I did not realize you could also read."

"Only English," I blurted.

Some of the text of the bonds was in Latin. I hoped he would believe I hadn't understood everything the documents revealed.

Father used to say that being able to read people was more important than deciphering the written word. It helped a soothsayer tell patrons what they most desired to hear. I had no trouble guessing that what Hornsby wanted was my death.

I swallowed convulsively.

To my surprise, he stepped aside, clearing the way to the door. "Get out. You can prove nothing. By the time you return with a constable, these papers will be naught but ashes. As for the earrings, they'll be back in Mistress Fitts's chamber. Your meddling will cost me some of the profit I counted on, but I will have the satisfaction of watching you hang."

His words sparked deep resentment and the conviction that if I was to die anyway, there was no harm in provoking him further. "Did you kill her to keep her silent about those bonds?" I crossed my arms over my chest, prepared to wait as long as needed for an answer.

He hesitated, but the temptation to boast proved too great to resist. "She begrudged my earning an extra bit of profit on loans she made."

"You quarreled?"

"We did. She dismissed me and threatened me with the law. Then she turned her back on me to wash her hands."

I shivered, imagining what happened next. "Villain!"

He laughed. "For killing her or for casting the blame on you? You made it easy, having quarreled with her the way you did. How could I not tell the authorities that you cursed her and swore revenge?"

"My curse on you will be far worse."

"I am not afraid of you. Neither your curses nor any accusations you make will trouble me in the least. No one will believe your word against mine. I am a respected scrivener. You are naught but a wretched figure flinger."

I had just opened my mouth to condemn him to Hades when the door creaked again. This time it opened all the away.

"They will believe *me*," Bates said as he entered the room, "and this good constable can confirm what we both overheard."

Behind him stood a man I did not know, but he was armed with a cudgel and looked as if he hoped Hornsby would attempt to escape so he could use it.

"I thought you were the cat," I whispered, weak with relief.

Bates grinned at me. "The cat," he informed me, as Hornsby was taken into custody and led away, "was but a portent of good fortune to come."

A Note from the Author

"The Curse of the Figure Flinger" was first published in *Alfred Hitchcock Mystery Magazine* in December 2004. The character of Bates first appeared in *Face Down Beneath the Eleanor Cross*. The character of Dame Starkey first appeared in *Face Down Below the Banqueting House*, where her relationship to Nick Baldwin is revealed. She also made a brief appearance in *Murder in the Queen's Wardrobe*.

The term "figure-flinger" for astrologer first appeared in print in 1601, which means it was undoubtedly in use in everyday speech several decades earlier. If not, it should have been.

Lady Appleton and the Yuletide Hogglers

Susanna, Lady Appleton sat at the coffin desk in her study on Christmas Eve, one hand holding a quill, the other idly toying with a length of multi-colored cloth. It was beautiful stuff, soft and smooth to the touch, more durable than it looked, and specially knitted for her by a silkwoman of London as an early New Year's gift from her foster daughter, Rosamond.

She sighed, feeling sorry for herself. She'd rather have had *Rosamond* at Leigh Abbey for Yuletide.

Her gaze drifted from the letter of thanks she'd started to write to the view beyond her east-facing window. She could just make out the track left in the snow by her servants when they had set out to fetch home the Yule log. Rosamond had always loved that part of the holidays.

So had Susanna, when she'd been younger, but this December had been uncommon cold and the drifted snow lay deep across the land. She was not of a mind to celebrate in any case. In this twenty-eighth year of the reign of Queen Elizabeth—1586—Susanna faced her fifty-second Yuletide season with a singular lack of enthusiasm.

The manor house felt empty. It was foolish to think so when she employed some thirty persons, but this year few of those dearest to her were in Kent to share the festivities. Rosamond was in London. So was Rosamond's husband, Rob. It was Susanna's fervent hope that they had mended the differences between them. It had been almost eight years since they'd married. Full of youthful self-confidence, they had confounded their elders' plans by eloping. Susanna had promised herself not to meddle, but it had been difficult to see those she loved so unhappy.

Stretching, wincing when she heard a shoulder joint pop, she rose and went to stand beside the window. The late afternoon sun still shone brightly, reflecting off the brilliant white carpet spread across Leigh Abbey's fields. Beyond were the orchards, and the wood where the Yule log was being decorated with ribbons.

On the other side of the forest was Whitethorn Manor, Nick Baldwin's home, but he, too, was in London. She could not begrudge him the reason. At long last he'd reconciled with his half sister. He was to spend Yuletide with her and a newly acquired husband. They had invited Susanna to join them. She'd nearly accepted but had come to her senses in time. Why willingly subject herself to unsubtle hints that she and Nick should wed when she never had any intention of remarrying? Nick understood. At least, she thought he did, but everyone else, even the local vicar, thought her an unnatural woman because she insisted upon retaining control of her own lands and goods and person. Widowhood had given her freedom to do as she pleased. She did not mean to relinquish that, not even for love.

The sound of music drew Susanna's gaze back to the edge of the wood. The revelers were returning, dragging the heavy Yule log behind them and singing about the holly and the ivy. The former was used to decorate the interior of the house; the latter adorned the outside of the door.

Susanna left the window meaning to return to her desk and finish the letter to Rosamond, but as she turned, she glanced through the corner room's other window and caught sight of a second group approaching Leigh Abbey. On foot, they came from the direction of the nearest village, Eastwold, and had nearly reached the gatehouse. She recognized them as the parish hogglers. They had come to solicit contributions for the church.

Plucking up the purse she had ready for them, Susanna made her way to the nearest stair and descended to the ground floor. The passage that circled the snow-covered inner courtyard took her to the great hall, already decorated with boughs of holly, yew, bay, rosemary, and box, but she continued on until she reached the small parlor, a comfortable room popular with the women of the household.

Susanna smiled when she saw the flowers twined through the spinning wheel in the corner. It would not be used again until Plough Monday, the first Monday after Twelfth Night. During Yuletide, all but the necessary work of cooking and caring for animals was forbidden.

Otherwise, everything looked the same as it always did. The broad wooden bench under the window was cushioned with embroidered pillows. The small, carpet-draped table held Venetian glass goblets and a crystal flagon. A portrait of Queen Elizabeth graced one wall. A chest held books, since Susanna often read to her maidservants while they sat and wrought.

A cheery fire blazed in the hearth. Susanna settled herself in the Glastonbury chair drawn up close to the warmth to await the little party of villagers.

They were singing when they entered the parlor, one of them off key. Since she had trouble carrying a tune herself, Susanna did not complain. As soon as they fell silent, she held out a small velvet pouch full of coins.

"For your trouble, good sirs, and for the betterment of the Parish of St. Cuthburga."

The local carpenter, Thomas Sparke, stepped forward to accept her contribution. He was a young man yet, having taken over his father's trade only a few years earlier. He bowed deeply as he took the money—so deeply that Susanna wondered if he might be mocking her. Electing a Lord of Misrule for villages had gone out of fashion along with choosing boy bishops in churches, but the Yuletide tradition of irreverence toward one's betters lingered on.

Susanna was well acquainted with all the men in the Hogglers' Guild. Eastwold had barely two hundred inhabitants and most of them had ties to Leigh Abbey that went back for generations. Nathaniel Lonsdale, vicar of the parish of St. Cuthburga, was Susanna's appointee and her kinsman as well.

Young Sparke reminded her of his father. He had the same splotchy face and bushy eyebrows, and Thomas was a churchwarden, as Gerald Sparke had been. So was Alan Peacock, the big-boned, fair-skinned fellow standing just behind Sparke. He had replaced his father, now deceased, as Eastwold's miller. Had it really been sixteen years, Susanna wondered, since young Alan's marriage to her tiring maid, Grace Fuller, had set the entire village buzzing?

Carpenter, miller, schoolmaster, baker, and town herdsman had been sent out to beg for alms. Absent was the blacksmith, Ulich Fuller, Grace's uncle, the most senior member of the hogglers, As such, he should have been the one to accept her offering, not young Sparke.

"Where is Goodman Fuller?" she asked.

"He's growed too old and infirm," Sparke said. "With so much ice and snow on the ground, he durst not brave the track hissel."

The smug expression on the young man's face irritated Susanna, as did the knowledge that Ulich Fuller was only a few years older than she was. She'd have asked more questions, but Alan Peacock called for another song and the hogglers burst out with "The Boar's Head Carol."

By the time they left Leigh Abbey, the Yule log had arrived and was ready to be placed in the hearth in the great hall. With exaggerated formality, Susanna's steward, Mark Jaffrey, presented her with a charred piece of the previous year's Yule log so that she could hold it to a candle flame until it caught fire and then use it to light the new one. A great cheer went up when the wood began to burn.

Another followed as an enormous bowl of spiced wine was carried into the room.

Some hours passed before Susanna thought of Ulich Fuller again. When she did, she made her way to the place near the hearth where Mark sat on a bench with his wife. Jennet was Leigh Abbey's housekeeper and Susanna's dear friend. They'd been together more than thirty years, ever since she first entered Susanna's service as her tiring maid.

It broke Susanna's heart to see how frail the other woman had become. Her spirit was undaunted, but her body had grown weak and wasted since she'd begun to suffer palpitations of the heart. None of the herbal remedies Susanna had tried had cured her condition, although they had allowed her to live many years longer than most people with the same symptoms.

"What ails Ulich Fuller?" Susanna asked, certain Mark would know. Fuller was married to his sister, Anne.

"His joints are all swollen, especially his hands and knees," Mark said. "He's turned most of the work in the smithy over to his apprentice."

"Is he finding it difficult to walk?"

"He manages well enough."

"Not well enough for the other hogglers, it seems. They left him behind in the village."

Jennet's eyebrows lifted in surprise.

Mark laughed. "The more fools they. He's still Eastwold's only blacksmith. I warrant those men will find they must take their horses to Dover the next time they need shoeing."

* * *

It was a tradition of long standing for the entire community to gather at Leigh Abbey on Christmas Day. Susanna's cook had outdone himself by making minced pies with dried fruits and spices and with mutton in remembrance of the shepherds. Each one contained thirteen ingredients, intended to represent Christ and his apostles. In addition to the pies there was brawn with mustard, bread, cheese, fruit, nuts, spiced ale that had roast apples floating in it, and the centerpiece, a large pastry case surrounded by jointed hare, small game birds, and wild fowl and carried in on a huge platter. Inside the pastry was a turkey stuffed with a goose that had been stuffed with a chicken that had been stuffed with a partridge that had been stuffed with a pigeon.

Ulick Fuller had walked to Leigh Abbey from Eastwold, a distance of a mile and a half, just to prove he could, and when the piper played a jig, he danced with his wife. Although he was clearly in pain by the time the music stopped, the triumphant look in his eyes told everyone present that he did not count the cost of demonstrating that he was not as infirm as his neighbors thought he was.

Well into the celebrations, Susanna noticed Alan Peacock and the vicar standing off to one side with their heads bent so close together that strands of Peacock's wheat-colored hair mingled with Nathaniel Lonsdale's graying locks. Their faces wore expressions out of keeping with the cheerful countenances all around them. Frowning, Susanna had already started their way when Peacock lifted his head and gestured for her to join them.

"There has been a theft," he said in a low voice. "Someone has stolen all the money the Hogglers' Guild collected."

"I told him he should not bother you with this matter," Lonsdale interrupted, "although you *are* clever at finding things out."

Susanna felt her eyebrows lift at the grudging compliment. Her cousin the vicar, whose bulging eyes gave him an unfortunate resemblance to a freshly landed fish, did not approve of what he was wont to call her "meddling."

"No doubt it was some vagabond who took the money," Lonsdale continued. "He'll be long gone by now."

"Perhaps. Perhaps not." She turned to the miller. "Where was the money kept?"

"In a leather pouch in a locked coffer in Tom Sparke's cottage."

"Is the coffer missing as well as the pouch?" she asked.

Alan shook his head. "The coffer was left behind." His shifted his feet and looked uneasy. "Tom kept the key on a nail by the door."

"Then anyone could have come in when the cottage was empty, opened the coffer, and taken the contents."

Looking miserable, he nodded. "We collected nearly five pounds in all. We counted the take when we returned from our rounds."

"You and Tom?"

He nodded again. "The others went home to their wives and their supper."

Susanna considered that Alan might have taken the money himself and sent a speculative look his way. As his father had, he'd expanded the mills he owned. If was possible he was in debt and had not wanted to go to a moneylender.

Susanna expected to discover the truth within a day or two. She was able to confirm that there had been no masterless men seen in the vicinity for many weeks and learned that Alan Peacock was in no need of ready coin. He had everything a man could ask for—prosperity, a loving wife, and a fine brood of children.

That left one other possibility.

* * *

Early the next day, Susanna rode into the village. She was accounted an expert on herbs and herbal remedies and took with her a small jar of powdered turmeric. The plant was a rarity in England, and used mostly as a spice in cooking, but it could also relieve the pain of inflamed joints.

"Good day to you, Goodwife Fuller," she said when Anne admitted her to a small, well-kept house in the center of Eastwold. Anne was also small and well-kept. A lively little bird of a woman, she had sharply defined features and the distinctively large ears, hidden beneath her coif, that marked her as a member of the Jaffrey family.

She bobbed a curtsy and offered a gap-toothed smile. "Good morrow, Lady Appleton. What a lovely hood that is."

Susanna reached up to touch the length of cloth Rosamond had sent her. Although the day was noticeably warmer than those that had gone before, she'd draped it over her bonnet to keep off the chill. She'd looped the trailing ends twice around her neck but they still dangled nearly to her waist in a waterfall of color.

"This was a gift from your nephew's wife. For reasons best known to herself, Rosamond has invested in the business of a London silkwoman."

"That is a profitable trade," Ulich Fuller said from his chair by the fire. "Mistress Rosamond always were a clever lass." He started to rise, but Susanna gestured for him to remain seated.

"I'm told your joints trouble you, Goodman Fuller. I have brought you something to relieve the pain." She handed the small jar to Anne. "Mix a teaspoon of this powder in a cup of warm milk and have him drink that amount three times a day."

Anne's eyes widened and Fuller muttered something unintelligible under his breath. Susanna could guess that he, like many people who did not know better, believed that imbibing milk caused sore eyes, headaches, agues, and rheums.

Fuller's gray hair was thinning and his face was deeply lined, but he'd lost none of his bulk. His biceps bulged beneath his shirt and his shoulders, although stooped, were massive. It must gall him not to be able to work at a forge, but one glance at his hands told her that he could no longer grip his tools. She doubted he could so much as shoe a horse with knuckles that badly swollen, let alone lift a small key from a nail, insert it into a lock, and turn it.

"Asses milk will do," she said briskly, "if you need what your cow produces to make cheese."

"Milk is a drink fit only for children and the aged," Fuller said. "I thank you, Lady Appleton, but unless your powder can be taken in ale, I'll not have any part of it."

After reluctantly returning the jar, Anne drew Susanna aside. "He's a stubborn old fool and suspicious of pills and potions." She hesitated. "I think he would let me apply a salve to relieve the pain, if such a thing exists."

"It does, but one of the ingredients is a deadly poison, the same one used to kill rats and mice, and it must be used with great care."

"Mousebane?"

"That is one of its names. The ground dried roots, mixed with oil and rubbed into aching joints, can lessen pains such as those that afflict your husband, but should even so little as a grain remain on your hands and you touch those hands to your lips, you could die of it."

"I will take the risk, and gladly, Lady Appleton. Never have I seen Ulich so distraught as when the hogglers refused to take him with them. They said he would slow them down, and then that dreadful boy, Thomas Sparke, suggested that he could follow after them mounted on an ass and wearing a gown, pretending to be the Virgin on her way to Bethlehem. They all laughed, mocking him after all the years of service he's given to the Hogglers' Guild."

"They are young and foolish," Susanna said. "They will learn in time to appreciate their elders."

* * *

Wassailing the apple trees on the first day of January, to ensure a good crop for the next year's cider, was an ancient tradition in the

Parish of St. Cuthburga and one Susanna particularly enjoyed. Even the church did not object to wishing the trees good health and abundant crops. The celebration would begin shortly after sundown. Torches set on poles all the way from Leigh Abbey to the manor's orchard would guide the villagers to a gathering place in front of the oldest tree.

Earlier on New Year's Day, Susanna had distributed gifts to her household and accepted presents in return. As she wrapped Rosamond's colorful length of cloth around head and throat, in preparation for the evening's festivities, she glanced through the window of her study in time to see Ulich and Anne Fuller arrive a little ahead of the others. By the light of the setting sun, she observed that Ulick was using a staff to help him walk and was glad he was being sensible. Warmer temperatures had continued throughout the past week, melting the snow and leaving mud and slush behind. The path was more treacherous than usual.

Unaware they were being watched, the Fullers crossed a narrow bridge lit by rush dips stuck into brackets at both ends. The stream below had been coated with a thick layer of ice when Susanna's servants dragged the Yule log over it, but that solid surface, too, had begun to thaw. As soon as they reached the other side, Anne left her husband to go on ahead, no doubt to lay claim to a convenient log for them to sit upon. More revelers from Eastwold were already in sight. Gathering up her cloak, Susanna went out to join them.

One of Alan Peacock's daughters, fourteen-year-old Jane, had been chosen for the honor of fishing the crust of bread out of the bottom of a large wooden wassail bowl and placing it in the crook of the tree. Wearing a wreath of greenery as a crown, clasping the crust in one hand and grinning at the crowd, she climbed a short ladder. With a dramatic flourish, she reached even higher to leave her gift.

As the crowd began to sing, the noise of drums and horns and people banging on pans with ladles filled the air. Tom Sparke poured mulled cider around the base of the tree.

"Old apple tree we wassail thee," those assembled caroled, "hoping thou will bear."

Smiling, Susanna's gaze roved over the crowd, She was delighted to see them enjoying themselves. She did not realize the Peacock girl was still perched atop the ladder until young Jane, fumbling about among the branches, nearly lost her footing. Curious, Susanna moved closer and was waiting at the foot of the ladder when she scrambled down.

The flickering light of the nearest torch illuminated wide blue eyes and a frown of consternation. When Jane realized who stood beside her, she gave a relieved cry and thrust a heavy leather pouch Susanna's hands. The clink and jingle of coins rubbing together was all but drowned out by the singing, but there could be no doubt about what it contained.

"I found it tucked into the hollow of the tree," Jane said. "Do you think someone left it as an offering to the orchard?"

"I think someone hid it there, and that you were a clever girl to find it."

Jane's father appeared at her elbow. The astonishment on Alan Peacock's face would have exonerated him of guilt even if Susanna had not already eliminated him from her list of suspects. Tom Sharpe was next to notice what they'd found.

"Give it to me." He reached for the pouch.

"I think not," Susanna said. "This money was collected for the church and to the church it will go." She looked around for her cousin and found him standing a short distance away, arm-in-arm with his wife and still singing. She handed the bag back to Peacock's daughter. "Take this to the vicar, Jane."

She surveyed the rest of the crowd with intense interest, pausing only once before Peacock reclaimed her attention.

"Who took it?" he asked.

"You would do better to ask who gave it back."

"It were took a week agone," Sparke said. "The thief never meant to give it back. It were hid amongst the branches of that tree."

"Yes, but in the one tree where it was sure to be found." Susanna considered that fact for a moment longer. "It was a jest, I think, and best forgotten now that the money has been returned."

Both men objected.

"Even supposing you could discover who took the pouch, would you truly wish to prosecute that person to the full extent of the law?"

They exchanged a look. The theft of more than a shilling commanded the death penalty, although juries were often moved to exonerate such offenders rather than send them to the gallows. It would be a serious step to press charges, knowing that the accused might be executed.

"In any case," Susanna said in her most soothing voice, "I doubt we will ever identify the culprit."

Reluctantly, Sparke and Peacock agreed to let the matter drop.

Unaware of the small drama playing out beneath the oldest tree in the orchard, the majority of the villagers continued to sing and dip into the wassail bowl. As soon as the two hogglers left to confer with the vicar, Susanna looked around for one person in particular.

Ulich Fuller was still where she'd seen him last. Having rejected a seat on the log Anne found for them, he stood with his back against one of the lesser trees in the orchard. His staff was propped up next to him. Apple trees did not grow as tall as oaks or elms, but the hollow where the pouch had been left was not within easy reach. Someone whose knees would barely support his weight could never have hidden the money pouch.

A smaller, more agile person had done so, someone who had been outraged on Ulich's behalf over the way the hogglers had taunted and demeaned him.

Susanna's suspicion solidified into a certainty when she realized that Anne Fuller was nowhere to be found. If she had been watching the tree, she'd have seen Jane find the bag and give it to Susanna. She *had* been looking that way when Peacock and Sparke were arguing. She'd stiffened and looked guilty when Susanna's gaze came to rest on her. That she'd fled seemed to prove she'd both stolen the pouch and returned it, and suggested that she had leapt to the conclusion that what she'd done was about to be revealed. She no doubt thought the hogglers would have her arrested, and that she would be hanged for theft. It was no wonder she had fled.

Leaving the revelers behind, Susanna set off along the path that led back to Leigh Abbey, the most likely route Anne would have taken. Although she had torchlight to guide her, it was difficult to see where to put her feet. The track had been slippery to begin with and had been made more so by so many people passing over it.

Just as she reached the footbridge, she heard an ominous cracking sound followed by a cry of distress. Dreading what she would see, she peered toward the expanse of frozen water. The rush dip on her side of the bridge provided enough light to reveal dozens of fissures scoring the surface of the stream. Mayhap in an attempt to avoid being illuminated by the torches, and thus elude the men she imaged were in pursuit, Anne had attempted to cross the ice. Her weight, slight as it was, had caused it to give way beneath her, leaving her balanced precariously on a floe.

"Stay still!" Susanna shouted. "I will go for help."

Anne started at the sound of her voice and nearly tumbled into the frigid water. "No! It is better if I die here and my death be accounted an accident."

Afraid that Anne meant to fling herself into the stream, Susanna abandoned any thought of returning to the orchard. Instead, she picked her way carefully down the bank. The water was not overly deep, but it did not have to be for Anne to drown.

The ice broke into even smaller pieces as she hesitated, convincing her it would never support her weight. She was wishing for a rope when she realized that she had something just as strong. Swiftly, she unwound the length of cloth from around her head. It was long and sturdy enough to pull Anne to shore, but she would have to cooperate in her own rescue.

"You do not need to die. I am the only one who guessed the truth and I have no intention of telling anyone else."

Anne was shivering so hard that her entire body shook and her footing was unsteady on an ice floe that bobbed erratically on the surface of the stream. "They will find out. I will be hanged. I would rather let the water take me."

"Did you intend all along to drown yourself?"

"I meant to go home and kill myself with the mousebane I bought to ease my husband's pain."

Susanna winced at the thought of such a horrible, painful death. "There is no need. No one will accuse you of any crime. It is not as if you meant to *keep* the money."

She felt along ground covered with half melted snow for something she could use to add weight to one end of the cloth. Her fingers were nearly numb before she found a rock of sufficient size, but it was ice cold and slippery. As she struggled to pick it up, she heard Anne shriek in terror.

The other woman narrowly regained her balance, but Susanna took heart from the fact that she made the effort. Despite her claim that she preferred to die by drowning, she had fought falling into the icy water.

Abruptly, the rock pulled free. Susanna hastily tied it in place. "Catch hold of this!" she shouted, and flung her makeshift rope in Anne's direction.

By some miracle, Anne did, but her hands shook so badly that she had great difficulty untying the rock. When she finally succeeded, she followed Susanna's directions and knotted the cloth around her wrist. Meanwhile, Susanna fastened the other end to a sturdy sapling. When all was in readiness, she took hold of a section between the sapling and the stream and ordered Anne to jump from her floe to one nearer the shore.

"It will not hold my weight. I will fall into the stream."

Susanna almost smiled. Anne's words proved she wanted to live. "Jump now!"

For once, Susanna blessed the fact that she'd inherited her father's height and sturdy frame. She'd become stout with age and lacked the strength of her youth, but she was accustomed to wielding a mortar and pestle in her stillroom and was no weakling. When the inevitable cracking sound heralded another break in the ice, she was ready.

Anne windmilled her arms in a desperate struggle to stay upright, but a moment later she tumbled into the water with a loud splash. Susanna planted her feet, braced herself to take the other woman's weight, and hauled for all she was worth.

She had forgotten how quickly clothing, especially long skirts, became waterlogged. Beads of sweat popped out on her forehead as the burden she sought to pull to shore grew heavier. Anne tried to crawl back onto the surface of the ice, but the edge broke off, splashing her with frigid water and causing her to cry out.

Susanna continued to pull. The cloth held, and so did her strength. After an interval that seemed endless, Anne clawed her way halfway up the bank and collapsed, whimpering piteously. Susanna hastened to her side and grasped her by the shoulders to pull her clear of the water.

Although she was short of breath from the unaccustomed exertion and nearing the end of her strength, Susanna had more to do. Anne could not stay where she was. She could die as easily from being wet and cold as from drowning. The knots in the cloth resisted at first, but came undone after a few frustrating moments. When Susanna had taken off her warm wool cloak and wrapped Anne in it, she helped the shivering woman to stand.

"You must walk. I cannot carry you to the house."

Anne's teeth chattered so hard that she could not speak, but as long as Susanna helped support her, she managed to take shuffling steps. They were staggering like a pair of drunkards by the time they reached Leigh Abbey.

Inside, in the small parlor where a fire had already been lit, Susanna helped Anne out of her sodden, ice-encrusted clothing and bundled her into a blanket. Since all the servants were still in the orchard with the villagers, she prepared hot possets herself, lacing them with a liberal dose of sherry sack.

Not long after, Mark Jaffrey appeared in the doorway. His eyebrows shot up at the sight of Anne's wet clothing drying by the fire and her still damp hair. "Ulich said you weren't feeling well," he said in a tentative voice.

"She is much better now," Susanna said. "She fell in a patch of slushy show. You will need to ask Jennet to lend her something to wear."

Mark looked doubtful but remembered why he'd come. "The wassailing is done and the villagers are on their way home. I've hitched a horse to the farm cart and persuaded Ulich to drive it so that some of the women and children do not have to walk so far."

"Excellent thinking, Mark," Susanna said.

Shaking his head but asking no questions, he left to find his wife.

As soon as they were alone again, Susanna took Anne by the shoulders and waited until she met her eyes. "Nearly an entire year must pass before the Yuletide hogglers make their next rounds. That is more than enough time for me to make clear to them that I will not donate a single penny to the cause unless Ulich Fuller is one of their number when they come to Leigh Abbey. Advise your husband of that, Anne, but if you are wise, tell him nothing more."

A Note from the Author

Hogglers and wassailing the apple trees were part of celebrating the Twelve Days of Christmas in the south of England during Tudor times. No one today, however, seems to know much about either of these traditions. This story presents a sixteenth-century country Yuletide as it might have been, including the traditional exchange of gifts on the first of January.

This story was originally published as a Crippen & Landru chapbook for Christmas 2010. Chronologically, it is the last appearance of Susanna, Lady Appleton in print.

For those of you who wonder what happened her after that date, I picture her living comfortably at Leigh Abbey, devoting herself to local concerns, and taking care of her long-time companion, Jennet. Despite a dicey heart, Jennet has many years yet to live. By sixteenth-century standards, since Susanna has reached her mid-fifties, she is a little long in the tooth to gad about solving crimes. At that age, in those days, an average person's physical condition would be similar to that of someone in their mid-eighties today.

Together, Susanna and Jennet share several grandchildren. Susanna's adopted daughter, Rosamond, and her husband, Rob, Jennet's son, are last seen returning to London with her young half brother at the end of *Murder in a Cornish Alehouse*. Although the text doesn't say so, Rosamond is already expecting her first child. I always planned that she would to have children. In fact, my other historical mystery series, set in 1888, mentions that the protagonist, Diana Spaulding, is descended from a famous sixteenth-century herbalist. Given the passage of several centuries, her knowledge of her own ancestry isn't precisely accurate. Susanna had no children of her own, but Diana is descended from Andrew Jaffrey, Rosamond and Rosamond's son.

About the Author

Kathy Lynn Emerson has had sixty-four books traditionally published and has self published several children's books and three works of nonfiction. She won the Agatha Award and was an Anthony and Macavity finalist for best mystery nonfiction of 2008 for *How to Write Killer Historical Mysteries* and was an Agatha Award finalist in 2015 in the best mystery short story category. She was the Malice Domestic Guest of Honor in 2014. Her *A Who's Who of Tudor Women* contains over 2300 mini-biographies of sixteenth-century Englishwomen. She also writes under the pseudonyms Kaitlyn Dunnett and Kate Emerson. For more information, please visit www.KathyLynnEmerson.com.